WHITETOOTH FALLS

JUSTIN JOSCHKO

JOURNALSTONE
YOUR LINK TO ARTIST TALENT

ISBN: 978-1-950305-12-4 (sc)
ISBN: 978-1-950305-13-1 (ebook)
Library of Congress Control Number: 2019943841

First printing edition: November 8, 2019
Printed by JournalStone Publishing in the United States of America.
Cover Design and Layout: Don Noble
Interior Layout: Lori Michelle
Edited by Scarlett R. Algee
Proofread by Sean Leonard

JournalStone Publishing
3205 Sassafras Trail
Carbondale, Illinois 62901

JournalStone books may be ordered through booksellers or by contacting:
JournalStone | www.journalstone.com

ADVANCE PRAISE FOR
WHITETOOTH FALLS

"Joschko's complex storytelling will keep readers hooked until the final bloody scene."

—*Publishers Weekly*

"With his stunning debut *Whitetooth Falls*, Justin Joschko explodes on the horror scene with a chilling tale of genuine horror! Highly recommended!"

—Jonathan Maberry,
New York Times bestselling author of *V-Wars* and *Rage*

"Joschko's prose is lyrical, but with bite. This book is gritty enough to wear your teeth down, with a full dose of noir and a fresh take on classic horror. I loved it."

—Sarah Read,
author of *The Bone Weaver's Orchard* and *Out of Water*

"Equal parts horror, mafia drama and hardboiled procedural and delivering on the promises of each, *Whitetooth Falls* is a werewolf story with teeth."

—T.L. Bodine,
author of *River of Souls*

"Joschko has created a diverse cast of multi-dimensional characters. A richly imagined, well-researched take on the traditional werewolf story."

—Laurel Hightower-Wells,
author of *Whispers in the Dark*

WHITETOOTH FALLS

To my mom

TABLE OF CONTENTS

PRELUDE: NEW MOON

1: THE TOUR

THE SMELL WAS the worst of it.

Detective David Moore held a rag to his mouth and stepped over the charred remnants of the transom and into the lobby of Stanford Acres. Much of the roof had collapsed, forming great yawning holes through which the blue sky gaped at the ruins. The drywall behind reception had burned away, revealing half-melted innards of copper pipes and electrical wire. The room ran thick and greasy with the noxious fumes of a dozen chemicals, wood varnishes and silicon and puffy pink clouds of insulation all spumed into the air by the vanquished flames. Yet worse somehow was the smell beneath them, a charcoal tang of roasted flesh that reminded David, appallingly, of barbeque. That human flesh once cooked would smell much as any other was a fact both obvious and abhorrent.

Noise from the street drifted through the gaps in the crumbling walls. David could hear the low murmur of rubberneckers gathering along the lines of police caution tape, the hubbub of reporters setting up on-location broadcasts, the monotone bellow of duty officers insisting the public stand back and not tamper with the investigation. As he made his way inside, these loose noises were replaced by the crisper, almost clinical sound of forensic analysis, as men in white gloves studied the destruction. A team of arson investigators picked their way through the wreckage, the lower halves of their faces obscured by paper masks. They nodded to David as he passed, shifting when needed to provide a clearer look at the bodies. He made his way down the hallway, stepping carefully around the debris. Rooster tails of ash rose in the wake of each footfall, adding their peppery sting to the already caustic air. Light tumbled in through empty window frames, igniting crystalline embers in the shards of shattered glass.

He entered a bedroom and spotted his partner, Walter. Mid-fifties, he had the large, softening frame of an athlete gone to seed. An unlit cigarette jutted from beneath the grey tusks of his walrus moustache. He touched a lighter's dancing flame to its tip and inhaled.

"Kind of in poor taste, Walt."

Plumes of smoke unfurled from the sides of Walter's mouth. "I guess it might stink up the drapes, huh?"

David approached the bed. Walter offered him a cigarette from his pack and David, pausing for a brief pang of guilt, took it. He bent towards Walter's lighter and studied the body through a sheer veil of tobacco smoke. The victim, though badly burned, was still recognizably female. A woman in her eighties or nineties, David guessed, from the wisps of hair and the wrinkled topography of her unblackened left cheek.

"How many, all told?" David asked.

"Twenty at last count, though there's a couple of spots the body boys haven't swept that closely yet."

"Jesus."

Walter shrugged. "Half these folks were bedridden, the other half in wheelchairs or walkers. Not the sort gonna be makin' dramatic escapes through windows. Staff did what they could, but we're talkin' one nurse for every dozen residents. It was the smoke did it more than the fire, so there's a bright side for you."

"Pretty damn dark for a bright side."

"True. But that's about as bright as she gets."

Walter smoked his cigarette down to the filter and snubbed out the embers on the pad of his saliva-dampened thumb. He readied himself to flick it, paused, and pocketed it instead. "Come on. I'll give you the tour."

They walked to the end of the hallway, their gazes drifting about in an ostensibly casual way that belied the true depth of their search. Years on the job had taught David that looking too closely could be as bad as not looking at all. Clues were skittish things, and too aggressive an approach was liable to spook them.

Walter led him down the stairs to the basement. Soot and ash lined the walls, giving the hallway a sepulchral, cavernous cast. David and Walter clicked on flashlights. Stalactites of fire-warped tile hung from the ceiling, strung with cobwebs of melted insulation and vines of dead wire. Pockets of smoke eddied about the ragged ceiling, flavouring the air with a bitter tannin stink. The damage grew greater as they progressed, culminating in a coal-black abscess gaping in the left wall. Flames had blistered the support beams and eaten a hole through the ceiling, allowing a column of soot-stained light to descend from the room above. David whistled in appreciation at the totality of the destruction.

"Utility closet," Walter explained. "Fire chief says this is where it started."

David leaned through the doorway and trawled the beam of his flashlight slowly about the room. Aluminum shelves slumped half-melted against the back wall, their contents burned to slag. He spotted an empty paint can and squatted to inspect it. He hooked the rim with one gloved finger and lifted it gently. "Plenty of fuel in here, by the looks of it."

"Sure. Paint, Varsol, all that good shit. Question is, what set it off?"

"Electrical, maybe?"

4

"Possible," said Walter. "Spoke to the manager and he said everything was up to code, inspected just last year. We'll need the records to prove it, but the place has a pretty good reputation. My mom stayed here."

David looked at Walter uneasily. "She wasn't . . ."

Walter waved David's concern away. "She died years ago. Alzheimer's. Fuckin' bitch of an illness. Compared to that, smoke inhalation's not so bad."

"Still pretty bad, though."

Walter nodded.

They emerged into the midmorning air, lungs sighing with relief. David immediately quelled their enthusiasm with another cigarette. They cleared out to the sidewalk to let the evidence boys work without feeling like homicide was peering over their shoulders.

"So what you think?" asked Walter. "This one comin' our way?"

David puffed on his cigarette contemplatively. "Not really for us to say, is it? Could very well be bad wiring, or maybe the janitor was sneaking a cig and forgot to butt out properly. Arson guys'll give their report, let us know if we should investigate."

"Yeah, but what's your gut tell you?"

David stared at the building, and the building stared blindly back. "It was deliberate."

"Yeah?"

"Oh yeah."

Walter flicked ash from the end of his cigarette. "Takes a special kind of scumbag to torch an old folks' home. What's it gain you?"

David held his cigarette aloft as if it were a tiny wand. He studied its burning tip, watched as embers took wing on the steady breeze. "That's the question, isn't it?"

It was a question he intended to have answered, eventually.

Though he doubted he'd like what he heard.

2: BLOOD SPORTS

IMAN YAWNED. Her limbs rose and stiffened in a semi-voluntary stretch, loosening joints torqued tight by slouching. The monitor on her desk displayed an open PDF, the text of which her mind had long since stopped following, even as her eyes dutifully scanned the lines. She blinked the document back into focus and started again. Gradually, her concentration wriggled its way into the flow of sentences. She swivelled side to side in a slow rhythm as she read, her office chair silently accommodating the motion.

A cup of green tea unspooled fragrant steam into the room. She took a sip, wincing at the heat, and set it down as Professor Motes arrived. He wore a starched white dress shirt and brown slacks with ironed creases. Wingtip shoes glinted blackly below neatly-hemmed pantcuffs. He was a consummate square, though tiny details hinted at a bohemian past. Iman sensed it in his round-rimmed glasses, the sprigs of black hair trimmed half an inch short of shaggy, the snippets of Sun Ra and Herbie Hancock that occasionally drifted through the gaps in his office door. A messenger bag hung from a strap around his shoulder. He held a Tim Hortons cup in each hand, the larger of which he set on Iman's desk.

"Good morning, Miss al-Qaddari."

"Morning, professor. And thanks. You didn't have to get me anything."

"I'd feel like a cad walking in here with only one cup. It's French vanilla."

"My favorite. Thanks again."

"Not a problem. I hope it doesn't clash too much with your tea."

"I can always reheat it." She set her mug aside and pulled back the lid on her cappuccino. A whiff of vanilla and foam tickled the tender skin around her nostrils. She blew on the steaming liquid and regarded Motes from over the cup. "I thought you had a faculty meeting all morning."

"It let out early, mercifully. Ullman's attending a conference in Glasgow, which left Pearl bereft of her favorite target for her complaints. She tried to take aim at me, but I've become adept at feigning bouts of convenient amnesia."

Iman laughed. Lydia Pearl was well-known around campus as a class-A shit disturber, the sort of woman who never met a text that didn't brim with patriarchal, heteronormative hostility. "Ah, Professor Pearl's okay. She taught my Introduction to Romantic Poetry class in first year. Anyone who loves Coleridge can't be all bad."

Motes rolled his eyes. "That's the trouble with you. You *like* everyone. Scorn is the spice of life. Without it, your day is just so terribly bland."

"I thought it was variety."

"Only for people with dull tongues and duller brains. Speaking of which . . . " He reached into his messenger bag and pulled out a stack of papers. "The dreaded day is upon us. Essays from the grammar gulag."

Iman groaned theatrically. In truth, she didn't mind grading papers, even those from Motes' Mechanics of Writing class, a first-year course for remedial students who fumbled commas and thought a semicolon was part of the human anatomy. But Motes loved nothing more than a bit of commiserative griping, and it was fun to indulge him from time to time.

"It'll go quickest if we divide and conquer. Be firm with them. No rounding up to spare feelings. A failed paper deserves a failing grade."

"Yeah, I know. But an F just seems so . . . harsh."

Motes shook his head. "Far, far too nice. I expect chipmunks and finches alight on your shoulder whenever you walk through a park."

"Better Mary Poppins than Ebenezer Scrooge."

His finger tick-tocked in mock admonishment. "Tsk. A life in academia will squeeze the kindness from you soon enough. Only curmudgeons make tenure, you know. You'd best crab up, or you'll find yourself in the private sector, earning vast sums and reading books for pleasure."

"It sounds awful," said Iman.

"You have no idea."

Motes rounded Iman's desk and disappeared through the door at the back of the room, which led to his private quarters. The setup suggested a more secretarial role on Iman's part than she liked, but it gave her a de facto office of her own and meant virtually constant access to Motes, who was her thesis supervisor as well as her boss—a level of accessibility most graduate students could only dream of.

Taking a drink from her cappuccino, Iman began settling back into her reading when a man stepped into the office. Her first thought was that he had the wrong room. He wore a leather jacket festooned with buttons and zippers, atop a jaundiced t-shirt spotty with pinhole burns. Bits of metal jingled in the pockets of his cargo pants, which bore the scars of hard use in their threadbare seat and ragged knees. His hair, thinning up top, ran long in the back, black curls spilling into bushy stubble two days shy of a full beard. Tattoos twined out his jacket cuffs and up his neck. He looked to Iman like a holdover from the 70s punk scene merged with a 1930s steelworker, a man built from angles and vices and scars. He held a battered leather briefcase in one hand.

"Can I help you?" Iman asked.

The man glanced at her, saying nothing. The tip of his tongue slithered across his lower lip, leaving a trail of spit. He walked past her without stopping and barged into Motes' office. A punky smell of pot smoke and car exhaust followed him like a great billowing cape. Iman caught a glimpse of Motes' expression of annoyance before the door swung shut, frosted glass panel rattling in its frame.

They spoke for several minutes. Iman caught the timbre of their voices, but couldn't make out anything they were saying. Curiosity goaded her towards the door while propriety held her at her desk. Curiosity proved stronger, and she was still in her seat when the man left Motes' office, his stride loose and cocky. He favored her with an up-and-down glance, concluding with a lupine smile. Iman stared back, unimpressed and afraid in equal measure, hoping the former sufficiently obscured the latter. When the man was gone, she leaned forward to catch a glimpse into Motes' office. The professor sat at his desk, clutching his coffee mug to his chest with both hands. His computer monitor, positioned to his left, divided his face into hemispheres of light and shadow.

"Who was that?" Iman asked.

"Hmm? Oh, no one. A student, enquiring about a grade." He smoothed a crease in his shirt with his thumb.

Iman raised an eyebrow. Motes wasn't the sort of professor who took kindly to students barging into his office unannounced. She opened her mouth to question this and closed it again. The exchange was really none of her business.

She'd almost forgotten about it by the time Motes left his office twenty minutes later. He carried a loose stack of papers under one arm, the individuals sheets poorly collated and threatening to spill with every hitch and fidget of his shoulders. His glasses sat precariously on the tip of his nose. He pushed them into place with the heel of his hand.

"Well, I'm off. I trust you have everything you need from me?"

Iman smoothed the furrow of confusion creasing her brow with some effort. "Um, yeah, I guess. You're going already? You just got in."

"Yes, I know, it's just that there's something I've forgotten that I must attend to."

"Is everything okay?"

"Oh yes, fine fine fine. Only a minor matter." Motes chuckled as if he'd told a joke. He fiddled with the pens on Iman's desk, fastidiously arranging them into parallel lines. "One other thing. I have a tutorial for my second year CanLit course in about an hour. I wonder, would you mind terribly if I asked you to cover it for me?"

"What, you mean teach it?"

"I wouldn't expect you to lecture. They're supposed to have read *Monkey Beach* and you'd simply need to chair a discussion on it. You've written on Robinson's work in the past, I'm sure you're more than capable."

"Well, I guess . . . "

"I hate to ask. It's just that something urgent's come up that I really must see to."

"It's fine. I know *Blood Sports* and *Monkey Beach* inside out."

"Perfect. I thank you kindly. Please take the rest of the day off after that. I shan't be in until tomorrow."

He was gone before Iman could say anything more. Her gaze lingered on the doorway as if regarding an afterimage of his sudden egress. *What the hell was that?* She tapped the end of a pen against her bottom teeth and pondered what could possibly have driven Motes away in such a frenzy. A sick relative, maybe? If so, she figured he'd mention it, at least generally. Motes was no oversharer, but nor was he the sort who refused outsiders any glimpse of his personal life. She'd met one of his boyfriends in the past and heard reference to a couple more, and knew his mother was living in a nursing home—though thankfully not the one that had burned down a few nights prior.

Her thoughts circled the question for some time, but could find no foothold, and eventually withdrew. It remained a curiosity, jutting from the topography of her afternoon like an obelisk in the shrinking distance. By the time she stood before Motes' bemused class, it disappeared over the horizon, not to be seen again for some time.

PART I:
HARVEST MOON

3: A COLD CASE

MANILA FOLDERS LAY open along the edge of the desk, their contents spread into jumbled patterns of incontrovertible yet inscrutable logic: a jigsaw puzzle with non-Euclidean pieces, several of which were missing. David worked them into fresh arrangements, occasionally picking one up to scan its contents or peer at a previously unscrutinized corner of a photograph. For two months, he'd acquired a steady stream of documentation concerning the Stanford Acres fire: witness statements, floor plans, victims' dental records, suspects' rap sheets, psychiatric assessments of every bedwetter and firebug in the province, a ninety-page report from the city's chief arson investigator. And photos. Hundreds of them, stark images of every burned bed and smouldering carpet, every blackened face and charred finger, all of them snapped from every conceivable angle. And what, from this wellspring of data, had David gleaned? What did this plethora of intelligence amount to?

Thus far, nothing but a couple of dead trees.

David raised his coffee mug to his lips and found it empty. Blackish sediment tarred a sticky ring along the edges of its convex bottom. He smacked his lips, his tongue a wad of dirty cotton. More coffee was the last thing he needed, more caffeine the first. As he let these conflicting needs argue their cases, Walter walked in with a full carafe in hand, snuffing out the anti-coffee movement with a single graceful pour. He stood over David, his bulk held in check by a powdery-grey suit gone threadbare at the knees and elbows.

"You're a good man, Walt."

"Just fluffin' you, sorry to say. We've got a case."

David rubbed his eyes. "Fuck me."

"More or less. Some inconsiderate bastard went and got himself killed on our shift."

David picked up a document at random and watched the writing ooze in and out of focus. "Can you take this one? I'm up to my elbows in Stanford Acres, and Delduca's been breathing down my neck."

"Mine, too," said Walter. "But for the moment, this takes precedence. Supposed to be a real clusterfuck."

"You sure know how to sell it."

"Stanford's a cold case anyway, Davey. Time for something hot and fresh."

"You think Delduca's gonna let this thing drop?" asked David. "The press are already eating him alive."

"Yeah, tell me about it. But he's gonna have to take it like a big boy. We got no witness, no lead, no motive. What's that leave you with?"

"A hunch."

Walter sniffed out a single small laugh. His moustache twitched. "That and fifty bucks'll get you blown on Ferry Street."

David looked up long and somberly. Walter's shoulders bounced with a conciliatory shrug. "Okay, tell me the fuckin' hunch. Then we gotta go."

"Smells mafia."

Walter smacked his forehead. "What, no CIA?"

"I'm serious, Walter. It's too neat for a firebug, and the insurance yielded diddly squat. Who else pulls that sort of job?"

"You still stink of Toronto, kid. Maybe the dons up your way do macho shit like that, but Ballaro's cautious. He wouldn't pull that kind of stunt. Not on a bunch of fuckin' retirees."

"Could be sending a message."

"Against a building full of fuckin' geriatrics? What, they been runnin' a racket on him, cuttin' into the tapioca business?" Walter shook his head. "You're too far into this shit sty, Davey. You need some air. Come on, let's go downtown and look at a corpse. You'll feel better."

David gave the ocean of papers a final forlorn glance.

Feel better? The fuck of it was, that might just be true.

4: PAPERWORK

DAVID STUDIED THE hand. A cigarette dangled from the right side of his mouth, its plumes of smoke a nebulous shield against the ugly smells of the Sundown Lounge parking lot. The worst of these rose from the hand itself, or perhaps the smudge of sticky pavement surrounding it. He slipped gloves over his own hands and hunkered down for a closer look.

It was an ordinary hand, as hands go—curls of black hair sprouting from between its first and second knuckles, calluses on the pressure points of its palms in a weightlifter's signature pattern, fingernails squared and trim and free of dirt. The strangeness began below the wrist, where slightly hairy flesh gave way to a ragged stump of bone and sinew. A wild fringe of tattered flesh described its edges, suggesting a less than clean cut. The last of its blood had long since drained to a tacky film on the pavement, giving the exsanguinated flesh a pale, marble cast.

"What you think, should we bring him in for questioning?" asked Walter. A cigarette jutted from beneath his grey moustache. He took a drag, filling his pudgy red cheeks, and exhaled a long jet of smoke through his nostrils.

"I dunno. You think he'll talk?"

David sketched a chalk outline around the hand and picked it up. Walter snapped on a flashlight and held it aloft, giving David enough light to work. Rings decorated its pinky and middle fingers, bands of solid gold bejewelled with tiny diamonds and an ostentatious ruby, respectively. David clucked his tongue. The hand had been out here for at least an hour before the cops had showed up, lying unprotected in the parking lot of one of the city's less reputable strip clubs—as if any strip club in Niagara Falls could be considered reputable—and yet its rings, worth thousands of dollars apiece by the looks of them, remained unplundered.

A few rubberneckers, obviously drunk by the look of their droopy-eyed grins and teetering postures, stood behind the yellow police caution tape. The first responding officer was in the process of brushing them off, a task impeded by their inebriation and the fact that at least one of them was busy hitting on her.

"Shit, that's fucked up, though, huh? You must be a pretty tough chick, lookin' at shit like that all day."

"There's worse parts of my job, sir, believe it or not. Now, I'm going to have to ask you one more time to move along. This is a crime scene."

"We're just lookin'," the second man said.

"Yeah, view's not all bad," the first man added with a wink.

The officer rolled her eyes.

"I'm going to speak to the detectives. Stay behind this line. If you're not well on your way home—in a taxi—by the time I'm done, then both of you are getting a ride with me. And not the kind of ride you're thinking of."

The two men giggled to each other as the officer walked over to David and Walter, shaking her head. "Idiots. This poor schmuck had to get offed at the Downer."

"Is there a better place?" asked Walter.

"A park. A church. Somewhere with less booze and testosterone. Forensics guys are on their way to bag and tag. I asked around inside, but no one seems to've seen anything."

"So they say," said David. "Hard to imagine something like this was quiet."

The officer shrugged. "Manager says he heard some shouting, but I guess that's about par for the course outside this place at two AM. Most of the regulars had already called it a night, so parking lot was pretty sparse. First guy says he saw anything claims he spotted the mess walking to his car."

David set the hand down gently where he'd found it and did a quick tour of the scene. The hand was far and away the biggest part of the victim in evidence. Otherwise. all that remained were a few scraps of cloth and denim.

And blood. Lots and lots of blood. A severed hand on its own wasn't necessarily evidence of homicide—David had seen folks survive some serious butchery in his time—but a quick glance at the breadth and depth of the red puddle drying on the tarmac told him that whoever had lost this hand wouldn't be stumbling into the precinct to claim it. That left the question of where the body went. And who took it. And why. As questions went, David figured he wouldn't encounter a shortage for some time to come.

Clicking on his own flashlight, David traced the perimeter of the puddle. He made it about halfway around before spotting an irregularity in its grim coastline, a few rivulets of dried fluid that had flowed mysteriously uphill. With slow, measured steps, David marked their trajectory, and after five or so paces noticed a few red droplets scabbing the otherwise dry pavement. He followed the dots to a field at the edge of the parking lot. Bulrushes and crab grass cluttered a shallow culvert, their blades bent double and dyed a deep shade of crimson.

Well, that answers one question. Probably. He snapped off the flashlight. "Call in a team," he told the officer. "We're gonna have to do a little exploring, and it'll be a hell of a lot easier once we get some daylight."

"You need me for that?" the officer asked. "I'm an hour past the end of my shift as it is, and this mess is sure to leave a bitch kitty of paperwork."

"I got the deets from her already, Davey," said Walter. "She should be good to go."

"Yeah, I think you're all set. Thanks for keeping the scene."

"No worries." A look of sudden disgust congealed on her face. "Ugh. Idiots."

Across the parking lot, the two drunks had wandered away from the police line and were climbing into their car. The lead one gunned the engine and peeled out of the parking lot, nearly scratching the fender of the manager's BMW on his way out.

David shook his head. "There's a traffic fatality in the making."

"Worse," said the officer, trotting off to her squad car. "Even more fucking paperwork."

5: CIVIC DUTY

"**T**ELL ME SOME good news, Walter."

David held the Styrofoam cup in both hands. A column of fragrant steam rose to his nostrils, filling them with the rich scent of slightly burnt coffee. He took a sip, wincing as the liquid scalded his lip. This was his third cup in as many hours. David savored every stimulating drop. He'd been up since eight AM the previous morning, clocking his current stretch of wakefulness at about twenty-nine consecutive hours. At this point, holding back his exhaustion with caffeine was like trying to dam a river with a sieve.

They'd found the body easily enough. It lay strewn through the field about twenty feet past the edge of the parking lot, streamers of skin and entrails threaded through the waist-high grass. The sun hadn't yet had the chance to put the spurs to decomposition, but the sheer volume of viscera alone smelled pretty ripe. David puffed away at a pair of cigarettes as he approached, grateful as always for the olfactory-deadening effects of a lifetime addiction to nicotine. He'd told his wife on numerous occasions that he'd quit smoking when he retired—and he sincerely believed that he meant it every time—but until that day, putting down the lighter would be tantamount to handing in his badge. He whistled, summoning Walter and the forensics team over, and brushed the grass aside to see what he had to work with.

The answer was very little. Calling the mess in the weeds a body would be like calling the Food Basics baking aisle a cake. The raw materials were there, but the end result was nowhere in evidence.

"Oh man," said Walter, rubbing his chin. "It looks like something tried to eat the poor son of a bitch."

"Looks more to me like something succeeded. Come on, let's get this over with."

The detectives crab-walked through the grass, snapping photos and turning up leaves to peek for clues, taking care all the while to keep any residual evidence off of their shoes. Dewy fronds dampened their pant cuffs and clung to their gloved fingers. The forensics team hung back a respectful distance, waiting for homicide to give the go-ahead to start bagging and tagging.

Organic tissues sprawled over tufts of dandelion and clover, stirred in a slurry of flesh and blood and bone. The face was unrecognizable, the jaw so badly shattered—at least half of it seemed to have disappeared altogether—that dental records wouldn't be of much help. A field inspection yielded no tattoos or obvious birthmarks. DNA samples abounded, but unless the victim was logged on a known database, they couldn't tell him much. The current tactic was to check on any folks who'd been spotted around the Sundown Lounge the night of the murder, to see if someone failed to turn up. The next step would be to put out a call to anyone in the region who'd filed a missing persons report. They wouldn't be of much use at giving a positive eyeball ID, but if they could scrounge up a bit of the target's DNA, the police forensics unit could check for matches. But even assuming the samples existed, all of this runaround took precious time. David could feel the case cooling while he sat on his hands, waiting for the bloodhounds to point him down the right path. As things stood now, all he had were untold miles of forest primeval and a couple of matches to light the way.

It was thus with a much-needed spark of hope that David watched Walter slap the file onto his desk. His pudgy fingers walked a rapid syncopated rhythm over the manila folder, a gesture that David's longstanding partnership made easy to read—a break.

"We got a match," Walter said. "Poor bastard didn't leave us much besides fingerprints, but fingerprints did the trick."

"The guy's a perp?"

"Not just any perp. Check the mug shots."

David opened the folder. "Holy shit."

A familiar face sneered up at David from the mug shot. Blue eyes glinted above a piggish nose, the chief flaw in an otherwise fairly handsome visage. A coif of frosted blond hair framed the face on three sides, while a square and dimpled chin rounded out the fourth.

"Eddie Ballaro."

"Rotten apple of his pappy's fuckin' eye."

David flipped through the pages. "We had prints on this guy? I thought he wasn't in his dad's game."

"He's not. But a guy as dumb and pampered as our pal Eddie can get into plenty of mischief without his father's say-so. Did six months for assault and battery on a Pakistani store clerk. Poor schmuck caught Eddie's girlfriend shoplifting a Snickers and actually tried to call her on it. The kid didn't even own the place."

"Civic duty's its own reward, Walter." David took a long sip of his coffee.

"Thirty-six an hour plus overtime don't hurt either. Anyway, Eddie kept out of trouble after his one little stint. He still gets up to the usual macho bullshit, but he keeps it focused on the sort of people don't go cryin' to the cops."

David's ears perked up. "You mean other families?"

"Pfff, Eddie don't got the stones for that. No, he holds court in the bars down on Main Street, cruises the strip clubs, throws cash around. Acts like king of the low-rent scum, takes it as his privilege to pummel the ones who look at him cross-eyed."

David fidgeted with the ring on his right ring finger, a sterling silver alligator coiled chin to tail, its snout a stubby protrusion that his thumb could catch, allowing the ring to spin endless revolutions around its flesh and bone axis. The ring had been a gift from his eight year old son—six at the time—purchased with pocket money at the region's annual Friendship Festival. As a piece of jewellery, it was, if David were to allow himself utter objectivity, cheaply forged and a little tacky. But it was the first gift his son had ever picked out and bought him all by himself, and he loved it more than just about anything he owned.

"So what if Frank ordered it himself? You know, got tired of his son making a mockery of his good name?"

Walter shook his head. "I ain't one to normally romance the wops, but I don't see the Ballaros whacking one of their own. Especially not hard enough to turn 'em into hamburger. A death like that ain't dignified. If there's one thing Ballaro believes in, it's dignity."

"So what, you think it was one of these low-rents that did Ballaro?"

"Sure. Guy on bath salts, maybe, doping himself up for the job? Someone like that wouldn't care who Eddie's daddy was."

David tapped a pen against the edge of his desk. "It could be we're overthinking this whole thing on account of the victim. Eddie looks like he was mauled by a wild animal, maybe he was. We should call up Marineland and see if they've got any missing bears, plus do a quick sweep of zoos and the like. What's that place up near Hamilton?"

"African Lion Safari." Walter sprechsanged the jingle in an off-key tenor. "I dunno, the whole thing feels awful deliberate to me. But we should probably cover our asses, make sure we don't end up puttin' out an APB on a perp turns out to be Yogi Bear."

"You wanna make the rounds, I can hit up animal control for details."

"Gonna scope out the local wildlife, huh? You get any ideas, you use protection, eh? That's how AIDS got started."

David rolled his eyes. "You're a real asshole, Walt."

Walter touched hand to heart. "I only put up with that 'cause I know, deep down, you love me."

"Real deep, maybe."

6: MORSELS OF GROTESQUERY

IMAN SLUMPED IN front of the computer, her head resting on the pillar of her forearm. Yawning, she rubbed the crusted yellow remnants of sleep from her eyes and checked the clock in the bottom right-hand corner of the screen, which confirmed—not for the first time—that it wasn't yet eight o'clock. A human hour for the nine-to-fivers, perhaps, but as someone who rarely rose before ten o'clock on weekdays and noon on weekends, Iman thought a seven-thirty start time was nothing short of cruelty.

She opened Microsoft Word and squinted against the fusillade of white pixels, shielding her eyes like a vampire before a cross. Her phone buzzed. She checked her notifications, saw a text from Brian, reading:

"Holy cow. U got up before me?!?!"

Grinning despite her exhaustion, Iman tapped out a reply. *"Showered ate and out the door by 7 sharp :S. Even made extra smoothie for you. In fridge."*

The response came a moment later: *"W almond milk?!?"*

In reply, Iman favoured a simple: *";)"*

"U R So sexy."

Iman laughed, texted back: *"Breakfast turns you on? Your mom makes it for you like every weekend. Is there something you should tell me?"*

"Not smoothies tho so its kosher."

Iman forced herself to put the phone aside. There was no point coming in at such an ungodly hour if she was just going to fritter the time away texting. She'd felt the crunch over the last month, as her RAship sprawled from fifteen hours a week to nearly thirty—not all of them compensated. In addition to her normal work editing papers and managing correspondence, Professor Motes had recently had her poring through obscure journals and fetching articles on topics far afield from Western Literature, which was supposed to be his area of focus.

As if summoned by her thoughts, the hallway door swung open and Motes stepped into the office.

"Morning, professor," Iman said, glancing at him from her screen. Motes' appearance had become steadily more alarming over the past month. He'd dropped a good twenty pounds from his fleshy frame, giving him the wrinkled look of a balloon partially deflated. His olive skin had a pale greenish hue, and pimples erupted in an oily tiara beneath his thinning hairline. His eyes retained their emerald intensity behind wire-rimmed glasses, but the flesh beneath them was baggy and bruised.

Motes grunted in reply to her greeting. He fished a key ring from his pocket and stabbed a key into the lock.

"How are things?"

"Fine, fine. Check your email. I've got more stuff for you."

"I did. I'm already on it. Do you want paper copies or PDFs?"

"Whatever. Just get it done. Oh, and here." He dug through the messenger bag for a notebook, tore a page from its spiral binding, and slapped it onto her desk. "Check these out for me."

"Sure. Do you want me to go now, or . . . " she began, but Motes was already heading for his office, his head down as if trudging against a strong headwind. He slammed the door behind him hard enough to rattle its pane of frosted glass.

Iman's hand drifted to her phone and brought up her news ticker app. She scrolled through a few articles, keen to read something not steeped in academia. Her eyes tripped over a headline: *Body Found Outside of Local Strip Club*. Intrigued (and a bit guilty at her interest), she clicked the link. The article served up a few juicy morsels of grotesquery—severed hand in the parking lot, viscera dragged into a nearby field—but little in the way of hard facts. No ID on the victim, no presumed motive. Just some rhetorical fluff and a few reaction quotes from the shell-shocked manager. She forwarded the link to Brian. He pinged back five minutes later.

"OMG sick!! WTF U think did it?!?!"

"Who knows? Some sicko probably. Though sort of sounds like body was mauled by animals."

"U think bears?! :O"

Iman shook her head. Though he'd moved to Canada from Hong Kong when he was only five, Brian hard-headedly retained stereotypes of the country as a sprawling backwoods, with wolves and moose cavorting behind every strip of new-growth forest lining the highway. *"No bears in Niagara Peninsula, hun."*

"What bout in Marineland?"

Iman typed a response, bit her lip, deleted it. Brian shot over a follow-up message:

"Check and Mate B ^)"

Snorting, Iman set her phone down and resumed her article-trawling between sips at her tea. Its bitter, fragrant taste rolled over her tongue. In spite of her best efforts, her mind kept veering back to the gory description of the body in the field. She wasn't alarmist by nature, but the fact that something so gruesome had happened so close to home was unsettling. Niagara Falls was only a ten-minute drive down the QEW, and on several occasions Iman had driven past (though never gone into, of course), the club the article had mentioned. She pictured the body lying in the waist-high grass, a shroud of flies rippling over its pulpy remains. Ludicrous to think a wild bear could make it all the way down the Niagara Peninsula unseen, but a cougar might manage it. And there were zoos nearby . . .

She shook these macabre thoughts from her mind and picked up the paper Motes had put on her desk. A dozen call numbers were scrawled across its upper half, sloppy but legible, if only just.

An itch corkscrewed into her sinuses and yanked out a sneeze. Droplets of moisture dappled her monitor. She grabbed a Kleenex and mopped the monitor clean. Another sneeze came, but she was prepared this time and directed it safely into her tissue. She dabbed her upper lip and worked a knuckle into the tender crux between the bridge of her nose and her left eye, where a histaminic itch burrowed into the membrane. *Damn ragweed. Shouldn't the season be over by now?* Her symptoms had tapered into mild irritation after prolonged periods spent outdoors. Why the sudden resurgence?

She rubbed her nose. Whatever its cause, an allergy attack offered all the incentive she needed to leave the office. She locked her computer with a few keystrokes and headed for the library.

7: CORNER POCKET

DEREK STUMBLED DOWN Lundy's Lane, singing a vague approximation of "Brown Sugar" by the Rolling Stones. That he had only the most nebulous grasp of the lyrics besides the chorus—and there were bits of that he wasn't quite sure of, either—did not in the least dampen his enthusiasm.

"Somethin' 'bout a slave ship, plowing the fields, cold in a market down in New Orleans. Scarred old Sally's doin' all right, somethin' somethin' somethin' *just around midnight . . .* "

Around him, bar rats filtered into their cars and taxis, or clustered into the few fast-food joints that stayed open after closing time. Derek could go for a burger, but he was cleaned out. He had an empty wallet, a forehead shaking with the first pre-tremors of what was surely to be a foundation-buster of a hangover, and a stride-stiffening hard-on that he had no satisfactory way of alleviating. The cause of all three factors could be attributed to a halter-topped brunette in her early twenties. She and her girlfriends had carpooled down from Brock University to see the Falls and "get a sense of the culture," as she put it, her words blending slightly one into another. Her cleavage had jiggled slightly as she'd sidled into the stool next to Derek, who was more than happy to impart a little culture on a willing pupil.

Things had gone great until about one o'clock, when Derek—who'd been guiding the conversation towards the motel room he had just down the road, replete with coffee and other euphemistic amenities—was interrupted by a pug-faced blonde, who'd collected her bouncy and be-haltered friend and led her into a car and away, leaving Derek without so much as a phone number or even, in fact, a name. To be fair, Derek was pretty sure she'd told him the latter, but he hadn't been listening very closely.

"Fucking cocktease," Derek mumbled aloud, though without any real malice. He'd known well enough the long odds he was throwing, and he'd tossed his chips in anyway. University girls were a bad bet. They slummed it at the Blue Lagoon readily enough, soaking up a bit of that underworld charm, but when it came to sealing the deal, they got cold feet nine times out of ten. They loved the proletariat, those university girls—just not enough to fuck them. Derek supposed that meant he'd been strung along, but he'd copped a feel or three in the process, so who was the victim? It didn't take a Machiavelli to manipulate Derek McCulloch. A pulse and a pair of tits did it every time.

Derek stumbled into the parking lot of the Jupiter Motel, sparing a glance at its gloriously tacky sign. Built in the halcyon days of the 1960's, the Jupiter Motel was one of those peculiar Niagara Falls institutions that embraced the faux-futurist optimism of the space age and looked dated about six months after they'd been built. A lot of people wrung their hands over the city's copious eyesores, but Derek, for his part, couldn't get enough of them. He found his room, conducted a brief survey of his pockets until retrieving his keys, and let himself in.

He pawed the wall next to the doorframe, but the light switch proved elusive. He was still fumbling for it when a yellow light sliced through the darkness. Two men occupied his small and dingy room. One sat on the foot of his bed, elbows propped on his knees, his sizable belly straining at the buttons of his suit jacket; the other, reed-thin and sporting an adolescent's wispy moustache, leaned nonchalantly on the television stand. Both men held automatic pistols, their barrels trained on Derek's chest.

A breaker tripped deep inside Derek's brain and the usual cold machinery whirred to life. Intoxication evaporated in the autoclave of his mind, leaving a vacuum of utter sobriety. Yet his next words came out in a slurred jumble, and he stumbled slightly as he spoke, as if standing on a ship in an uneven keel. He'd already adopted, without consciously intending to, the mannerisms of a much drunker man.

"Man, that escort service's got some explainin' to do. I *specifically* said no ugly chicks."

The man on the bed smiled thinly. "Look at this lush, Lou. He thinks he's people."

Lou nodded. "Real cute, he is."

"No need to get nasty, girls. I'll still do you. But expect a stern letter to yer manager."

"You can tell him to your face in a minute."

Derek dropped his lecher's grin. He injected a look of delayed understanding into his features, a sudden widening of the eyes, a faint twitch beneath the lower lip. In truth he'd had a pretty good guess what this was about the moment they'd flicked on the lamp, but dumb was a role that got acclaim no matter how often you played it. "Whatta you mean?"

"I mean," said the man on the bed, "that Mr. Ballaro requests the privilege of your company."

"Yeah," added Lou. "And he ain't askin'."

Derek suppressed a smile at the look the man on the bed shot Lou. Lou, for his part, was oblivious. But thick or not, the man knew his business, as did the man on the bed. Both guns kept a pin on Derek's torso, their different angles giving at least one of them a clear shot regardless of which way he dove. He overbalanced right and took a stagger-step towards the closet, bringing him within grasping distance of his jacket, in the pocket of which resided a fully loaded .45 calibre revolver. Derek could picture the weapon clearly in his mind's eye, an image verified down to the last detail when the man on the bed reached beneath the covers and dangled the selfsame gun between thumb and forefinger.

"Good effort, Derek. We know your little tricks."

"Wish I'd known yours, Joey."

The fat man nodded. "What can I say? I keep it close to the vest. So, about this meeting."

"Right. 'Course." Derek cleared his throat. "Duly noted. Thanks for deliverin' the message. I love that personal touch. I can pencil him in for, say, next Tuesday?"

"Fraid this is a, whattayacall, rush order. You'll be comin' with us now."

***

There were two types of meetings you could have with Frank Ballaro: those you showed up to on your own—on time, respectably dressed, and stone sober—and those to which you were escorted. The former type tended to end with a lot of money changing hands, though other outcomes were possible—from stern lectures to shattered kneecaps—depending on your current standing, past actions, and general comportment at the meeting in question. The latter type only ended one way: a bag over the head, a bullet to the temple, and a tumble into the Niagara River. Derek had attended enough of these meetings to know—though mercifully never as the guest of honor.

Now it seemed that invitation had arrived. The question was, how could he tactfully turn it down?

"Guys, this ain't right," he said, lubricating his voice with crocodile tears. "I ain't caused Mr. Ballaro any trouble."

"That's for him to decide, not you."

"Come on, Joey. We're pals, ain't we? Just tell me what the big guy thinks I done. Whatever it is, I'm sure there's an explanation."

"You go on and explain it to him, then. We ain't the judges 'round here. We're just the delivery men."

Derek sniffed. "You . . . you think he'll listen, then?"

"Sure, sure," said Lou. "He'll listen."

Right. Not that I'll be saying much with my brains splattered across his parquet.

Joey, ever the cagier of the two, managed a more plausible lie. "Mr. Ballaro ain't no softy, Derek. You know that well as anybody. But he's fair. He don't ice folks for the fun of it. He don't tell us why we fetch a guy and we don't ask. He says jump, we jump to the fuckin' moon, you get me?"

"Yeah?"

Joey nodded. "Yeah. But another thing about Mr. Ballaro, he don't like to be kept waiting."

Derek nodded hard enough to make himself dizzy. "Okay. Okay, let's go then. Only hold on, I gotta . . . " Derek clutched his stomach and squeezed his balls between his thighs until the nausea he was faking turned real. "I gotta . . . " He staggered into the bathroom and dropped to his knees over the toilet, splashing the water as he cut loose a retching, gagging furor. It was a convincing performance; by the end of it he actually felt like puking. A few strings of bile hung from his lips.

Footsteps rang against the bathroom tile. Just one set, heavy and graceless. Lou, Derek was willing to bet. The sound of his voice proved him right.

"Okay Derek, enough fucking around. You cleared some room, now get up before we haul your ass outta there ourselves."

Derek retched harder by way of reply, his vocal cords straining. Cramps wrung his overworked diaphragm. He placed a hand on the cistern and made to stand, then doubled back down for another go. Lou took another step closer.

"All right, you asshole, that's enough." He grabbed the scruff of Derek's shirt, began hauling him to his feet.

The spin was swift and fluid, more dance than combat. Derek yanked the lid from the cistern one-handed and smashed it against Lou's head, his free hand sweeping the pistol aside, where it discharged harmlessly into the wall above the bathtub. A hail of porcelain shrapnel exploded through the room. Several slivers pricked Derek's face and burrowed into his hands; he would find himself digging them out over the next two weeks. Lou raised his hands to his jaw and let out a wail of pain, cut short as Derek jammed the broken edge of the cistern lid into his throat. He sawed back and forth until the porcelain turned red, grabbed the gun from Lou's numb fingers, and spent two quick shots into the thin man's head.

Derek sprang backwards before the shell casings hit the tile, sliding his ass onto the sink counter until his back was flush with the wall. With the slow motion clarity of soldiers and great athletes, he watched Joey lumber into the bathroom, gun brandished at nothing. The half instant it took him to figure out where Derek went was a half instant too long. Derek grabbed Joey's extended arm, bent it sharply against the doorframe for leverage, and fired a single point-blank shot into his elbow. The joint blew out in a jubilation of blood and bone. Joey let out an ululating scream. The gun dropped from his hand and skittered behind the toilet.

"Well shit," said Derek, inspecting the wound. "Now there's a hole I'd pay full price for. You've been holding out on me, Joey." The slur in his voice was gone, shed like so much snakeskin. He gave Joey's arm a gentle tug and the fat man dropped to his knees. The bathroom echoed with his incessant wailing.

Derek bent the arm upward. "Shut up, Joey. You're irritating me."

27

Joey shut up, his screams replaced by a low and steady blubbering.

"Question time, tubs. We both know how this meeting with Ballaro was supposed to end, so don't bother denying it. I don't hold a grudge. We're professionals, you and me, and that shit's just business. What I wanna know is what the big guy thinks I did to *earn* my invitation."

"I dunno, man, I dunno. You think he tells me anything?" Joey's eyes were red and glossy with tears. He wiped his face with one pudgy hand. A runner of snot clung to his index finger. Derek yanked a length of toilet paper from the roll and handed it to Joey, who wiped his face with a small nod of thanks. *Shoot a guy in the elbow and he thinks you're Hitler reincarnate. Hand him a hanky after and he thinks you're a god. People are funny.*

"No, I don't think he tells you jack shit. But you hang around that club of his an awful lot, and I know you ain't quite so brain-dead as your ex-partner over there." Derek motioned to Lou's body, dangling grotesquely over the lip of the tub. "I'm guessing you hear shit. So what I'm asking for is an educated guess. Why does Ballaro want to see me?"

"It's Eddie."

Derek blinked. "Eddie? His dipshit son? Since when's he been orderin' muscle around? Last I knew of things, Ballaro wouldn't trust the kid with his own cock and a tub of Vaseline."

"Eddie didn't order shit. Ain't you heard? Eddie's fuckin' *dead.*"

Derek giggled. Oh, this was *rich.* "Humanity's fuckin' loss. What'd he do, grope the wrong biker's favorite stripper? Wrap his fuckin' Beemer around a tree? Drink his dumb self to death?"

"Ain't what he did that counts. It's what was done to him. Shit was ghastly, Derek. I seen pictures. Ain't nothin' left of the kid but some guts and his fuckin' hand."

The situation got a whole lot less funny. "And Ballaro thinks *I* did his son?"

Joey clenched his jaw against a wave of pain. It crested, dropped. The tendons in his neck lost their guitar-string tautness. "You got the meanest rep outside the family. You been known to leave some . . . uh . . . souvenirs behind. And Lord knows you and Eddie were on the outs."

That's a fucking understatement. "Eddie's pissed off half the peninsula in his time. Why me?"

"Well, there was, you know . . . the whole scene at Vintage . . . "

Derek gritted his teeth. Time had yet to dull the memory's jagged edges. He'd been shooting pool at a bar on Main Street, a dive hangout for bikers and metalheads. It wasn't the sort of place named men like the Ballaros normally showed their faces, but Eddie fancied himself pure street and got a kick out of getting tippled alongside the city's riffraff underclass.

He came in with his usual abrasive swagger, a phalanx of cronies at his shoulders, tipping winks at waitresses and generally acting like he owned the place. At a glimpse of the prick Derek's stomach went sour, as if the several pints of beer he'd drunk all spoiled at once. "Fuckin' prick," he muttered under his breath. His opponent, a wiry guy called Corey with thick-framed glasses and a braided beard, gave Derek an uneasy look over this blasphemy.

"Careful, man. That guy's dad owns like half of the Hill. Cosa Nostra and shit."

"That so?" Derek asked, feigning ignorance. "Then I guess he could stand to lose a few bucks."

Derek waited until Eddie had spotted him, offered a small wave, and missed his shot. The cue ball careened off the seven and landed with a muted thump in the corner pocket.

"Skee-ratch!" cried Eddie, to tepid laughter.

"Not my night," Derek admitted. "Look at all these solids." He gestured to the table, where a constellation of five low balls spread out around the eleven and thirteen, the only high balls left on the felt. Derek was, in fact, shooting stripes for this particular game, but Corey picked up their swapped allegiances quickly enough and didn't protest. It did, after all, provide him with a substantial lead.

Derek hacked his way through the rest of the game, allowing himself to pot the odd ball so as not to appear unrealistically awful. Corey was a competent player. Not gifted, surely, but possessed of enough raw skill to leverage his sudden lead into a reasonably truncated victory. They shook hands and exchanged pleasantries, Corey's gaze shifting uncomfortably between Derek and the posse by the bar. He downed the remains of his beer in a rolling swig and left.

"What do you say, Eds?" Derek called across the bar. "Up for a game?"

"I dunno, man. I like to play someone who can offer a bit of a challenge, at least."

"Come on," coaxed Derek. "It was an off table for me. I'll even make it interesting. Say five bucks a ball?"

Eddie blew dismissively through his lips. "Pffff. Chump change. You wanna play? Let's do it. Fifty bucks a ball. Plus a hundred for a win."

Derek forced a look of apprehension across his face. "Okay, I guess." He racked the balls and swivelled some chalk onto the tip of his cue. "You wanna break, or should I?"

"Go for it, chief."

Don't think I won't, you arrogant prick.

Derek went for it, all right. A true shark job called for feints and artifice, whittling out a few slight victories and goading the opponent, through frustration or arrogance, into raising the stakes. But this wasn't about fattening Derek's wallet; it was about busting Eddie's balls—and not the ones on the table. This was Derek's first major miscalculation, but it felt so damn good that, were he given the chance to relive the night's events, he'd probably do the exact same thing all over again.

His break sank two balls, a stripe and a solid, leaving an open table and even odds on both suits. Derek put nose to felt and pledged his allegiance to stripes with a bank shot into the corner pocket. He potted two more and found himself pretty snookered by the four ball, which placed a solid defence between the cue ball and the thirteen. Rather than risk it, Derek tried a glancing shot off the ten at the quiet end of the table, failing to sink it but leaving Eddie with nothing. Eddie took a gamble on the three ball and scratched, giving Derek ball in hand. In friendly games Derek would place scratches behind the line in a gesture of sportsmanship, but there was nothing friendly about this game, despite the smiles plastered to both players' faces. He placed the ball kissing distance from the fifteen, which teetered on the lip of a side pocket, nudged the ball home, and set the nine ball caroming into the corner, where it landed with a clack atop the previously potted eleven.

In three short turns Derek faced the eight ball on a table where three of seven solids still stood. He treated himself to a quick glance at Eddie, who stewed beneath his smile like a lidded pot approaching boil.

"Corner pocket," Derek said, pointing to the target with his cue. He sighted the ball, chin grazing the felt, and took the shot. The eight ball bit the pocket's back bumper and sank like a stone in a well. "That's game, chief. Eight sunk against four at fifty bucks a ball, plus a win, that's me up three even. Care to go again?"

Wordlessly, Eddie racked the balls into a slightly off-kilter triangle. "Got lucky," he mumbled.

It was Eddie's turn to break. He struck the cue ball at a bad angle and sent it spinning into the broad side of the triangle with an ugly scraping sound. The shape took on a rumpled, fender-bender look. Eddie fixed it and took another shot from behind the line, this time scattering the balls. Anger crippled his already shoddy game. Derek scored an extra four hundred bucks, then a remarkable four hundred and fifty. He started to think he might have a new business going when Eddie finally yanked out his wallet and, with stiff, shaking fingers, tossed out twelve one-hundred dollar bills. They fluttered down one after another, landing in a loose pile at Derek's feet.

"Keep the extra fifty."

Derek knelt down to collect the bills. For twelve hundred dollars, he was willing to let Eddie claw back a bit of his lost dignity. As he gathered the money into a pile, he heard a wet, plosive sound. A droplet of warm liquid plopped onto his head. Eddie bent over him, a gleam of spittle on his grinning lips. A few members of his posse chuckled, elbowing one other at the spectacle. Derek rose, his good humor long gone. He looked Eddie square in the eye, noting with pleasure the faint glimmer of apprehension there.

"Watch yourself, Eddie."

Eddie thrust his chest out, shoving his way into Derek's personal space. "Or what? What the fuck you gonna do, eh?"

"Why don't you ask your daddy? He's seen enough of it."

Eddie's mouth shrank to the size of a half-healed scar. "You threatenin' a Ballaro, Derek? That it? You ice a few guys, torch a few buildings, all on my dad's say-so, and you think you can step to, act a big shot in my town? You're a fuckin' *janitor,* man. You clean up our shit and collect your paycheck. That's where it ends."

"Your father doesn't need a janitor, Eddie. He can keep his own house in order. You're the one who makes the messes in the family, usually in your pants. You don't need a janitor, you need a fucking babysitter."

Under most circumstances, Eddie's tough talk deflated into a queasy just-joshin' bonhomie at the first real sign of resistance, followed by a smouldering period of behind-your-back trash talk. But the presence of his posse made him bolder than anticipated, and where Derek expected a snide remark, he got a right cross to the temple. It was a clumsy punch thrown by a novice welterweight, but its sheer unexpected nature helped it land. Derek staggered back, jags of light bursting before his left eye.

Eddie landed no second punch. At least, not until three of his goons had peeled Derek off of him, snorting rage and flicking blood from his knuckles. Eddie pulled himself upright on the pool table. Twin rivers of stringy red mucus streamed out his nostrils.

"Hold 'im" Eddie said, his voice clotted with the smudgy sound of a broken nose.

"Yeah, you boys hold me tight," Derek said. "Wouldn't want your precious little angel to risk his ass in a fair figh—"

Derek's last word broke off, snapped in two by Eddie's fist. He played some chin music, rattling Derek's teeth and splitting his lip like an overcooked sausage, and threw a volley of quick rat-a-tat jabs to the abdomen. His rings left nicks and gauges in Derek's skin. The goons knew their business, holding Derek taut and steady, but with enough spring to take the sting out of it for Eddie's knuckles. The animal dwelling in the depths of Derek's mind gnashed its teeth and pulled furiously on its chains, but Derek refused to let it free. Fighting back could only make a bad situation worse. Eventually the pummeling eased up. Eddie, winded and nursing his raw knuckles, told his posse to toss Derek out.

"Don't let me catch you around here again, Derek. You hear me?"

The goons dragged him onto the patio and tossed him over the railing, where he landed in a heap of scrapes and bruises. They didn't even spare him a second glance as they went back inside. A few abrasive measures of amphetamine-soaked death metal shrieked out the door before it swung shut. Derek lay where he'd fallen for a moment, patting down the pockets in which he'd stuffed his winnings before the worst of the beating. It seemed to be all there. He slouched down the road to a neighbouring bar with a danker, quieter air and soaked his hurts with several successive shots of Jack Daniels.

So that was it. Eddie gave him a public humiliation, and a few weeks later had wound up a corpse in a theatrical and deeply messy fashion. It wasn't exactly hard evidence of guilt, but nor was Ballaro beholden to the finer points of jurisprudence. Still, he had a good working history with Frank. With some kowtowing and a bit of luck, the whole misunderstanding could potentially be straightened out.

Before, that was, he'd killed one of Ballaro's men and crippled another. Neither action spoke volumes towards his innocence. Had he submitted meekly to his capture, he might've been able to talk himself out of his death sentence. Instead, he'd seized what had seemed like his one chance at survival—violence; a personal specialty—and in so doing effectively signed a warrant for his own execution.

It was almost sort of funny.

While Derek mulled over the finer points of his situation, Joey slumped onto the floor, his injured arm still held loosely in Derek's hand. The tiles were slick with blood. The soles of Derek's shoes made an unpleasant smacking sound every time he shifted position.

"Well, Joe, I guess I've gone and made a mess of things."

"I'm really bleedin' here, Derek. You gotta get me to a hospital."

Derek tapped the barrel of the pistol to his lips. "When Ballaro sent you to collect me, he call on anyone for backup?"

"No, man. Just me and Lou."

"Don't lie to me, Joe."

Joe peeled his face from the floor. Threads of blood and snot clung to his cheek. "It's God's honest truth, Derek. Really. He expects his name to carry enough weight that it don't matter we got no backup."

Derek made a hook of his index and middle fingers and sank it into the hole in Joey's elbow. Joey writhed like a man undergoing electroshock, bellowing like nothing human. Derek withdrew his fingers.

"Let me hear God's truth one more time, Joey."

"I swear it, Derek, I swear it," Joey blubbered. "It was just me and Lou. He's gonna expect us back pretty soon, though, so we don't show up I wouldn't be surprised he sends a couple guys to check up on things. You know how he is."

Derek nodded. "Cautious. Cautious and smart."

"Hey man, I'm losin' a whole lot of blood. Can you drop me at the hospital? I won't look where you go after that, for real. Everything's sorta dim and all anyway. Or call an ambulance on your way out. It won't cost you nothin'. I won't hit you back Derek, I swear it. I swear it. It really hurts."

Derek chewed his lip, gave a quick glimpse around at the scene, and sank to one knee. Tenderly, with the solemn movements of a man proposing to his fiancée, Derek tucked the barrel of the gun under Joey's chin.

"I just want you to know, Joey, that you were always one of the better ones."

"Derek, wait, I—"

Derek made it quick and clean. As clean as possible, anyway.

8: LINES OF STATIC

WALTER TOOK OFF his hat and ran his chubby fingers through his thinning grey-brown hair. His moustache twitched.

"Well, here's one we can wrap our head around, at least."

David lit a cigarette. The proprietor raised a finger in protest, opened his mouth, and thought better of it. He stood on the motel room porch, wringing his hands and glancing nervously from side to side as if attending not a crime scene but a crime in progress. David exhaled a plume of smoke into the room, watched it eddy off the cheap wallpaper and twine around the slowly-twirling blades of the ceiling fan. He clamped the cigarette between his teeth and looked over his partner's shoulder into the bathroom.

The room resounded with the buzz of flies. Blood clung to every surface, rivulets of it dried to a tacky paste. The owner could scrub all he wanted, but he'd never get those tiles clean.

The two bodies formed a crude J shape. The lanky man curled semi-fetal in the tub, his akimbo legs intersecting with the truncated cross of the heavy man collapsed on the floor beneath him. His head nestled in the narrow gap between tub and toilet while his feet poked out the doorway into the hall. David crouched down and inspected the man's leg. Blood soaked his pants from shin to knee, but the soles of his shoes were pristine save for a bit of road grit caught between the treads. The cigarette danced and jigged from one corner of David's mouth to the other. He removed the yellow caution tape crisscrossing the doorway.

There was scarcely any spot to stand that wouldn't involve compromising the crime scene. David eventually found a sliver of unbloodied tile and set one foot there, balancing the remainder of his weight on the bare rim of the toilet. The heel of his shoe hooked snugly against the porcelain, providing enough leverage for him to bend forward and examine the body in the tub. A bullet hole gaped from his right temple. It expanded to a gaping crater on the head's opposite hemisphere. A spew of bone and brain clung to the wall like an ugly silhouette, a pantomime exhibit of the force and angle of the shot. Another wound split the man's neck, which had been rendered to raw meat between chin and collarbone. Pale shards poked from the desecrated flesh. David plucked one free with a gloved hand and held it to the light. Porcelain.

He shifted the body to one side, revealing the shattered remains of the cistern lid.

"A nasty gash to the neck and a bullet to the head to finish the job. Your guy?"

Walter stood with a small grunt, his knees popping. "Same capper, though this mook took a bullet to the elbow first, point blank."

"Eesh."

"I'll say. Skin's peeled back, too. Buddy was poking around in there."

David took a look for himself. "Trying to make him talk."

"I'd be singin' any tune the bastard called out, it was me."

They stepped from the bathroom into the annex by the double bed, free from the contortions of preserving evidence. David tapped his cigarette into an ashtray he found on the nightstand.

Walter lit a smoke of his own. "Let me paint you a picture."

David gestured for him to go on.

"Our perp finds himself cornered in his room. Maybe he owes money, maybe he made it with the wrong girl. Anyway, it's two to one and the guy's spooked. He holes up in the bathroom, clocks the first guy who comes in with the toilet lid, takes his gun, bu-blam." Walter cocks a finger at David's temple, mimes pulling the trigger. "Body number two charges in after his friend, gets one in the elbow. Maybe he begs, maybe there's a bit of a struggle. The perp pumps him for info, kills him, and gets the hell out of dodge."

David nodded slowly. "Sounds about right. Only I don't think we're dealing with your run-of-the-mill deadbeat here. Whoever pulled himself out of this scrape knew his business."

"Or he got his blood up and got lucky."

"That's a lot of luck for one little bathroom."

A curtain of smoke descended from Walter's nostrils. "Guess we'd better see whose room we're standin' in."

They found the owner in the reception room lobby, running his fingers compulsively over the rubber fronds of a fake palm tree. He was a compact man, his lip shadowed with a wispy black moustache, his otherwise bald pate bisected by a peninsular widow's peak. A large mole sprouted from the soft flesh above his chin. Its bulbous weight pulled the right corner of his lower lip down slightly, giving his face a perpetual pout.

"You are done with room. I clean now, yes?"

"Not just yet, I'm afraid," said David. "We've seen all we need. The forensics guys'll be here soon. They'll get everything bagged up for you. Once they're done, someone'll let you know."

"Until then, that room's occupied," added Walter. "No maids, no guests—though I'm guessing you'd need to offer a pretty cheap rate, eh?"

The owner didn't find this funny. He tugged at the mole on his lip.

"They come already. They take picture."

"Different guys. I'm sorry, it won't be much longer."

"No good for business," the owner said. "No good at all for business."

"You kiddin'?" asked Walter. "All sortsa whack jobs get off on that stuff. 'Stay in the Murder Room! Commune with the spirits of the dead!' You get the place spruced up a little, you're gonna have lines around the block."

David gave Walter a small waving hand gesture. *Enough.* He put a guiding hand on the owner's shoulder. "Listen, sir. We appreciate your patience. We're just about ready to go, but before we do, we're wondering if we could get a look at your guest registry."

The owner led David—or rather, David subtly led him—to the motel computer, an ancient desktop faded to the yellow-beige of a smoker's teeth. A fan wheezed dusty air over the heat sink as the processor grumbled to life. The owner clicked about the screen, bringing up a primitive spreadsheet of names and room numbers. He highlighted a name and pointed.

"There. This one."

David leaned forward and read the name Krist Novoselic. "I guess I shouldn't be surprised." He straightened up and looked at Walter. "Fake name."

"Yeah? What'd he go for? Hugh Jazz? Seymour Butts?"

"No, our guy kept it classy. Unless the former bassist for Nirvana's made someone very angry lately."

"No one's ever cared enough about a bassist to blow one, let alone try an' off one. Especially not from a second-rate band like Nirvana."

"Watch your mouth," David said, still studying the screen. "They defined my generation."

"Yeah, and The Stones and Zeppelin defined mine. Three guesses which one of us wins the culture war."

David shot Walter a surreptitious middle finger and turned to the owner. "I'm guessing it's too much to hope for, but this guy didn't pay with a credit card, did he?"

The owner shook his head. "Cash deposit. This I will not be returning. It will cost twice so much to clean the room, not to count the lost business."

"Absolutely. If he should come back to claim it, you're under no obligation to give it to him. We'd appreciate if you gave us a call immediately, though." David's eyes flicked to the corners of the lobby. Cameras sprouted from the drywall like mechanical flowers. "You guys got closed circuit TV?"

"Yes. But the tape is deleting itself every twelve hours. Mr. Novoselic comes in here for the last time on Tuesday when he rents the room. This is five days ago."

"This Mr. Novoselic, you remember what he looked like?" asked Walter.

"He is young guy. No beard or moustache. Brown hair in short haircut. Light skin. Same height as you, maybe taller." He pointed to David. "His clothes are not so nice. Not like bums, but like young people. The baggy t-shirts and jeans."

"Any tattoos? Piercings?"

"I see none of these."

Walter jotted the responses down on a small notebook. "Would you mind coming down to the station to speak to one of our sketch artists? See if we can paint a clearer picture of this guy?"

"I have no time for this. I am busy running my business."

"It won't take long."

The owner seemed unhappy about this, but didn't protest further. David toyed with the alligator ring on his finger. "One more thing. Would you mind making us a copy of the surveillance tape?"

"I am telling you, the film is being deleted every twelve hours. You will not see him."

"Probably not, but we might get lucky. And if we do, we won't need you to come down to the station after all."

The owner reached under the counter and pulled out a blank VHS tape. "Please give me fifteen minutes."

They piled into David's unmarked Impala fifteen minutes later on the nose, tape in hand, and drove to his house. Dandelions peeked through hairline cracks in the pavement. David's house was humble but well-kept, two storeys of 1930s red brick perched above an amended veranda and garden. Steeps gables gave the roof a high-browed, inquisitive cast. He'd purchased it two years ago when he'd moved back to Niagara Falls from Toronto, amazed at what the combined might of a detective and realtor's salaries could fetch him outside the megacity's vortex-like pull. Inside, a narrow hallway fed into a network of cozy, closed-concept rooms. Vistas of open-concept space were more fashionable, but David appreciated the way older houses compartmentalized domesticity, partitioning life into discrete chambers. Categorization appealed to the investigator in him.

A woman sat in the living room, leaning sideways against the armrest of the couch. Mid-thirties, slender, curtains of brown hair draped over either shoulder. She looked up from her book at the sound of their entry, smiled.

"Oh, hey, hun. What's up? Hi, Walter."

"Good to see you, Nancy," said Walter. "You mean you haven't left this bum yet?"

"No point, he hasn't found out about the two of us."

"I've been too damn discreet, that's the problem."

Nancy arched her back, meeting halfway as David stooped down to kiss her. "What are you two doing here?"

David held up the VHS tape. "Official police business."

"What, from 1998?"

David smiled. "Exactly. VCR at the precinct went bust last year. Tape heads all worn to hell. We could probably dig one up somewhere, but if I'm gonna watch a movie I'd just as soon do it on my own couch."

Nancy's gaze drifted back to the tape, their cast solemn. "It's not about, you know . . . that strip club murder, is it?"

"No, nothing like that. It's security camera footage from a motel. Not a murder in sight." *But maybe, if we're lucky, a murderer.* "Shouldn't take us more than an hour, then we'll be out of your hair."

"Take all the time you need. I've got a house to show at eleven, so I should start getting ready anyway." She set her book down with its pages splayed open over the armrest and gave David another quick peck as she passed. "Good seeing you again, Walter. You and Rose should come by for dinner again some time."

"Make ribs like last time, you got a deal."

Walter settled on the couch while David queued up the VCR. A varnish of dust coated the lip below the tape slot. He wiped it away with a pinky finger and slipped the tape home. Gears whirred and crunched as the tape heads slotted into position. It occurred to David how strange and alien this technology must seem to his son, much the way a Victrola would have seemed to him as a boy.

David set the tape to rewind and plopped on the couch next to Walter. The older detective ran his fingers over the ribbed ledge of a glass ashtray—purely decorative, as David had cut out smoking inside years ago.

"Hey, since we're loungin' and all, how 'bout a beer?"

"It is"—David checked his watch—"9:43 in the morning."

"Scotch?"

David shook his head and went into the kitchen. He came back with two bottles of Mad Tom, coils of frosty carbonation rising from their uncapped lips. Walter sniffed his before drinking, his face puckering at the sting of hops.

"There somethin' wrong with Budweiser?"

"There's everything wrong with Budweiser. Now can we watch the tape?"

Walter took another swig of his beer—his disgust, as David had suspected, was largely feigned—and twirled his hand in a go-ahead gesture. The VCR let out a mechanical hiccough as the tape reached its starting point. David hit play on the remote.

The lobby of the Jupiter Motel filled the television screen, its colours wan and muted. The camera peered onto the scene from a steep isometric vantage point that gave the room a warped appearance, as if the angles of the walls had been tweaked. A dull but steady tape hiss comprised the sound. Despite these limitations, the picture itself was crisp, allowing David and Walter to make out the finer details of patrons' faces as they filtered to and from the desk. The overnight receptionist fumbled in the register for change and passed keys indifferently to customers. He was a young kid, high school probably, greasy hair tied back in a ponytail. His shirt, wrinkled and poorly fit, bulged from his belt in patches where he'd half-heartedly tucked it in. David's detective eyes cycled into full-on profiling mode: five-eight, one-twenty pounds, a skinny burnout in the making, hadn't dropped out of school yet but thinking about it.

He scored Ds and Cs, plus maybe the odd A in shop or art. Worked bum hours to avoid the hardscrabble duties of fast food or retail, scrubbin' through midnights for pot money. He'd turn around come college, given a kick in the ass and parents who gave half a fuck. David considered imparting these deductions to Walter but decided against it, his focus too keenly honed on the goings-on depicted by the juddering half-speed tape.

"We should talk to the kid."

"Clemens and LaFleur already milked him dry. Kid heard a couple of shots, but says he figured it was a punk with the TV up too loud. More like he was too drunk or stoned to care and don't wanna cop to it."

"Still. Set the kid in an interrogation room and his memory might get a bit sharper."

Walter shrugged and sipped his beer. "Suit yourself. Once we watch this tape I'm catchin' a nap."

"I suppose you want to use my spare bed."

"Well, I'd drive the Impala home, but I've been drinking."

"Do you not want to solve this thing? Between the Stanford Acres fire and the Sundown Lounge murder, this city is starting to look like Sarajevo in the nineties. You've seen the memos." Circulated by email to all PR personnel, with Walter and David deliberately CCed, they included the text of forthcoming articles from the *Niagara Falls Review*, in which crime and politics reporter Dawna Lane covered the proceeding investigations, her prose aflame with increasingly incendiary comments about the force in general and Chief Delduca in particular. The memos refrained from editorializing, but the subtext was clear: get Stanford Acres and the Sundown Lounge off the front page and into the dustbin with the other old news, or else.

Walter waved his hand in David's general direction, his eyes on the screen. "I'll go about it my own way. Now hush up. I'm tryin' to watch this thing."

"There isn't even any sound."

Walter's hand flapped more vigorously and David hushed.

The tape stuttered on. The recorder captured images at a reduced frame rate to save space, but the VCR wasn't designed to compensate, so everyone on screen moved with the herky-jerky franticness of pratfall artists in old silent movies. The urge to fast-forward was overpowering, but it was easy enough to miss something as it was, given the playback speed. A clock in the corner counted forward the minutes: 11:51, 11:52, 11:53 . . .

"Hold it," Walter said. David hit pause. The image onscreen froze, lines of static carving it into horizontal segments. Two figures could be seen through the plate-glass window at the front of the lobby: one tall and lanky; the other muscled, giving way to middle-aged fleshiness. Both wore neatly-cut suits.

"Our boys?" David asked.

"Looks like it. Check out that swagger. They didn't know what they had coming."

"The receptionist puts the shots at what, three?"

"Two-thirty or thereabouts. Other guests nearby give the same time, more or less."

"But none call the cops, of course."

"'Eh, I hear a bang, it ain't none of my business'," said Walter, aping a middle-aged Italian they'd come across on their brief and fruitless canvassing of the motel.

"Good Samaritans abound."

"Warms the cockles of my heart, man."

David pulled out a notebook and jotted down *11:53 -> Victims arrive.* He fast-forwarded to two o'clock and resumed playback.

"So our boys show up first, let themselves into the room somehow. Through a window, maybe, or maybe it's just unlocked. They're still there two or three hours later when Mr. Novoselic arrives."

"Late to the party," said Walter, tsking. "Typical rock star."

"Our boys are dressed too nice for burglars, so we're talking ambush. Only they let Novoselic get to the bathroom, which means they did some talking first. No way the guy just bumbles in there and dives into the john without them so much as firing at the door."

"Could be they weren't there to kill the guy. Just put a scare into him, break his legs, that sort of thing."

David shook his head. "They didn't seem to have the tools for that."

"Could be the guy took them when he booked it."

David nodded. "Or could be they were there to take him someplace else."

"Yeah, I'd buy that. Guy uses a fake name to book a motel, he's either fucking around on his wife or he's into something he shouldn't be."

"Or both."

Walter tapped the end of his nose knowingly. He snapped his fingers, pointing excitedly at the screen. "Hey hey hey, we've got some movement."

David snatched up the controller and hit pause. A blur of cloth and denim haunted the outer ridge of the frame. David walked the scene back with a tap of the rewind button and played through again. He and Walter focused on the screen with grim intensity.

The second pause was quicker and better timed, but revealed little more than the first. Unlike the two victims, who'd sauntered along the slab concrete walkway running the length of the building, the lone figure cut diagonally across the parking lot, putting him only partially in frame, and at a bad angle to boot. Even if they cut open the tape and had a photographer blow up the frame to poster size, they'd never get a clean look at his face.

"Might not be the guy, anyway," Walter said.

David shook his head. There was no way he could know for sure, but he did. The compass needle whirling in his mind found true north at his first glimpse of the faceless figure on the screen. He hit play and set the remote beside him. His index finger hovered over the pause button. The minutes skittered past. Walter took occasional sips from his beer, the lip of the bottle hovering inches from his face, his gaze lacking David's overt intensity but no less keen.

At 3:01 a figure passed the window, this time heading in the opposite direction. He walked briskly, a hurried stride that wasn't quite a run. David hit pause, freezing the man in place. His light hair stuck up at odd angles. A bag, hurriedly packed, dangled half-zipped from one hand, the hem of a pair of jeans poking out like a denim tongue. A line of pause static obscured his neck and jaw, but his face was clearly visible—early thirties, clean-shaven, handsome but showing the first folds and tears of hard living. David guessed the ladies came easy and still would for a while to come, until the guy's bad habits scrawled their usual graffiti over his features. He struck his open hand with his fist.

"Fucking A. Let's get this bad boy to the photo lab. They can grab a still, get it blown up for us. We'll hit the skin bars and other dives tomorrow, see if we can scrounge up a positive ID."

"No need," Walter said. A tiny smile hid beneath the fronds of his moustache. "I know exactly who that motherfucker is."

"Yeah?" David watched the wheels turning behind Walter's hazel eyes. "And?"

"This shit just got a lot more interesting."

9: BLACK MAGIC

IMAN TRUDGED HER way to the third floor, clutching a stack of books under one arm. Their hardbound corners dug divots into the soft flesh of her bicep, and the axis of pressure binding them into a single column shifted perilously with each riser, giving the load all the stability of a tightrope walker with a clubfoot. Her backpack—stuffed to bursting with more books—provided an awkward counterbalance, its nylon straps pinching the tendons that ran from shoulder to neck. For roughly the thousandth time since she left the library fifteen minutes earlier, she regretted not bringing a canvas bag or three with her. Loaded down as she was, she felt like a bottle of nitroglycerin balanced atop a Jenga tower— and the players stacking the bricks weren't exactly pros.

She staggered into her office and, drawing on some miraculous reserve of previously unplumbed dexterity, managed to set the books down delicately on the cushions of a nearby couch. She slumped the backpack from her shoulders and set it down next to the books. Her upper body groaned with blissful relief. She pushed the books aside and plopped down next to them, letting her over-tightened muscles uncoil. *If these library runs keep up their pace, I'll be bench-pressing two hundred pounds by the time I get my Master's.* There was no way Motes was reading everything he was having her fetch. Even skimming them all would be a daunting task, given the papers she poured into his email inbox. She scanned the titles, wringing her brow at the panoply of bizarre texts: *Der Hexenhammer, Concernant la Sorcellerie et la Magie Parmi les Amérindiens; Chilling Tales Volume II: 1931-1934; La Bête du Gévaudan; Den Hrafnsmál Saga; Virgil's Bucolica.* For a man who read Dickens on the beach and considered Gogol's *The Nose* to be an unfortunate dip into absurdity, this was a deeply bizarre reading list.

She rose to knock on Motes' office door when a sound caught her attention. She paused, hovering in a squat halfway between sitting and standing. The sound came again, low and wet, a tumbling of glottal stops followed by a sibilant inhalation of breath.

Motes was sobbing. The unmistakable sound of a tissue torn from its box preceded a honk as the professor blew his nose. Iman shivered with the symbiotic mortification she felt whenever she unwittingly peered through the cracks of an acquaintance's composure. As she cringed, the topmost book in her tenuous tower slipped from its perch and struck the couch's armrest. Motes' sobbing ceased mid-breath.

"Hi professor," she called, her voice spangled with false cheeriness. "I got the books you wanted."

"Fine," Motes said. "Leave them on the table. I'll grab them later."

"Sure." Iman wiped her nose with a finger. A few stray hairs crept up her nose, setting off a volley of sneezes. She studied the hairs.

Dog fur?

Maybe his dog died. Not that he ever mentioned having a dog. She touched her fingers to her eyelids and worked them in slow, gentle circles, waiting for her tear ducts to kick in. Her corneas felt like under-greased skillets, their scored cooktops crackling with heat. Part of her discomfort came from Motes' coat dander, but most of it was simple fatigue. For the past two weeks, Iman had waded across an endless quagmire of murky academic prose, hacking through thickets of arcane syntax and peeling back paragraphs sticky with jargon in the no doubt vain hope of spotting the faint glimmer of some lost jewel. The saddest part was, she wasn't even getting paid for a lot of this. She tucked her Motes work into her schedule wherever it would fit, cramming bits and pieces into crevices between meals or after workouts.

Resigned to another eye-abusing four hours, she booted up her computer and settled into the latest and most bizarre task Motes had assigned to her. Today she was reading about werewolves. Or rather, werewolf lore. You'd think it would be an interesting subject, but academics could desiccate the juiciest topics, wring dry the drippings and leave leathery husks of bland mental nutrition. She chewed these without pleasure, mulling through case studies and anthropological dissections of folklore from every corner of the globe.

"It's for a paper," he'd replied tersely when Iman asked why his reading had taken such a sudden divergence. "Give me a summary. The myths, the tropes, all of it."

She hoped to find a basic archetype, something clean and clearly delineated she could hand Motes before getting back to her painfully neglected thesis. Instead she found patterns of the desultory sort one sees in clouds, contrivances of shape or texture that made a scene, but could shift into meaninglessness with the slightest change in the wind. The werewolf was a victim, a sorcerer, a spirit, a witch's familiar. They changed in moonlight, under a curse, as punishment for sin, through gris-gris or incantation or ritual. The ancient Greeks wrote of a Scythian tribe that transformed into wolves once a year, the Romans of a man who hung his clothes on an ash tree and donned a wolf pelt in their place. Whispers echoed through the Balkans and the Caucasus, flitted through Scandinavia and Western Europe, passed the lips of the Haitians and the Navajo. African tribes spoke of men who morphed into lions or leopards, The Indians and Chinese of were-tigers, the Aztecs of were-jaguars. Shapeshifters wore wolf-skin belts, anointed themselves with magic salves, drank from enchanted streams, slept outside in the light of a full moon. Cures ranged from the brutal—driving spikes through the afflicted individual's hands—to the laughably simplistic—exercise, reciting the Lord's Prayer.

An email notification popped onto the bottom of her screen. She checked her inbox and saw nothing. She switched to Motes' account, to which she also had access. Journals often reached out to him with news about submitted papers or requests to review manuscripts, and replying to these missives was one of Iman's myriad duties. She found no new email here either. Puzzled, she noticed the trash bin folder, which indicated three recent deletions.

"The hell?" she whispered to herself. Motes never touched his email except to send her articles. Messages sent to him often went unchecked for months unless Iman goaded him into reading them. The trash folder purged itself each week, which meant the messages were no more than a few days old. Fighting a riptide of guilt at her intrusion, she clicked on the trash bin and reviewed the deleted emails.

All three came from the same account, blytzkreegbop123@hotmail.com. She read the oldest one first and worked her way forward:

sup motes? ive been mad busy but we need to take a trip. two months max, u know the day. gotta see Majka again and i need u there. no bodies this time, so no worries :) peace L

u avoidin me bro? wont do any good. u got our gift and u owe us. L

yo motes. good talkin to ya ;) next time email back and u wont get a late night visit lol.

That was it. Iman checked the dates. The first had arrived three days ago, the second last night. The third was only a minute old.

Nervous energy impelled her to stand. She paced the office, sifting through snippets of text in her mind and hovering over the monitor to reread bits she'd forgotten. *U got our gift and u owe us.* What could that be? Some sort of bribe or payoff? For what? It all seemed a little dramatic for a better grade, but what else could Motes really offer?

One phrase in particular pierced her like an icicle, frozen and deadly sharp: *no bodies this time, so no worries.*

No bodies this time.

So what the hell happened *last* time?

44

10: SUGAR DADDY

THE IMPALA PUTTERED up Montrose Road, cruising past bungalows and strip malls clinging like barnacles to major intersections. *The Immigrant Song* chugged out of the stereo system, fuzz-soaked downstrokes beating the relentless rhythm of a war galley's oars. It was a hard song not to speed to, and David forced himself to ease up on the accelerator.

"You're gonna hang a left a little past Thorold Stone Road," Walter explained.

Interviewing Frank Ballaro had been on their to-do list since they'd first IDed Eddie, but the man could be hard to reach, especially if you wore a badge. The intended flavour of the meeting had changed a good deal since David had first planned it, given the events at the Jupiter Motel. It was bound to be a whole lot tastier given that particular addition—but also more apt to be poisonous for all involved. Ballaro was a cautious man, but dangerous. David and Walter would walk out of there untouched, no question, but if they left a sour taste in Ballaro's mouth when they did, any number of misfortunes might befall them down the road.

"So tell me a little about our shooter," said David.

"You mean you've never heard of Derek McCulloch?"

"Should I have?"

Walter shook his head. "You embarrass yourself, kid. The mope's from your neck of the woods."

"Toronto's a big city, Walt. We don't get on first-name basis with every scumbag who comes through central processing. This guy got a serious record or something?"

"Nah, the usual dickhead bullshit. Grand theft auto, a few burglaries, bar fights. The guy's rap sheet ain't what makes his name. It's his reputation."

David smiled. "What, he's a good lay or something?"

"We find him, you're welcome to see for yourself. I don't know how well he fucks, but he's a goddamn Da Vinci of fucking people up."

"So he's an enforcer?"

Walter seesawed his hand back and forth in a so-so gesture. "Hitman, mostly. Freelance. Puts bullets in people when a payin' customer feels a certain someone lacks enough lead in their diet."

"How many people are we talking?"

"No one we can prove, but enough to build a bit of a legacy on the street. Some of the newer stories are probably bullshit, you know how these things go. Guy pulls a few hits and doesn't get caught, he turns into Paul Bunyan, so big his footsteps make lakes."

David nodded, contemplating. "You're thinking this Derek guy did Eddie Ballaro?"

"I'm thinkin' daddy Ballaro thinks as much. The timing's suspicious, I admit." Walter smoothed his moustache against his lip, pulling the hairs taut enough to stretch the skin. "First Stanford Acres burns, then Eddie gets hamburgered, now two wise guys gunned down in a fleabag motel. This whole fucking city's going to the dogs."

"I suspect it's as good or bad as it ever was. We're just seeing it a little more clearly."

Walter smirked, his eyes rekindling their sardonic glitter. "You're a fucking poet, Dave."

"You're a fucking asshole, Walt."

"Hey, best to play up your natural talents, am I right?"

Walter guided David along a winding street lined with oversized McMansions aping styles from more prestigious ports of call: faux-Tudor, faux-Mediterranean, faux-Victorian, they stood cheek by jowl in their cookie-cutter splendor, gaudy peacocks preening for some unseen mate. Marble fountains sat atop carefully manicured lawns, hosting alabaster cherubs pissing rainwater. David couldn't for the life of him understand the rich. Did money corrode taste?

They rounded a bend, coasting past BMWs and Mercedes parked nonchalantly on the curbside, chrome fixtures flashing in the sun. Walter pointed to their left. "This is it. Pull over."

David whistled. Even by the elephantine standards of the neighbourhood, Ballaro's house stood out. Not just in size, but in class. A Georgian façade offered symmetrical splendor, a symphony of geometry playing in its lintels and mullions and eaves. Marble columns quadrisected the manor's width. A granite staircase funneled visitors to a pair of oak and iron doors, its splayed fan shape creating an illusion of greater distance between columns two and three. This wasn't faux-Georgian; this was an *homage*. Every surface glimmered with the impossible whiteness of a Hollywood actor's teeth. David guessed that Ballaro had the walls power-washed on a monthly basis to maintain that kind of shine.

"Jesus. We can't nail this guy on tax evasion?"

Walter snorted. "Please. Ballaro ain't a stupid man. His dirty money don't flash. That house is all paid for on the level, taxed and squeaky clean."

"Seriously? How?"

"Dude owns half of Clifton Hill, about ten hotels, and two dozen properties besides. You ever been to Scream Manor? Twenty-six bucks for forty minutes walking through a dark hallway while some kid in a costume plays grab-ass with your girlfriend. Thing's a fucking money factory."

David licked his teeth, studying the house. "If the guy's got so much money, why's he still in the game?"

"Why's an alcoholic keep drinking after he sees blood in his piss?" Walter rolled down the window, spat on the roadside, rolled the window back up. "Ballaro's old-school mafia, goin' back to when his granddaddy stepped off the boat. That shit don't just wash out."

A burst of sunlight stabbed through a chink in the clouds. It glanced off the marble columns, leaving parallel scars of brilliant white.

"How're we going to play it?" David asked.

"I'll lead. Ballaro and me go back a ways."

"That a good thing or a bad thing?"

Walter's hand seesawed. "Depends. We'll get what we can about Eddie first, swing it 'round to McCulloch once the udder runs dry."

An iron ring hung from a grinning bronze face set in the center of the door, its lowest arc bulbous and rounded where it was poised to strike a raised metal circle. Walter lifted the ring and let it fall. Assisted by nothing but gravity, the knocker still made a considerable bang. He gave it another two goes for good measure and waited, hands stuffed in the pockets of his jacket. Anonymous shapes whirled behind panes of frosted glass. The shapes coalesced into a single grey-black figure and opened the door.

The man who greeted them was serious business. David could see it in the way he held his shoulders—back and squared, as if harnessed to a heavy burden that he was more than a match for—and the jutting cast of his jaw. He was fortyish, clean-shaven, black hair slicked back against his skull, a few threads of grey visible among the roots. His suit hung trim on a muscular frame, complementing his proportions intelligently. No off-the-rack number, this—a tailored job if ever there was one. He stood dead still save for his eyes, which flicked from Walter to David and back again.

"Yeah?" He neither frowned nor smiled, as if suggesting that whatever direction this conversation took rested squarely on his visitors' shoulders.

Walter extended a hand. "Detective Walter Pulaski. This here's my partner, David Moore. We're here to talk to Frank Ballaro. You must be his boy. Vincent or Joseph?"

The man pursed his lips, prodded his teeth with his tongue. "Hey papa," he called, his eyes still set on Walter. "You know a Detective Pulaski?"

"This ain't a social call. But yeah, he knows me."

The man continued staring as if Walter hadn't spoken. Footsteps made their way to the door, punctuated with the sound of heavy breathing.

"Quit bein' a hard ass and let the detectives in, Vinnie. Show some hospitality."

Frank Ballaro had Vinnie's large stature and impressive shoulders, but he bore them both with slinky confidence, as if his joints were looser than his son's. A few more pounds had settled around his neck and middle, sheathing his muscular frame in fat. His hair, ashen grey, had retreated to the top of his skull, where it maintained a peninsular stronghold against his encroaching baldness. His fingers glittered with rings. They jingled one against another as he shook Walter's hand.

"Forgive the boy, detective. We're on raw nerves around here these days, you understand. Good to see you."

"Nothin' to forgive. I understand. This here's my partner, David Moore. Been with the force goin' on two years now. Came to us from the big leagues up in Toronto."

Frank displayed a flawless set of teeth. "Must seem awful sleepy down here."

"We keep busy," said David. "May we come inside?"

"Of course, please, follow me. Leave your shoes on. Mare-mare! We've got guests!"

Frank led them into a long but cozy parlor, walled with brick and granite along its exterior walls, pine and maple accents on its interior. He took a seat in a red wingback chair. Walter and David sat across from him on either end of a couch. An oak coffee table straddled the gap between Frank and the detectives.

A woman entered carrying coffee. She was fit and top-heavy with silicone, her skin blanched and tucked with the usual bulwarks against time's inexorable tide. Youth's veneer wore thin around the eyes, where the first cracks of age broke through the Botox and makeup. David pinned her at mid-forties—same age as Vincent Ballaro, give or take. Frank's daughter-in-law, maybe? Her tomato-red nails danced up Frank's arm as she passed him his coffee, lingering at the nape of his neck. Eddie Ballaro's impertinence haunted her hushed smile, and the picture fell neatly into place. Second wife of long standing, mother to Eddie and stepmom to Vincent. Frank patted her hand and nodded his thanks for the coffee. He extended an arm to David and Walter.

"Sweetheart, these are detectives Pulaski and Moore. Detectives, my wife Mary-Anne."

She offered them a smile that didn't quite reach her eyes. David's first thought was an inherent dislike of policemen, but her indifferent greeting seemed unconscious rather than deliberate. Grief hung like leaden weights from her extremities, made every movement slow and shaky. He would bet any money that she'd already forgotten both of their names.

"Can I get you a coffee? We've got a whole pot. You boys take cream or sugar?"

"Nothing for me, thanks," said Walter. "A cup after noon and I'll be up pissin' and jitterbuggin' half the night."

"We've got decaf, too," Mary-Anne said.

"Thank you, but I'm good."

Frank turned to David. "What about you, Junior? Surely you don't got a bum prostate like gramps here at your age, eh?"

"A coffee'd be great, thanks. I take it black."

"That's my boy. Mare-mare, what's say we break out the espresso for the kid, eh? Give him a taste of the old country. You mind?"

"Not at all."

"Thank you, sweetheart." He watched the door swing for a moment after she'd gone, ribbons of steam rising from his coffee. He sipped it, smacked his lips.

"We're real sorry for your loss, Frank," Walter said. "I know us cops weren't Eddie's favourite people, but ain't a man alive deserves to go out like that."

"Can't say I agree, but I thank you for your sympathies." His gaze drifted back to the kitchen door. "I ain't about to claim I'm doin' fine just yet, but it's harder on her than me. Vinnie and Joey are like sons to her, and Bernice is closer to her than me half the time, but Eddie's the only one drank at her breast. He had her looks, her temper too. Maybe we coddled him too much, who knows? Boy liked to throw dice, whore around. He ruffled his share of feathers."

"It's them ruffled feathers we're here to talk to you about. Dave and I drew your boy's case. We saw the scene, and I'm sorry to say it don't offer much in the way of firm leads. No witnesses to speak of, no security footage, no shell casings or explosives residue. We're pretty well on a ledge with our dicks flappin' in the wind. You turn us onto anyone mighta harbored a grudge against Eddie, it could help us track the bastard down and get you some justice."

Frank smiled. "You policemen and your justice. You reach for it, but it's always just beyond your grasp, eh? In the old country, we knew what justice was. Someone wronged you, you wronged 'em right back. None of these lawyers and courts and due process."

"What old country is that, exactly? Way I heard it, you were born down the road at Greater Niagara General."

Frank shrugged. "Italy gets in the blood, detective. I'm a wop same as my *nonno* and his *nonno* before him. You work your job in this town as long as you have, you should know that."

"Funny. We Polacks couldn't give a fuck about the home country. Must be all that sunshine down there, makes you people sentimental."

"What can I say? We're poets, you're peasants."

Mary-Anne returned carrying a miniscule cup of coffee on a saucer. Islets of foam floated on a tiny black sea. David took the cup gingerly, as if afraid he might pinch the handle too hard and snap it off. "Thank you. This looks great."

"My pleasure. You boys need anything else?"

"We're fine. Thank you, ma'am."

She left, her heels marking each footstep with a crisp tap. Her exit was polite but prompt; David sensed she was keen to avoid hearing more than she had to about the circumstances of her son's death. He could hardly blame her. Frank waited until she was well out of earshot before continuing.

"I could give you a dozen names before my coffee cools, detective, and think up another dozen before lunch. All will mean less than nothing. Ballaros have enemies. Niagara is a town of little ambition, full of weak, squalid, envious people. My Eddie enjoyed their company. Why, I've no idea. I think to remind himself how big he was, since the rest of us made him feel small."

"There's no shortage of scum on the streets, I'll give you that. But what happened to your boy, it weren't no tweaker or second-rate pimp did that. It ain't my intent to upset you, but I'm sure you know enough about what happened to know it was messy. Twenty-five years baggin' and taggin', I've never seen somethin' like that before. You factor in the means as well as the motive, you might be able to narrow things down a little."

Frank tapped his finger on his chin like he was thinking about it, eyes turned up to the ceiling. He exhaled through closed lips. "'Fraid not. I'll be sure to let you know if anything comes to me."

David took a sip of his espresso. Its rich bitterness flowed across his tongue. He nodded his head approvingly. "Very nice."

"Enjoy it. We don't skimp on coffee in this house."

I imagine you don't skimp on much. David let his eyes take a quick tour of the room, soaking in the delicate patterns inlaid along the moulding, the teak and mahogany furniture, the watercolours—originals, not prints—on the walls, depicting scenes of urban and pastoral Italy. Everything arranged to be refined without feeling stuffy, roomy but not sparse. Money could buy taste in the form of a big-name decorator, but David thought the arrangement was a Ballaro original. It had a personal touch belying the detachment of a professional, evident in the few tacky but charming quirks—a ceramic Ziggy statuette, a slab of the Berlin wall purchased from a German tourist shop, a saucy plaque reading "Tact: The ability to tell someone to go to hell and make them feel happy as they go on their way."

"Okay," Walter interjected. "We'll move on. Next question: you have any idea what Eddie was doin' at the Sundown Lounge that night?"

"Proselytising, I suspect. Goin' up to the strippers and sinners and askin' them if they've found Jesus. What do you think he was doing?"

"Could be he was there to meet somebody."

"Sure. Probably a bunch of bodies. But I doubt he had much to do with them beyond tradin' cash for skin."

David studied the interplay between Walter and Frank. The two men looked casual enough, both of them sitting back in their chairs, arms draped over armrests or folded in their laps. Yet David sensed a coiled alertness beneath these facades, the spry, balls-of-the-feet tension of pro tennis players. Whether they were playing doubles against an unseen opponent or singles against each other, however, David had yet to determine.

"Easy, Frank. We gotta check all the angles here. How often did Eddie go to the Downer? He a regular?"

"I didn't keep the boy on a short leash. What he did on his own time was his business. I know he liked the clubs, but what I heard, he preferred Mints to the Downer. A little classier, higher calibre of dancer. You want a good ballpark figure, I'd ask the manager."

They already had, of course, but there was no sense in bringing that up. Walter jotted something in his notepad—probably just scribbles; the pad was as useful as a prop as it was at recording information—and gestured for Frank to continue. "And leading up to the night in question, did Eddie act strange at all? Maybe seem nervous, angry, like there was somethin' on his mind?"

Frank shook his head. "Eddie was just Eddie. He wasn't one to sweat the small stuff. I loved the kid to death, but he was a bit of a layabout. Comes from bein' the youngest, I guess. Vinnie and Joey, I made sure they knew the ins and outs of the business. Bernice could always take care of herself, so she didn't need much shepherdin' from her mother and me. Eddie came along, didn't seem so important I had an heir. Why not let the kid get his rocks off how he likes? We got the money."

"So basically, this whole thing is totally out of the blue? No precursors, signs, even in hindsight?"

"You don't wake up expectin' your baby boy to be torn to bits in a strip club parking lot. I can't think what kind of sign you might find for that, 'cept maybe rainin' frogs or the Niagara River turnin' to blood." Frank's voice stayed calm, but his tension showed in the stiff way he held his coffee, elbow and shoulder rigid as soldered joints. Walter noticed it too, for he dropped the subject and moved on to their next round of questions—albeit on a subject not likely to make Frank any less tense.

"While I'm here, I'd also like to ask you a few questions 'bout Derek McCulloch."

Frank raised an eyebrow but said nothing.

"You know Mr. McCulloch, correct?"

"Sure I know him."

"You mind me askin' how?"

"He works for me."

David nearly choked on his coffee. Frank's less-than-legal activities were an open secret among the three of them, but admitting to employing a hired killer—even a non-convicted one—seemed exceptionally candid.

Walter continued his questioning as if merely ticking through a telephone survey. "Doing what, exactly?"

"Odd jobs. He fixes games at my arcade, makes sure all the spooks and scares are workin' in my haunted houses, that sort of thing. Boy's good with his hands, has whattayacall, mechanical aptitude."

"So he's an employee of yours?"

"More like a contractor. I call him when I need him."

"On the books, of course?"

Frank smiled. "Certainly. Payin' under the table's a crime, ain't it?"

"Not the kind is any of our business. Pour everything you got into the Cayman Islands for all I care. I just do bodies. Which is what makes me ask about Derek."

"Something happen to Derek?" Frank asked, sitting forward in his chair. A cloud of concern passed across his face. David all but knew it for a lie, but still felt himself convinced of its sincerity. *Christ, this guy should be in Hollywood.*

"Not that we know of. He seems to have disappeared. He'd rented a room from one of them divey joints out on the Lane, one called the Jupiter Motel."

"Hey, hey there. A few of those divey joints, as you call 'em, paid for this house."

"Fine. Divey cash cows. Happy? Anyway, seems a couple of guys showed up to Derek's room a few hours before he did. There's some commotion, shots fired, and next morning the two men are dead and Derek's in the wind. Poof, gone."

Frank scratched a piece of freckled skin beneath his lower lip. "Jesus. I hope the kid's okay. I haven't heard a peep from him in weeks. He reaches out to me, I'll let him know you're looking for him."

"I don't think that's likely to happen. Our best guess is the kid's on the run. See, the two guys we found in Derek's room are also on your payroll—or were, anyway. Louis Perone and Joseph Santino."

Frank crossed himself and muttered a small prayer in Italian.

"I take it this comes as news to you?"

"Of course. I don't keep tabs on the men work for me."

"Still, they'd worked for you a long time. It says here . . . " Walter flipped through his notepad, struggling to find a page David knew for a fact he could pinpoint in half a second if the situation warranted it. "Okay. Lou since '89, Joey since '84. Management of Horror Hill and the Sleep EZ Motel, respectively. Positions like that, you musta put some trust in them."

"I don't hire a guy 'less I trust him. But there's different sorts of trust. I've known all sorts of guys who do good work but can't keep their noses clean. Some guys have a need eats them up, makes them useless for anything but nabbing the next fix. Others live whole lives showin' up for work on time, doin' a good job, then goin' home and getting baked on smack or whorin' their way from here to Windsor. Man's personal business ain't no business of mine."

"Sure. So you didn't have any sense that they might be up to something, I guess you'd say . . . unsavory in their personal lives? Any clue as to what this meeting might've been about?"

"Like what?"

"I dunno. Drugs? Prostitution? Protection racket?"

"Please. What would I know about any of that sort of thing?"

"You tell me."

Frank smiled. "No. I can't say I knew anything about it. But that's different than saying I'm one hundred percent surprised. Lou and Joey were their own men. What choices they make off the clock, I can't be responsible for 'em. Joey does surprise me, I admit—he seemed like a straight and narrow sort of guy, good head on his shoulders—but Lou and Derek I can see cookin' up the kind of scheme ends with people gettin' shot. Lou, God bless him, was too damn thick to see the risk in such a thing. You flash some dollar bills in front of the guy, he forgets what he might have to do to earn 'em."

"And Derek?"

Frank stared into his coffee mug, swirling the liquid in a slow gyre of foam. "When it comes to work, Derek's a real pro. Diligent. Professional, Thorough. You give that boy a job and he sees to it it gets done right. But in his personal life, he's reckless. Given to vices, bad choices. Am I saddened to hear he's gotten himself in that kind of trouble? Absolutely. Am I surprised?" Frank bobbed his head from side to side. "Some crashes happen blink of an eye, like. Others you see comin' a mile off. It don't mean you can stop them. Derek's a 'live fast, die young' guy if ever there was one. Kid has a James Dean thing about him, sort of guy courts danger with an eight inch hard-on, gonna bang it or die trying."

"So you're sayin' whoever hit Lou and Joey might've been after Eddie all along, simply caught the other two on an off chance?"

"Wouldn't surprise me, but I ain't sayin' it's the only option, either. Could be Derek and the boys had a falling out, one owes the other, things come to a head. I'd like to think better of all three of 'em, but I'm a realist. Or could be any number of other things happened, too. You're the detectives, not me. I ain't got no crystal ball."

"Neither do we. But what you're sayin' is, whatever Lou and Joey were doin' in that motel room, it weren't bein' done on your behalf."

"I send a guy to do a job, detective, rest assured it gets done. Whatever business was goin' on in that room, sounds to me like it was unfinished."

"So you don't think Derek had anything to do with what happened to Eddie?"

"If I thought he did, believe me, I wouldn'ta sent someone to him on my behalf. I woulda dealt with that business personally."

Walter flipped his notepad with a quick jerk of his wrist. He tucked his pen into the spiral binding and slipped the pad into his jacket pocket. "Thanks for your time, Frank. We'll let you know soon as we find anything."

"Always a pleasure, Walter." They shook hands. Frank extended a hand to David next. His grip was firm, his palm callused and dry. He gave three sharp pumps and withdrew, all business. "And nice meeting you, son."

"Likewise. Please, thank your wife again for the coffee."

"I'll be sure she gets the message. Keep up the good work, gentlemen. *Ciao*."

Back in the car, Walter lit a cigarette. "Well there. You've met Niagara's big cheese. Was it everything you'd dreamed it would be and more?"

"Sublime, certainly." David lit a cigarette of his own. He never used to smoke in vehicles, but Walter couldn't make it a block without lighting up, and even with the windows down the smell beckoned him incessantly. The old guy really was a bad influence. "They're holding up pretty good, considering."

"Ballaro's all about pride. It wouldn't do to go blubberin' in front of the law. But yeah, he's a tough nut. You don't survive in his business for long, bein' overly emotional."

"I didn't expect tears and chest beating or anything, but the guy was just so . . . relaxed. His son's dead, and it's like he's over it already."

Walter smiled around his cigarette. "Don't let him fool you. Frank is anything but over it.

Ballaros are the only family in the country south of Toronto with a name that means a damn, and they got that way by bein' the biggest, baddest, meanest motherfuckers on the block. Frank's shrewd, but that don't make him a lightweight. He keeps the body count low 'cause he knows too much blood'll raise the heat on his operations. But when the man's got a point to make, he makes it. It's best you don't forget that."

"So you expect a point's forthcoming?"

"I'd be shocked if it wasn't. Unless it has already, and we just didn't see it."

David puffed on his cigarette, reflecting. "And what about McCulloch? You buy he didn't know anything about it?"

Walter raised his eyebrows. "You have to ask?"

"I'm trying not to make any assumptions here. This mob business is a little out of my depth."

"He knew. Lou and Joey would've never made that kind of move without his say-so. Joe Santino was way too cautious for such a thing. Lou Perone was a dim bulb, I'll grant that, but even he'd know enough not to try and cut in on any side business without Frank's express consent, unless he'd developed a sudden urge to be parted from his balls. No, they were there on Ballaro business, and shit went south. Question is, what'd they botch? A hit, or just a bring-him-in-for-questioning thing?"

"Does it matter?"

Walter took a final rolling drag on his cigarette and flicked the butt out the open window. It landed on the curb, spewing sparks over the sodden leaves and road grit. "At the time, maybe. Not now. All I know is, that moke McCulloch better pray we find him before Ballaro does."

"We got half our patrol keeping an eye out for him."

Walter waved the point aside. "He's long gone, man. Scurried back to some familiar hole. If he's got half a brain cell in his skull, he won't show his face in this town again anytime soon."

David tapped his lip with his index finger. "You said he hails from Toronto, right?"

"That's the word we got on 'im. No family to speak of, though, no one we can lean on. Guy's a classic lone wolf."

David fished his smartphone out of his pocket and flicked through his contact list. He clicked the dial button and listened to the digitized sound of ringing. The third ring cut out early, replaced by a woman's voice.

"Well, I'll be goddamned. David Moore. That really you, or some perp knock you off and take your phone?"

"It's me all right. How you doing, Wanda?"

"How am I doing? That all you got to say to me? If you have the nerve to try a booty call after I ain't heard from your ass in going on two years—"

"I was up there six months ago."

"Been six months too long, then, huh?"

David smiled. "Call it seven. Now, really, how are you?"

Wanda dropped the sass from her voice as if tossing off a pair of brass knuckles. "I'm good. Been a hell of a summer, gangbangers lightin' each other up like a bunch of dope-dealin' birthday candles, but it keeps me busy. How's life down in tourist town?"

"We've been keeping pretty busy ourselves."

"I heard about the fire. Nasty business. And that body outside the strip club. You catch that one?"

"'Fraid so."

She whistled. "Got any leads?"

"One second, let me ask my partner." He held the phone to his chest, turning the receiver out so she could hear. "Hey Walt, would you say we got any leads on the Ballaro case?"

Walter rubbed his chin in contemplation. "Well, I got my dick in my hand *and* my thumb up my ass, so I'd say we're making progress."

"You hear that?" David asked, back on the line. "Wheels in motion."

"Sounds like you got a crack squad down there."

"No doubt. But even the pros need help every once in a while."

Wanda clucked her tongue. "Typical man. Only call when you want something."

"Why would anyone call anyone else, unless they wanted something?"

David could practically hear her eyes roll at that. "Lay it on me, partner."

"How are you guys stocked for CIs these days?"

"Pfffff, up to our elbows, boy. Condo construction's shot, Labor Ready's turnin' people back left and right. Half the city's itchin' for a quick payout, seems like."

"Well, you put the word out that there's a new sugar daddy in town."

"You say the word, honey," Wanda said. "Who we looking for?"

David told her.

11: SOMEONE WHO LIKES THE RAMONES

IMAN THRUST HER fingers into her hair and slumped forward, her chin inches above the keyboard. White pixels fired mercilessly into her unprotected irises, making her already red-rimmed eyes water. She sipped her lukewarm tea without peeling her gaze from the screen, as if the image it displayed were a wild animal she'd pinned down, and a moment's lost concentration was all it needed to buck her grasp and dart into the protective underbrush.

"Hey, everything okay over there?"

Iman let out a nervous yip. Brian arched his eyebrows, his face betraying a mix of amusement and concern.

"Jeez, jumpy much?"

"Sorry, I guess I was kind of zoned out."

"I'll say. You look like you're checking out Faces of Death videos or something. What's up?"

"It's nothing, really. Work's just weird."

Brian clucked his tongue in sympathy. "Another book run today?"

"He's got half the library in there with him by now. The weird half, too. You should see some of the stuff he's had me check out for him. Occult books in half a dozen languages, collections of pulp magazines from the '20s and '30s."

"Well, he *is* an English professor. Aren't they supposed to be, I dunno, quirky?"

"Not Howard Hughes quirky. And it's not just the books. Look at some of the websites he's been checking out. There's forums on Wicca and voodoo, YouTube videos on sympathetic magic, firsthand accounts of exorcisms and demon possession. And then there's this."

Iman pointed to the screen. A crude forum filled the browser window, comprised of colourful text atop a starscape background. The page stretched for thousands of entries by users named Starkin and Faefolk411 and NosferatuReborn, their avatars drawn from luridly-rendered fantasy paintings or sketches of people with horns or hooves or wings.

"You ever heard of otherkins? They're people who identify as part animal or spirit. They claim to be dragons, vampires, elves, that sort of thing."

"You mean, like, roleplaying?"

"No, I mean seriously believe it. It's even got a clinical term. Species dysphoria. Look." She clicked the tabs on her browser, bringing up a few clinical abstracts in PubMed and Wikipedia articles discussing terms like *Therianthropy* and *Supernumerary phantom limb* in frank, earnest prose. "There's whole communities of these people, Bri. And Motes has been spending a lot of time with them."

Iman brought up the browser history and scrolled back over the last two days. Innumerable pages flew by like suburban streets beneath an ascending plane's undercarriage, nearly all of them identical hits for a few forum sites distinguished only by page number. She looked to Brian, hoping for an expression of horror to match her own. He met her gaze side-eyed.

"This is *his* search history?"

"Yeah."

Brian leaned closer to the screen. He put his finger to the track pad and minimized the map, revealing a small application in the bottom corner.

"You're *VPNing* into his computer?"

Iman bit her cheek. "So?"

"That is seriously not okay."

"Why not? It's not like I broke into his office or hacked his passwords or anything. He gave me access months ago."

"Yeah, so you can get files from his hard drive and check his email. Not so you can snoop around his personal search history."

"I'm not trying to blackmail the guy or steal his identity or anything. He knows I have access to his computer. If he really didn't want me seeing this, he'd've deleted his search history."

"Jesus, you sound like CSIS."

"Not a fair comparison." She motioned to the screen. "Doesn't this strike you as strange, though?"

"It's weird, sure, but I guess I don't see what the problem is. If he's not going on there for research, then he's got a weird hobby. So what?"

Iman shook her head in frustration. "It's not that. You haven't *seen* him. He's just . . . he's in bad shape. The other day, when I was dropping off some books, I heard him in his office crying. I mean full on *sobbing*, like his mother had just died."

"And you think it has something to do with this occult stuff?"

"I don't know. I try not to be judgemental. It all seems like a bunch of bull to me, but I'm not about to try and tell someone what to do, not if it makes them happy. But Motes is anything but happy. He's frigging miserable and I'm afraid he might be cracking up and I don't know what to do."

Brian rested his hand on Iman's shoulder. She took it gratefully, pressed his palm against her own.

"Have you considered talking to him about it? I'm sure it'd be uncomfortable as hell, but maybe it'd be good to clear the air a little."

Iman bit her lower lip. "There's something else. This I didn't mean to find, I swear to God."

She brought up the three emails from the trash folder. Brian read them over a couple of times. "Okay. That's . . . weird, I'll give you that. Who's this 'Blitzkrieg Bop' guy?"

"No idea. Someone who likes the Ramones, I guess."

"Whoever he is, it's none of your business."

"Yeah, but did you read the part about bodies? What if Motes is in some sort of danger?"

"What if he isn't? It could be a prank. It could be some sort of sick in-joke between him and a friend of his. You don't *know*, Manny."

"I guess it could be," she said, though she wasn't convinced. Whatever those emails were, they weren't a joke. Brian gave her shoulder a reassuring squeeze.

"I just want you to be careful. If you're gonna be prying through a guy's personal info, ask yourself why. Make sure it's for the right reasons. Otherwise you may regret it later."

"It is. It definitely is." Iman chewed her fingernails. "I mean, there's a bit of honest curiosity in there too, sure. But I'm not on the hunt for anything sordid or juicy. If I start to stumble on anything that looks truly private, something he wouldn't want me seeing, I promise I'll stop."

Brian grabbed the remote from their coffee table—built from milk crates and sanded plywood into a piece of boho kitsch—and turned on the TV. "The only problem is, by the time you realise you've found something like that, it'll probably be too late."

12: MATCHBOOK

THE COPPER PENNY smelled a hell of a lot worse than Derek remembered. He recalled the look of it as if he'd never been away, its buckled floors and sagging stools and sleek U-bend bar stained a murky piebald ebony-ocher by decades of sweaty elbows and spilled beer and fingers greasy with buffalo sauce. Neon signs depicting beer and liquor logos flickered in the gloom. He knew every warp and tear on the felt faces of the three pool tables—could even work a physics-busting acute bank shot off a chip in the bumper of the one nearest the slit window, to the double-take vexation of unschooled opponents—and could chart the topography of ruined cork circumscribing the bar's lone dartboard. The whine of blues guitar on the jukebox, the clatter of billiard balls, the laryngitic wheeze of the beer fridge's bum compressor, he could hum it all like the title track of a beloved old album. But the smell was another matter. It burbled beneath the more recognizable odours of fryer grease and draught foam and sickly-sweet soft drink mixers, a subterranean trickle of stale piss and damp vinyl, of broken teeth and rancid sweat, of knuckle-busting machismo and ugly, pointless sex, all of it mashed into a bilious slurry and seeping, drip by foetid drip, into the bar's groundwater.

Derek wafted his pint of 504 beneath his nose to block the worst of the smell, taking long, slow sips and sloshing the hoppy liquid against his tongue. He'd chosen a booth in a corner cobwebbed with shadows, affording him a near-complete view of the bar. An exit to the bar's compact patio stood a mere three steps away. The door swung shut and locked automatically, meaning Derek could slip out while Ballaro muscle couldn't slip in. His .45 nestled against his chest, its front sight digging into his ribcage. A baggy coat slightly too warm for the season obscured its telltale bulge and hung loose enough for an easy draw. With these precautions in place, Derek was willing to allow himself to get moderately drunk—a fairly large concession, as the situation called for nothing less than black-out intoxication.

Far safer would be to hole up in his little nest with a mickey of Jack Daniels and a twelve pack of beer, but Derek was and always had been a social drinker. In the absence of other people, his buzz inevitably sputtered into a sloppy melancholy, driving him to squander the night listening to Springsteen and feeling sorry for himself.

Not that Derek was feeling especially gregarious. He was content to sit in his corner and let the other patrons mingle among themselves, filter-feeding on whatever morsel of conversation drifted his way. It was thus with mixed emotions that he saw Bugs Merrithew strutting into the bar. A baseball cap sat backwards on his head, a youthful affectation belied by the lines in his face and the scraggle of beard hanging under his chin. Twiggy arms poked out from a baggy t-shirt, both covered wrist to forearm in tattoos depicting some mescaline-tinged pandemonium, a lunacy of cackling demons and big-breasted women and classic cartoon characters with melty sideshow faces. He wore steel-toed boots two sizes too big for him. Together with the t-shirt and backwards cap, he had the air of a child stricken with some dreadful aging disease, his features withering before they'd even reached full bloom. He spotted Derek and came over, his outsized shoes clomping over the warped floorboards.

"Yo, Matchbook, 'sup? Long time no friggin see, eh?" He smacked Derek an exuberant high five and slipped into the booth opposite him. Bugs skittered about the outer fringes of Toronto's criminal enterprise, dealing weed, breaking into cars, running the occasional number for the smaller loan sharks. He shied from violence and had no ambition—he seemed content, as far as Derek could tell, to feast on the scraps the big fish left behind—but was, in his own peculiar way, one of the most connected men in Toronto's underbelly. Every don, dope fiend, and dealer in the GTA knew Bugs, though not better than Bugs knew them. He recited rap sheets the way kids of a bygone era traded baseball cards, fawning over stats and debating the fine points of hardness, rep, profile. Bugs normally made decent company despite his more irritating qualities, but Derek was too on edge to tolerate his frenetic discourse. Yet he found it difficult to take a hard line with Bugs. Something about the scrawny loser brought out an almost parental instinct in Derek; he supposed a lot of players in town felt the same way, which was as good an explanation as any as to why Bugs had yet to get his face pounded into the pavement.

"How's it hanging, Bugs?" Derek said, his eyes locked on the bar over Bugs' shoulder. Bugs seemed not to notice his distracted tone, or else chose to ignore it.

"Real good, man, you know. Rocking. So you back in town?"

"Nah, man. I'm on the International Space Station. This shit you see here's just a hologram. I send it down to dives like this to get pissed up in my absence."

Bugs let out a stuttering laugh. "Yeah, man, yeah. You're in orbit. Cool, cool. So what's up with you these days, man? You got somethin' on the go, or . . . ?" He let the sentence trail off, its upward lilt suggesting a question.

"Nah. Just back for a few. Keeping a low profile. Don't want shit to get too hot, you know what I mean?"

"Cool, cool, respect. Hey, you know who else I've seen around? Lucky Luke!"

In the pit of Derek's stomach, some clumsy caretaker upended a bucket of ice water. "Luke Volchyin?"

"Yeah. You know him, right? He was gamin' down there in Niagara for a while."

Derek ran his finger through a bit of spilled beer, drawing nonsense figures over the table. "Not well, but yeah. I remember the guy."

"We all thought Ballaro had wasted him. Guy fuckin' vanished, chief. I'd heard rumors Ballaro had him, whattayacall, incinerated, and torched an old folks' home just so he had a place to hide the ashes. So there'd be no motive, like."

That would be among the dumber reasons to torch a building, thought Derek, who knew from arson. "You don't say."

"That was the word. But he's back now, and word has it he's headin' back to Niagara. I saw him chattin' up some of your boys from down that way, guys on the outs."

"Yeah, like who?"

"Remember Nails?"

Derek swished beer between his molars, savoring the sting of carbonation against his gums. He knew Nails (née Earl Parks) in passing, a mid-level bookie and loan shark on the Ballaro roster with a trailer-park complexion and punk sensibilities. The sort of guy who wore leather vests with too many zippers and earlobe spacers threaded with iron nails (hence his street name), listened to sludgy metal, and read comics about pregnant chicks getting murdered. He considered himself cutting edge, but Derek found him tiresome. In his experience, that sort of counterculture death fetishist posturing was a wrinkly shell hiding a nugget of cowardice.

"I thought you said on the outs. Nails is a Ballaro man."

"Nah man, you really have been out of it. Nails and Ballaro are history. Didn't you hear?"

Derek shook his head. "What happened?"

"He was getting' mouthy, man. Started steppin' on toes, doin' his own Shylockin' on the sly, actin' a big shot. You know Nails, man, guy's a two-inch cock in a ten-inch condom. Ballaro caught wind of it, told him to knock it off. Know how that crazy fucker responded? Mailed Ballaro a package with a dead rat in it, its belly all stuffed with shit. *Parks'* shit, man." Another burst of hiccup laughter. "Ballaro didn't like that."

"I wouldn't want to meet the sort of guy who did."

"Yeah, for sure. So anyway, Ballaro sends a couple boys up to Hamilton. They find Parks and send him a message. Held him down, got some pliers, and ripped the nails outta his ears. You know how he had them studs? Well, he ain't gonna be danglin' no metal from there no more. His ear lobes look like paper you tear it out of the receipt machine wrong. All ragged. Nasty."

Derek sipped his beer. "He learn his lesson?"

"Maybe, man. But he ain't happy. Been talkin' all sorts of shit. I'd keep my mouth shut, I were him. You do *not* mess with the Ballaros, man. Every player and wannabe in the province should know that."

Thanks for the tip, you dipshit. Derek felt his smile curdling. He did his best to skim the sour skin from it, not wanting Bugs to sense something amiss and burrow deeper into his business.

"I'm pretty tired, Bugs. Think I'm gonna polish off this beer and head home. It was good talkin' to you."

"Yeah man, for sure. Always a pleasure. Look, so . . . " Bugs leaned in close enough for Derek to catch a whiff of his breath, a thunderhead of menthol cigarettes and eggs two weeks past their prime. He spoke his next words in a conspiratorial whisper. "Whatever it is you got on the go, you can cut me in. You need a spotter, someone to run a message, maybe gather some friendly names, I'm your guy. You can ask anyone in this town, Bugs don't shirk a job. I'm like one of them, whattayacall, *mercenaries*, man. I get in, get it done, get out."

Derek shifted in his seat, partly out of general discomfort and partly to put some distance between his face and Bugs'. "Sorry, man, but it's like I said. I'm not here on business. All I've got on the go is some heavy drinking and maybe a little pussy on the side." Derek expected a laugh at this, but Bugs didn't smile. He licked his lips, beads of moisture clinging to strands of dead, chapped skin.

"Hey, c'mon, man, you didn't come back into town just to drink in this pisshole, eh? You got somethin' on the take. I got connections, I can make things happen. Frig, I was *built* for this shit. You cut me in, whatever you got goin', you're gonna get double profits. Triple, even."

Bugs clutched Derek's forearm, his fingers rigid with bony strength. His wrist turned upward, revealing track marks amongst the cacophony of artwork. Derek looked from them to the purple-black shadows under his eyes, to the yellow-brown rubble of his bottom teeth.

"You dumb asshole. You're using again?"

Bugs winced as if struck.. "So I take a taste every now an' again, man. What's it to you? Ain't done a thing to my game. I keep it straight when I'm workin', man. I ain't gonna punk out on you. Ask anyone. Bugs don't punk out, he's on the street."

Was there anything more stubbornly pathetic than a junky after cash? Derek didn't think so. He'd seen men begging him to spare their lives who showed more dignity. It would be a kindness to pull out his .45 and spray the miserable bastard's brains over the bar. But Derek was in too tight a spot to indulge in charity. Bugs would have to go about dying his own way—a path he'd set more than his first step upon, to look at his arms. He locked eyes with the junky, his face awful in its blankness. "You'll want to be lettin' go of my arm now, Bugs."

Bugs' tongue made a fresh circle of his lips. His hand skittered back to his side of the table. "My bad, Derek. You get somethin' on the go, you call Bugs, eh?"

"No doubt, man." Derek took a long slow sip of his beer. Bugs, taking the hint, slid out from the bench and found a fresh target on the far side of the bar. Derek sighed and slouched deeper into the bench. A crick worked its way into his hunched spine and Derek, after a few half-hearted attempts to shift his weight into a more accommodating position, ignored it. The puddle of good cheer he'd accumulated, as sad and shallow as it was, had evaporated. He wished he hadn't bumped into Bugs. That idiot would be blabbing to half the city about how he saw Matchbook McCulloch down at the Penny, probably back in town on a job. Word of mouth was the last thing he needed right now. Toronto wasn't Niagara, but Ballaro had a long reach and could easily stretch across the lake and swat Derek into oblivion, given the inclination and a bit of intel. And now fucking *Volchyin* was back in the picture? There was a name Derek had hoped never to hear again. He was pretty sure ol' Lucky didn't bear him a personal grudge— he'd always got on okay with the guy, and knew enough to cover his tracks during that final dust-up—but the guy was bad news all the same.

The intelligent thing to do would be to get on a bus and not get off again until he'd reached the coast. Hole up in Vancouver, maybe, or down to the States, if he wanted to risk the border. But what would he do then? He didn't know anyone out west, or out east for that matter. The GTA was his *home*, for fuck sakes, the golden horseshoe shining from Toronto to Niagara the extent of his charted cartography. He'd be damned if he was going to let some bigshot wop force him into exile. Let Ballaro's goons come for him. They'd find ol' Matchbook a wilier rat than they were used to, the sort that can sniff out poison before it's even been laid. That might, with a bit of luck, even manage to nudge that poison into daddy Ballaro's morning coffee.

Derek downed the rest of his beer in a long, rolling swig. He pulled out his wallet and began counting up his bill, paused, and slipped the wallet back in his pocket. He flagged down a passing waitress and pointed to his glass.

"Another pint, please."

He flashed the waitress a smile as she set the pint down, sneaking a quick glance at the wink of cleavage she showed as she bent over. "Wonderful. Thanks." The first sip, foamy and frigid, filled his mouth with citrusy hops. He licked a bit of foam from his upper lip and let his hand fall naturally on the masked butt of his revolver.

Let the wops come find him, they wanted to see him so bad.

PART II: HUNTER'S MOON

13: HIGH STAKES POKER

DAVID STAGGERED DOWN the dim corridor, hands thrust forward like feeble antennae. He wasn't sure how long he'd been walking, only that it had been a long time. Some terribly pressing business spurred him onward, step by fruitless step down the unchanging hallway. To his left ran a series of kennels with doors woven of stiff wire, some unoccupied, others holding a motley assortment of dogs. There were Corgis and Pekinese, German Shepherds and sleek-legged Greyhounds, terriers, and retrievers, mutts of every size and description. All of them were mangy and underfed, and many were marred by various mutilations or deformities—missing paws, truncated tails, eye sockets scooped clean or blighted by cataracts thick as egg whites. They paced and whined and whimpered, an orchestra of misery hopelessly out of tune. There seemed no end to the kennels. They ran beyond bends in the hall to either direction, and stacked one atop the other by the dozens, rising until they disappeared into a haze of gloom.

The wall to David's right was a vista of flat featureless grey, marked only by the occasional locked door or inscrutable sign. He studied the signs when he saw them, but the words sloshed and smeared like inky liquid, running through his fingers every time he strove to grasp their meaning. As he pondered one such collection of fluid hieroglyphics, the disjointed sounds emanating from the kennels swelled in volume. Whines and whimpers became howls and wails, which burst apart into a cacophony of savage barking. Dogs hurled themselves at the doors of their kennels, bloodying their paws and breaking their teeth against barriers of crisscrossed metal. The wire doors groaned against their weight.

"Hang on!" David cried. "I need to find the right one!" He ran down the hallway, scanning the kennels in a desperate search for the dog who'd first started barking. If he could find it, calm it down, the others would follow.

The shrill bleating of an alarm rent the air, dialing up the dogs' aggression to an even higher pitch. Muzzles drew back in monstrous snarls, revealing foam-flecked jaws that gnashed in David's direction. A million pounds of canine fury battered the kennels' doors, snapping wire and bursting hinges. David heard a protracted squeal of shorn metal as the doors gave in as one, unleashing a tsunami of fangs and fur. It crested over him, a thousand thousand dogs roiling and snarling, crushing him—

He awoke with a snort and a muffled cry. Nancy's hand clutched his shoulder, shaking him gently. She pointed to the nightstand, where David's cell phone sat ringing. He grabbed the phone and nearly dropped it, his hands clumsy with sleep. The ring cut out mid-bleat as he thumbed the talk button. "Yeah?"

"Hey, Dave. It's Walter." Even in his fuzzy state, David noted the absence of jocularity in Walter's voice.

"Walt," David said, blinking crust from his eyelashes. "What's up?"

"You get a call from me at three in the morning, only one thing it could be about, no?"

Swinging his legs out of bed, David grabbed a pad of paper and a pen from his nightstand. He balanced the pad on his thigh and posed the pen to write. "Where are you?"

Walter recited an address. "Sorry to wake you, pal, but you're going to want to see this. I mean, you won't *want* to, but, well, you'll get what I mean. Just get down here."

"Everything okay?" Nancy mumbled.

David rubbed his eyes. "We'll see, I guess."

He dressed in the dark and left, grabbing a coffee from the Tim Hortons drive-thru on his way. He turned onto Stanford Street and checked the address he'd scrawled in his notepad. He struggled to read his handwriting by the flicker of passing streetlights, but the address proved unnecessary. There was little doubt which house he was looking for. Police cruisers straddled the curb, lights flashing silently, while an ambulance idled in the driveway. Police caution tape cordoned the house in streamers so thick they formed a web. A clutch of neighbours and curious onlookers—the former distinguishable by their bathrobes and pyjamas, the latter by their post-closing time stagger—peered over the barrier, their faces dyed alternating shades of blue and red by the twirling police lights. A pair of uniformed officers walked the line, imploring the onlookers to move along and return to their homes. A few people shuffled off when confronted, but the others mostly ignored the officers' pleas, and some even tried to pester them for information.

Members of the crowd spotted David, but he was plainclothes and they paid him little mind. A lone exception emerged from the fold: a woman in her mid-thirties, blonde hair pulled back in a ponytail, slim legs descending from a tweed skirt. She drew a pen and paper from her purse with a gunslinger's speed and poised to write.

"Detective Moore? Dawna Lane. We've met before, shortly after the fire at Stanford Acres?"

"I remember," David said, his voice bereft of inflection.

"Care to comment a little on what happened here tonight?"

"I couldn't tell you. I haven't even been inside yet."

Dawna jotted. "This is the third crime of horrific scale in the last few months. Should the public be concerned for their general safety?"

"No more than usual."

"There's growing frustration that these cases aren't being treated seriously. What are the police doing to ensure the public are safe?"

"I really can't comment on any investigations at the moment. Now, if you'd excuse me."

He ducked under the caution tape, flashing his badge at the uniformed officer who'd come to send him back. The officer backed up, hands raised. "Sorry, detective. We're having a hell of a time here."

"No worries. Seems like half the neighbourhood's up in our business."

The cop shook his head. "It'll only get worse once word gets out." His narrowed eyes glanced towards Dawna Lane, who continued her scribbling. David nodded, eased the door open slightly to offer the smallest possible view to the crowd, and slipped inside.

Shit. This one's making the front page, all right.

The destruction was on a scale so massive it seemed staged, a director's wet dream of domestic mayhem. In the long, L-shaped room stretching from front hall to dining room, maybe one or two pieces of furniture remained unbroken. David spotted an ottoman leaning face-down against the hearth, toppled but otherwise undamaged, and a wooden chair that stood entirely undisturbed, miraculously pristine amidst the chaos. The rest of the room was a maelstrom of splintered wood and shattered marble and smashed electronics. In his days as a Toronto cop, David had been in some scuzzy places, but this was something else altogether. It looked like some well-meaning eccentric had tried to housebreak a hurricane.

Walter stood beside the remains of the dining room table. Built of solid oak by a craftsman worth a damn—no IKEA junk in sight in this place—it had nevertheless broken neatly in the centre, as if a drunken Paul Bunyan had cleaved it in two with his gargantuan axe. Playing cards and plastic chips filled the valley between the table's severed halves, a stream of them partially covered by a man's headless body. The head, David was pretty sure, had landed in the curio cabinet, roosting in a nest of broken porcelain figurines. Though it was possible the head belonged to someone else: the floor was strewn with bodies, few of them whole. A quick count put it at six in this room alone, but they'd need forensics to say for sure.

"Quite a sight, eh?" Walter said. "When these guys play high stakes poker, they really play high stakes poker."

David paced the length of the room with his hands clutched behind his back, stepping carefully to avoid disturbing any evidence, organic or otherwise. The bodies were still pretty fresh—no more than two hours dead, he guessed—but their ripe smell was already unfurling through the room. David considered lighting a cigarette but decided against it. It seemed disrespectful somehow, even if the house's occupants were far past caring about the adverse effects of secondhand smoke.

He passed his measured gaze over the walls, the floor, the furniture, a single long sweep of a prospector's sieve, panning for nuggets of meaning amidst the murky rubble. He paused at the dining room window, or rather, what was left of it. The panes had exploded inward in a shower of glass and splintered wood, both sashes torn clear from the frame and smashed to kindling on the carpet below. Something huge had leapt or been thrown inside from the back patio, where muddy prints described a running leap that suggested the former option. Deep gashes scarred the sill and, to a lesser extent, the transom. He took a small flashlight from his pocket and peered through the ruined window, careful not to cut his hands on the glass shards littering the sill.

"It doesn't make much sense, does it? They came through the window—or at least one of them did. But I'm not seeing any shell casings."

"I don't think our guy was packing. Not with anything automatic, anyway. Only casings we found match the guns lying next to 'em. At least a couple of the victims were armed, but the heat didn't seem to do 'em much good."

"So what, you're saying these guys we're attacked by a mob with, I dunno, machetes?"

"Axes, maybe? Whatever it was, it wasn't a firearm. Only way you'd cause this kind of mayhem'd be with a machine gun. And even if they'd rigged up some mechanism to catch the casings, there ain't a sharpshooter alive who could pour bullets into a room full of people and not mess up the walls. Coroner'll say for sure, but I'll bet you a six-pack of your hipster beer we don't find a single bullet in these guys, unless they panicked and started shootin' each other."

David knelt down and lifted half a broken plate out of the way, uncovering a muddy smear much like the ones he'd spotted on the patio. It was definitely a footprint, but the guy who left it must've been pivoting or really filthy, for the shape it left was nothing like a human foot. It flared in the front in a starburst pattern and tapered to the back into a sleek arrowhead.

"All this remind you of something?"

"You mean a certain scene outside a certain strip club? You don't know the half of it. Look."

Walter led David to the hearth, where a body lay slumped again the stone fireplace. Something huge and immensely sharp had raked him scalp to sternum, tearing flesh and scoring bone down to the quick. His upper body resembled a piece of roadkill, a slurry of ruined tissue. Walter picked up the wallet lying nearby with gloved hands and held it up, open, to David. A clear plastic window displayed a driver's license belonging to Vincent Ballaro. David's gaze snapped back to the body.

"Jesus Christ, you mean—"

"Our best guess, yeah. Again, we'll need a blood test to be sure, but take a look at the hair. The build. It matches near enough to convince me. First responders already talked to some neighbours, found out this place belongs to a couple named Hank and Stella Mirano. Hank's got a cozy job in upper management at one of Ballaro's hotels, or at least he did. Several of the other guys got similar pedigrees. It seems Saturday night poker was a bit of a tradition with these guys. Took turns hosting, played for decent stakes. Ten-buck antes, I heard. Not high rollers per se, but not pocket change, neither."

David pictured Vincent Ballaro as he'd last seen him: proud, sternly handsome, unintimidated by the two homicide detectives showing up unannounced on his father's doorstep. He tried to reconcile this image with the charnelhouse scraps lying before him and found he couldn't do it. It shouldn't have been so difficult—powerful men died just like any other; David knew that better than most people—and yet the two facts wouldn't gel. They mingled uneasily as oil stirred in water, globs of one image repelling swirls of the other.

"Fuck me."

"You got that right. Goddamn place looks like the scene of a bear attack, but I ain't never heard of a bear who had it in for a mob family."

Walter reached for his cigarette pack, contemplated the filters for a moment, and put the case away unsmoked. He tongued the tip of his moustache until the hairs grew slick and matted with saliva. "I'll tell you one thing. Someone's sending Ballaro a serious fucking message. And subtlety ain't exactly their strong suit."

David hunkered next to Vincent's body. A piece of metal glimmered amongst the wreckage of splintered wood and shattered ceramic a foot or so from Vincent's fingers. David brushed the debris aside and gently withdrew the object. He held it up with thumb and forefinger to avoid smudging any latent prints. As best he could tell, it was a letter opener in the shape of an ornate dagger, its handle and blade molded from the same bar of tarnished silver. A bit of waxy, blackish blood clotted on its bladed tip.

"Whatever message this fucker is sending, I think the Ballaros are getting it loud and clear."

14: A CHORUS OF SCREAMS

IMAN SHOWED UP to her office at quarter after nine, her ceramic travel mug exuding its pleasant warmth into the palm of her hand. Green tea, brewed strong and flecked with leafy sediment, sloshed in its belly. She tried the door and was surprised to find it locked. For the last two weeks, Professor Motes had been arriving before she got in and staying after she left, typing and clicking maniacally at his office computer. His constant presence had grown increasingly stifling, especially since she'd come across those deleted emails.

She booted up her computer. The sound of students playing Frisbee on the quad leaked intermittently through the office windows, cheers and groans and laughed exchanges filtered to a hissing white noise by the double-pane glass. Sipping her tea, she opened the *Toronto Star* website to trawl for a bit of light reading to ease her into the workday. A jolt rattled through her as she read the homepage headline: *Seven Niagara Falls Residents Killed in Brutal Slaying.*

Repulsed yet inexorably curious, Iman read the article with one hand pressed to her stomach, which twitched at each fleck of gore hinted at by the article's breathless author. Seven people dead. A chorus of screams. A mysterious assailant of superlative ferocity. Intimations of a serial killer, a pack of feral dogs, an escaped exotic pet.

An email notification interrupted her reading. She checked her inbox, an unconscious reflex she barely registered. There was nothing in hers, so she switched to Motes', where a fresh message from blytzkreegbop123@hotmail.com struck her in the belly like a dagger of ice. Moving of its own volition, her hand positioned the mouse over the email and double-clicked.

hey motes. how u feelin? have a good night? ;) i did (read the papers? lol). This is just a warm-up. see u soon. L

Iman read the message a dozen times, parsing it with greater fervor than she would a line by Ezra Pound. Read the papers? Which ones? A warm-up for what? How soon? She looked from the email to the article in the *Star*, still open on her desktop. *Ridiculous. You're grasping at straws.*

The office door opened with a click. Professor Motes leaned on the doorframe, an overcoat hanging loosely from his shoulders down to his knees. Its baggy cut served only to emphasise his recent weight loss. He looked like a tall, gangly child playing dress-up with his father's wardrobe. A frizz of stubble masked the lower half of his face, its grey-black hairs appearing sooty and ungroomed. Some tufts were longer than others, and a corona of crumbs clung to the whiskers around his lips. He blew his nose into a tattered Kleenex and staggered to his office, slipping his coat from his shoulders and tossing it onto the coat rack as he went. At no point did he so much as acknowledge Iman's presence with a word or glance.

Bracing her elbow on the armrest to stop her hands trembling, Iman quickly closed the email and marked it as unread. She breathed a sigh of relief as the text reverted from plain to bold. Motes was no computer whiz, but even he knew the difference between a new and a read email.

Motes' coat, hung in haste, slipped its hook and landed in a heap on the floor. Iman hung it back up for him, wrinkling her nose at its sour-sweet odour of stale rainwater and old sweat mixed with something dank and earthy, the smell of winter vegetables left too long in a root cellar. Her fingers brushed the cuff of one sleeve and felt something tacky and damp. A trace of sticky red liquid clung to her fingertips. She sniffed the substance seemingly against her own volition, part of her wanting nothing more than to lop her fingers off at the second knuckle lest the fluid taint the rest of her.

Blood.

Gagging, Iman encased her fingers in a wad of Kleenex and wiped off the worst of it. Her knuckles cracked from the force. She swished her fingers in her tea, wincing at its residual heat, and used the water to scrub them clean. After thirty seconds or so her fingertips grew chafed, the stain reduced to a reddish tinge in the whorls of her fingerprints. She upended the tea in a potted plant and sat down at her desk, her eyes locked on the screen but registering nothing.

"Okay," she said aloud, repeating the word like a mantra. "Okay. Okay." The sound of it calmed her. There was no need to jump to conclusions. The . . . *stuff* she'd touched could've been all sorts of things. Maybe Motes got a bit of food on his sleeve when preparing lunch. Or maybe he brushed up against something freshly painted, smeared a bit of red pigment on his cuff. It could be anything, even transmission fluid. Iman seized on this idea with particular excitement. Transmission fluid had a rusty red colour and was thick enough to leave a tacky residue on a piece of clothing. Maybe he was having car trouble and had taken a look under his hood.

A single phrase strutted through the back of her mind, gleefully kicking the legs out from this comforting premise: *no bodies this time, so no worries.*

Ludicrous, Iman thought. *You're being paranoid.*

"God fucking damn it!" Something heavy and breakable hit the floor with a brittle crack. Motes, a spectre of free-form colour behind frosted glass, delivered a savage kick to whatever he'd thrown. The object let out a fatal crunch, synchronized with a grunt of pain from Motes. He threw open the door. For an instant his face looked twisted and vulpine, his upper lip drawn back to reveal an arsenal of teeth buried in white and spotty gums. The rage tumbled from his face and lay in pieces on the floor. Beneath its shell hunched a look of bewilderment and raccoon-eyed exhaustion. His cheeks were as cracked and worn as the heel of an old catcher's mitt. He wiped his nose with his sleeve, dragging a runner of snot from elbow to wrist.

"We're . . . out of coffee," Motes explained, studying the carpet. He drew pictures in its grain with the toe of his leather shoe. "Would you mind running out and getting me one? From the place I like downtown."

"Y-yeah. Um, sure, professor. No problem at all." She sidestepped away from the coat, aware as she was moving of how transparent a gesture it was. Luckily Motes was too shaken to notice.

"Great," he said, rummaging through his pockets. "I'd like a couple of scones, too. One vanilla and one cheddar. Lots of butter on them. And, uh, something for yourself, too, if you'd like. You can take my car." He passed her his keys and a ten-dollar bill. She took them both, taking inadvertent care not to touch his hand in the transaction.

"Okay, sure. Will do."

With mumbled thanks, Motes retreated into his office, closing the door with pointed softness behind him. Iman let out her breath in a long, steady stream. She wrapped her hand around the keys until their saw-toothed edges bit her palm.

15: A DARK ROAD

THE LIVING ROOM looked very much as David remembered it, but the feel of the place couldn't be more different. The air of cordiality in spite of grief was gone, razed by the calamity in the poker house. In its place gaped a charred and barren strip of hurt and aimless hostility, spiny and brittle and choked with ash. David received no offer of expensive European coffee, and the cord of repartee between Walter and Frank—a subtle twine of words and gestures that betrayed, if not mutual affection, then at least a certain mutual respect—lay severed at their feet. Mrs. Ballaro flitted about the house like an uneasy phantom, carting loads of laundry and mopping floors and scrubbing tables.

As if to balance his wife's flurry of activity, Ballaro himself sat motionless. His head sank into his shoulders, corrugating his neck with a series of bulging folds and plumping the wattle of slack flesh under his chin. He cradled a wine glass in his hand, its fluted base tucked between his middle two fingers. Only the gentle clockwise swirl of the wine in its clear belly betrayed the fact that Ballaro moved at all. He could otherwise have been nothing more than an ugly and awkward piece of furniture.

"Frank," Walter said, taking up his half of the severed cord at their feet. "I dunno what to say. You've got our deepest sympathies. I mean, it's just . . . "

"Terrible beyond words," David tried. Walter's minute nod signalled a good effort, but Ballaro didn't seem to have heard. His wine glass began a more pronounced swirling, the gyre of Merlot deepening. Walter leaned forward, elbows braced on his hefty thighs.

"I want you to know that we're doing everything we can to investigate. In Vincent's case and in Eddie's."

Watching the tiny whirlpool in his glass, Frank gave a single guttural laugh. "And how is that going for you?"

"God's truth? Not that well, Frank. I'd usually slather on some platitudes about how our best minds are on the case, and strides are being taken every day to bring us closer to the truth, but we're men of the world, you and me, right? So I'll spare you the bullshit. This is a stumper if ever there was one. I mean, it doesn't take a genius to see both attacks are connected, but how and why? We're fumbling around in the dark here. You're the common denominator, Frank.

Whoever's doing this has got it out for you bad, and I don't see them stopping any time soon. Anything you can tell us, any suspicions, altercations, reasons someone with this kind of capability would be after you—"

"What kind of capability is that, detective?" Frank's eyes snapped up from his glass, the skin beneath them puffy and bruised. "Skinning a man like a deer in a strip club parking lot? Ripping seven men to shreds—seven *armed* men—and walking away unscathed? You ask if I know a man such as this? Your office has watched me a long time, Walter. Do they think me a *Mafioso,* or a voodoo priest?"

Walter swallowed, saying nothing.

"My family and I will deal with this in our own way, detective." He drank his wine in one long, rolling swig. "If we can think of something that might assist you in your investigations, we will be sure to let you know," he added, in a tone that suggested he would do anything but.

It was then that David noticed a few things that *had* changed in the room besides its tone. The loose collection of art and keepsakes that had decorated the hearth was gone, replaced by a network of Catholic iconography. A procession of saints lined the mantle, a tea candle burning before each one. They faced inward towards the mantle's centre, where a large crucifix hung from a nail a few inches from the ceiling. It was solid wood, cross and savior alike carved from a single piece of mahogany. A crown of dried thorns—real, from what David could see—encircled his head, rivulets of glossy blood frozen mid-trickle down his face. It was a fabulous piece of devotional art, though David figured such a compliment wouldn't land well under the present circumstances.

"Frank, listen. I don't want to cheapen your grief—God knows that's the last thing I'd want to do—but we can help each other. I'm not asking for a handout, and I'm not trying to weasel up to you and get you to compromise yourself. Any side business of yours is entirely outside my interest here; I'll swear an oath to that if you like. Right now all I want is to nail this scumbag who's terrorizing my town. I know you want that too. We're on the same side here."

Frank's laughter pounded the silence. David jumped in his seat, fingernails digging into the armrest. His face flashed red. *Christ, you ninny. Way to show some balls here.*

"You're on my side, detective? That so? Trust me, you don't want to be. This is a dark road I'm walking. I don't need any pussyfoot badges holding my hand." He stood with a groan, one hand braced against the small of his back. "Show yourselves out," he said, and walked into the kitchen without another word, leaving David and Walter alone in his living room.

"Christ, poor guy," said David. "Losing two kids in the span of a month. That's gotta be a dark road. I can't think of one much darker."

"I don't think he was talkin' about grief, Davey." Rubbing his chin, Walter approached the shrine running the length of the hearth. He picked up a book lying next to an icon of Saint Christopher, ran his finger along the binding, underlining the book's title: *The Book of Black Magic and Ceremonial Magic.* "I think that path of his leads somewhere else altogether."

16: ONE HELL OF AN ASSERTION

"YOU STOLE HIS KEYS?!"

They sat opposite one another in their tiny apartment, Iman on the futon, Brian on the nylon folding chair that served as a piece of econo accent furniture.

"I didn't steal them," Iman said. She palmed the strip of brushed nickel and held it to her chest, as if afraid Brian might try and snatch it away from her. "His set is back in his pocket or wherever, where it belongs."

"So what is that you're holding, then?"

"It's a copy. I got it made at the hardware store."

"I . . . " Brian raked his fingers through his fine black hair, revealing a high forehead with a hairline in the first stages of retreat. "You can't just copy someone's keys without permission. I'm assuming you don't have permission?"

Iman's silence was answer enough. Brian threw up his hands in an exasperated sigh.

"You *have* to realise how crazy this is. Prying into the guy's business is one thing. Probably wrong, yeah, but at least you're savvy enough that you're not likely to get caught. But this, with the key . . . what are you planning on doing with it?"

Iman hefted the key, enjoying its slight but palpable weight in her palm. "Well, really, there's only so much you can do with a key, right?"

"You can throw it out. That's something you can totally do with it. Or . . . " Brian went on, pacing and thinking out loud. "My dad has a vice in his garage. We can take it there and smash it with a hammer, get it all busted up before we toss it. That way it can't, you know, fall into the wrong hands."

"Fall into the wrong hands? Christ, Bri, it's not the nuclear launch codes I've got here. It's a front door key."

"But you obviously planned to use it when you copied it, right? I mean, it had to have entered your mind as a possibility. So why?"

Iman pulled an afghan from the foot of the futon and draped it over her legs, her toes probing through the gaps in the wool. "You know how when you were a kid, and you had a loose tooth? The kind that's just hanging on by a little flap of skin? You'd keep prodding it with your tongue, and every time you did it'd hurt like hell. But you'd do it anyway, over and over, until you finally worked up the guts to just pull it out once and for all?"

"O . . . kay. Sure."

"Something's been bothering me. It's this worry I've had. It's crazy, I know it's crazy, but I keep going back to it. Just like with the tooth. I'll be eating breakfast or reading or trying to sleep, and I'll catch myself mulling it over again and again. And I'm just gonna keep doing it until I rip it out and take a good look at it." She held the key up to the light. Whorls of fluorescence bounced off its brushed nickel finish.

Brian removed his glasses and gingerly nibbled on the arm. "And that's what you need the key for?"

"I guess. I dunno."

Moving to the futon, Brian put a hand on Iman's knee. "You could try talking about it. That might be an approach that's a little less, you know, illegal."

Iman set her hand on his and squeezed gently. "You're going to think I'm a lunatic."

"You think I don't already?"

Iman gave Brian a playful slap on the arm. "You ass! I'm being serious."

"Okay, okay. No jokes."

Iman sifted her hands through her hair, twined a lock around her index finger. "You remember those websites Motes has been reading? The stuff in there? I think it's more than just an online fantasy for him. I think he's starting to act on it."

"Based on what, exactly?"

"Based on all sorts of things. The way he's been acting. The books. The crying. The emails. And the other day, when he came in, there was blood in the cuff of his jacket."

Brian chewed a bit of dried skin on his upper lip. "How do you know it was a bloodstain?"

"Not a bloodstain. Blood. Fresh, dripping.."

"So what? Maybe he cut his arm on the way into work."

"I checked. When I brought his keys back, I made a point of looking. No cut."

"And based on this, you're saying . . . he's . . . "

"I'm saying something's wrong. I've felt it in my bones for months now. And maybe I *am* crazy, but if I don't do something to settle this feeling one way or another, I'm gonna crack."

"And by *do something,* you mean . . . ?"

"Motes has back-to-back classes this Tuesday afternoon. He's been blowing off his first-years, but his fourth-year seminars he still makes it to religiously. He won't let the seniors fall by the wayside. That gives me a solid six hours where I know he won't be coming home."

Brian opened his mouth to speak, closed it, chewed his words contemplatively. "I want you to think really carefully about this. I'm not going to tell you not to, and I'm definitely not gonna call the cops on you or anything like that. But you need to ask yourself if your suspicions are really firm enough to justify violating this guy's privacy. I know you're not trying to blackmail him or anything, but this is some serious stuff we're stumbling into."

Iman's hand found Brian's, her fingers lacing through his. "We?"

Brian's Adam's apple trembled like some strange oscilloscope measuring anxiety, but his hand didn't slip away from hers. If anything, it gripped hers tighter. "Hell, a clean record can only get you so far, right?"

She felt a rush of affection for him like heat from an oven door. Her hand left his and ventured somewhere more intimate. Brian's cheeks burned crimson.

"Feeling better?"

"A little bit, yeah. But I expect to feel a whole lot better still in a minute or so."

17: FOURTEEN BULLETS

SOME DAYS DAVID felt like a machine crudely retrofitted to run on coffee and cigarettes. As a fuel they burned dry and foul, grinding gears and backfiring pistons and clotting on belts in a bitter tar-like film, but at least they gave a good kick. He swallowed the soupy black dregs of his current cup, snubbed out the dog end of his smoke, and waited for the cocktail of nicotine and caffeine to send him trundling back into something like awareness.

He glanced over at his partner and felt a shameful comfort in the fact that he wasn't the only one coasting on fumes. Walter's head rested in his hands. His whole body seemed to sag beneath its weight, as if his skull had been replaced with a facsimile forged from solid lead. The older detective usually shouldered sleeplessness with the stoic resolve of a well-seasoned pack mule, but today he seemed blindsided by a backlog of exhaustion, as if all those skipped hours of sleep had ganged up and struck as a single marauding horde. He rubbed his face, shedding Danish crumbs from his moustache, and poured himself a fresh cup of coffee.

"Okay," he said, rubbing his hands together. "Let's talk this through one more time. What have we got?"

David rubbed his eyes. "The phrase 'fuck all' springs to mind."

"Humor me, kid. We're missing something here, and I ain't gonna get a decent rest until I find it."

"Fine. Coroner says Vinnie and his pals all died of blood loss caused by massive internal trauma. Toxicology reports turned up the usual mishmash of booze, tobacco, and prescription drugs, plus a bit of cannabis in one of the younger guys. The woman of the house was on Effexor, an antidepressant. They found the brand name in the medicine cabinet. Bodies received a combination of blunt force trauma and lacerations. No bullets, no metal shrapnel, no burns, which means no bomb. Ruling is that they were severely mauled by some sort of wild animal. I talked to the manager of African Lion Safari, who says they've never had an escape as far back as he can remember, and an animal head count as of this morning comes back full. Same story from the zoo down in Stephensville. Toronto Zoo too, though that's way too far to be credible anyway."

Walter made a steeple of his fingers, pressed them to his lips. "What about exotic animal dealers?"

"Hard to say for sure, since they're off the books. I talked to Delduca about it and he's got a few officers asking around. So far, zilch." He extended his hand to Walter in a "your turn" gesture.

"DNA tests are still pending, but so far all the blood we found comes from the victims. There's no clothing fibres on the windows, and the footprints are a smeary mess. Eyewitnesses are uniformly unreliable. A couple of neighbours report seeing something resembling a bear, others say a wolf. None of them got a good glimpse, just a silhouette among shadows."

"It seems to me, if it walks like a duck, and quacks like a duck . . . "

"We've combed that neighbourhood up and down, Davey. Every garage and shed swept, every alley inspected, every dumpster probed. If the Queen had misplaced a pube somewhere within those six square blocks, we'd've found it and returned it to Her Majesty days ago. There's no way we could've overlooked a wild animal. There'd be another sighting by now.

"That leaves murder, which seems just as crazy, if not crazier. How the hell could someone leap through a window and murder eight people, at least three of 'em packin' loaded pistols, armed with nothing but a blade—one, I might add, that leaves wounds indistinguishable from the sort left by teeth and claws?"

David counted off the dead ends on his fingers. "So we rule out man, we rule out beast. Doesn't leave us with much, eh?"

Walter sucked the end of his moustache. "You're gonna laugh at me for this. I know it."

"What?"

With uncharacteristic timidity, Walter reached into his collar and pulled out a crucifix on a long golden chain. A tiny pewter Christ hung from nails smaller than thumbtacks, his expression of quiet anguish rendered in impressive detail despite his small size.

"So it's a cross. So what?"

"I haven't worn this in thirty-eight years," Walter said. "I found it in my bedroom drawer, in a basket with my wife's jewellery. I wasn't even sure I still had it anymore, thought maybe it'd gotten sold at a garage sale or mixed up with some stuff we sent to Goodwill. When I found it yesterday, Davey, I felt like a guy who knows he left the oven on comin' home and findin' his house still standing. I felt *saved.*"

"I didn't know you were religious."

Walter's moustache couldn't quite hide his smile, small though it was. "Neither did I. I've been in this business a long time, man, and I've seen some strange shit. Some evil shit. But when it comes to out-and-out kooky, this has to be a new record. I don't know what the fuck's going on, but it scares me."

David gave Walter a reassuring pat on the arm. "We're gonna figure it out, Walt. Give us a bit of time. Someone'll spot a mountain lion or escaped tiger or something and the whole thing will start making a lot more sense."

"A tiger, huh? Got quite a vendetta for a kitty cat. Who are the Ballaros, Siegfried and Roy?"

"Then it's some psycho with a werewolf fetish, okay? There's a rational explanation here. We just need to find it."

"No one'd love that more than me, pal," said Walter. "Trouble is, where do we look?"

"I can think of one place. McCulloch. He's wrapped up in this somehow."

"You seriously think he's behind all this shit?"

"Maybe. Maybe not." David twirled his silver alligator ring, its tiny feet catching on the callused webbing between his second and third fingers. "But even if he's just blundered into this same as us, the guy's got a very different vantage point. Maybe he sees something we don't."

"It certainly couldn't hurt to bring the little fucker in, but I don't see him leading us to our creature."

"Give it time," said David.

"Did you count the bullets?"

"Huh?"

Walter cradled his coffee in his lap, both hands wrapped tightly around the mug. "There were eighteen shell casings on the floor of the poker house. We pulled three bullets out of the walls, and one of the forensics boys found another one buried in a tree out back. That leaves fourteen bullets unaccounted for. Where are they?"

David chewed the inside of his cheek. Walter, his interrogator instincts ever honed, had asked a question with only one answer. David couldn't quite put voice to it. Walter continued as if he had.

"What the fuck takes fourteen bullets and doesn't die, Dave? What takes fourteen bullets and doesn't even fucking *bleed?*"

As he spoke, Walter's fingers scurried up his chest to his crucifix necklace. They clung to it the way a toddler holds her mother's skirt in the dark, hoping for a protection she may or may not be able to provide.

18: LET ME OUT

THE DUSTER IDLED on the curb, belching exhaust from its rust-dappled muffler. Its engine rang with the audible clatter of pistons. They set the whole car to shaking like a hyperactive child confined to a school desk ten minutes before the final bell. Iman's leg jiggled in sympathy until Brian's hand settled on her thigh.

"Which one?" he asked. Iman pointed to a bungalow three down from the corner, a squat brick house with white trim. Its freshly asphalted driveway and crisp, unweathered shingles hinted at quiet prosperity, though the grass had grown too long and a thicket of dandelions and creeping Charlie besieged the front garden.

"Thanks for driving me," Iman said.

"Yeah, well, what's a B and E without a getaway car, right?" He drummed his fingers on the steering wheel. "You nervous?"

Iman ran her tongue over the roof of her mouth. Her saliva had taken on the pliant tackiness of wood glue. "No way. Check it out." She held up her hand and gave it an exaggerated shake, partly for comic effect and partly to hide the very real tremors rippling through her fingers. "Solid as a rock."

"You don't have to do this, you know. Avondale Dairy Bar's only about ten minutes from here. We could grab sundaes and call it an afternoon."

"Don't tempt me."

"I don't think a little temptation is such a bad thing, under the circumstances."

Iman ran her fingers along the wisp of hair at the back of his neck, smiling at the faint quiver of his jaw. "Thanks for trying. But I need to do this."

He nodded as if expecting this answer. "If I see him come home, I'll honk the horn."

"I think that'd just draw his attention, hun. He won't come home, trust me. I'll be fine."

"Said the protagonist in every movie like this ever."

"Tell you what. If you see someone pull into the driveway, text me." In truth, she'd most likely hear the car pull in before the message had even arrived, but having a plan seemed to put Brian at ease. He pulled his phone out of his pocket and set it on the dashboard, ready for action. "Good luck."

"Thanks." She tried to think of something else to say that suited the circumstances and realised that unless she got it over with, she'd keep nattering forever. With a decisive nod aimed at no one in particular, she stepped out of the car and slammed the door behind her.

Iman had been to Professor Motes' house only once, when she'd come to talk over her decisions on a stack of term papers she'd helped him grade. This had been before his mini sabbatical and subsequent metamorphosis into an irascible loner, and he'd invited her in for a drink and a chat while the papers sat ignored on the counter. She'd seen little more than his living room—clean, sparsely furnished, tasteful paintings and indigenous folk art dotting the walls— yet even this small knowledge of the house's geography comforted her. She understood why vampire lore held that creatures of the night required invitation to enter a dwelling, but upon receiving it could come and go at their leisure. A sense of fractional ownership accompanied the return to a known place, as of a foot slipped into a doorway, preventing it from closing all the way. It was a foolish thought but a powerful one, and if she hadn't been here before, she wasn't certain she'd be able to slide the key in the lock, as she did now.

The tumblers sounded loud as a gunshot in Iman's overclocked ears. She wasted no time getting inside, performing a pantomime of a woman who had every right to go where she was going, in case some nosy neighbour was peeking through his blinds at her.

The threshold crossed, her heart slowed from a gallop to a trot. Motes lived alone and his car was gone, leaving no logical reason why the house would be anything but empty. A reasonable assumption, though a tiny saboteur taking residence in the deepest folds of Iman's brain gleefully poked holes in it. *What if he has a houseguest? What if he lent his car to a friend? What if it's at the shop?* All possible, though given Motes' recent attitude, a houseguest seemed highly unlikely. And he had his classes, she knew that for a fact. *What if they got cancelled?*

Shut up, she hissed silently. Then, aloud: "Hello? Professor? You home?" It seemed prudent to announce herself just in case he or someone else was home. That way she couldn't be accused of sneaking around. The fact that she'd unlocked the door and had absolutely no story to support her presence occurred to her a few seconds later. As such, the silence that greeted her question was more than welcome.

She went to the living room first, perhaps because it was the only room she knew. It was much as she remembered it, only less clean. Pizza boxes lolled across the coffee table, pools of grease saturating the corrugated cardboard. Scabs of tomato sauce clotted in the warp and weft of a Turkish rug. The whole place felt unwashed and unvacuumed, the smell of it rank and itchy in her nostrils. She sneezed, coating her fingers in snot.

"Ugh," she said. Another reason to be glad of her solitude.

She found the bathroom next, seeking to clean herself up. Her hand paused over the tap. A red stain discoloured the porcelain basin. Similar stains speckled the tile floor and the rim of the bathtub. But the stains, ominous as they were, weren't what caught her attention. Stranger, in its way, was the hair. It covered the tub like a furry grey moss, locks of it glued in damp clumps to the shower walls and carpeting the tub's sleek bottom. Between the blood and the fur, it looked like Motes had tried to shave a large and disgruntled dog and had at least partially succeeded, earning himself a few less than playful nips for his efforts.

The main section of the house described a loop, from entrance to living room to dining room. A hallway branched off to the bedrooms, but Iman left them for now and continued along the circle to the kitchen. Drifts of dirty dishes spilled over the sink and onto the counter. A halo of flies circled the overflowing garbage. The smell of rotting food and sour water hung heavy. Iman tamped the pile down with a wad of paper towel and shut the stainless steel lid. She knew how foolish it was to mess with these things while poring uninvited through someone's house, but she couldn't help herself. She might be here a while, and the smell was bringing tears to her eyes.

The kitchen table was conspicuously free of clutter, save for a pencil and a stack of papers bound with a paper clamp. Greasy thumbprints dotted the cover, and multicoloured tags erupted erratically from the margins. She flipped through the pages, which depicted photocopies of a handwritten manuscript. Motes' jottings brambled the margins, and dark pencil strokes slashed underlines beneath various sentences. She tried to read a few of them, but after scrutinizing the scraggly lettering, she realised the whole thing was written in French.

She checked the first few pages for publishing info and found nothing. The thing seemed to be just a diary, and an old one. Iman's academic radar prickled. This was different than the books she'd checked out from the library. It wasn't the sort of thing you'd find in an indexed search. Motes had sought it out deliberately. The question was, why? Flipping back to the cover, she jotted down the title on a bit of scrap paper she nicked from the garbage: *Le voyage de Lucien Chevalier, coureur des bois, dans le bouclier de Nouveau France, 1621-1625.*

At the end of the kitchen, opposite the back entrance, stood a door unlike the others in the house. It was built to a different dimension, about half as wide as it was tall, giving it a bulky, broad-shouldered cast. Unlike modern interior doors made from thin sheets of wooden laminate glued to a hollow frame, these boards were solid oak and bound with strips of iron. Stranger still was the mechanism beside it: an automatic feeder standing astride an upended bucket. The chute that normally led to the pet's bowl had been lengthened with several feet of PVC pipe halved lengthwise, forming a crude slide that led from the device's mouth to the foot of the door, where a sudden curve funneled it to the half-inch crack between where the oak boards ended and the kitchen tile began.

Brow furrowed, Iman opened the feeder's reservoir, expecting to see several inches of dry kibble piled inside it. Instead she found nothing but an empty plastic chamber. Whatever the machine was meant to dispense, it was gone. She scoured the floor to see what it might have been, which was when she spotted the trail of fur leading away from the door. Iman bent down and grabbed a tuft of it, rubbed it between thumb and forefinger. It was downy and soft, a smoky grey that shone like polished steel where it caught the sunlight.

The various bits of evidence began to assemble themselves in her mind. Could Professor Motes be sheltering a wild animal of some kind, a coyote maybe, or a bobcat? Something distempered and a little dangerous, the sort of thing that might molt all over the place and leave you scratched up, poorly rested, and more than a little irritable?

Maybe even something big enough to tear a guy apart in a strip club parking lot?

Stop it, she thought, scolding whatever malicious voice inside her head had spoken. *You're being paranoid.*

No bodies this time, so no worries, the voice replied.

Bending down, she cocked her ear to the gap at the bottom of the door and waited for a sound—growling, scratching, the restless shift of limbs or tail—that might clue her in to the room's strange inhabitant. She heard nothing, save the soft hum of the refrigerator motor and the distant putter of cars.

Leave it, Iman. It's a wild animal, for goodness' sake. But curiosity's splinter sank in deep. If she was going to remove it, she'd have to get right in and dig it out. *Just a peek. Whatever it is, it's probably sleeping.*

The doorknob turned. Iman eased the door open a crack and peered into the gloom. A rank, sour odour unfurled through the doorway. At the first whiff Iman nearly slammed the door shut, but curiosity stayed her hand. *Just a peek,* she thought again.

Inch by inch, the door swung open into darkness. Iman strained her ears, searching for a hungry growl or the rustle of something large and deadly readying itself to pounce. She heard nothing save for the faint squeak of the door's fat steel hinges. Gradually her eyes adjusted. Wooden stairs led down to a concrete floor, a drain dimpling its approximate center. No animal presented itself, predatory or otherwise, though Iman could only see a narrow sliver of the basement, as the stairwell walls served as blinders to either side.

"Hello?" she called, feeling foolish but not knowing what else to do. "Anything down there?" She waited several seconds without response. "I'm not going to hurt you!" *Oh, good one, Iman. I'm sure the poor thing's gasping with relief.*

With the door open the smell grew stronger, wrinkling her nose and settling in an almost palpable film on the back of her throat. It stank of compost after heavy rainfall, of meat gone bad.

As she had in the car, Iman realised that she could stand here forever, balanced on the threshold between advance and retreat, weighing hypotheticals with all the pompous conjecture of philosophers debating over angels and pinheads. There was either something down there or there wasn't. She could go downstairs and know for sure, or she could turn around and wonder. The former option threatened a sting of fear, the latter an ache of uncertainty. She could rip the bandage off, or leave it on while the skin beneath it turned wrinkly and fish-belly white.

With a final shove of resolve, Iman darted halfway down the steps, crouching to see around the stairwell walls while retaining some semblance of cover from them.

The room was tiny, maybe ten feet square, and low-ceilinged enough to make a tall man stoop. Its concrete walls radiated a late autumn chill, sinking needles of gooseflesh into Iman's exposed forearms. This was clearly no basement but a cold cellar, though what food it once held had either been carted away or rotted into nothingness. The room was bare save for the ruins of a few wooden shelves smashed to kindling.

The door swung gently shut behind her. Iman thrust a fist against her chest, bracing her ribs against the frantic battery of her heart. Her mind wobbled on the precipice of panic. She nudged it backward to safety and waited for her racing heart to resume a more relaxed pace.

Two small windows tucked against the ceiling provided the room's only light. Heavy iron bars divided the light into even strips. Iman hadn't thought to seek out a light switch, and even if she had, it wouldn't have mattered; the lone bulb affixed to the ceiling had shattered, leaving a jagged stump of glass. Shadows covered the floor like a great rumpled blanket, its dank folds forming pockets where anything could hide. But despite the poor visibility, Iman could sense she was alone. She felt it like a vacuum in her chest, a sucking emptiness pulling inward on the rest of her. Something had been living down here, but that something was gone. The knowledge should have comforted her, but it didn't.

A drift of straw piled waist-high in the corner behind the stairs. The floor around it was damp and discoloured, shallow puddles of unknown fluid lying in stagnant pools where the concrete had set unevenly. Iman approached the pile, putting her certainty in her solitude to the test. An itch wormed up her nostrils and down the back of her throat. It settled in her lungs, heavy as wet wool. She coughed into a closed fist and rubbed her eyes with the heels of her hands. Whatever had been down here, it shed like a bastard.

She prodded the straw with her toe. Her hay fever was even worse than her pet allergies, and she knew she'd pay dearly for every stalk that so much as brushed her skin. The dampness gave everything a mouldy, foetid odour, but at least it kept the finer fibres from wafting up her nose in a histaminic cloud. She waded knee-deep in the stack. Her foot struck something hard and light. She probed her toe into the thicket more slowly, brushing the straw aside when she rediscovered whatever she'd kicked. Bending down, she grabbed the object and pulled it into the light.

It rose long and pale and limp in the middle. The end nearest her concluded in a node of fur and gristle, the far end in a blossom of thorny protrusions mossy with residual hair. A thin band of connective tissue joined foreleg to aft.

The severed leg fell from Iman's fingers. She clutched fruitlessly at air, unsure where the leg had gone. Her fingers were numb, the sensation of gripping oddly absent. She staggered backwards and her heels caught on something solid. The straw broke her fall somewhat, but her tailbone still struck the concrete with a painful jolt. She kicked herself clear of whatever had tripped her. Her escape caused the straw to shift, unearthing the head and ribs of an adult deer. Flesh, skin, and organs had all been stripped away from the neck down, leaving only scraps of tendon and cartilage clinging to the bones. The head, by contrast, was undisturbed, save for the lower jaw, which had been torn free. Its tongue lolled limp and obscene from its cavernous throat, its eyes glossy as the buttons on a dead man's suit.

I don't want to be here anymore. The thought landed in the center of her mind: a plain declarative sentence, almost childlike in its simplicity. She'd seen what she needed to see—though what it told her was an open question—and she could ponder it at her leisure at home, in bed, with the lights on and the blinds shut and the door locked tight.

Iman scrambled up the stairs. Let Motes keep his wolf or his bear or his goddamned fucking *wolverine*, whatever monster he'd wrangled up that had managed to strip that deer so clean it hardly stank. He was welcome to it, as far as she was concerned. Let him lose a hand feeding the damn thing.

She reached the top of the stairs, hand hovering inches from the doorknob, and stopped cold. A pocket drought struck her mouth, leeching every drop of moisture from lips to throat.

Nicks and gouges marred the door from top to bottom. Not an inch of grain was left unscarred. But set atop the patina of splinters ran deep slashes in a crude but conscious pattern. They shrieked their plea in letters a foot high and eight inches across: LET ME OUT.

Iman couldn't possibly agree more. *He's insane,* she thought simply. *I'm in an insane man's house right now, uninvited.*

She turned the knob, pulled, and met sudden and intractable resistance. The door didn't budge. She tried again, leaning backward to hang her whole weight against the door. Still nothing. She spied the chunky latch set a few inches above the knob, its empty keyhole leering at her. Understanding hit her like a cudgel to the temple, nearly spilling her down the stairs. She braced herself against the stairwell, sliding her hand along an unfinished rafter. Splinters dug into the meat of her palm. She would feel these only later, musing over exactly when and how she'd gotten them.

"Oh, no," she said. "Oh no oh no oh no." The words looped back on one another, a Mobius strip of anguish. She shoved her hands into her hair, raking her fingers against the roots and pulling until the pain wrung tears from her eyes. The sensation dragged her back into the present.

Her hand fell to her pocket and felt the bulge there with a flash of triumph. Her phone! She pulled it free, nearly dropped it, and keyed out a text to Brian. It took several tries, her trembling thumbs sloppy on the tiny touchpad, but she eventually managed it and hit send.

Help! Locked in cellar! Come inside and find door in kitchen. ASAP Please!!!!!!!

A response pinged back a few seconds later: *on it.*

Relief embraced her, balmy as bathwater. Thank goodness for sweet, sensible Brian. She'd no doubt earned some teasing from him over the next few weeks, but she'd take it gladly in exchange for an escape from this creepy subterranean kennel. Her phone rumbled against her palm, signalling a new text from Brian.

Front door wont open. Did u lock it behind u?!?

Iman felt as if she'd stepped from her nice warm tub into a pool of ice water. She threw her mind back to the front hallway, pictured every movement of her body during those first few steps. Could she really have locked the door? Why would she do that? She always locked her apartment door out of habit, but this was a different house with a different latch.

A door's a door, dummy. Do you remember consciously deciding not *to lock it?* No, she didn't. She bit her lower lip hard enough to leave imprints in her skin. Her phone chirped out a fresh text.

U need me to break in?

YES!!! She typed. Her thumb poised over the send button, hung there a moment, and touched down on the backspace instead. She composed a fresh message: *not yet.* A break-in was a last-ditch option. At best it would tip off Motes that someone had been snooping around his house, which was hardly a good feeling. At worst, she and Brian could wind up in jail. Neighbours weren't all that likely to call the cops over a girl with a key entering Motes' house through the front door, but she suspected they'd react very differently to a young Asian man smashing his way through a window.

"Okay, Iman," she said. "Think. Think think think." Fingers drumming on her thighs, she scanned the room for possible escape. There wasn't much to go on. The windows were heavily barred, the door too solid to kick down, the lock a steel fist wrapped tight around the latch. Any tools Motes might have stored down here were long gone, leaving nothing but a few lengths of splintery wood from the broken shelves.

And a deer carcass, a sardonic voice in her head chimed in. *Don't forget that!*

Kneeling down, Iman brought her eyes level with the gap at the bottom of the door. A veldt of shed fur stretched across the room, fading to bare tile at the far edges. She scanned the fur for foreign objects, expecting no surprises. Her mind turned to its next plan when a glint of metal caught her eye. She torqued her head from side to side, straining for a better view, but the object remained mostly hidden, visible only as a winkle of silvery light three or so feet from the door.

Wishful thinking, Iman, the voice chastised. *A key, just lying there?*

It was a lot to hope for, sure. But it wasn't impossible. Whatever strange shit had gone on in this cellar, the place wasn't built as a dungeon. Motes hadn't locked anyone down here to act out some slasher flick B-roll looping through the murky caverns of his psyche. The lock was on the wrong side of the door, for one thing, and there was no body, no restraints, no sign of struggle. Someone was down here and got out. How? The simplest explanation was that they had a key, or that they received one at the right time. The automatic feeder started to make a lot more sense. Motes could load it, come downstairs, do . . . whatever the hell it was he did down here, and wait for the key to come sliding down the chute the next morning. But what did he do with it then? It didn't go back in the feeder. Did he pocket it? Hang it on a keyring? Or did it slip through his fingers, landing amongst the dirt and dander littering the kitchen floor?

Only one way to find out.

Iman reached for the object, wedging her arm into the gap under the door. It fit up to her wrist. Further effort yielded maybe half an inch, and even that was hard-won, the oaken planks digging gashes into her forearm. She needed a longer reach.

She rifled through the smashed remains of the shelves, hoping for a narrow strip of timber that could function as a makeshift arm. But the damage to the wood had been thorough, and every piece she turned up was either too fat or too stumpy. Pipes ran along the ceiling, partially visible where the plaster had rotted away, but she'd never get one free without a wrench or a hacksaw. Iman could see only one other option. Stifling a shudder, she returned to the pile of straw and picked up the deer's severed leg. The joint sagged limply, the frayed bit of tendon that bound foreleg to aft grinding against the broken socket. Iman swallowed the bile rising up her throat and carried the leg up the stairs, holding it as far away from her body as possible. The naked bone felt slick and awful and strangely alive against her fingers. She slipped the leg beneath the door. It fit easily, but its ruined knee made a direct approach impossible. With every stab forward the leg folded back on itself, abrading the gristly binding still further. A few more twists and it would snap, leaving Iman with a tibia too short to do the job.

With a delicate flick of her wrist, Iman whipped the leg to the side, careful not to overshoot and rip it in two. She brought it around in a smooth arc, her eyes pinned to the small glitter of metal amidst the fur. When the leg eclipsed the object, she began to reel it back, agonizing over each inch. Her wrist worked back and forth, making minute adjustments as the leg slid through the carpet of fur. She positioned the hoof directly over the object and paused. This was where it all counted. Slowly, slowly, she trawled the leg along the tile floor, raising it slightly to put more weight on the hoof. The object snagged on the hoof's rigid tip. It slid along with it for half a foot before slipping free. The hair around it parted as Iman pulled the leg back the rest of the way, allowing her a clear view for the first time. It was definitely a key.

Sweat settled over Iman's palms, slickening her grip. She wiped them on her jeans and cast the leg a second time, overshooting in her excitement. The hoof skittered over the tile, ploughing up drifts of dirt and fur. Iman bent the leg slightly, nestling the key in the hollow of its broken knee, and let the full length of its calf drag over it, bringing to bear every inch of friction at her disposal. The key slid towards her in short bursts before catching on the grouted furrows between tiles or slipping off to one side or another. At each derailment Iman would carefully adjust the leg, working in serpentine patterns to keep the key centered. Eventually she ran out of leg and found the key a tantalizing eight inches from the door. A quick swipe with the deer's foreleg brought it within reach of her fingers.

Iman clutched the key in both hands. She traced her thumb over its teeth, their peaks and valleys dimpling her skin. Never before had she been so *aware* of something, so alert to its properties of mass and shape and texture. She tried to fit it in the lock, panicked when it wouldn't go, turned it right side up, and slid it home. The tumblers rattled within their metal chassis. Light washed over her as the door swung open. She blinked it back, shielding her eyes behind the crux of her elbow. It took every ounce of restraint she possessed not to dart out the nearest exit—to leap through a window if necessary—and keep running until her lungs burst.

She slipped off her left shoe and wedged it beneath the door. Satisfied it couldn't swing shut, she hobbled down the steps and tossed the deer leg into the pile of straw. Back upstairs, she unwedged her shoe and shut the door behind her, listening for the sharp click of its lock engaging. She dropped the key where she'd found it, kicked some fur around to hide the more obvious drag marks, and left through the front door, being sure to lock it behind her.

Brian paced up and down the front lawn, checking windows and tugging experimentally on a trellis. His head whipped around at the sound of the front door closing. He ran up to Iman and threw his arms around her, making an even bigger spectacle of himself than he doubtless already had. Iman couldn't have cared less who was watching. She hugged him back fiercely.

"Are you okay?" he asked.

"I guess so, yeah."

Brian's Adam's apple bobbed once up and down. He pushed his glasses up his nose. "What the hell happened in there?"

Iman warded the question off with a raised hand. "Not now. Sorry, but I can't. Soon, okay?"

"Yeah, sure. Okay." His arms fell to his sides. "So, uh, what do you want to do now? Do you need anything?"

Iman chewed the corner of her lip. The answer, absurd as it was, came to her without prompting. "You still up for Avondale Dairy Bar?"

19: DOCTOR GUTS

DAVID SLOUCHED HIS coat from his shoulders and hung it by a hook in the breezeway. A patch of sweat dampened the space between his shoulder blades, staining his white dress shirt an overcast grey. It had started out freezing that morning, but the sun broke neatly through the clouds by noon, sending forth supply lines of summer heat before the clouds regrouped and hemmed in their flanks. Such were the caprices of autumn weather in Southern Ontario: wear whatever the hell you like; at some point you're going to be uncomfortable.

Tugging his shirt from his clammy skin, David sat on the kitchen chair and watched with bemused gratitude as supper assembled itself around him. Nancy brought plates heaped with rigatoni in meaty red sauce, while Brandon carried forks and knives in a single mass of cutlery. He wielded them like some improbable medieval weapon, parrying and thrusting before dispensing them in their proper places under a reproachful look from his mother.

"Well, look at this," David said, pulling Brandon in for a kiss on the cheek. Brandon tolerated the paternal affection, though he scrunched his face and wiped the affected spot with the back of his wrist shortly after.

"Hi, dad."

Nancy ran her hand from one of David's shoulders to the other, lingering briefly over the downy hairs on the back of his neck and pinching the wad of tense muscle cresting above his collarbone.

"Jeez, this is like wood. Tough day in the salt mines?"

"Spent eight hours or so banging my head against a wall." It was really more like twelve, if you counted the hours David spent lying awake and puzzling over the latest murders, but David didn't want to worry Nancy unduly.

"Anything to show for it?"

"A cracked skull count?"

Nancy made a sympathetic noise and left to fetch drinks. Brandon took his place at the table, fork in hand. He stared longingly at his plate but didn't eat. *How'd I get such a well-mannered kid?* David wondered. At Brandon's age, David would have been halfway through his meal already, shrugging off his mother's blandishments for him to slow down and hold his fork in a civilized grip. Brandon, perhaps sensing David's contemplative gaze, looked up at his father.

He really was a good-looking kid, his skin smattered with freckles and creamy with preadolescent smoothness, his limbs slender and lithe. Eyes the bright blue of glacial waters peered out from beneath a mop of sandy blond hair that would make girls swoon if he ever bothered to comb it—though the moment when this would occur to him was still a few years off. David brushed his thumb over his silver alligator ring.

"How was school?" David asked. He remembered how much he hated being asked this question as a boy, how dull and irrelevant it seemed. And now here he was asking it of his own son, startled by the realisation that he really wanted to know the answer.

Brandon shrugged his shoulders in the lax, loose-jointed manner of children. "Okay, I guess. Kinda boring."

"Boring?! What sort of stuff are they teaching you?"

"Math, science. Spelling."

David furrowed his brow. "You mean they haven't taught you any skydiving yet?"

Grinning, Brandon shook his head.

"What about flamethrower class? Or maybe that's not until high school." David tapped his chin with his index finger. "Hun? When do they start teaching kids how to use flamethrowers?"

Nancy returned, drinks in hand. "The same day they get a very unpleasant visit from yours truly." She set a bottle of Mad Tom in front of David, already uncapped. Beads of condensation bejewelled its slender neck. He took a long swig, letting the pleasant sting of hops crash over the root of his tongue.

They settled into a companionable silence, enjoying the meal and each other's company. David untethered his mind from work, but the rigging snagged and he found thoughts of the case dragging behind him. He and Walter had canvassed the neighbourhood five times over, prodded every bereaved family member, cased funerals, waded hip-deep through old files on the Ballaros, spoken to every wildlife expert and criminal pathologist in the Niagara region, and their weeks of work had turned up precisely nothing.

"Everything okay, hun?"

"Hmm?" David snapped to attention. A piece of ravioli hung pierced from his fork, dangling inches above his plate. He ate it and found it cool. How long had he been holding it there?

"What's up?" Nancy asked. "You seem far away."

"Nothing," said David. "Just daydreaming, I guess. Had a long day at work."

"Was it Doctor Guts?" Brandon asked.

"What?"

"Doctor Guts. Did you catch him yet?"

"Brandon, please," said Nancy, her fork pausing in front of her mouth. "I'm trying to eat."

"Who's Doctor Guts?" David asked.

"The guy who killed all those people last month. And the other guy too, at the strip club."

Nancy set her fork down and put her head in her hands. "Who teaches him these things?"

"Pete said they call him Doctor Guts 'cause he kills people and takes their guts. You know, for experiments and stuff."

"What sort of experiments?" David asked.

Brandon shrugged. "You know. Just experiments. Like in a lab."

David shook his head. "No, we haven't caught him yet."

"But you will, right?"

"I hope so."

"You will."

David ruffled Brandon's hair. "Thanks for the vote of confidence, kid."

"Can we change the subject, please?" pleaded Nancy. "You two may have iron stomachs, but I don't much like to talk about doctors or guts when I'm eating. Especially not pasta in tomato sauce."

"You just don't appreciate sophisticated dinner conversation, do you?"

"Clearly."

David took a bite of pasta. "How'd the showing go?"

Nancy mimed sticking a finger down her throat. "These people don't know what they want. They tell me they're looking for something central near Drummond Road, a place with some age and good bones. They'll go as high as three hundred. I find them this beautiful place, solid brick, restored finishings inside, a coal room converted to a root cellar, just gorgeous. Seller wants two-sixty, I say I can probably get her down to two-forty. The couple take a five-minute walk around and turn up their noses at it. Too closed-concept, they say. Too stuffy." Nancy threw up her hands. "They want heritage, but without the whole 'heritage' part."

David's phone buzzed in his pocket.

"Shi—dang," he said, catching himself. *God, overtime with Walter really drags your vocab through the gutter.* "Sorry. I should take this."

"No phones at the table," Brandon trumpeted. He'd been blasted by that rule too many times not to call it out when he found himself on the right side of the law.

"We'll make an exception for dad," Nancy said.

"No fair," groaned Brandon.

"What if it's about Doctor Guts? You'd be sorry I didn't answer then."

"David, please."

With a sheepish grin, David answered the call. "Detective Moore here."

"Shit, baby, you all business, huh?"

Sweat prickled David's palms. "Wanda," he said, keeping his voice even. "What's up?"

"You know I wouldn't call just to tease you, Dave. I got news."

"McCulloch?"

"He's in town. Got a CI can place him at half a dozen spots over the past three weeks."

"Three weeks?!"

"Yeah, believe me, I wish we had this guy years ago. He squirts positive IDs the way most junkies squirt piss. But we got what we got."

David did some quick mental arithmetic. "What about the tenth of October?"

"Hold on, let's see." David heard the crisp sound of notepad pages turning. "That's a Saturday, yeah? Uh huh, I got him at a piece of shit dive called the Copper Penny."

"You're sure?"

"That's what Bugs told me. He's good with dates."

Bugs, thought David. *Who names these people?*

"I've got him in Toronto as early as September twenty-sixth," Wanda went on. "My guy's seen him off and on since then. Says there's a few hangouts he likes, we stake one out, shouldn't be more than a few days we can nab him. You wanna send a warrant, get a couple of our guys on it?"

"No thanks, Wanda. I'd prefer to settle this one myself."

"It's outta your jurisdiction. You could get yourself in a mess of nasty paperwork, you're not careful."

"I gotta take the risk. You got a couch I can crash on if need be?"

"Please, babe. There's a bed for you here anytime. But you sure you don't wanna put our boys on it?"

"Thanks, Wanda, but this one needs a personal touch."

"Your call. When you showin' up, tomorrow?"

"Better make it tonight. I'll see you in a couple hours."

"Damn, you don't play. I'll put the kettle on, 'cause your ass is gonna need coffee."

"Bless you, Wanda."

He clicked off, his face tilted to his phone but his eyes cutting over for a glance at Nancy. He caught a glimpse of her face before she had it quite composed, her disappointment only partially paved over. "Work?" she asked.

"Work."

"I guess it's urgent, huh?"

"If it weren't, I wouldn't have even picked it up."

"Liar," she said, smiling to show she was only teasing, hiding her teeth to show she wasn't.

"Can't be helped, Nance. I'm sorry."

"I know. Someone's gotta do it. How long will you be gone?"

"I could even be back tonight," he said, withholding the slimness of the odds.

"Was it about Doctor Guts?" Brandon asked, excited.

David wiped a bit of pasta sauce from the side of the boy's mouth. He'd need a word with the CI to be sure, but given what he'd heard, McCulloch wasn't seeming like the main attraction. "I don't think so. But it could be one of his nurses." Nancy rolled her eyes, a gesture Brandon failed to catch in his gape-eyed wonder.

"He's got *nurses?!*"

"More than you know, kid."

20: PERMIT

CHRIST, DEREK WAS getting sick of bars. Such a concept would have seemed downright absurd to him a few weeks ago. Bars were his natural habitat, a biosphere of wood and glass and neon where the flora fermented in kegs and the fauna danced and screwed and scurried from happy hour to closing time, where the alphas wore studs in their noses or tattoos on their necks or polo shirts with popped collars and the omegas always bought the next round. Derek fit in neat as a puzzle piece, a keystone species holding the barmaids and bouncers aloft, an apex predator with .45 calibre claws. Derek revelled in their hominess, the ebb and flow of faces as he moved from one to the next, the niches and specials and quirks. But gradually he'd begun to realise that once you pare away the ornamentation and inebriation that rendered in them a shine bright as polished jewellery, bars were pretty much just boxes filled with booze and shitty lighting. The folks who danced in and out of view weren't lively characters in some hip play. They were just a bunch of drunk and horny losers looking to kill time. And what was Derek but the drunkest, horniest loser of them all? Yet he kept going to them throughout his protracted epiphany—first out of habit, then out of denial, and finally out of spite. He was damned if he'd cower from the likes of Ballaro, and drinking at home felt a little too much like hiding.

But if sitting in the back corner of a dive bar wasn't hiding, what the fuck was it, exactly?

Derek found his thoughts circling this bitter gyre more and more often, kicking against the current in a vain attempt to keep from drowning. He thought often of striking back at the Ballaros, carving space for himself in Niagara's meaty interior, but his imaginings lacked the iterated precision of true planning. They existed rather as operatic fantasies, grandiose and unworkable, a tizzy of gunfire and pyrotechnics. Derek had worked his trade long enough to know the gunslinger model never paid off for long. The meatheads who thought otherwise ignored a simple fact: somewhere in a magazine was a bullet with your name on it. The trick was to keep something solid between it and you.

The asshole hadn't even given Derek a chance to explain himself. That was what really got him. You have a cordial working relationship with someone for ten years, mutual respect on both sides, and at the first sniff of trouble a couple guys show up at your motel room at two in the goddamn morning. No discussion, no explanations, just a metal slug and a dip in the river. How's that for loyalty? How's that for mutual respect?

Brooding into his glass, Derek didn't see the man until he was at his table, hand resting on the backrest of the chair opposite him. A bulky silver ring circled his third finger. Derek's first thought was mafia, but the man was otherwise unadorned save for a wedding band, and his rumpled overcoat and off-the-rack khakis screamed *cop*.

The man pulled out the chair and slid neatly into it. He leaned forward, elbows propped on the table. Derek pinned him at mid-thirties, six foot, a slender one-eighty, soft features but eyes like chips of flint. Shitty cops—and most cops, in Derek's experience, ranked among their number—came in two flavours: pencil-necked desk jockeys and knucklehead sadists. Derek didn't think this guy fell in either camp. He got a similar feeling for the woman who took the seat to his right. A uniformed officer, she was late thirties, heavyset but carrying it fairly well, her skin that rich West African ebony that almost seemed to glow under certain light. Derek could make her as a beat cop by the badge, but the guy remained a mystery.

"You Derek McCulloch?" he asked.

"I say no, will you leave me alone and go bother another table?"

"I dunno. You're welcome to give it a try."

Derek swirled his beer. Islets of foam orbited the rim, leaving streaks along the edge of the glass. "What are you, narco or something? I'm not holding, haven't done any of that shit since high school."

"I don't particularly care if your colon's packed with forty pounds of China white, Derek. That's not my deal."

"No?" Derek sipped his beer with a satisfied smacking sound. "What's your deal, then?"

"Why don't we go and talk about it someplace more private?"

"You arresting me? What's your probable cause? I got a whole bar full of people here saw you come up to me. I haven't been starting any shit, and you know it."

"That's how it has to be, huh?" The guy looked at the lady cop, shaking his head at the sorry state of things. The lady gave a what-are-you-gonna-do shrug, building an easy pantomime between them. These two had history together, then. Policing or a con game, it amounted to the same thing from opposite angles, and Derek had run enough scams to know that sort of rapport couldn't be purchased prefab; you had to grow it from sweat and dirt.

The guy stood up, smoothing out the lapels of his jacket. The lady followed suit, shimmying her legs out from under the table.

"One thing, though, before we go," he said, leaning down until his mouth was level with Derek's ear, very conspiratorial. His face eclipsed the right half of the room, swallowing Derek's field of vision. Derek caught a bitter whiff of coffee on his breath. "You got a permit for that?"

The man's hand shot out on "permit," quick but calm, and wormed into the cavity between Derek's shirt and his jacket. Cold weight drew across Derek's ribs, and the man's hand withdrew holding a pearl-handled revolver. He set it on the table, the barrel pointing to a spot just to Derek's left. The bore winked its dark eye at him.

"Oops," said the woman. It was the first time she'd spoken. Her voice was gentler than Derek expected, almost musical. The man waved to a passing waitress, who eyed the gun uneasily as she approached but didn't say anything. The man took out his wallet and flashed a badge at her.

"We'll take the cheque, please," he said.

21: LOYALTY

DAVID SNUBBED OUT his cigarette on the bottom of the glass ashtray. The butt rose from the ashes like a crooked tombstone, a sardonic image if ever there was one. He watched eddies of smoke flow about the ceiling, batted by the languid revolutions of a ceiling fan. The room felt strangely dated, as if years of tobacco smoke had preserved it. Fluorescent lights buzzed in metal cages, casting a yellowish tinge over the stark, utilitarian desks. Steel file cabinets stood sentry in the halls. Everything was either grey or pea green or that nauseous yellow-brown no-colour that grew inexplicably popular in the 1970s, which David thought of as Bureaucratic Beige. Flat-screen monitors perched atop the desks, sleek black anachronisms giving the lie to the office's timelessness.

Wanda walked over and handed David a manila folder.

"You read all of it?" he asked.

"Skimmed it. No warrant in there."

"Don't need one just yet."

"You sure? You aren't gonna be able to hold the boy, you don't charge him with anything. We could nail him for the forty-five, at least. A public defender even half-awake could shake him out of it, probably, but at least it'd give you some ground for the time being."

David shook his head. "I'm playing this one a little different."

"You're the boss. I hope you aren't draggin' me into any bullshit, though."

"You're squeaky clean, I promise you."

"He know you're not a Toronto cop?"

"If he asks, I'll be sure to tell him."

Wanda rolled her eyes. "You Niagara boys play by your own rules, huh?"

"It's the Wild West, baby." David tapped the folder on the desk to line up the papers inside it. He slipped the folder in his briefcase. "You think the kid's stewed long enough?"

"It's been damn near two hours. You hold him much longer, he might buck on you, start whining for his lawyer."

David nodded. "Thanks for your help, Wanda."

"You got it. I'm headin' home. You've got the address, come by once you're finished up with big boy in there."

"Thanks, but I'll probably just suck it up and drive back to the Falls."

"Fool, it's two in the damn morning already. You grill this guy properly, you could be here for hours. I don't want you fallin' asleep at the wheel and goin' off the road."

"That's sweet of you."

"Sweet nothing, my luck they'll ring my ass up and have me respond to the scene. You interrupt my sleep by dyin', I'm not gonna be too pleased with you."

"Hands at ten and two until I'm out of Toronto, you got it."

Wanda gave David a quick hug. "Don't you beat that boy too badly, now."

"I was always better at teasing, anyway."

She left David in her cubicle, alone save for a few night-shifters plugging away at their keyboards and a belligerent suspect with an interesting story to tell. The trick was to make him feel like telling it.

David squared his shoulders and set his jaw. He let every trace of emotion, good or bad, drain from his face. It flowed away slowly as syrup from an upended bottle, smoothing out lines and sanding down any corners that might betray a sneer or smile. He checked himself out in the mirror and saw 186 pounds of anonymous, granite-faced law enforcement.

Derek McCulloch sat low in his chair with his arms crossed casually over his chest. The room was small and windowless, bordered on all sides by bare concrete walls, and empty save for a small metal-framed chair and Lucite table, both of them bolted to the floor. David brought his own chair in with him: a stately tall-backed piece of oak, bigger, higher, heavier than Derek's. He dragged it along the floor, its legs capped with iron rivets to make the journey that much louder. The chair was a good prop; he hadn't realised how much he'd missed it. He set it down with authority—not quite a slam, but making his presence known—and made himself comfortable. A lone bulb in a wire cage provided the room's only light, and David could use it to great effect. He leaned forward, tilting his head to lay a band of shadow over his eyes.

"How you doing, Derek?"

Derek looked at him evenly, unimpressed by the theatrics. "I've been better."

David breathed a small laugh. The man was cool as coffin dirt, he had to give him that much. Bullying him into talking wasn't going to cut it. Better to throw him off balance, see if he trips.

"Can you tell me where you were on the night of September 8th?"

Derek blinked, his face otherwise unchanged. "I dunno, man, probably not. Do you remember what *you* were doing that night?'

"Yeah, I do. Investigating a murder."

Derek rolled his eyes. "Okay, wise ass, you remember what you were doing the night of, I dunno, September 3rd?" David paused, his face neutral. Derek gave a smug smile. "Exactly. You come at me with some date that gives you a hard-on, but it don't mean shit to me."

"Cute, Derek," David leaned forward on the table, giving his best no-bullshit cop shtick. "But I'm not the one in the hot seat. You are. So you'd best rack your brain."

Derek bit his lip, his gaze cocked to the side. "What day of the week was it?"

"Thursday, going into Friday."

"Then yeah, as a matter of fact, I do know what I was doing that night. I was at the Blue Lagoon."

"Were you with anyone else who can corroborate your story?"

"There were other people there, but I wasn't with them."

"So what were you doing there, exactly?"

"Drinking. Eating. Singing karaoke."

David cocked an eyebrow. "Singing karaoke?"

"That's right, asshole. I rule the mike. Go down there tonight and ask around about the guy who sang 'Can't Get No Satisfaction' by the Stones. I owned that shit, man. Someone'll remember."

"And that's what you were doing September 8th?"

"That and maybe getting laid. Don't put that down as a statement, though, 'cause I don't remember one way or the other."

"Struck out a few times in your day, huh?"

Derek shrugged. "You win some, you lose some, right?"

David flipped open his briefcase. "You enjoy your stay at the Jupiter Motel?"

Derek straightened up in his seat, adjusting the collar of his shirt with a tug. Tells, definitely, but minor ones. His face was a sculpture of bemused indifference, as if the question were so much small talk.

"Please, man, that place is a rathole. I pick better accommodations than that when I go to the Falls."

David had to give the guy credit. He didn't rattle. His fingers hesitated over the sheet of glossy paper in his briefcase and let it lie for now. There were a few avenues he wanted to pursue before things got openly hostile. "You visit the Falls often, do you? You a big gambler? Or just a sucker for haunted houses and wax museums?"

"I'm a contractor. Maintenance and shit. I got a couple of clients down that way, I work for 'em sometimes."

"Maintenance I understand. Never heard of a contractor getting paid to shit." David rifled through the papers in his briefcase as if queuing up a key piece of evidence. It occurred to him that when he started going for the jugular in interrogations, he was basically doing his best impression of Walter Pulaski. *Christ, the old guy must be contagious.* "By clients, you mean Frank Ballaro."

"He's one of them, yeah."

"He must be pretty shaken up lately, all things considered. You send him your condolences?"

"We don't got that kind of relationship. I see the guy again, I'll say a few kind words."

"I'm sure he'd appreciate that. Did you know Eddie Ballaro, Derek?"

Derek's lips split in a wide grin that failed to meet his eyes. "Okay. Fuck this. We're done here."

David sat back in his chair, legs casually crossed. "Is it something I said?"

"Yeah, nice try. Lawyer time, motherfucker."

"We could certainly go that route, Derek, if you want to. But you might want to give it some thought. Now normally, here's where I would put on a gentle, slightly hurt tone and say something about how we're just having a chat, ask you why you want to get lawyers involved. We're pretty sure this is all some misunderstanding, but you start hiding behind a lawyer, we cops get suspicious, et cetera ad nauseam. But you and I, we've danced to this tune before, right? So let's cut the bullshit. In a normal situation, hell yes do you want a lawyer. Tripping you up and making you say stuff you didn't mean to say, that's my job. That's what gets me up in the morning. But in your case, we've got what we like to call extenuating circumstances."

Derek crossed his arms. "Lawyer, please."

"Hold on, hold on." David held up his hand. "Let me talk this through, okay? You don't have to say a single word more. I'll talk, you listen. And when I'm done talking, if you still want a lawyer I'll have one here pronto. Hell, I'll even let you use the phone, call one of your choice. But if you lawyer up now, you're still gonna hear my offer, but it'll be too late to take me up on it. You might walk out of here a bit sooner, but you might be kicking yourself with every step. So what do you say? Can I give my little spiel?"

After a moment's thought, Derek's head tilted forward in a barely perceptible nod.

"Great. I'll keep it short and sweet. Last month, two men were found dead in a motel room in Niagara Falls. It turns out these guys have known connections to Frank Ballaro. Considering this little rendezvous happened three days after Ballaro's boy was found torn to shreds in a strip club parking lot, my finely tuned detective instincts sensed a connection. You don't know anything about this, of course. Which is why I find it so strange that we pulled this picture of you from the motel's surveillance cameras."

David tossed the photo to Derek. It had been blown up to the size of a sheet of printer paper, the distortion and noise whittled down through digital trickery. Derek glanced at the photo, at David, at the door, his face betraying all the high emotion of someone waiting for a bus. *Some brass balls on this one, all right.*

"Doesn't do it for you, huh? Sure, the picture's a little blurry. Maybe a good defense attorney could pour enough doubt over an accommodating jury to let you slide. Unfortunately for you, this here photograph is just the spark that started the fire that's about to burn your ass to a crisp. The receptionist knows who was staying in the room where Ballaro's boys got done, and he gives a pretty good description of the guy, who bears a striking resemblance to the smug young fella sneering back at me this very moment. We pop you in a lineup and have him pick you out, I don't suppose we're gonna have a lot of trouble. And then there's the DNA evidence. Yeah, I know, hotel gets cleaned every day, right? But a place like the Jupiter Motel doesn't do all that thorough a job. We've got hair, blood, a bit of spit-up toothpaste on the sink basin. Even a Kleenex full of good stuff from a one man love-in. No condoms, though, which surprises me for a ladies' man. Though someone with your pedigree probably had enough sense to nab those before he left.

"In a nutshell, we've got more than enough evidence to bring you in, and a better than fifty-fifty shot at conviction. Even if we blow that one, I'm sure a search of whatever hole you've burrowed yourself into up here will turn up something interesting. And if not, we've always got this." David reached into his briefcase and pulled out a plastic evidence bag. Derek's gun lay inside, next to a note card recording the time and place of apprehension.

David swung the gun from side to side, letting his comments stew for a minute, which Derek passed by blowing a series of long, slow breaths through pursed lips, picking at a scab below his chin, and engaging in a number of other small gestures broadcasting boredom but not fear.

"But here's the thing, Derek. I don't especially want to do that. Not because I'm a nice guy—I'm not—and not because I think you're a good kid who might've gotten in a little over his head—I don't. No, the truth is, I just don't give that much of a shit about Lou Perone or Joseph Santino. I was there before the mess was cleaned up, I saw the scene, and it seems to me like it was them or you. I'm not sure if they were planning to do you there or bring you to some quiet place out of town, but I don't doubt that the end result would've been pretty much the same. So you made your move, and you were quicker. Good on you. That's self-defence, far as I'm concerned.

"The trouble is, I don't get to make those distinctions. That's for the law to decide. But sometimes upholding the law comes down to nothing more than some shitty utilitarian math. What happened to Lou Perone and Joey Santino may or may not be a crime, but either way, it's over. What happened to Eddie Ballaro, on the other hand, I don't think that's over. If I only get to solve one of the two crimes, then seems to me I'm doing society a favor by focusing on Eddie's.

"So here's what I'm asking. I want a name. Get me to the bottom of this Ballaro business, and we can write Lou Perone and Joey Santino off as self-defence. No one's clamouring for justice on their behalf anyway. But things are getting ugly in Niagara, and I want it stopped."

Derek drummed his fingers on the table. "You want me to tell you who killed Eddie Ballaro?"

"Or at least a solid lead in the right direction, yes. You're clearly involved to some degree. It's no secret you and Eddie didn't get along—"

"Half the fucking city didn't get along with Eddie. I can barely think of someone who did. If everyone he ever pissed off knows who offed him, why don't you just knock on a few doors at random? You'll find someone in fifteen minutes, I guarantee you. No, you know what? Fuck this. Lawyer lawyer lawyer lawyer lawyer."

David clamped a cigarette between his teeth. He struck a match and touched the flame to its tip. "You sound pretty sure."

"I don't know shit about what happened to Eddie Ballaro. I dunno what fucking memo got circulated, but you all got some pretty fucked-up ideas about what I get up to in my spare time. I can't answer your question, so cuff me if you've got the PC or let me the fuck out of here, please, officer." He half stood, hands braced against the table, tendons in his neck taut. His posture hung a hair below threatening. David was used to braggadocio, particularly with young male perps, but Derek's restraint was atypical—and impressive.

"I never said I needed the answer now," David said. He sent a cloud of tobacco across the room. "Ask around. You can get into places I can't, talk to people who look at cops like we carry the plague. I've worked enough cases to know that whoever was vicious enough to pull a murder that gruesome, at least part of them is proud of it. And who's gonna worry about spilling some dirt to Matchbook McCulloch, right?"

Derek closed his eyes and rested his head against his chair. It must have been a supremely uncomfortable position, given the hardness of the chair and the angle of his neck, but Derek looked as if he was close to drifting off. "Let me get this straight in my head here. And for the record, this is just me testing out your little hypothetical scenario. I don't know anything about no motel murders, nothing about Eddie and Vincent Ballaro I didn't read about in the paper. Basically, you're approaching a guy who you claim shot and killed two men, both of whom have presumed connections to the Niagara underworld. You then ask that guy to go poking around that very same fucking underworld to dig up clues about yet another murder, which may have spurred off the whole gunfight in question. Do I have this right?"

"That's pretty much the long and short of it, yeah."

Derek held his arms up with his palms face up and his wrists parallel, bound by invisible shackles. "Lawyer."

David tapped ashes onto the interrogation room floor. "You disappoint me, Derek. I didn't think a guy like you'd be scared of some Main Street riffraff."

"Oh, please, don't question my manhood. My poor ego can't take it."

"I've got no opinion of your manhood one way or the other. But I do question your intelligence. You think you'll be any safer in lock-up than you will on the street? Ballaro's got friends on the inside as well as the outside. And in there, you won't be able to grab a Greyhound once things start going south. You know who we locked up not six months ago? Dino Malone. He was another 'contractor' for Ballaro, only he was a bit more like family, the way I hear it. He cut a guy's head in half with a chainsaw, top to bottom. Peeled his skull like a banana skin. He's never seeing sunlight again except through bars, but his family's doing just fine. Got a wife and two kids in a plush condo off of Thorold Stone Road, courtesy of Ballaro enterprises. Makes you wonder what he did to inspire such loyalty, and what he'd be willing to do to keep it."

For the first time since David had stepped into the interrogation room, Derek looked uncertain. "If I say yes, I just walk out of here?"

"I'll hold the door for you myself. Of course, I'm counting on you not to just up and disappear. No catching planes or hopping over to the States. I've gone ahead and got you flagged as a person of interest with customs, so you won't find a smooth crossing. I'll expect weekly check-ins with me and my partner. Somewhere discreet where you won't be seen mingling with cops. But show up five minutes late and your ass will be APBed so hard there'll be squad cars looking for you on the moon."

Derek reached across the table and took the glossy photo from David's briefcase. He studied it for a while, tilting it forward to better catch the light. "This arrangement, how long does it go on for?"

"Until I've got my man."

"And what if you don't get him? What if there's no *him* around to get? Some people are sayin' it's some sort of wild animal doin' this shit, and I ain't exactly Davey Crockett."

"If I'm satisfied you've scoured every corner and studied every angle, I'll call us square. I'm not setting you up to fail, Derek. Hard as it might be for you to believe, I want to see you succeed."

Derek flicked the photo, making a stiff cracking sound. "No offense, man, but I'll believe that when I fucking see it."

22: SAFE AS HOUSES

DAVID ENTERED SIMON'S Restaurant to find Walter already waiting, patting the vinyl cushion of the seat next to him. A rampart of junk rose behind him, stacks of newspapers buttressed by cardboard boxes full of tourist knickknacks and garage sale fodder. It ran the full perimeter of the room, pausing only—at the health inspector's insistence, David assumed—for the length of the open kitchen, where griddles bloomed with the smell of frying eggs and bacon. Shelves had been installed a foot or two shy of the ceiling to better display the forest of ceramic statuettes and cracked picture frames and defunct toys inhabiting the restaurant's upper quarters. Amidst the dunes of junk, enough room had been carved out for half a dozen tables—many no doubt salvaged from the same rummage sales as the stuff surrounding them.

Walter dabbed his face with a napkin and set it on his plate, where a yellow smear and a few toast crumbs comprised the sole remains of his breakfast. He burped once, contentedly, and pounded his chest with a closed fist.

"You ever heard of waiting?" David asked.

"You said you were only gonna have coffee."

"You still wait."

"Whatever, Miss Manners. I'm hungry, I eat. Here, top me up, eh? I saved room for another cup just for you." Walter wiggled his coffee mug. The dregs sloshed about inside, black as tar. David took the cup over to the coffeemaker and filled it along with a fresh mug for himself. He'd found the self-serve process uncomfortable on his first visit, but Walter had dragged him here enough times that he'd gotten used to it.

David brought over the coffees and slid in next to Walter. He shook a sugar packet and poured the contents into his mug.

"When's your guy supposed to get here?"

David checked the time on his phone. "Should be here in a minute or two."

"Unless he bugs out on us."

"Yeah." David added some cream to his coffee and stirred it until it took on a mahogany hue.

"You think he will?"

"Depends on how smart he is, I guess."

Walter tugged at his moustache. "You're opening up a real can of worms when you turn around and nail him."

"He gives me what I want, we won't have to go there."

"You're not seriously thinking of dropping him as a suspect, are you?"

"Way I see it, there's a good chance the whole thing can play as self-defence."

"He shot two guys."

"What do you think they were gonna do to him? Clean his room? A decent DA could spin it without my help. He gives me the Ballaro killer, least I can do is nudge it along a little."

Walter pinched the bridge of his nose with his thumb and forefinger. "Dave, the guy's a monster. Do you know some of the heinous shit he's done? I don't care if Santino and Perone were scumbags. If we have a chance to nail McCulloch, we should fucking well nail him."

"It's a weak case, Walter. I spun some shit about DNA evidence, but who knows how that'll pan out? The lab's backed up for months, and the place was a sty. Probably got thirty different hair samples from the mattress alone. We bring him in on Santino and Perone, we're back at square one. And if he walks, it'll all be for nothing."

"So you ride him 'til he's sore and then bust his ass. What's the big deal?"

"It'd make a liar out of me."

"You're homicide police, Davey. Lyin' to perps is half the fucking job."

David thumbed through the newspaper topping a nearby stack, its pages stiff and yellowing. "This is different."

Walter held up his hands. "Whatever. It's your call, chief. I just hope you know what you're dealin' with, is all."

"Neither of us has any idea what we're dealing with, Walt. That's kind of the point."

The bell above the door jangled. Derek scanned the restaurant, his face wrinkled with bemused apprehension. He took a seat opposite David and Walter, while his eyes kept wandering among the labyrinthine shelves and junk-packed crannies.

"What the hell kind of place is this?" he asked.

Walter snorted derisively. "You mean to tell me you've never been to Simon's? For shame. The place is a goddamn Niagara Falls institution."

"For what? Hoarders?"

Walter slumped back in his seat. A puff of musty air escaped through cracks in the vinyl upholstery. "Davey, educate this savage, would you?"

"You wanted discreet, right? I doubt any of your gangland buddies will be wandering in here."

"Whatever, man. Let's get this over with." Derek draped his arms over the chair and let his limbs hang limp. It was a childish gesture, expressing a boredom so powerful it unhinged your joints. David had seen his son do the exact same thing while awaiting a slow meal or silently admonishing his parents for spending forty-five minutes debating over paint samples. The connection troubled him in a way he found hard to define.

"How's it going?" David asked. "You staying safe?"

Derek snorted an incredulous laugh. "Yeah, safe as houses. It's only a crime lord who owns half the city wants me dead, what's to worry about?"

"Don't tell me a guy like you doesn't know how to take care of himself."

"Sure I do. Why you think I went to Toronto?"

"Cause you're too stupid to go somewhere less predictable?" suggested Walter.

"Seriously, though," said David. "If you need some sort of protection . . . "

Derek snorted. "Sure, why not? 'Hey, Butcher, Tyrone, you guys off Eddie Ballaro? Oh, don't mind the officers, they're my escort.' Please, man. You might as well paint a target on my ass."

"I was thinking something a little more subtle."

"You could give me my piece back."

"Nice try."

Derek crossed his arms. His legs stretched and folded under the table, groping in vain for a comfortable position. He rubbed his neck with one hand and glanced out the window, sinking lower in his seat.

A waitress came over to their table, her grey hair pulled back in a loose bun. "Can I get you boys anything?"

"I'm fine with my coffee, thanks," said David.

Derek either missed this cue or chose to ignore it. "Yeah, I'll take a black coffee and two eggs, over-easy with bacon and toast. Oh, and some hash browns."

"Separate bills," David added as the waitress left.

Derek raised his hands, palms up, in a what-the-hell gesture. "You're not even pickin' up my fuckin' tab?"

"We go Dutch for now," David said. "See where this takes us."

"Sure," added Walter. "We don't want you to feel pressured to go all the way."

David wiped his face with a napkin and set it on the table, masking a subtle calming gesture to Walter. *Easy.* "Let's get this over with, shall we? It's been a week. What have you found for us?"

"I've been doin' like you asked me to, hittin' up the bikers at the south end and the street gangs out in St. Catharines. Talked to half the dealers in the damn city, chatted 'em up real casual. Dealers hear shit, got people in and out at all hours, most of 'em too fucked up to keep their mouths shut."

"You score anything?"

"What's this, entrapment? I'm not about to run your errands to get brought up on a few grams of coke."

"We're homicide police, Derek. I don't care if you mainline MDMA into your eyeballs. I just want to make sure you're being cautious."

"Please, man. Let me take care of myself. I made some deals so no one gets suspicious. They just think it's a little more junky chitchat while the guy in the back cuts in more baking soda. Believe me, I got no interest in bein' found."

"Glad to hear it. So you've made the rounds. Anything odd pop out at you?"

Derek shrugged. "I can tell you some of the regulars haven't been turning up lately."

"Got names?"

Derek rattled off a few. "Riffraff, mostly, but these guys come and go all the time. Could be a bunch of 'em got a Labour Ready gig up in the woods or went west to the tar sands. Could be they got nailed in a narco sweep, though I guess you'd know about that."

"So you don't got a line on any of these names, we could maybe look into 'em?"

"Look, man, this shit ain't easy. We're not talkin' about a bunch of forwarding address kinda guys, ok? You asked I tell you what I see, so I'm telling you what I saw. Take it or leave it."

David jotted down a few notes. "Is there anything else you can think of? Anything you find a little strange or suspicious?"

Derek drummed his fingers on the table. "I dunno, man, I . . . hey, okay. Lucky Luke's supposedly comin' back to town."

"Lucky Luke?" David looked at Walter for assistance, who only shrugged.

Derek rolled his eyes. "I thought you guys were supposed to know the streets."

"I know a name if it's worth half a shit," countered Walter. "Who's this Lucky Luke?"

"Lucky Luke Volchyin. He ran a bit of a racket for a couple years, out down Highway 20. Girls, weed, numbers. Started nibblin' on the edges of Ballaro territory."

"And got his balls handed to him in a pack lunch?" ventured Walter

"Nah, man, they call him Lucky Luke for a reason. Guy was fuckin' untouchable. Any time Ballaro tried to send a message, guy wasn't where he was supposed to be. Got him pretty pissed off."

"So what'd he do about it?"

Derek probed his tongue along the pocket between gum and cheek. "Nothin', man. I dunno. Guy just took off."

"He took off?"

"Yeah. Couple months ago." Derek fidgeted with his paper placemat, tapping the corners until the bottom edge lined up with the table just so.

"And Ballaro let that be?"

Derek shrugged. "Problem solved, right?"

"But if he's back, that could ruffle some feathers, am I right?"

"I dunno, man. Maybe. Maybe buddy's smartened up. Look, are we done here?"

"We're getting there. You told me you haven't seen much. What've you been hearing?"

"Nothing."

David took a pointed sip of his coffee. "Eight guys in a mob house got turned to hamburger. You can't tell me no one's talking about it."

"Everyone's talkin' about it, that's the problem. Haven't you been readin' the papers? You can't fuckin' move for all the pet theories and speculatin' horseshit out there. Every two-bit slinger and hustler knows a guy who knows a guy who arranged the hit. Got people sayin' it was Russians, Asians, Iranians. Heard one guy talkin' about how it was coyotes, someone slippin' 'em PCP. Another guy thinks it was a trained tiger out of the circus, same one performs with the lady some nights at Mints. You got your serial killers, your government cover-ups. Who the fuck you *want* to've done it? I can find you a guy'll tell you that's how it went down."

"What about people actually taking credit? Anyone you believe?"

"That's just it. Everyone says they know who did it, but when it comes to names, they get all vague. Usually a few wannabe tough guys'll act all mysterious about that stuff, try and build a rep for themselves without givin' anything away, but I'm not hearin' any of that. I think what happened in that house, it's too heinous to cop to."

"Sorry, I don't buy it," said David. "When it comes to human misery, there's no such thing as 'too heinous.' Whoever did it's gonna talk, and word is gonna spread. These are your people, Derek. Network with them."

"Man, what d'you think I've been doing this week? You've got me wading through a sea of bullshit, lookin' for one little nugget of corn. What do you expect?"

Walter shook his head. "First it's horseshit, now you're tellin' me bullshit? Better keep your stories straight, kid. That stuff won't play well in court."

"Please, man, I'll suck your dick if this case ever legit gets to court. It ain't gonna happen."

"I dunno, now that I'm good and motivated . . . " Walter gave a lascivious bump-and-grind in his seat.

Derek turned to David. "Y'know, I should've pulled my piece when you came up to me in the Penny. Getting' gunned down by cops in a dive bar'd still be a million times better than lunch with this asshole."

David raised his coffee cup in a salute. "There, my friend, I can agree with you."

23: BRIGHT AS A SHAVED COIN

IMAN SAT AMONG the din of the cafeteria, pushing overcooked—and overpriced—butter chicken around her plate. The sauce had congealed to tar-like stickiness. Strings of it clung to the tines of the fork. She pushed her tray aside.

A familiar face emerged from the fog of students and slid onto the bench seat opposite her. She brushed a rogue lock of hair from her forehead and set her backpack on the table beside her, fingers working the zipper.

"How'd you even find me in this mob?" Iman asked.

The girl shrugged. "You get a sixth sense for it after a while. It's good to see you, Manny."

"You too, Em." The two girls smiled at one another: Iman slender, coffee-skinned, straight black hair hanging heavy as crepe; Emily a vision of Teutonic supremacy, the sort of buxom, cream-skinned blonde you'd find in Nazi propaganda. Only Hitler's dream girl likely wouldn't have taken French Literature and Women's Studies at Brock University, nor audited a couple of Arabic courses to branch out from her study of European tongues—Romantic ones, no less. The girl was a panoply of languages, an effortless polyglot who, with a year's casual study, could read the Quran in its native script—a feat Iman, to her shame, couldn't even come close to managing. They'd met during a couple of English Lit classes they'd shared in undergrad—Postcolonial Women's Narratives and Gender and Race in the Victorian Era—and struck up a fast friendship that had softened but not broken when they pursued graduate studies at separate universities: Iman continuing at Brock, Emily drifting to Holy Sceptre.

"So, no offense, but I won't be coming to you next time I want someone to recommend me a good beach read."

Iman gave a sheepish smile. "Was it that bad?"

"Bad? No. It was actually pretty interesting, as a historical document anyway. Prose wasn't much, but what can you expect?" Emily reached into her bag and pulled out a stack of paper. Notes and scribbles fuzzed its margins. Some bits of text were highlighted, others underlined, giving them the beleaguered look of a manuscript that had undergone a major pummeling in the editing room. She rested an arm across the title page, allowing Iman a glimpse of the first few words of the title only: *Le voyage de Lucien Chevalier.*

A shiver went through her. Somehow, she felt this book was important. It was too esoteric, too outside the scope of Motes' other readings, not to be. Iman clutched her hands to avoid snatching it from Emily's grasp. *It's in French, dummy. It won't do you any good.*

"What do I owe you for copies?" Iman asked, reaching for her purse. Emily waved the question away.

"Please. Didn't cost a thing. Being a grad student has its perks."

"At a posh school like Sceptre, maybe. Anyway, thanks. I appreciate it."

"No worries. Where'd you even hear about this thing, anyway? It's not on the public system at all. Our archives have what might be the only copy."

"It's for work." The lie rolled effortlessly off her tongue, greased as it was with a thin veneer of truth.

"Well, I guess there're worse ways to earn a few dollars. Like I said, it's sorta fascinating from a Canadian perspective."

"So what's it say, exactly?"

"Well basically, this Lucien Chevalier was a French fur trader, and a bit of an amateur explorer to boot. I couldn't tell much about the guy's background, but he seems pretty fascinating. You wouldn't think some French bushman out scoring furs would be literate, let alone sophisticated enough to keep a whole diary, though I guess Champlain did it, so there's precedent. Anyway, the journey he talks about brought him up to the Canadian Shield. He's got a few fellow voyageurs with him, but he doesn't seem too big on their company. He calls 'em rude and hard-headed, and uses 'free-thinker' like a curse word. There aren't a lot of specifics on their quarrels, but my take on it is that Lucien's superstitious and they're not. Or at least, not in the same ways."

"What sort of ways do you mean?"

"Okay, the thing is, humans never really settled the Boreal Shield. Explorers have passed through it, and some First Nations people probably hunted around the outskirts, but it's never supported a substantial population. It's too rugged. The ground's all outcrops and limestone and too tough to farm, and the winters are seriously harsh. The voyageurs had all been around long enough to know they weren't about to run into more than the odd Beothuk or Iroquois camp. But Lucien kept insisting he saw people. Lots of them. He'd spot them mostly at night, haunting the outer fringes of their campfires, standing and silently watching. They'd vanish whenever he pointed them out, and as far as he could tell none of the voyageurs ever saw them, or believed that he did either."

"But it could've been Iroquois or whatever, right? I mean, they had cause enough to be wary of white folks—no offense—so it's no surprise they'd hang back and watch what happened rather than stroll right up to them."

"Fair point, normally, but at this point in history, voyageurs and Native Americans were actually pretty chummy. They did a lot of trade together."

"Maybe these ones were more cautious."

"Sure. But here's where the story gets weird. Lucien spends a lot of time describing these 'encounters' or whatever. The watchers were absolutely silent, and they stayed far enough back from the fire that they were little more than silhouettes. Most of the time, the only reason he'd even notice them was their eyes. They flashed, flecks of blue or grey or green. 'Emeralds set in a band of deepest night,' he called them, which was a pretty sweet phrase, I thought."

Iman ventured another bite of her butter chicken. The taste remained subpar, but it was at least edible. She dabbed at the sauce with her naan bread. "What's so weird about that?"

"Name me a blue-eyed Iroquois."

Iman nodded. "Ah. I get you."

"Lucien only got a proper look at the watchers twice. The first time he was scouting ahead with his canoe, charting the course of a river. He took a sharp bend and spotted a man dressed in ratty furs, face covered in a thick brown beard, European as can be. He called out in French and a spotty bit of German, but the guy just stared at him. He dropped his gaze for a second to try and navigate the canoe to a shoal so he could beach it and get out to greet the stranger. But when he looked up, the guy was gone. He called out after him and scoured the riverbanks for half an hour, but never caught another glimpse of him.

"After that he started seeing the silhouettes. They came pretty much nightly for about two weeks. And that was all he saw, right up until the last few pages of his diary. He'd been in the woods for about three months at this point, and it was starting to wear on him. He started venturing out onto smaller tributaries and spending nights away from his main party—he never comes out and says it, but I'm guessing he was getting pretty sick of their company.

"On one of these jaunts, he set up camp on a small clearing partially shielded by a limestone outcrop. The last mention of the figures is several days ago at this point, though he makes a point of noting each night that he ate his preserves cold and slept without lighting a fire. I'm guessing the watchers have something to do with it.

"Anyway, he hears some growling in the middle of the night, snaps awake, grabs his rifle. Bears are common in the Shield, especially back then, and grizzlies aren't unheard of. He loads a round and creeps around the outcrop to the source of the sound, which came from the bank of a river nearby. As he gets closer, he notices not one growl, but two. The first is constant, and it doesn't take him long to place it as a waterfall. For a moment he feels relief, assuming the other growl was nothing but his imagination piling onto the sound of running water. But then the second growl rises to a roar, then a whimper of pain, then silence, followed by some wet smacking sounds that Lucien doesn't like at all. He sidles up to a cluster of cattails growing along the edge of the river, and very carefully peeks out.

"He sees a bear, but its days of being a threat are done. It's dead, its belly torn open, its head flopping back like a rag doll's. Hunched over the bear is a man who could be the older brother of the bearded guy he'd seen months earlier. Wider shoulders, darker beard, but the same hooked nose and silver-blue eyes. He's naked save for a few straps of fur draped haphazardly over his chest and belly. Lucien looks for the weapon the guy used to fell the bear, but as far as he can tell the guy didn't have so much as a sharpened stick. He shoves a hand into the bear's belly, pulls out a wad of entrails, and bites into them. No fire, no knife, no nothing. Just fingers and teeth and raw meat. He scarfs down the handful in a few quick bites and licks his fingers clean, and that's when Lucien notice's the guy's fingernails. They're the yellowy-beige of old bones, and inch long, maybe a quarter-inch thick at the base, and tapered to gnarled points. As Lucien watches, the guy uses one of them to slice through fur and gristle and peel back a flap of bear skin.

"As you might expect, Lucien's had enough. He breaks camp that night, tracks down his comrades, and tells them he's quitting the expedition. They put up a fuss, threaten to confiscate his furs and cut him out of his share of the profits. He haggles them down until they let him take enough furs to pay his passage back to France, and counts himself well rid of the lot of them."

Emily turned up her hands and rested them on the table. Iman waited for more information and, when she received only silence, asked: "And then what?"

"That's it. That's the end of the diary."

Iman scratched her head. "Okay."

"I mean, obviously he made it back to civilization, since he managed to get his diary bound and into the Holy Sceptre archives via who knows what roundabout process. Some canny librarian probably dug the thing out of a rummage sale. And I'm pretty sure he made it back to France at some point. I found some online historical records on an archives site, and it has a record of one *Lucien Chevalier, Voyageur, né en 1586, mort en 1645*. The diary includes full names for three of the other voyageurs, and I checked those guys out too. I found birth records, but no death dates for any of them. All are marked as last seen 1621, *disparu à la mer*."

"Lost at sea?" Iman ventured.

"I think more 'lost beyond the sea.' Weird, eh?"

"Yeah, weird about covers it. But doesn't some of what he says call the whole thing into question? I mean, mysterious figures in the darkness? A man killing a bear with his, um, bare hands? No pun intended." Iman scratched her head, fingernails making a scraping sound against her dry scalp. "With stuff like that in there, it's hard to take the rest of it all that seriously."

Emily bit her lower lip and glanced aside, a gesture Iman knew meant she disagreed but wanted to say so in the gentlest possible manner. "I know I've made the guy sound like a bit of a nutjob, but most of his diary is so sane it hurts. Pretty much every entry is just recordkeeping. He describes the weather, charts the distance and direction they travelled each day, points out landmarks for future references, describes the local flora and fauna, keeps inventory of catches. He even talks about his meals, especially when they involve wild edibles. Talk of strange shadow people is few and far between, and when it comes the tone is more curiosity and growing unease rather than stark raving lunacy. When his colleagues don't believe him, he reacts with frustration, not paranoia. He doesn't start building up conspiracies or suspecting the other voyageurs of having it in for him, both thoughts you'd expect from someone having a schizophrenic episode in the woods."

"It could be fake."

"Sure it could. But to what end? If the guy was trying to write a thrilling account of his adventures in the savage new world, he did a lousy job of it. Half the diary is clerical blather, and the denouement just sort of flops there. There's no climactic showdown or brush with death. He just gets spooked and goes home. If you're gonna make something up, you might as well go big."

Iman slurped a bit of butter chicken sauce off her fingers. "You sound like you really believe the guy saw this stuff."

"I believe that *he* believed it, which is a different thing altogether. But do I think he's lying or insane? Frankly, no. I don't know enough about the region's history to offer a convincing explanation, but whatever it might be, I bet it'll make for a hell of a story."

"For sure." *But not as good a story as what happens in Professor Motes' basement.*

"One more thing. I mentioned that Lucien gives a detailed account of how far he travelled each day. He also spends a fair bit of time pointing out any landmark he comes across. Big rocks, lakes, river forks, hilltops stripped bare by lightning. Between the two, I did a little Google mapping and put together a rough outline of his trip." Emily handed Iman a black and white printout showing a map of northern Ontario. A thick grey line described a lopsided horseshoe through the wilds to the west of Hudson Bay. Iman traced a finger along the route, skimming over trees and rivers.

"Em, this is great." A bizarre thought occurred to Iman, the sudden pressure of it forcing a question to her lips. "Hey, when Lucien saw the man eating the bear, did he happen to describe the phase of the moon?"

Emily leaned forward, her brows furrowed. "It's funny you should ask. I noticed the same thing."

"What's that?"

Emily zipped her bag and looked at Iman, her expression oddly blank. "That it was 'bright as a shaved coin,' as Lucien put it. Meaning a day or two short of full."

24: A THREAD

THE OFFICE GREW stuffy and silent, lost in its mid-afternoon lull as the detectives chased leads and the lieutenants schmoozed their way through protracted lunch meetings. A desk fan batted tufts of stale air around the room. Walter amused himself by exhaling lungfuls of smoke into its whirling blades, coating everything in its path in a funnel of carcinogenic mist. He studied papers in between puffs, his cigarette working its way jauntily from one side of his mouth to the other.

David stared at the file spread open on his desk. In it rested the life story, from a law-enforcement perspective, of one of the missing perps Derek had mentioned. Thin stuff, as leads went, but the meaty bits of this case had long since been gnawed to the bone. David felt like a man sifting through a joke word search, the kind where the goal isn't to find as many listed words as you can among the thicket of characters, but to figure out there aren't any words hiding in there at all.

"Anything interesting?" asked Walter.

David scanned the text, hoping to snag something he'd glossed over on previous read-throughs. "Nah. You?"

"Pfff. None of these guys scream 'vengeful assassin' to me. No associations with Ballaro, good or bad, no crimes more serious than a bit of petty bullshit."

David grabbed the next file. Luka Volchyin. Old Lucky Luke, as Derek had called him. *Guy doesn't look so lucky to me.* Volchyin had a pretty thin rap sheet, nothing out of the ordinary for a Niagara Falls thug. A couple of rescinded juvenile charges, a bust for possession of marijuana, some drunk and disorderly. Only real time served was eighteen months for beating up a fellow lowlife in a downtown bar. This sort of riffraff drifted in and out of town all the time, riding the winds of whatever con or easy fix they could sniff out. David wasn't sure why Derek might find his arrival noteworthy.

David chewed on the lid of his pen, gnarling the plastic. "Hmm."

"What's up?"

"Something about this guy seems familiar."

"You run into him on a case or something?"

"No, nothing like that. I'd recognize his face if I did. It's something else. Luka

Volchyin. Volchyin . . . " The pen lid tapped out a snare beat on David's desk. It paused mid-strike, trembled like a compass needle finding magnetic north.

Volchyin. Could it . . .

Calmly, David set the pen on the desk and rifled through his file cabinet. A clutch of folders bulged from a section marked *Stanford Acres*. David's fingers danced nimbly over its carefully alphabetized index, gliding past *Photos* and *Suspects* to *Victims*. He withdrew a slim manila folder, inside of which sat a list of the names and pertinent facts associated with the twenty-one residents who'd died in the fire. His gaze skipped to the Vs, where a single entry rested in faded typeface: *Volchyin, Sonya.*

"Well, shit," said David.

Walter, ears honed to catch the sound of leads, ambled over. "What you got?"

David passed the folder to Walter. Walter clucked his tongue.

"Well, shit," he agreed.

"Lucky Luke rubs Ballaro the wrong way in the spring. An old folks' home goes up in flames in the summer, counting among its victims one Sonya Volchyin. Volchyin goes underground, and nasty things start happening to Ballaros a couple months later, right around the time Lucky rears his not-so-lucky head."

"I'd hold off typin' up the warrant just yet, Columbo. This ain't exactly a smoking gun."

"Of course not. But it's a thread. A clear motive running through all the bullshit we've shovelled." David's fingers felt like worms beneath an overturned rock, wriggling in the sudden burst of sunlight. He clamped them between his thighs. Walter noticed, squeezed David's shoulder.

"It's a good catch, Davey, but don't go off the rails here. We don't even know she's related to the guy."

"There a lot of Volchyins in this city that you're aware of?"

"I'm just saying. Even if the motive pans out, this thing's still far from solved. We got a pissed-off goon with an axe to grind. How does he go about butchering a house full of wise guys and skip off scot-free?"

David ran his fingernail under the word *Volchyin.* "That's the question, isn't it?"

One of many, anyway.

25: ANGELS

DEREK CAST HIS eyes around the bar. He tilted his beer this way and that, building towers of white foam along the inside of the glass and watching them slowly tumble, sandcastles swallowed by an amber sea. A waitress with shocks of blue and pink hair set a plate of nachos in front of him. He ate quickly and without pleasure, his head bent low to the plate, shovelling handfuls of grease into the burning hole of his belly.

It had been a long and largely fruitless evening of probing every rathole and greasy spoon in town, trading rounds of drinks for gossip and taking the pulse of the city's underclass. He found nothing worth reporting, apart from an almost undetectable dulling of the atmosphere. It seemed quieter somehow. Business wasn't down noticeably from what he remembered, but the rowdier element seemed absent, skimmed off the top to leave the thinner, more tepid brew behind. He riffled through his memory for a sense of who might be missing, but he couldn't come up with anyone worth noting.

His nachos eaten, Derek downed the last of his beer, slapped a toonie on the table, and left. A fresh crop of burnouts would bloom along the bars after midnight, and he'd need a couple hours' rest to face them. He squinted against the streetlights and pulled up the hood of his windbreaker. A chill breeze came hard off the river, putting a nip in the air despite the brightness of the day. Four pints of beer sloshed uneasily in his belly. A piss before leaving would've been just the ticket, but a creeping malaise had forced him out the door and left his bladder like an overfilled bucket, threatening to spill with the slightest jostling.

Christ, what a clusterfuck he'd stumbled into. Ballaro wanted him dead, the cops had his balls in a vice, and he couldn't skip town unless he wanted to be subject to a province-wide manhunt. He'd scraped by thus far by his wits and his wallet, and the latter was fast approaching empty. Normally he'd score a quick job to make some cash, but he couldn't even do that. The cops had him under the microscope. Anyone in the city ate a bullet, he'd be the first mook they'd turn to. Anxiety hung about him like a swath of flies, whining in his ears and flitting at the edges of his peripheral vision, persistent and unswattable. He patted the side of his windbreaker, where a Smith & Wesson Governor nestled cozily in the waistband of his jeans. A .38 calibre, the gun felt like a toy against his hip compared to the .45, but he cherished its company all the same.

With the bow-legged stride born of a bulging bladder, he walked to the corner of Bridge Street and Victoria Avenue, where he entered an all-night gym and flashed his card—expired but passable—to the tan, leanly-muscled woman behind the counter. She let him pass without protest. He slipped into the change room, found a free urinal, and unleashed a torrent of yellow piss, his moan of relief harmonizing with the tinkle of running water. His bladder appeased, he staked out an empty bank of lockers and changed from his thrift store windbreaker and dirty jeans into khakis and a light tweed jacket (also thrift store, but more respectably so). He pulled a black wig down over his close-cropped blond hair and covered the wig with a knitted toque, adjusting the elasticated band to expose enough wispy locks to make his phony hair colour evident. Donning a cheap pair of aviator sunglasses, he doubled back the way he'd come and legged it to the bus station, moving as swiftly as he could without drawing undue attention to himself.

At the station, he grabbed the first bus heading south and took a seat near the back. He found a used copy of the *Niagara Falls Review* and pretended to read, using the pages as parapets to block his face while affording a surreptitious look at his fellow passengers. They were mostly pensioners and scruffy teens half a step from homeless, not the sort Ballaro was likely to have on payroll. He cast regular glances out the rear window, noting the make and colour of cars to flag any that might be following him.

The wig's cheap synthetic fibres itched madly against the back of his neck. After a few stops he ripped it off and stuffed it into his duffel bag when he thought no one was looking. A less than subtle ploy, but fuck it—anyone who'd followed him for this long would have to have seen through the disguise anyway.

Once the bus ventured onto a side street within a short jaunt of his neighbourhood, he changed out his tweed jacket for his windbreaker—turned inside out to mask its stormy grey with the lighter-toned lining—and signalled a stop. He scanned the street for idling cars, saw none, and walked briskly through the back roads to the fleabag low-rise apartment he'd rented over the phone. He climbed the stairs to the third floor, stepping around the soggy stains and discarded junk mail. An infant's soprano wail sliced through the alcove. The kid's mother tried unsuccessfully to sheath the sound with increasingly irate admonitions. "Stop it, Joey. Stop it! Joey, you *stop it right now!*" Derek massaged his forehead with the heel of his hand. He could feel the seeds of a forthcoming headache being planted.

The apartment was a decent size but hopelessly run down, its floorboards buckled and scratched, its plaster walls yellowed and blistered. Mildew and old cigarette smoke lent the air a sour tang that clung to his clothes and followed him for blocks every time he left. He'd crashed here for four nights now and was already sick of the place—just as well, since four nights in one spot was pushing his luck. He wondered if he could somehow skip out on rent *and* finagle his damage deposit back. Without it, he'd have a hard time finding another place to take him in.

Among the many skills and talents that had contributed to Derek's survival in his particularly risky line of work, perhaps the most important was his finely honed sense of looming danger. He felt it now, a bright twang in the depths of his cerebellum. It guided his hand to the butt of the Governor hidden beneath the hem of his t-shirt before his eyes registered the peculiar shadow on the wall. He drew the gun as he stepped into the kitchen, raising the barrel to chest height and squaring it on the figure before he'd even registered who or what it was.

The man stood near the fridge, thumbs tucked into the pockets of his ragged blue jeans. Zippers grinned up and down the arms of his leather jacket, which hung open over a t-shirt sporting the album cover of Television's *Marquee Moon*. His teeth glinted white within a bushy black beard. He extended one hand in a friendly two-fingered wave—a gesture that nearly got him shot by Derek, who flinched at the sudden movement. His index finger cinched tighter, putting three pounds of pressure on a four-pound trigger pull.

"Matchbook McCulloch," the man said, his words untainted by the slightest hint of worry.

"Lucky Luke," Derek replied, aiming for a similar nonchalance. He studied Luke's eyes, panning their murky waters for nuggets of malice. His sieve came up empty, but that was far from enough to make him lower the gun.

"It's Luka now. Like my babushka called me." The humor bled from his face in an instant, leaving a corpse-white pallor that brought every scar and crease and wrinkle into stark relief. He shot a glance at Derek's gun, and the smile returned. "You won't be needin' that bad boy, bro. This ain't gonna be that kinda meeting."

"All the same, I think I'll keep it."

"Suit yourself, but I'm tellin' you there's no need. I ain't packin." The man spread his arms out, planted his legs shoulder-width apart. "Pat me down if you want, bro."

Derek shuffled forward, his gun squared on Luka's chest. He traced the man's outline with his free hand, checking his waistband and probing beneath his jacket for a hidden shoulder holster. Apart from his clothes and some spare change, Luka didn't have a thing on him. Derek took three steps back and allowed his stance to relax slightly, though the gun's sights remained locked on Luka's sternum.

"You here about Ballaro?" he asked. "Cause if so, you should know that he and I are quits."

"So I heard. Way folks tell it, the big man's even got money on your head. He'd like it in his presence, and he don't particularly care if it's still attached to your body, if you catch my drift."

"It's not all that hard to catch."

Luka laughed again, just a chuckle this time. "I always liked you, bro. You know why? You never bought into your own fuckin' hype. Too many guys do what you do, they start to think they're James Bond or that *Day of the Jackal* motherfucker. Nah, bro, you got nothin' to fear from me. I'd sign a pact with the devil himself before I'd do that fat wop's dirty work."

It's not his I'm worried about, so much as yours. But it was possible Luka was playing it straight. He had no direct beef with Derek, after all—at least not that he knew of.

"Not to be rude or anything, man, but you mind gettin' to the point? My arms are gettin' tired and I'd just as soon get to the 'me shooting you' or 'you leaving' part."

"Sure thing, bro. Ballaro's been swinging his dick around this town for a long time, right? Someone pisses him off, he has a little chat with 'em and they go for a ride over the falls without a barrel. We know the drill. A guy like that tends to piss a lot of people off, but he's got so much muscle it don't matter. That's about to change." Luka spread his arms in a grandiose gesture. Derek's finger tensed on the trigger, pausing an ounce of pressure shy of firing. "I had a vision, bro. I saw a way to get back at him. To pay him back for my babushka, and everyone else he's stepped on."

"Not that I plan to cry any tears over the Ballaros, but you've got your work cut out for you there. As targets go, you won't find one much trickier than Frank Ballaro."

Luka buffed his nails on the front of his t-shirt, inspected his cuticles. "I got at his kids, didn't I?"

"So you say. Some folks out there think the fuckers got offed in a bear attack."

Luka flashed a smile. "Pretty choosy bear, ain't it? Got a taste for Italian?"

A droplet of sweat oozed into Derek's eye. He wiped it away, careful to keep the gun trained on Luka. "Okay, assume you're tellin' the truth. You nailed his kids, used a trained circus tiger, went nuts with a hatchet, whatever the fuck happened. You've still got poppa to deal with, and poppa's awful mad. His back's to the wall, and he's gonna be under tighter guard than the pope at Mecca. How the hell do you expect to compete with that?"

"That's just it, bro. It ain't gonna just be me for much longer. I'm gettin' myself a pack."

"A pack?"

"Ain't no shortage of people run afoul of Ballaro in this town, bro. Lotta muscle, but no one to put it to good use. I've been taking these guys under my wing, and I've just about got everyone I need. All I'm missin's a lieutenant. Someone with brains and savvy, the kinda guy who knows how to do more than just pull a trigger. The kind of guy can send a strong message."

Derek wiped first one hand on the seat of his pants, then the other, taking care to keep the gun raised all the while. The barrel trembled as he held it one-handed. "Wait. So that's what this is about? You're . . . recruiting me?"

"You could put it that way. What d'you say? Ballaro's got it in for you. I'm offerin' a chance to wipe him off the map for good. Get you a clean slate."

"Did it occur to you that I could just as easily sell you to Ballaro myself? I bring him your head, it might put him in a forgiving mood."

Luka shrugged, not in the least perturbed by the threat. "You could try. I dunno if he'd be willing to hear you out, but you never know. First you gotta get my head off my shoulders, though, and I kinda like it where it is."

"This thing I'm holding? It's called a gun. You might not've heard of it, but it gives me a bit of an edge in the whole 'kill or be killed' department."

"What kind of bullets you packin'?"

"Just .38s, but they're hollow points. I put four or five in you, your guts'll be chop suey."

Luka smiled. "Maybe. Maybe not. Care to give it a try?"

Another bead of sweat ran into Derek's eye. He blinked it away, his grip on the pistol tightening. "Excuse me?"

"You got the piece, right? Shoot me."

"Buddy, my life's complicated enough right now without having to dispose of a body. Could we not and just say we did?"

In response, Luka raised one arm with his palm facing outward, as if being sworn in to testify. He drew the nail of his index finger down his forearm from wrist to elbow, digging a culvert of split flesh. A thin ribbon of blood wound downward to his bicep, where it pooled until distending in tear-sized droplets and falling to the ground. Derek counted four of them—maybe a half a teaspoon of blood in total—and looked up to find the wound already closed, a months-old scar in its place.

Derek felt his grip on the pistol falter. The butt grew slick and viscous, as if formed from soft wax that was melting in his hands. The barrel drooped, pulled down by an impossible weight. "What kind of Criss Angel shit is this?" he asked.

"Trust me, bro. Angels got nothing to do with it."

26: SÉANCE WITH THE BABA YAGA SET

THE ROOM RUSTLED with the furious scratching of pen on paper. David bent over his desk, right hand scribbling. The tendons in his wrist twisted ever-tighter, begging for reprieve. He finished his jottings with a final flourish and tossed the pen aside. His arm muscles sighed. He probed a thumb into the bony groove at the back of his wrist and massaged the tender meat there. The figures were rough, the lettering chicken-scratch, but it was all there. He ran his tongue over his parched lips, and signalled Walter over with a flap of his hand.

"What you got, Davey?"

"I went through the case files over the past couple of years, looking at arrests for drug dealing, prostitution, assaults, the usual scumbaggery. I took all that, plus all the stuff's been going on over the past few months, and I put together a timeline." David motioned to the paper, which depicted a long rightward-facing arrow. Lines leading to notes or doodles branched off its length. He tapped the leftmost side. "Luka Volchyin seems like a bit player at first. His name doesn't get much traffic. But comb close enough, and something seems off. Like here, last February. Ted Bailey pulls in a couple of guys caught slinging dope out near the Sundown Lounge. Guys are bush league, and they roll over like puppies, tell Bailey they're selling for a mid-level guy called Lucky Luke. The Downer's Ballaro territory, so Bailey figures they're cooking up some bullshit, but the guys stick to the story, say they'll testify, whatever they gotta do."

"Yeah? Then what? They clam up?"

"Then nothing. No follow-up. One of the guys gets picked up on a possession charge six months later, no connection. The other guy's gone."

Walter sucked the curly tip of his moustache. "You talk to Bailey about it?"

"Yeah. He looks at me kinda fuzzy, says he sort of remembers. The whole thing fell apart before it got to trial. I push, but all I get's more waffling."

A frown creased Walter's face. "You think Bailey's bought?"

David laughed. "A bought cop would have a better story up his sleeve than that. There's a million smarter ways to graft, if that's what you're into, and Bailey's no dummy. What's more, this same thing happens more than once. Each time, a couple of toughs mention Lucky Luke, and the trail goes quiet. That's when I realise that for the last year and a half, this guy's been selling coke, dope, escorts, all on Ballaro territory. And getting away with it. Look." He traced the men along the arrow, stopping six inches from its tip. "All this time, with impunity. No retaliations. No messages. I checked hospital and police records for all the guys who got brought in selling for Luka. A few got arrested for dumb shit outside the game, but no one's thumbs got broken, no one took a tumble over the Falls in a burlap sack."

"Ah, come on," said Walter. "There must've been something."

"Nothing that worked. You remember the case back in April, three mooks dead in a room at the Regency Inn?"

"Tainted coke. Simmons caught it, got ruled accidental death."

"But not 'til the lab results came back," corrected David. "We still did some nosing around, right?"

"Sure."

David reached across his desk and grabbed a black notepad. "I read back over my notes on the case. I talked to some friends of the deceased, looking for motives, clues, the usual. Asked a bunch of them what three bambinos might've been doing in a hotel room together, considering all three of them had houses in town. I got the usual runaround, guys clamming up. A few suggested they were having a little party, which makes sense, given the coke. But one guy tells me they were talking about a problem they needed to deal with. Some guy stepping on their toes, whom they needed to teach a lesson. A guy called Lucky Luke."

Walter blinked once, the sound of it audible in the office stillness. "You serious?"

In reply, David handed Walter the notepad, flipped to the appropriate page. Walter ran a thumb over the jottings, as if convinced they were some kind of illusion. "Why the hell'd you never say anything about it?"

"I don't know. I don't remember doing it."

Walter scrunched his eyes. "What you mean, you don't remember? You just told me about it."

"It was the note that brought it back. When I think really hard, I can sort of recall it, but the whole thing's sort of . . . slippery. I've usually got a good head for this stuff. but I dropped the ball here completely, just like Bailey. And it wasn't just us two." David took another notebook out of his back pocket. He flipped it open to a page marked with a sticky tab and jabbed the paper with his finger. The words *Lucky Luke* were written and underlined, the handwriting unmistakably Walter's. "Sorry for snooping on you, buddy. But I had a hunch."

Walter took his notepad back and gripped it in both hands, as if struggling to hold it aloft. His lips worked soundlessly behind his moustache.

"Well, what the hell you make of a thing like that?" Walter fixed his notepad with the sour stare he normally reserved for his most recalcitrant interrogation subjects.

"The general trend continues until August, when Stanford Acres burns to the ground. After that, no mention of Luka whatsoever. He vanishes. Then the Ballaro murders."

"I still don't see the connection, Davey. So Volchyin fucks off. So what? His granny just bought it—assuming she *is* his granny."

"She is." David waved his hand at another folder. "I dug out the obituary. Survived by a single grandchild, one Luka Volchyin."

"Damn near twenty people died in that fire. What makes you think granny Volchyin was the target?"

"A hunch. And this." David slid a photocopy of the Stanford Acres floor plan over to Walter. He pointed to a small room halfway down the eastern wing of the building. "This was Sonya Volchyin's room, number 113. Can you guess what was directly beneath it?"

Walter's tongue circled his lips. Though they were parched, the action left them no damper than they'd been before. "The utility closet," he said. It was no question, but David nodded all the same.

"I did some digging on granny," said David. "Asked a few old folks who survived the fire. Turns out she had a bit of a reputation. Sharp mind, but didn't talk much. Read books with funny titles. Didn't make friends. Kept a lot of strange herbs, ointments, that sort of stuff around her room."

"Sounds like just about every old bag I've ever met in my life."

"I'm not talking Gold Bond powder here. Granted, these are secondhand accounts, but they were pretty consistent. More than one person suggested she was into witchcraft."

"You're not breaking out the tinfoil hats on me, are you?" Walter asked. He absently fingered a spot on his chest, tracing the perpendicular contours of a small crucifix hanging around his neck.

"Please. I sure as hell don't think anybody was hexed here. It's just a new angle, a little window into Volchyin's head. What I think we've got is someone really sly, the sort of guy who knows how to clean his tracks. Someone with a serious fascination with the occult, either because he legitimately believes in it or because it's a convenient prop for him."

"All because grandma liked to play with Ouija boards, huh?"

"It's not just grandma. Think back to the murders. Can you recall anything connecting them, apart from the victims?"

"A shitload of paperwork?"

"A full moon. Two brutal murders a month apart, each targeting a Ballaro, each taking place on the night of a full moon. There's a message there, and we aren't the only ones picking up on it. Remember the book on Ballaro's mantel? Remember the silver knife?"

Walter rubbed his eyes. "This is beyond fucked."

"Tell me about it." David walked over to the coffee machine and began brewing a fresh pot. "I've started making a list of possible sources in the region.

Occult bookstores, Wiccan meet-up groups, that sort of thing. See if any of them know anything about Volchyins senior or junior."

"Those should be some fun interviews."

David stuck his tongue out. "If it gets me Volchyin, I'll even submit to a palm reading. I don't know what weird voodoo this guy's into, but I very much want to have a long chat with him."

"So that's your plan, huh? Séance with the Baba Yaga set?"

"For the next two days, at least. We'll get a chance to test my little theory then. If it doesn't pan out, I might drop it."

Dark liquid trickled from the coffee machine's reservoir. David watched the carafe fill drip by drip, his fingers performing a rolling tap on the table.

"Why, what's in two days?" Walter asked.

When the first cupful of coffee appeared, David switched out the carafe with a spare cup and poured the contents into his mug. He took a sip of the bitter liquid, grimacing with pleasure.

"The next full moon."

PART III: BLOOD MOON

27: ENABLER

DAVID STUDIED HIS dwindling stack of playing cards. He flipped the topmost card over, revealing an eight of diamonds. Walter countered with a nine of clubs and snatched them both with a small cackle. David rotated his head in a figure-eight motion, working out the kinks in his neck. The front seat of a car was hardly conducive to playing cards, necessitating he hold his head at an awkward angle to observe the action. A pizza box, its contents long since devoured, provided a workable playing surface, albeit one regularly upset by the tectonic shifts of Walter's hefty thighs.

"This game is so stupid," David observed.

"You're just mad 'cause you're losing."

David scratched the back of his neck. "It's war. Everybody loses."

"Don't give me that hippie noise. Turn over your damn card."

"I wasn't being poetic," David said, turning over a seven and scooping up Walter's five. "I just mean because it's such a shitty game."

Walter flipped over a nine, ceded it to David's jack. "You're the one who didn't want to play poker."

"Never got the knack." David and Walter put down simultaneous tens. Walter cocked his elbow and circled his forearm in a chug-a-lug motion, chanting "War! War! War! War!" Sighing, David counted out three cards and turned over a fourth. A king. He looked from it to Walter's four, and with a small smile raked all ten cards into his pile.

Walter's moustache twitched. "Stupid fuckin' game."

David paused to glance out the windshield at Ballaro's house, visible half a block down the road. They'd camped here since a little before sunset, smoking cigarettes and keeping casual watch. The evening grew cold, and with the engine shut off to conserve gas and the windows rolled down to vent the worst of the smoke, a chill soon crept into the cab, draping its heavy arms over their shoulders in a gesture of presumptuous overfamiliarity. A steady wind rattled the twining branches of the young maples that demarcated the strip of no-man's-land between street and sidewalk.

David clamped a cigarette between his teeth and lit it, cupping the newborn embers to block the breeze. The cider-sweet smell of autumn mingled with the abrasive tang of burned tobacco. He leaned out the window and exhaled a zephyr of smoke into the mottled black firmament. As he watched his latest breath dissipate, his eyes were drawn from the fading smoke to the full moon hanging overhead. It looked ugly and bloated, an egg sac bulging with the night's sinister offspring. *Christ, David, get a grip.*

Walter followed David's gaze, motioned with his chin towards the Ballaro house. "You really think something's goin' down over there tonight?"

David threw one hand open as if tossing an invisible ball. "Beats me. It looks locked up pretty tight. Don't see how anyone with ill intent could get in and expect to get back out again, but I would have said the same thing about Vincent Ballaro's place."

Walter brushed his thumb against his chest, smoothing a crease in his shirt. He tossed down a two, which lost to David's seven. "Could be the nutjob's made his point. Or he feels like changing it up, get the old element of surprise."

"Could be."

"Shit, look at us," snorted Walter. "Real fuckin' detectives."

"Niagara's finest."

Walter shifted in his seat, nearly upsetting the piles of cards stacked atop the pizza box. "Hey, you mind if I put on some tunes?"

Nodding, David turned the ignition one notch to trigger the battery. Walter fished a CD case from the inside pocket of his coat, popped out the disc, and slid it into the car's sound system. Jaunty piano chords bounced from fifth to root, a syncopated honky-tonk tickled out of yellow-white keys. A crisp baritone orated over the chords, pleasant and on-key in spite of the sprechsang approach.

"Walter, is this 'Werewolves of London'?"

"Good tune. Why d'you ask?"

"God, you're such an immature asshole," David said with affection.

Walter gave David a look of theatrical hurt. "You got something against Warren Zevon?"

David rolled his eyes.

"What, you mean because of this whole full moon thing? Please, Dave, give me a little credit. It's a coincidence."

"Right."

"No, I'm serious." Walter put a hand to his meaty chest. "Hand to God."

David was just credulous enough to entertain this as possible. He could even, if in his most charitable frame of mind, write off the second track—"Bad Moon Rising"—as a subliminal or coincidental choice. The first strains of "Clap for the Wolfman" that followed settled any doubt with the subtlety of a ball peen hammer to the temple. Walter's barely restrained giggling in the passenger seat lent little credence to his proclamations of innocence.

The strains of "I'm a Werewolf, Baby" by the Hip bellowed through the sound system when Walter's phone buzzed in his pocket. He turned the stereo volume down to silent and answered the call.

"Pulaski here." The corners of his moustache turned down. "Shit. Really? Where?" He tucked his phone against shoulder and pulled out a notepad. "Uh-huh. Uh-huh. No, that's not too far from here. We can be there in ten. Get forensics and the coroner down there. Right, yeah. Thanks." He clicked off the call and flipped his notepad shut. "This shit is seriously getting old."

The hairs on the nape of David's neck trembled, stirred by a nonexistent wind. Never had he less enjoyed being right. "Another body?"

"Mincemeat, just like the others." Walter looked up at the moon and flipped it the middle finger. "You know what you are, you fat bitch? You're an enabler."

28: HOWL

IMAN RUBBED HER biceps, arms hugged tight to her chest. Her jean jacket had seemed entirely adequate when she'd left the apartment, but the passing weeks had sharpened autumn's fangs, giving bite to the evening air. She hiked up her collar and held it shut with one hand to trap the heat.

"You want me to start the motor?" Brian asked. He'd dressed more sensibly in a padded jacket and scarf, the latter of which he'd already offered to her twice. If he offered it a third time, she'd probably take him up on it, though she hoped he didn't. It was her own stupid fault for thinking summer's last breaths would linger forever.

"Maybe for just a minute," she said. "I don't want to waste gas."

Brian turned the ignition, and the engine juddered to life. The car trembled on its aging suspension, loose bolts rattling. A whiff of exhaust trickled into the cab—another argument against idling for too long—followed by a puff of warm air from the vents. Iman wrung her hands in front of the heater until the numbness left her fingers. The upper vents pushed back the condensation glazing the windshield, giving Iman a clear view of the house across the road.

They'd parked a few houses down to avoid suspicion, but it was hard not to feel exposed anyway. Brian's rustbucket clashed with the neighbourhood's palette of modest affluence like a mustard stain on a blouse. She hoped no one called the cops—they had no intention of doing anything illegal, but it would be embarrassing and spoil the stakeout.

"How much longer do you think we should stay?" Brian asked, which was his polite way of asking when they could get the hell out of there.

Iman studied the sky. A riot of reds and yellows fringed the horizon, fading as it rose to a lush purple-black. The moon sat bright and full overhead, a polished cue ball resting on the felt of the night.

"Not too much longer," she said. "I'd say it's pretty much after sunset, wouldn't you?"

"Does it need to be?"

"I don't know." She looked down at her hands, which she pinched between her knees to conserve their heat. "Look, I know you think I'm crazy—"

"I don't think you're crazy. I think *this situation* is crazy. It's an important distinction."

Iman stroked Brian's cheek. "Oh, Brian," she said, her voice soft with affection. "You're so full of crap."

"I do what I can."

She'd told Brian about her experience in Motes' house, detailing the converted cellar and the dead deer and the path of hair. He'd listened with rapt attention tinged with disbelief, a fact that irked Iman until she realised it wasn't distrust of her story, or even her perceptions. It was simply that the events didn't seem real to him. The shape they took was too bent and odd to slot within the parameters of his worldview. Iman faced a similar challenge, though her run-in with Motes' basement had hammered the knowledge home, pounded it against her brain until its square pegs fit through the round holes of her incredulity, and her beleaguered mind needed to shift in order to accommodate this forceful and unwelcome intrusion. She assumed such unceremonious amendments were what drove some people mad, their minds insufficiently ductile to handle the logjam without cracking.

Naming the sickness helped, bending its amorphous edges into established parameters. She called it clinical lycanthropy, though she was no psychologist and afforded no window into Motes' mind. In truth, she knew only that he was very ill, and that such an illness could, conceivably, manifest itself as violence. If she was going to share an office with the man, she wanted to know what that might entail.

"So do you think he, like, dresses up, or . . . "

"I really have no idea, Bri. It's just a hunch. This seems like the best time to pursue it."

Brian looked straight ahead, drumming his fingers on the steering wheel. His mouth shrank to a skinny lipless line, a sign that he was going to say something serious. He opened his mouth, closed it, paused to regroup, and tried again. "I'd just like to go on record to say I'm against this. I'm not trying to talk you out of it, and I'm here if things go wrong, but I still think you should leave the guy alone."

"He's *sick*, Bri—"

"I believe you. I do. People go unhinged for all sorts of reasons, and I trust your judgement to spot that sort of thing when it happens. That's why I'm worried. Whatever Motes is into, it's definitely weird. And I guess weird isn't necessarily dangerous, but . . . " He shook his hands dismissively. "I don't know. I guess I'm just saying be careful."

Iman took his hand in hers, squeezed it gently. "Thanks. I will." She looked up at the sky. The whorls of red and yellow had faded to a dull, bluish grey.

"Is it time?" Brian asked.

"Who knows? But it's as long as I'm willing to wait." She unbuckled her seatbelt. "Wish me luck."

"You're not gonna, you know . . . go inside again or anything, are you?"

Iman shook her head. She had no intention of setting foot inside Motes' house ever again. "I'm just going to do a quick circuit of the house, see if anything looks strange."

"And if it doesn't?"

She shrugged. "Then we're just about where we started, aren't we?"

She stepped from the car into the vacant night. The streetlight above her flickered, its circuits jarred by rain damage or passing traffic. She crossed the street, hands stuffed in the pockets of her jacket, and approached Motes' house from the sidewalk. The wind rustled the leaves of the maple trees overhead. She stood for a moment, listening for other sounds beneath the susurrus of foliage. In the distance a dog barked, high and mournful. Iman shook her head and shivered.

She walked diagonally across the front yard, every muscle poised to betray casual confidence. She passed by the living room window, the room beyond hidden by drapes closed tight against the autumn evening. The kitchen and dining room curtains were likewise shut, though sheer enough to reveal that no light shone within. The house was, by all accounts, totally dark. If Motes was home, he was sleeping, though it was barely eight o'clock. *He's probably out,* said a voice in her head.

Then why is his car in the driveway? asked another.

Iman rounded the house to the backyard, wincing as twigs and fallen leaves crackled underfoot. Using the back door as a guide, she found the cellar window around the side of the house and hunkered down. She cupped her hands around the glass to cut the glare and peered inside, frowning at the vista of red-brown grain. Her eyes adjusted, and she realised there was a slab of plywood blocking her view. Strangely, it had been mounted to the inside of the window, leaving the exterior glass exposed. Squinting, she studied the sliver of darkness between the plywood and the window frame. Was there something moving in there, a flicker of motion against the shadows? She swore she saw it, though was aware her imagination could easily be playing tricks on her. Shifting her weight, she inched closer.

Something huge slammed into the plywood. It buckled towards her, smacking the iron bars with a resonant *pang.* Iman fell backwards onto the grass. Its damp fronds left a cold stamp against the seat of her pants. She scurried backward, terrified, yet too transfixed to stand and run as the invisible force hammered the plywood again and again. A crack appeared in the board, widening with each successive blow. A low, furious growling rumbled through the glass, rising to a staccato yelp with each slam. There was a pause, followed by the brittle snap of splintering wood. Something black and sharp stabbed through the cracked plywood.

Three somethings.

They curled to the right, revealing themselves to be long, hairy fingers, each capped with a twisted black nail. They blazed against the muted backdrop of the plywood, rendered in impossibly high definition by Iman's overclocked senses. She could see each hair sprouting from its follicle, chart the ragged shoreline where cuticle met nail, sense the pulse of blood through capillaries loud as bass from a cranked amplifier.

The fingers tensed, ripping a chunk from the plywood. There was a thud as something large struck the plank, and the darkness of the crack was eclipsed by a single yellow eye, its socket fringed with thick grey-brown hair. Its gaze met hers. Its pupil yawned open like an aperture to the molten madness churning in the deepest depth of the earth, where fire wyrms burrowed through rock and damned souls bathed in magma.

That's not a costume.

Iman scrambled to her feet and dashed into the road, oblivious to lights or neighbours or traffic. Had a car been coming, she would have surely been hit. But Motes' house stood on a quiet suburban side street, and the only running car in view was Brian's. She threw herself inside, nearly slamming the door on her own leg. Her hands reached for the seatbelt, tugging hard enough to trigger the locking mechanism and leave her gripping a useless stretch of rigid nylon. "Go."

"What—"

"*Go.*"

"Okay, going." Brian shifted into drive and attempted a U-turn, but the street was too narrow and he had to stop short of the curb. He threw the car into reverse and did a three-point instead. Iman balled her hands into fists and bit back a scream. Finally, Brian righted the car and drove off, pushing the car to twenty over the limit—a breakneck speed, by his almost prissily law-abiding standards.

It took her hours to fall asleep that night, a small eternity staring at the phantasmal shapes flitting across the ceiling and the walls and the backs of her eyelids. She thought the sight of that eye would stay with her for the rest of her life. But what haunted her most wasn't a sight at all, but a sound. She'd heard it as she'd run from Motes' backyard, after the board had ceased its splintering and the hairy fists their pounding. A high, savage, dreadful sound echoing backwards through time, filling her with the same dread that once chilled the hearts of her Neolithic ancestors.

A howl.

29: ALIEN STARS

DAVID AND WALTER drove north up Montrose Road, hooking along the highway and spilling out onto Kalar Road. Walter turned up the stereo and listened briefly to his mix CD, but the humor was gone and he quickly turned it back off. The streetlights and houses fell away, leaving them adrift on a sea of moonlit fields and distant silos. Hydro poles rose like masts from the roadside, running volts to St. Catharines and Grimsby. A gravel road led them to Firemen's Park, where a parking lot spotlit by orange lights stood like an asphalt island amidst the trees. A cruiser's lights bathed the surrounding grass in strobes of red-blue. David pulled up beside it.

The officers stood nearby, a short distance from a rust-flecked blue Taurus. One of the doors had been ripped clean off its hinges. It lay on the grass a dozen or so feet away. David cut the engine, and the officers walked over. He recognized the first one immediately: Tom Nichols, late twenties, decent build. A beat cop since before David had joined up with the NFPD. David considered him solid enough, but his eyes bore a harrowed look the detective didn't like. Orange light reflected off the sheen of sweat glazing his forehead. He shook Walter and David's hands—quick pumps, his palm clammy, his gaze roving this way and that.

"Detectives. 'Bout time. No offense, you got here quick and all. It's just, well, I guess you should check it out, huh?"

"Not a bad idea, Nichols." David turned to the second officer. She struck him as familiar, but it took a moment to place her. There were a lot of people on the force he knew only by sight, or didn't know at all. This girl, he felt he'd talked to. It came a second later. "Myers, right? You caught the Ballaro case."

She nodded. "You can call me Melissa. First responder on two maulings in as many months. Some girls have all the luck."

David held her gaze for a few seconds, appraising her comment. Between her and Nichols, he pegged Myers as the better go-to for questions about the scene. "So what do you think? Better or worse than the Sundown Lounge?"

"Hard to use a word like 'better' for a scene like this, but at least this spot's a whole lot easier to secure." She looked from David to Walter. "I was wondering if you two were gonna draw this one. I guess it's sort of your case now, isn't it?"

"Yeah, and about as welcome as a case of gonorrhea," said Walter. "You get an ID of the victims?"

"Found drivers' licenses and OHIP cards for both of them, plus the vehicle registration. The guy's named Bryce O'Connor, the girl's Sally LeChance. No priors on either of them. Came up here for some action, by the look of things, when whatever the hell got 'em came by."

"Whatever, or whoever?"

"I'll leave that to the detectives. Come on."

They walked over to the Taurus. On their way, Walter edged up to David. "You catch the names?"

David nodded. "O'Connor, LeChance."

"Don't sound like Ballaro blood, does it?"

"Could be a niece or nephew, grandkid, something like that."

"Yeah, but that piece of shit look like somethin' Ballaro's grandkid would drive around in?"

A rank humid heat escaped through the car's open side. David clicked on his flashlight and shone it into the car, Walter peering over his shoulder. The uniformed officers looked away. The woman officer's face retained a steely professionalism. The man's, more emotively limber, turned a pale green.

The bodies in the car were badly mangled, their genders identifiable mostly by their clothes and the girl's long blonde hair. They leaned towards the passenger side, belts unbuckled, hands reaching for the door handle. David worked the beam of light over the cab, checking for bullet holes he knew he wouldn't find.

"So these two hook up, come out here to do some parking, and find themselves in the wrong place at the wrong time?"

"I don't think it was a hook-up," said Melissa. She handed over an evidence bag, a wallet splayed open inside. A couple of glossy photos filled the laminated slot meant for IDs. They were the kind of pictures you'd get taken in mall photo booths, a young couple making goofy faces and falling all over each other. "Those're our pair. You can't tell from the bodies, but the driver's license photos give it away."

David clucked his tongue. *The kid's sharp,* he thought, realising as it crossed his mind that she was maybe two years younger than him at most. "So, what, you guys stumble on these two on patrol?"

"That'd be about our luck. But no, some kid came across it and called it in."

Walter looked around, perplexed. "And you let him go home?"

"Please, I'd know better than that. We got here, it was just us and the body."

"Then who called it in?"

"Male, mid-twenties by the sound of him. Called 911 from a payphone, said he saw a bunch of blood near a car by the parking lot. Dispatch told him to stay put, but he must've legged it."

David turned a slow circle, casting his gaze along the parking lot. The spaces were empty save for the cruisers and the car full of corpses. He studied the treeline, oaks and elms and maples like ripples in a curtain of night.

"There's no payphone here," he said. A blade of ice sank into his belly. "Officer, get on your radio and call for backup."

"Backup?" She raised an eyebrow. "It's ugly, sure, but whatever did this is long gone."

There's that "what" again. "I don't think so."

David drew his pistol, pointing vaguely at the trees. He scanned the darkness beyond them, searching for the wink of a gun barrel or the white crackle of a muzzle flash. The uniformed officers stepped back, hands raised warily. Even Walter looked uneasy, his moustache twitching. He put a hand on David's shoulder. "Christ, Davey, relax. You feelin' okay?"

David felt a wave of shame, the weight of it nearly enough to lower his gun, but the blade of ice twisted in his belly, cinching his stance tighter. "Where the fuck's the payphone, Walter? You see one around here? And who uses a payphone these days? You mean to tell me the guy didn't have a cell on him?"

"So what if he didn't?"

"He stumbles on two bodies, calls 911, gives 'em just enough information so they don't send half the first responders in town, then disappears? That sound right to you?"

Walter opened his mouth to answer, but his words were severed at the root as the night tore itself open and hell poured in through the wound.

It took Nichols first, barrelling out of the trees and mowing him down. He let out a scream snipped short by the wet crack of his head striking the pavement. Two quick slashes opened him neck to pelvis, a gasp of steaming red mist drifting on the brisk autumn wind.

The thing atop Nichols dipped its head to his neck and munched, a satisfied growl issuing low in its throat. It turned its reddened muzzle to the three cops. David felt the bolts securing his sanity spin loose a couple of turns. Even with his instincts screaming *setup*, even with the paranormal inklings bleeding into the edges of his investigation, nothing had prepared him for this. This was no wolf, no bear, no trained circus tiger. This was the sort of thing mad monks raved about on the cusp of Armageddon, a plague of fangs and sinew shod in nappy grey-brown fur. He smelled its musk needle-sharp in his nostrils, pheromones of mustard gas rolling over the parking lot. His eyes watered; his gun sight drooped.

To either side of him, Walter and Melissa pulled their pieces. The girl was quicker, her Beretta snapping out five rounds before Walter's gave its first cry. The thing gritted its teeth and swatted, as if beset by a swarm of bluebottles. It charged for Walter, raking its dinner-plate paws down from face to crotch. Walter grunted and fell backwards, the entire front of his body soaked red. The thing pounced on him, and David's gun found its mark. He emptied the clip and kept firing, the impotent click of the hammer lost beneath an inhuman scream he only vaguely recognized as coming from his mouth. He charged the thing and it smacked him aside. A casual blow, but it landed like a sledgehammer, snapping ribs and stealing breath. He crumbled to the pavement, lungs flopping in his chest like fish on a grimy deck, twitching for oxygen.

The thing rose over him, its eyes level with his, and David saw in its bone-white pupils the cataclysmic fires of alien stars. Its teeth—too many teeth, no mortal mouth could ever need so many—glinted beneath harsh fluorescent spotlights. Blood dripped from its pearly gums. He heard Melissa reload and fire, though the sound seemed unimportant and strangely muted, a television blathering in another room. He saw the slugs hammer the thing's left flank, watched the puff of blood rise from each entry wound, more dust than liquid. The thing didn't seem to care. It traced a claw crosswise along David's chest, playful, almost tender. Cloth and skin parted like tissue paper as it passed. Its breath reeked of abattoirs and madness, of bodies rotting in jungle heat.

David brought the butt of his pistol down on the thing's head, succeeding only in knocking the gun from his blood-slick grasp. The thing blinked in annoyance, snarled, and lowered its muzzle to feed. Its jaws spread impossibly wide, an upended chasm yawing over him. He flailed helplessly beneath its weight, fists pounding its nose, its head, its muzzle.

A beam of radiance burst from his right hand, bright as a magnesium flare. Heat bloomed in his palm, molten yet painless. It felt as if he were holding a star. The thing above him screamed, smoke curling from a glowing white gash in its cheek. It reared with pain, allowing David to roll free. He scrambled for his gun, knowing its uselessness but running on pure instinct. His hands fumbled to reload, spilling bullets across the asphalt. Any second those jaws would close on his skull, pulping brain and splintering bone.

The bubble of panic burst, and the world rushed in to fill the vacuum. David dropped the gun. The thing was gone, its flank disappearing into the darkness beyond the trees. Melissa stood at the squad car door, screaming into her radio. The light in his hand had been extinguished. He studied his palm, the skin there unburnt, and saw a glow like dying embers fade from the alligator ring his son had given him.

The sterling silver alligator ring.

David stood up, a band of misery squeezing his chest. He hobbled over to Walter, who lay supine on the pavement with his arms spread. Blood flowed from his gut in a hundred little rills and rivulets, saturating his shirt and feeding a pebbly red delta near his right hip. He looked at the wound, at the pale cast of Walter's face, and sat down next to him. Walter's hand twitched, fingers curling and uncurling. David took the hand in his and held it. The older cop looked up at him and coughed, bits of red phlegm speckling his chin.

"This sucks, Davey," he wheezed.

David patted his hand. "Better not talk, Walt. There's an ambulance coming."

"I thought of another one." The words came out haggard and parched, as if they had to drag themselves over gravel to get there.

"Another what?"

"'Bark At the Moon.' By Ozzy Osbourne. Good tune."

For a moment David figured he was delirious. Then he got it. "Real fucking funny. You can put it on your next mix CD."

Walter shook his head. It seemed to cost him a great deal of effort. "No way, man. You tell 'em to play 'Over the Hills and Far Away.' Led Zep. Classic track."

"You can tell them yourself, Walt."

Walter laughed soundlessly, a minute trembling of the shoulders. "Don't think so." He took a long, rattling breath. "It's so cold out here, I . . . "

"Hang on, I'll give you my jacket." David began shrugging his coat from his shoulders, each motion wringing fresh agony from his ribs. Walter's hand squeezed once, relaxed, and fell still. David put a hand to Walter's lips, counted to sixty. He closed the older cop's eyes and lay down beside him, listening to the approaching wail of sirens.

30: DEBRIS

IMAN CLOSED THE lid of her laptop, listening to the gentle purr of its hard drive winding down. She'd emailed Motes to tell him she wasn't feeling well and would be out of the office for a day or two. Writing it took the better part of two hours, punctuated with hand-wringing and compulsive parsing of words and phrases, her finger hovering over the track pad. The message was innocuous, a mere two lines, yet admission of what she'd seen seemed to leak into the text. It clung to serifs and dripped from descenders, a mephitic glaze that no amount of deleting and retyping could purge. When she'd finally closed her eyes and pecked *send* with a trembling index finger, she felt as if she'd just run uphill beyond the limits of her endurance.

Setting her laptop aside, she slithered beneath the covers of her bed, her eyes sour and stinging with sleeplessness. The events of last night played out in a continuous loop, a grim palimpsest scrawling its ugly image across her ceiling. She dimly remembered Brian's entreaties that he tell her what she saw, the gentle weight of his hand on her back, the worried gaze from the bathroom doorframe as she vomited every scrap she'd eaten into the toilet. Eventually, with much insistence from her—dimly remembered but earnest, as well as she could recall— he left for school, insisting she call him if she needed anything.

She closed her eyes and rubbed her temples, willing the mild ache to recede. What she'd witnessed in Motes' back yard was clearly impossible, yet every rational explanation she could think of broke against the anvil of her certainty. The only answer was that she'd hallucinated the whole thing, but then why did everything coming before and after feel so normal? Surely one couldn't ascend from the foggy depths of such delusion into clear-skied lucidity without some haziness in between.

Longing for distraction, she grabbed her phone and keyed in the *Niagara Falls Review*. The homepage headline read: *Police Officers Among Those Killed in Savage Animal Attack.*

Iman read the article, her fingers too numb to feel the screen of her smartphone. She scrolled on anyway, processors humming, blankly transferring data from corneas to ocular nerves to brain. There seemed to be no flavour to the information, no editorial colouring by her higher faculties. She was a fax machine transmitting signals, seeing the shapes but blind to their meaning.

Four officers from the Niagara Regional Police Department had a bizarre and tragic encounter with a wild animal last night. Duty officers Melissa Myers and Dan Nichols responded to an anonymous report of an animal attack in Firemen's Park. They arrived on scene to find the bodies of Brock University students Bryce O'Connor and Sally LeChance in O.Connor's vehicle. The bodies were badly mutilated. Paramedics called to the scene were dismissed, as the duty officers contacted homicide detectives David Moore and Walter Pulaski, who have been investigating the wave of similarly brutal attacks occurring over the last few months.

The attack left Detective Pulaski and Officer Nichols dead. Detective Moore was taken to Niagara Falls General Hospital with serious injuries. Officer Myers was unharmed in the incident but has gone on paid administrative leave. Chief Aldo Delduca insists the leave is voluntary.

"Officer Myers faced a horrendous situation bravely and competently and has our full support. The moment she sees fit to return to active duty, we'll be behind her one hundred percent."

A pool of saliva collected at the base of Iman's tongue. *They know. Whatever it is I saw, they saw it too.* Her belief in this fact was absolute. She held it the way a shipwrecked sailor clings to debris, white-knuckled and desperate to stay afloat.

Sweat prickled her palms. She wiped them on the seat of her pants one by one, her free digits dutifully scrolling through the story. She needed to talk to these people. To warn them about Motes. To share what she knew. But most of all, to look another human in the eyes and see the small nod, the signal of affirmation that said, "Yes. I saw it too."

Or they'll ship you off to the funny farm. That's always an option.

Iman dismissed the warning with a shrug. If she was wrong, if they'd experienced nothing more than an attack from a bear or a mountain lion, let them commit her. It would probably be the right call. She continued reading.

Detective Moore declined to speak to reporters, citing a need to recuperate. Officer Myers could not be reached for comment.

Iman grunted. *Otherwise known as 'go fuck yourself.'* Myers was out. She could be anywhere, and even if Iman could somehow get hold of her address, she seriously doubted the woman would want to speak to her. The press would be beating down her door hard enough already.

Moore, on the other hand, had a fixed location, at least for the next little while. And the beat reporters would likely hold off on him until he was out of the hospital, out of fear of reprisals if not professional courtesy. A young relative, on the other hand, might just be able to sweet-talk her way past reception.

Iman wondered what the odds were that Detective Moore was brown. Probably not that great. *I doubt he's that kind of moor, har har.*

A niece by marriage, maybe? Yeah. She liked the sound of that.

31: A LUCKY PUNCH

THE MOST PAINFUL part of David's stay at the hospital was watching his wife cry. It sounded like so much cornball Hallmark sentiment, but it was true. David chalked part of this fact up to the morphine, which coated his pain receptors with its wonderful spongy syrup while leaving the higher precipices of emotion unprotected. He stroked her hand softly, making an effort to hide how taxing he found the movement.

"How's Brandon?" he asked.

"Worried sick, but okay. I think your legend's grown exponentially in his mind since last night, and it was pretty grand to begin with."

"Gonna be a hell of a letdown once he hits his teens."

"I let him stay home from school today. Mom's watching him. I'm gonna bring him by later this afternoon for as long as the doctors let us visit. I just wanted to come by myself first. In case it was, you know . . . bad . . . "

David nodded, approving. "How bad is it?"

Nancy made a sound halfway between a laugh and a cry. "I dunno, you're the homicide detective, you tell me."

"Well, I'm not a case yet, so that's a good sign." He shifted back in his bed, grunting at the pressure it put on his ribs. Nancy put a guiding hand on his shoulders. Relief softened the bags under her eyes, but it was still clear she hadn't slept much, if at all. "You should go get some rest."

"I'm fine."

"You've been sitting here since what, one AM?"

"More like 1:30."

David checked his watch. "That's almost ten hours."

Her eyes swung to the left, a signal David recognized as her intention to change the subject. "Mom called my cell this morning. She said someone from the *Review* came by the house, asking questions about what happened."

"I doubt she had much trouble driving them off."

Nancy twirled her wedding band around her finger. "I guess they want to get your side of the story."

"The precinct already issued a statement, didn't they?"

"The papers are saying it was some sort of wild animal."

David looked at the tubes and needles probing the back of his hand. A strip of medical adhesive held the tubes in place. Saline dripped down from a plastic bag suspended on a steel pole.

"David?" Nancy asked, gently summoning his gaze to meet hers. "Was it a wild animal?"

"Sure it was."

Nancy gave him a long, silent look.

"It was big and hairy. A bear, by the looks of it. Or a wolf."

"You couldn't tell a bear from a wolf?"

"I wasn't exactly able to take notes," he snapped, instantly regretting it. Nancy flinched at the sound of his voice, so rarely raised. He took her hand with his and squeezed it. "It . . . it went for Walter first. Of the three of us, I mean. Dan was closer to the woods. It killed him and we were all in a line and it went for Walter. It could've gone for Melissa or me, but it didn't. It picked Walter. And I stood there and I watched . . . "

"Don't. I know you, David. You did everything you could."

David didn't answer. He ran his thumb back and forth over the strip of medical adhesive. Nancy touched her fingers to his cheeks and kissed his forehead. He smiled up at her, wan but sincere.

"I should probably go," she said. "I've got a deal closing today and I'm sure Brandon's itching for a full update."

"Do what you have to do. I'm totally fine here. They said I shouldn't need to stay for more than a few days. Have a rest for a few hours and bring Brandon by this evening."

"I'll see what I can do, rest-wise." She gave him a final kiss, on the lips this time, and flapped her fingers in a wave—a gesture so distinctly Nancy it nearly brought tears to David's eyes. "You need me, you call, okay?"

"You got it."

David tried to clear his mind of images from the night before. It wasn't easy. Every inhalation seemed to carry with it the charnel house stink of the thing's breath, and the whirring of central air fans evoked the growl of its throat.

That afternoon, Officer Myers paid him a visit. She looked strange to him in her civilian clothes—a green blouse atop a tan skirt—despite the fact he'd seen her only a few times before. The uniform did that to people. He straightened up in bed, smoothing down the sheets against his legs and ensuring nothing untoward was peeking out from beneath the covers.

"You mind my stopping by? I don't mean to intrude."

"No, yeah, it's fine."

Her eyes flicked to the floor, back to him. "You okay?"

"I've been better, I guess, but yeah."

"Good." Another flick, away and back. "I, uh, you've heard about Walter?"

David nodded. Melissa closed her eyes, her sympathy almost successful at masking her relief. She met his eyes evenly this time. "Dan got it, too."

"I know. I'm sorry."

"Me too. You guys were close?"

"You could say that."

Melissa nodded. They were cops; nothing more needed to be said. "Delduca made an official statement on our behalf. About the attack. He said it was a wild animal of some kind, likely a bear, though we couldn't say for sure."

"I heard."

"I guess it was dark and we had trouble making a definite identification."

"You know how it is. Heat of the moment and all that."

Melissa bowed her head. "I get it, okay? Clam up or get a one-way ticket to desk duty for the rest of your career, if not forced medical retirement. But since it's just the two of us, can we cut the bullshit for a few seconds? That thing was a bear the way Hulk Hogan is a typical retiree. We dumped thirty rounds into it between the three of us and it didn't even slow down. If it weren't for that fucking voodoo of yours, it would've devoured all four of us."

David fiddled with the alligator ring. "A lucky punch, that's all it was. I must've startled it."

"Lucky punches don't *glow*. I saw what happened. It was like you threw a handful of the sun at the damn thing."

"I didn't see any glow," David said, even as the sublime spark relit itself in the theatre behind his eyes.

Melissa pursed her lips. "You seriously expect me to believe that . . . *thing* was just some Hulked-up bear?"

"It could be. Who knows? We were both pretty hysterical. Our memories can't be trusted." He looked down at his ring, his free hand worrying it in jerky circles around his finger.

Melissa grabbed his hand. "It's silver, isn't it?"

David snatched his hand back, cradled it against his chest. "So what if it is?"

"It fits," she said. Her voice cracked with an uneasy alloy of laughter and sobbing. "It's fucking lunacy, but it fits. All of it."

"What fits?"

Melissa leaned forward until her face was inches from David's. "Do *not* give me that bullshit, okay? Do not. You know damn well what I mean. You've thought it too. I get why you're denying it, but it's in there, and don't you dare try to tell me otherwise."

David stared up at the ceiling, looking at nothing but keen to avoid Melissa's eyes. "There's a lot in there at the moment. That doesn't mean I can trust it all, and neither should you."

"What other choice do I have? Check myself in at the psych ward, tell them I've gone nuts?"

David closed his eyes, shook his head. He wished Melissa would go away.

The more he spoke, the more his own bent logic grated on his ears. "Nothing like that. Just that we shouldn't cling to any delusions—"

"*Cling?* You think I *like* thinking this shit? You think it feels good to come in here and talk about what happened to Dan? To believe—no, fuck believe, to *know*—that what ate him was a, a . . . " The word dangled from her lips, unsaid, before climbing into her mouth and down her throat, where its intrusion nearly choked her.

"So don't think about it. Maybe some things are best if you just let them be."

She sat in the visitor's chair, one leg crossed over the other. She closed her eyes and took a deep breath before speaking.

"Look, if we can't even admit the truth of what we saw to ourselves, the next person who dies, we'll have their blood on our hands. I can't just sit—"

David silenced her with a raised hand. Someone was coming into the room. She was early twenties, Middle Eastern extraction, no scrubs, and dressed too casually to be hospital staff. He placed her as second-generation Canadian, at least by the way she dressed—low-rise jeans and a red V-neck top—and the measure of her stride. Her voice confirmed it: soft, slightly nasal, and devoid of the rounded inflection of accented English.

"Excuse me, are you Detective Moore?"

Melissa answered before David got the chance. "Excuse *me*, kid, this is a closed ward. You can't just wander in here uninvited. I'd turn around now before you find yourself under arrest."

The girl looked back and forth between the two of them, her face betraying the shocked delight of an unexpected brush with celebrity. "You're Officer Myers, right?"

Myers didn't appear to find this attention the least bit amusing. She bristled, her stoic cop stare hardening her features like a fast-set cement mask. "You got a hearing problem? I don't intend to repeat myself."

"I know, I'm sorry, but I need to talk to you about what happened last night. Both of you."

Melissa grabbed the girl's wrist. The girl, obviously unused to the less pleasant side of the law, tried to jerk back. Melissa clamped down harder, spinning the girl halfway around and bringing her arm up behind her back.

"No, *I'm* sorry. I've had a long day already and I really don't need to be dealing with this shit. I'm going to walk you to the hallway now. You give me any trouble, this is going to get a lot less pleasant for you, in the short and long term. University kids can get busted just like anyone else."

"Melissa," David said. "It's okay—"

"It's definitely *not* okay. Visiting hours are for family and invited guests only. That means miss nosey here snuck past reception."

"I don't think that's an arrestable offence."

"Like I need more paperwork. No, no arrest, but it *is* enough to throw her out on her can."

"Look," the girl said. "I'm not trying to upset you guys, but it's very important I talk to you—"

"You're not good at instructions, are you?"

"It was a werewolf, wasn't it?"

Melissa froze. David didn't think he'd even seen someone do it more literally. Every muscle and tendon seized; even her breath seemed to clot in her throat.

"You can't tell anyone, I know that. But it was, right? That's what attacked you?"

"Is this some sort of joke?" Melissa growled, but it was too late. Her composure was laudable, but the girl had landed a perfect sucker punch. There was no smooth recovery possible. Realising her brief advantage, the girl went on.

"I know you feel crazy. I feel the same way. I saw it too. And I know who it is."

Melissa glanced over at David, lost for words. He gave a single nod, and she let the girl go. The girl took a couple of steps away from Melissa, her fingers kneading her kinked shoulder.

"Sit down," David said. "I think the three of us should talk."

32: HEAVY SHIT

IMAN SPOKE FOR the better part of an hour. The story dribbled out at first, thick and slow and clotted with *ums*, but as the improbable details piled up and the cops showed no signs of incredulity, the trickle became a steady flow. A nurse interrupted them at one point to change Detective Moore's dressing, and the detective asked her to come back later, citing police business. Iman took this for a good sign. When she finished, the two officers looked at one another. Iman sensed silent messages passing between them, but lacked the training or intuition to decode them. She could only hope that earnest, slightly troubled stare didn't mean *lock this crazy bitch up before she pulls a scalpel.*

"Something's still missing. The attacks haven't been random, which means there needs to be a motive. This Motes guy doesn't seem like the type to go in for the mob."

Iman rubbed her hands together. "It's a lead, though, isn't it?"

"Under normal circumstances, sure. But the identity of werewolves isn't exactly the sort of thing you usually grill a guy about. I've got nothing to hang over him and no logical reason to go to him for a report."

"Trust me. This whole thing is eating away at him. I've seen him deteriorate over the past few months. He's a wreck. If you put any pressure on him at all, he'll crumble."

"Or go to the papers claiming two lunatic cops accused him of being a werewolf."

"Not exactly the kind of reputation that helps you make Major," Officer Myers added.

"And the papers print it, sight unseen?" asked Iman.

"Point," agreed Moore.

Myers clacked her teeth together. "Still, this is some heavy shit we're laying at his door. If he's so keen to help us, why hasn't he contacted the police about it?"

"If he had," Iman asked, "would you have believed him?"

Myers looked at Moore, who shrugged.

"Point," he repeated.

33: THE PACK

DEREK AWOKE. Consciousness struck him with the car-crash dislocation of deep sleep interrupted, its impact hurdling him through the years and miles. His arm flapped vaguely at the impediment lodged against the crux of his shoulder. He was nine years old and sleeping off a night of Nintendo and off-brand cola at Michael Rothstein's house. He was sixteen and late for another Saturday morning shift at FreshCo, his mother's voice wheedling through the nappy drywall. He was twenty-one and passed out on his girlfriend's couch, the remnants of a mickey of Jack Daniels evaporating into a sticky film on his shirt. He was twenty-eight in Montreal, dozing semi-conscious in a hotel on St Viateur after completing the biggest job of his life, Miguel Santiago's gangster blood drying beneath his fingernails.

The pressure on his shoulder, vibrating savagely. His perceptions snapped into focus with a mucusy snort. He was thirty-one years old, sleeping off the jagged edge of a hangover in a shitty apartment in downtown Niagara Falls. And Luka Volchyin was standing over him, his face split in a madman's grin.

"Mornin', Matchbook. Thought I'd let myself in."

"Of course. *Mi casa es su casa* and all that shit." Of its own accord, Derek's hand drifted casually to beneath the bed's second pillow, where his Governor lay snug against the sheets, safetied but loaded. He thought of the way Luka had cut his own wrist with his thumbnail, how the skin had stitched itself back together as quickly as it had torn. Could his brain tissue do the same thing? Derek noticed an ugly weal of discoloured flesh bracketing the gap between Luka's nose and mouth. *That didn't heal up quite so fast. Why is that?*

"You read yesterday's paper?" asked Luka.

"Yeah. Fuckin' Leafs blew it again, eh?"

Luka's grin lost some of its width, but none of its intensity. "Funny guy. I was thinkin' of a more local story."

Derek said nothing. He'd read the story, of course. Had, in fact, bought about six different papers and read each account, then logged onto the library computers and read half a dozen more. Even to a professional killer, that kind of brazen balls-out recklessness was unthinkable. Almost awe inspiring, in a freak show, see-a-man-eat-a-tire sort of way.

"You could say thanks," suggested Luka. "But I know that's not really your style. So no worries, bro. That's the way things roll when you're part of the pack."

"Thanks for what, exactly? It seems like butcherin' people is its own reward for you."

"Hey, you take what you can get. You said those two homicide cops were tyin' you down, keepin' you from hittin' back at Ballaro. I took care of 'em for you."

"The fat old one, yeah," said Derek. "And good work to you there. But the younger guy's just in the hospital."

"Yeah well, things went south a bit. It's no big deal. He's outta commission, is the important thing."

"Not as out of commission as he could be."

"Hey, back off, okay? The asshole nailed me." Luka pointed to the gash on his left cheek. It carved a naked slash into his beard, its skin pink and puckered.

"Yeah, I noticed. You gonna make it?"

"You're pushin' your luck, McCulloch," Luka whispered. Derek checked the man's eyes and decided he was overplaying his hand a little. He raised his arms, palms out.

"Hey, man, I hear you. I'm sorry, okay? I guess I'm just a little wound up. You did me a major solid, and I appreciate it."

The flinty edge fell from Luka's gaze. "No worries, bro. Truth is, I shoulda ended that fuckin' cop. But the light." He closed his eyes, pinched the bridge of his nose. "I don't think so straight when I'm ridin' the moon. Things feel, I dunno, *lower*."

"Sounds pretty intense."

Luka grinned. "It's a trip, bro. Now you best get dressed. You're runnin' with the big dogs now. I think it's time you meet the rest of the pack."

The pack, it turned out, were sitting in his living room, making short work of the beer he'd bought himself the night before. Derek recognized many of them. There was Salvador Aguilar, an Ecuadorian grifter who used to pull three-card monte down by the falls. Beside him was Bear, a Quebecois juggernaut who spoke little English and communicated mostly through grunts. Nails stood in the corner, his earlobes tattered much as Bugs had described them. Derek counted nine, including Luka: eight men and only one woman—a rangy, sallow-skinned thing, all elbows and stringy brown hair, her eyes drowning in thick gobs of eyeliner. She had ugly, mannish hands made uglier by the fake green nails adorning them, though the rest of her wasn't bad. Her gaze met Derek's and flicked away, unimpressed. He placed her as the one-time girlfriend of Johnny Hall, head of the Hells Angels chapter that attempted to start up in town, much to Ballaro's distaste.

As he put names to faces and rap sheets to names, Derek realised the common thread: every single one of them had stepped on Frank Ballaro's toes and paid the price. Though not afraid to waste bullets and burlap sacks to make a point, Ballaro often relied on other forms of punishment to keep the city's underbelly in line. His restraint kept the body count down and the cops off his back, but it also made him a lot of enemies. Outcasts flung to the city's fringes, they'd clung to Luka as some hirsute Robin Hood, an outlaw keen to strike back at the establishment—even though said establishment was itself technically outlawed. They studied Derek darkly, their faces ranging from amused curiosity to contempt.

How many of their friends did I kill? he wondered. *And how many more of them were told to kneel down and kiss Ballaro's ring or wake up one morning to find Matchbook McCulloch's smiling face overhead?* He honestly couldn't say. Regardless of the exact figures, he didn't expect to find many friends here. His right hand itched for the comforting heft of the Governor, still sleeping peacefully beneath his pillow.

Luka wrapped his arm around Derek's shoulders. Derek could feel the muscles of the bigger man's bicep tight against his neck, full of dormant strength he had no interest in awakening. "Boys," he said, tipping the woman a wink, "I want you to welcome Matchbook McCulloch to the pack."

A rumbling of discontent roiled through the crowd.

"I dunno 'bout this, Luka."

"That guy's in Ballaro's pocket, man. How we supposed to trust him?"

"He iced my fuckin' brother-in-law!"

"Yeah, and Stitch, too. Blew the poor SOB's brains out while he was takin' a shit!"

"He's no good, Luka!"

"Shit and brains everywhere!"

Luka quieted the din with a raised hand. "We've all got our pasts. Every one of us has stepped on some toes, done some dirt, caused some hurt to someone else in the room. Today we leave all that shit behind us. You can fight against a man in a war and admire the grit he fights with, even if you hate the flag he's fightin' under. Grit is grit. Matchbook did what he did 'cause it was his job. He was smart. He was tough. And he was loyal. And what'd all those years of loyalty buy him? Two goons in his room at midnight, ready to give him a one-way trip on the lead express. But ol' Matchbook was too quick for 'em, and Ballaro's loss is our gain. This is forgive and forget time. Whatever beef you thought you had, that wasn't with the guy standin' in front of you now. All that bad shit, you lay it straight at Ballaro's door. It's him who needs to pay for what he's done, and with Matchbook here as my number two, I'm ready to make it happen."

The looks Derek caught from the crowd didn't seem to embrace the forgive-and-forget attitude Luka was promoting. Luka himself might have sensed this, for he continued his speech to end on a different note.

"Ballaro's been callin' himself king of this shithole for a long time. He's gotten fat, and he's gotten greedy. He don't run things fairly. That's all about to change, thanks to us. There's a new family gonna run the Falls, and the ties that bind it are thicker than blood!"

They let out a cheer that dissolved into a hoarse melee of catcalls and interlocking chatter. Derek saw Bear conclude an exchange by grabbing another man by the beard and slamming his head into the man's nose. The crunch of cartilage ricocheted through the room. The first man wiped his face, laughed, and broke the seal on another beer.

What the hell was he getting himself into?

34: A COUPLE STOPS

DAVID'S FEW DAYS in the hospital stretched into a week and a half, elongated by a poor reaction to an antibiotic followed by a flare-up of clandestinely infected tissue in his abdomen. The cut along his chest had a tendency to weep and weep without healing over, the surrounding skin alight with strange bacterial fires the doctors struggled to put out. He was allowed out only once, for Walter's funeral, and chastised upon his return for staying away the whole afternoon. Eventually the doctors capitulated to his constant insistence that he was well enough to go home, warning him away from any strenuous activity.

"I expect you to be off work for at least the next two weeks," intoned Dr. Bianchi, a slender woman with stern glasses and a smattering of freckles across her cheeks. "And riding a desk for a few weeks after that. No strenuous exercise, and try to keep off your feet."

David, whose ribs felt as if they'd been crushed in a vice, didn't think this advice would be hard to follow. He patted his side gingerly in recognition. "Believe me, these guys are all the reminder I need."

"Whatever works, but honestly I'm more worried about that infection." She glared at the troubled spot through David's shirt, as if observing it through some extra sense available solely to doctors. "Your ribs seem to be healing up nicely."

"Good to know."

On the mend they may have been, but recovery didn't stop his ribs from screaming like rusty hinges every time David shifted position. He paused twice on his way to the elevator, gripping the railings that lined the hospital hallway and breathing steadily until the shriek abated. His slipped into his pocket to confirm the presence of the prescription chits the doctor had given him. One was for an antibiotic he'd never heard of. The other was for Oxycontin.

David spotted the cruiser idling on North Street. He huffed his way to the curb, masking the strain on his ribs as best he could, and got inside.

"Your wife couldn't pick you up?" Melissa asked.

"She doesn't know I've been released."

Melissa raised an eyebrow. "Won't she wonder how you got home?"

"Probably."

"In her shoes, I'd be pretty pissed off."

"Probably."

Melissa exhaled. "It's your life. Where do I drop you?"

"My house isn't far, but we've got a couple stops to make first."

"Where?"

David guided her using directions he'd scribbled on the back of his antibiotics prescription. They pulled up to a modest brick bungalow on a quiet St. Catharines street. David checked the number against his notes and hoisted himself out of the car, moving his torso as little as possible. His ribs twanged as he straightened up and walked casually around the house, mentally comparing what he saw to Iman's slightly fevered description of Motes' property.

He found the cellar window and crouched down to inspect it. The scene was much as Iman had described it: a slab of plywood set on the inner frame, a hand-sized chunk torn from its approximate center. In front of the plywood stood a grill of iron bars, beyond them a double-glazed pane of glass. Neither had been disturbed or damaged. The same could be said for the house's other windows.

A final tour of the perimeter revealed no other obvious signs of escape. He lit a cigarette and smoked it down to the filter, pondering the dark windows shrouded by thick red curtains. Here dwelled his monster, so he was told, but how did the thing get out? He couldn't picture the beast that had attacked him and killed Walter using the front door. The sign of his egress should be obvious, but David didn't see a thing apart from the split plywood around back. He flicked his spent cigarette into the gutter and eased himself back into the passenger seat.

"Home?" Melissa asked.

David shook his head. "Brock University."

"You just got out of the hospital. You really think this is wise?" Her tone was disapproving, but she pulled away from the curb and towards the highway without further prodding. Clearly she was as keen to meet Professor Motes as he was.

35: ALCHEMY

CHRIST, WHAT A DUMP.

The street was worse than Derek remembered it: a procession of ramshackle brick houses with mangy roofs and rotting verandas, their overgrown lawns littered with fallen shingles and children's toys bleached by the sun. The houses were pre-war, solidly built but battered by decades of neglect. They bore the broken posture of prizefighters past their prime. Surely not that much could have changed since he'd been here last, yet the place felt strange and hostile in its working poverty. He felt like these houses deserved better. Their decline saddened him.

He turned onto a cul-de-sac and ventured to the second-last house on the right. What cursory effort the neighbourhood's other homeowners made at maintenance was absent here. The lawn rose in a knee-high tangle of crabgrass and clover, the thicket brightened with dabs of ox-eye daisy and slashes of purple loosestrife. Tendrils of swallowwort clung to the wire links of a cyclone fence. A plywood cataract blinded one window, and the glass in the others was grimy and cracked. He climbed the stairs, the punky runs buckling ominously, and rang the doorbell.

The man who answered had broad shoulders and a sagging belly. Curly black hair spilled haphazardly over his head, and patchy stubble covered his cheeks.

"How's it goin', Mike?" Derek asked.

Mike greeted the question with the sort of white-eyed shock Derek had fast been getting used to since his forced return to Niagara—a look of mingled dread and discomfort, as if Derek were a ghost crossed with a panhandler. His run-in with Perone and Santino was an open secret in the circles he frequented. Mike must have noticed his own gawking, for he quickly buried it beneath a grin.

"Matchbook! Hey, wow, good to see you man! I didn't know you were in town."

Probably figured my corpse was halfway down the river by now. "Yeah, well, business, y'know?" They stood there for a minute, Mike grinning stupidly, Derek awaiting an invitation inside, a coil of frustration winding ever tighter in his belly. "You mind if I come in for a sec?" he asked, keeping his voice pleasant.

Mike laughed. "Yeah, sorry, no problem. Come in, come in!"

He led Derek into the living room. Thrift-store furniture stood atop nappy yellow carpet. A stink of old food and cigarette smoke clung to every fibre. Mike swept an old pizza box off the couch to make room for Derek to sit.

"You want a beer?"

"No thanks."

"Scotch? Vodka?" Mike shook a bottle on the hutch and a few drops sloshed around inside. "No vodka, sorry. Rum?"

"I'm fine. I really just wanted to know if I could use your garage for a few." Though a bit gormless, Mike was a welder by trade, when he wasn't dealing rock or breaking into houses. His temperament kept him from steady legit work, but he still had a decent workshop that Derek had taken advantage of more than once when he required discreet access to power tools.

"Sure, sure," Mike said, too nervous to hide his relief. "Take all the time you need, man. Want me to show you the way?"

"I can find it, thanks."

Mike's garage and his house could have belonged to two different people. The grungy floors and disorderly furniture and haphazardly-strewn trash were nowhere in evidence. A procession of wrenches and hammers and saws lined the pressboard behind a freshly swept workbench, regiments grouped by tool and arranged from small to large. Labels festooned every drawer and cubby; not a screw was left out of place. Saw blades and drill bits gleamed beneath fluorescent light. Even the smell was different, the must and smoke replaced by the scents of steel and sawdust.

Derek ran his hand over the workbench. He'd done some good work in this garage over the years: sawed a shotgun short enough to hide beneath a quarter coat, jury-rigged a car bomb, built single-use silencers for half a dozen pistols. The contemplative nature of shopwork agreed with him. He enjoyed the precision, the alchemy of adding and removing components to make something new.

He pulled a box of .38 calibre shells from his left pocket, removed a bullet, paused, and grabbed a second as well. He placed them point-side up in Mike's vice and spun the lever clockwise until the clamps touched the casing. He grabbed a butane torch from the opposite wall, checked the fuel gauge, and set it next to the bullets. From his right pocket he removed a ceramic dish he'd lifted from a neighbour's potted plant, a four-inch spiral shank nail, and a short length of silver solder. He coiled the solder in the dish, lit the flame, and danced it back and forth. The silver coil wept and sagged, melting into viscous slurry. He dipped the nail in the solder and worked it briskly over the head of the first bullet, repeating the process several times. After a few minutes both bullets bore slightly bulbous crowns of silver maybe a quarter millimetre thick. The end result was a little choppy—probably not great for the ballistics, but over a few dozen feet it wouldn't make much difference. He could have got a cleaner coating by melting the solder on the bullet directly, but he didn't want to risk applying that kind of heat to live ammo.

Derek didn't intend to use the bullets, anyway. As things stood, Luka was the only ally he had. His "pack mates," though pacified by Luka's support, didn't hold Derek in high esteem, and the few who did trust him weren't about to stick their necks out on his behalf. Ballaro remained a threat, and the cops weren't about to offer safe haven—short of a life in solitary, maybe—as long as Detective Moore was around to connect him with his partner's death. Taking out Luka would be tantamount to putting a bullet in his own head.

But it was good to plan for all contingencies.

As the last of the solder cooled, a familiar itch of intuition curled itself around Derek's brainstem. The world grew sharper, all cold lines and hard surfaces glazed with an antiseptic sheen. He switched on the circular saw and left its blade buzzing pointlessly, tucked the Governor into the back of his pants, and crept back into the house, slipping the door shut behind him.

The carpets made slipping out of his shoes unnecessary, but he did it anyway—old habits and all that. A bassy burble carried through the wall, punctuated by long bouts of silence. He took slow, measured steps on the balls of his feet until the words became clear enough to catch.

"—don't know how long he's going to be. A silencer or something, I guess. Usually a few hours at least, but I can't make any guarantees. On my own? Are you fucking nuts? Get over here and we'll split it, okay? Look, I got to go."

Derek frowned. He'd always found Mike to be a little slow on the uptake, but he was decent company. He wouldn't have pegged the guy as treacherous. Shit, he didn't seem clever enough for duplicity. Pulling his gun from his waistband, he rapped on the living room doorframe and stepped into view.

"Hey, Mike, I thought I'd take you up on that beer after all."

Mike sat in a wingback chair near the rabbit-eared television, a cordless phone in one hand and a sleek black automatic pistol in the other. Derek kept his own gun dangling at his side. He was curious as to whether Mike would have the stones to pull on him. He guessed not, and Mike proved him right. He dropped the phone and shoved the gun out of view, tucking it between his hip and the arm of the chair.

"Hey, man! That was fast, eh? Sure, help yourself. You wanna grab me one, too?"

Derek smiled but made no move toward the kitchen. The Governor remained hanging from his side. His index finger traced the trigger guard.

"Why d'you got a gun there, Mike?"

Mike shifted in his seat, his hand still cocked awkwardly beneath the opposite elbow.

"Mike? Why do you have a gun?"

He chewed his lips, eyes roving about the carpet. "I dunno what you mean, man. You're the one come into my home holdin' a revolver in your hand. I could ask you why *you* got a gun."

"I think you know the answer to that."

Mike wept quietly, his eyes shut tight. Derek sighed.

"This is so fucking disappointing. How much am I worth?"

"Thirty grand, last I heard."

Christ, I hang around much longer and every scumbag in the city'll be crawling up my ass. "Decent chunk of change for shooting a friend in cold blood."

"You're one to talk, man. Doin' what you do for a living."

"You're not me, Mike. You were, I'd be handlin' this a lot differently." He grabbed a throw pillow off the couch and tossed it to Mike. Mike caught it, leaving the pistol tucked against his hip. Either he was so out of his depth he lacked the presence of mind to try and draw on Derek even now, with their cards laid flat, or he simply knew he'd never work it in time. Derek, feeling charitable, chose to assume the latter. He raised the gun, his grip on the butt still casual. "Hold that up to your face."

"Derek, hey, listen, I hadn't decided nothin' yet, okay? Money's tight, the bank's tellin' me they're gonna take the house."

"Hold the pillow up to your face."

"I was confused, okay? Desperate, even! Just go, forget it, I won't say nothin' to anyone, I swear!"

"I could shoot you in the belly instead. Takes a day to die, sometimes. Your intestines, stomach, all that shit, it's under pressure in there. You make a hole and it all squirts out."

Mike raised the pillow. He sobbed more openly with his face covered, his shoulders hitching. Derek pressed the Governor into the quilted fabric. The pillow dimpled where the barrel touched down. Mike made a high, mewling noise in the back of his throat.

"Hey, Mike?"

Mike pulled his head from the pillow to reply. Derek shoved it back in his face with a prod of the Governor's barrel.

"Thanks for letting me use the garage."

He fired a single shot, the sound of it muffled by the pillow. Mike jerked once and slumped to the side. Smoke curled from the hole in the pillow's upholstery, its singed cotton innards sizzling faintly. Cordite sliced through the musty air, followed by the stink of piss trickling down Mike's leg.

Back in the garage, Derek was pleased to find the solder had set nicely. He ran his thumb over the silver caps. Their cold smoothness felt pleasant against his skin. He loaded the bullets into the Governor and spun the cylinder until they reached the fifth and sixth chamber. He'd have to remember not to unload on any old target.

36: A RED BLIZZARD

IMAN HAD BEEN at her desk for about six hours, give or take, and had accomplished exactly nothing. She'd checked no emails, read no articles, edited no text, managed no files, written no notes, sent no correspondence. She hadn't even dicked around online checking blogs or news sites. For someone as compulsively busy as she was, that sort of protracted unproductivity was almost impressive. It was also agonizingly dull. But anytime she touched fingers to keyboard with the aim of accomplishing something, her mind would return to the conversation she was soon to witness. Her stomach would shrivel, and any idea or initiative she might have had would shrivel right along with it. She sat there, waiting endlessly, and yet when the office door opened and the officers stepped inside, she felt caught totally off-guard.

Myers came in first, dressed in full uniform. She tipped Iman a small nod, one hand resting on her hip—and, by accident or design, a few inches from the butt of her Beretta. Moore limped in behind her. His steps were small and tottering, those of a man twice his age, but as he entered the room his stride lengthened, years sloughing away like so much dead skin. His back straightened as his lower lip slipped beneath his teeth, a bridle to rein in the pain his swagger cost him. He motioned with his head to Motes' door. "He in there?"

"Since before I got in. He's rarely anywhere else."

Moore nodded, shifting his weight from foot to foot. A grimace flickered across his face, there and gone quick as a windblown leaf. "You can wait out here if you want, you know. Or go to the cafeteria, have a coffee. If this goes anywhere at all, you'll have already done your duty a hundred times over."

Take the out, cried a small voice in Iman's head. *Listen to the man and take the out!* She shook her head—at the voice or at David, she couldn't quite say. "I'm in this whether I want to be or not. Besides, I might be able to help if he clams up." *And if he takes it badly, he's liable to fire me whether I'm here or not. Who else could have fingered him to the cops?*

"Suit yourself." Moore gave a cursory knock on the door and let himself in.

Iman's first impression was shock at Motes' appearance. It was a strange sensation, since she bumped into him on an almost daily basis—indeed, she'd last seen him this morning on one of his brief food excursions—and couldn't reasonably say she didn't know what he looked like. And yet her recollections of the professor were fleeting, an impressionistic blur. She hadn't looked—really, intently *looked*—at him in a long time. Weeks, maybe. And the change that had occurred in the interval was profound.

Pimples traced a greasy constellation across his forehead, a splash of adolescence that clashed with and deepened the aged creases around his lips and nose. Bags of purple flesh waddled beneath his red-tinged eyes, fat as overstuffed purses. The sour funk of body odour mingled with the cartons of half-eaten takeout orbiting his desk. The computer monitor cast a blue-white pallor over his face.

Motes' eyes flicked to Moore and Myers and back to the monitor, as if the officers had been nothing more than a trick of the light. For all Iman knew, that might be exactly how he saw them.

"You Enoch Motes?" Moore asked. This earned another two seconds or so of consideration from Motes, who grunted an inarticulate reply and returned his attention to the screen. Moore reached across the desk and gently shut off the monitor.

"Do you mind? I'm busy." His tongue performed a nervous circuit of his lips. A fidgety tremor shook his fingertips. "If this is an official matter, I advise you to speak to the administration."

"As a matter of fact, it is what you'd call an official matter, professor," Moore said. "But I don't think your administration has much to do with it. I'm Detective Moore, and this here is Officer Myers. We have some questions for you about the Ballaro family."

"Who?" The fear on Motes' face sank beneath the surface, submerged beneath a wave of annoyance. "I don't know anyone by that name."

"I guess you haven't been following the local news," Myers said. This statement brought the fear bobbing back to the surface, though Motes still seemed far from having grasped the complete situation.

"As I said, I've been busy," he grumbled, his voice stiff.

"There've been some pretty nasty attacks lately," Moore went on. "Two months ago, a man by the name of Eddie Ballaro was mauled to death in a strip club parking lot. A month later, his brother was killed in pretty much the same way, along with six of his poker buddies and one of their wives. The third attack didn't seem to fit the pattern, until you consider I'm the guy running the investigation on the first two." Moore undid a button of his dress shirt, revealing a heavy strip of gauze wrapped across his chest.

Motes' mouth hung open. He closed it with an audible clack of teeth. "You were attacked?"

"My partner, too. Plus Myers and hers. Plus a pair of unfortunate Brock students we figure might've been bait. A busy night for our guy. I guess you'd call Myers and me the lucky ones. We fought the thing off before it could get us."

"How?" Motes whispered. The last corpuscle of blood had drained from his face, leaving his skin white as virgin canvas.

Moore smiled. "Strange you're so interested, being a man too busy to follow the news." The detective studied his right hand, the fingers of his left making minute adjustments to his alligator ring. "It was this, actually, since you asked. My son gave it to me. Not exactly fourteen-karat gold, but a lot, considering his allowance."

"Sterling silver?"

Moore nodded. "Do we understand each other, professor?"

For a moment Iman thought it was going to be that easy. Then Motes' face, quivering like so much jelly, crusted over in a recalcitrant sneer. "I understand that you're here outside of any official capacity, and that you have to leave if I ask you to, which is exactly what I'm doing. If I'm mistaken, then I'm under arrest or suspicion of arrestable behavior, in which case I'd like a lawyer present."

"A smart call, under normal circumstances." Moore leaned forward on the desk. Iman figured the posture must be causing him considerable pain, given the state of his ribs, but it had a withering effect on Motes' impertinence. "But everyone in this room knows that this situation is well beyond the scope of any lawyer."

Iman felt Motes' eyes on her at Moore's mention of the word "everyone." She studied the carpet. Telling Moore and Myers was the right decision, she had no doubt about that, but knowing as much didn't make meeting the professor's wounded gaze any easier.

"From a legal standpoint, I can't prove a damn one of my suspicions about you. Hell, if I even voiced them I'd have to turn in my badge. But if that's the road we go down, all I'll have to live with is a bit of embarrassment. What'll you have to live with, Motes? And what happens if Officer Myers or I place an anonymous call to the St. Catharines police department about a domestic disturbance at your address? Just a bullshit prank, right? Unless we were to do it in a few weeks' time, say the night of the next full moon?"

Motes drew nonsense patterns on the desk with his index finger. He peeked beneath a piece of paper, smoothed down the crease. "I don't know what you're talking about."

"Motes. Look at me."

Slowly, as if hoisted by a winch, Motes raised his chin until his eyes met Moore's.

"We have a responsibility here. Anyone who truly didn't know what I was talking about would've checked out of this conversation after about five seconds. You'd think we were off our rockers, and rightly so. If this wasn't ringing any bells for you, you'd have dived out the window, called 911, asked for my badge number at least. You're in this, and so are we. People are dying. Sure, the Ballaros are dirty, but murder is murder. And even if you think that sort of mob justice is okay for mobsters, that doesn't excuse what happened to those college kids. It doesn't excuse what happened to my partner, or Myers'. So you can man up right now and tell me what you know, or I will make it my personal mission to hound you to the fucking grave. Understand me?"

Watching Motes crumble was a lot like watching a building implode. There was a slight but palpable shift in the foundation of Motes' composure, a subaudible crumbling of bedrock into sludge. Next came a moment of stillness, followed by the sudden and inexorable toppling of a proud edifice into rubble. He wept with breath-stealing force, his upper body collapsing onto the desk. A clutter of displaced papers and takeout boxes washed over the edge. Runners of mucus dangled from his nostrils, giving his breathing a wet, rattling quality. He wiped his face on his sleeve until Myers handed him a wad of tissue. The cops seemed sympathetic but unwavering. If they felt discomfort at seeing a grown man dissolve into a whimpering heap, they didn't show it.

Motes gripped the desk hard enough to whiten his knuckles. He inhaled sharply, sucking loose snot back into his sinuses. When he spoke his voice was clear, though his eyes remained pinned to the carpet.

"It wasn't me. I don't expect you to believe it, but it's true. There's another, the one who did this to me. A man named Luka Volchyin."

Moore's reaction was marked but subtle. Iman didn't think Motes caught it, but she certainly did. A stiffening of the spine, as if a wire threaded through each vertebra were tugged suddenly taut. He reached into his pocket, pulled out a small notepad and pencil, and set the tip against the paper. "Tell me about him."

Motes cleared his throat. "He found me a few months ago. I figured he was a student, one of those slackers who never comes to class, then begs you for a passing grade at the end of the semester. Instead, he asked if I spoke fluent Russian."

"Do you?" asked Moore.

Motes nodded. "Social realist literature is one of my main areas of academic interest, outside of English. He wanted to know if I could speak it instead of just read it."

"Why?"

"He told me his family had come to Canada from Siberia in the wake of the Russian Revolution, a group of peasant landowners fleeing communism. They moved to Northern Ontario before splitting up. Luka's grandmother moved south, while her sister and brother-in-law stayed in their village. As Luka told it, this decision caused hard feelings on both sides. His grandmother never spoke to her sister again. And she'll never have the chance now, as she died in a fire earlier this year."

"Jesus," Iman said.

"Stanford Acres," said Moore.

Motes nodded. "The very same. Luka told me he was very close to his grandmother. He said one of her chief regrets was never reconciling with her family. He did some digging and found her sister—his great-aunt—still living in a northern township called Timber. He said the town itself, Whitetooth Falls, has maybe three hundred people, so he didn't think she'd be too hard to track down. However, from what his grandmother told him, he suspected his great-aunt may never have learned English. The town, it seems, is largely composed of Russian settlers, a Slavic answer to the Pennsylvania Dutch in miniature. He wanted my help to speak with her, give her the news of her sister's passing, and perhaps make amends on behalf of his grandmother's memory."

"And he wanted you as what, an interpreter?" asked Moore.

"So he said."

"You believed him?"

Another humorless smile flashed across Motes' lips. "Not for a second. It's probably stupid for me to tell this to two police officers, but I'm finding it difficult to care just now. This must be how you have so much success with confessions, I suppose. You stroke the inborn storyteller's impulse." He shook his head free of this digression. "To be honest, I assumed the man's real interest had something to do with drugs. A connection from Russia, someone who slipped in the back door, so to speak, took an elicit plane or simply chugged across the Bering Strait. The ancestors of our First Nations people did it; why not some gangsters? It seemed like a logical enough plan to me, though I confess I'm no criminal mastermind. Who would expect a drug deal to occur in Canada's hinterland?"

"So he asked for your help as translator, and you accepted?"

"No. I told him to get out of my office. That's when he showed me fifty thousand dollars in a leather briefcase." Motes removed his glasses, wiped the lenses on the hem of his shirt. "It was actually in a briefcase. I didn't think people really did that. It seems an inefficient means of carrying money. Why not envelopes, or a bag? It wasn't a nice briefcase, either. He probably got it at Value Village for a song. It cheapened the whole thing. That sort of money should be kept in something nicer, don't you think? I suppose going cheap makes sense economically, unless he deducts the cost of the briefcase from the total sum." Motes paused, index fingers steepled together. "I'm rambling, aren't I?"

"So you decided to take his offer," Moore prompted.

"It wasn't as quick as all that. I told him to come back in a few days, and gave the matter some serious thought. I also did a little digging into my supposed benefactor's story. I knew there was a lie in there somewhere, but I wanted to see how close to the surface it might be. A Sonya Volchyin really did die in the fire at Stanford Acres, and her obituary lists a Luka Volchyin as a surviving grandson. What's more, there is a Timber County, though no atlas or logging map lists a village of Whitetooth Falls, and the telephone listings for the region give mostly Irish and French surnames. No Russian at all."

"You had your suspicions, then."

"I would have to be pretty thick not to, given the man's story."

"What was your next encounter like? Did he change his tone?"

"Are you asking if he threatened me? It wasn't necessary. In the end I took his money, lies or no lies. Have I regretted this decision since? More than you could ever know." Motes coughed into a closed fist. Petals of colour bloomed on his pale cheeks.

Moore jotted something in his notebook. "How soon after the deal did you leave?"

"A couple of weeks. Luka had an exact day he planned to leave, and there could be no flexibility on that score. I took a brief sabbatical, which involved foisting off most of my summer classes during the last two weeks of the semester. My faculty wasn't pleased with me, but I knew I wasn't about to lose my job over it, and fifty thousand dollars is worth a few annoyed glances in the hallway."

"You drove together?"

"Yes. We took his car, a dreadful old Dodge Shadow. I offered to use my car even though it was sure to get dirty and dinged up on the logging roads, simply out of fear of breaking down in some backwater with no cellular reception. Everything rattled, the engine spewed grey smoke, and I kept hearing strange bangs and shifts from somewhere behind me." Motes shivered at the memory.

Moore jotted this down in his notes. "How long was the drive?"

"About twenty hours total, split over two days. We spent the night in a sleazy motel in North Bay."

"Did you share a room?"

"I paid for my own out of pocket. I had no interest in seeing the man's grooming habits."

More jotting. "But he was with you at the motel that night?"

"As far as I know. I shut myself in my room as soon as we got in and wondered what the hell I was doing."

Moore gave an encouraging nod, his gaze still fixed on the stream of details he was recording in his notebook. "If it's a motel, you would have parked out front. Did you hear him drive off at any point? Maybe go meet up with someone?"

"If he did, I slept through it."

"Do you think that's likely?"

"It's possible. I'm a fairly deep sleeper, though that night I didn't sleep particularly well. So no, I don't think it's likely."

"Did anyone come to see him?"

"Again, I'm not sure. Our rooms connected, so I probably would have heard. But who knows? It was the furthest thing from my mind."

Moore nodded. "Day two. Did you leave early, or did you have a lie-in?"

"Practically with the sunrise. He came and got me around five AM. Pounded on the door until I answered. I wanted a shower and a coffee, but he wouldn't hear of it. Said we had a schedule to keep to."

"On the drive north, you took highways?"

"For a while. We turned off the main road around Timmins, spent the afternoon bumping down logging tracks and dirt roads. There were a couple of washouts I thought we wouldn't make it over, but the Shadow managed it."

Moore's next question seemed like a non-sequitur to Iman, but clearly the man's internal radar was twitching, as it proved to be eerily on point. "You mentioned a strange knocking sound in the car. You ever figure out what that was?"

Motes drummed his fingers on the desk in a desperate tempo. "You have to understand. I didn't know this guy from Adam. I was greedy, yes, I admit it. Greedy and selfish and stupid. But I didn't, I mean . . . " He wiped his face, gratefully accepting another tissue from Myers. "Eventually the road petered out into brush. I thought we'd turn around, but Luka stopped the car and got out.

"I asked him what we were doing, and he said we walked from here. That's when I realised for the first time—not the last—how stupid I was being. What sort of town doesn't have at least one access road? I asked if there wasn't another route, but he ignored me. Instead he opened the trunk. Inside, there was . . . " Motes' hands twirled the Kleenex into a tight cord. They kept working until it grew taut in the middle, sheer tissue tearing. "A girl. A woman, I mean. A young woman. She was probably about your age, Miss al-Qaddari."

He looked at Iman, his eyes yawping with hollow self-loathing. It was the look of unlikely killers too shell-shocked to be penitent, those poor evil souls who wake from a daze to find they've drowned their children in a tub or stare blankly at the hammer in their hands, its business end matted with blood and hair. Meeting that gaze was like handling some awful jungle insect, all wriggling legs and slimy belly. She dropped it, repulsed beyond reply.

"You have to understand," Motes pleaded. "I didn't know she was there! By the time I found out, we were in the middle of nowhere."

"The entire trip, you had no idea there was someone in the trunk?"

"She was gagged and bound, and from the look of her, quite sedated. I know you're all likely accusing me of stupidity or wilful ignorance—and perhaps a bit of the latter goes into it—but I swear it never crossed my mind. I was thinking the man needed to make a deal to buy or sell drugs, or at most maybe some sort of illegal firearms trade. But the actual reason for his trip, you can't reasonably expect me to have anticipated that, can you?"

Moore didn't respond.

"I wanted to help her, I truly did. My cell was getting no reception, and he had the keys to the car. I'm not a strong man; I could barely carry her to the end of the lane, let alone the nearest town. Luka was bigger, ruthless, the sort of man who knows how to fight, how to hurt."

Moore met the professor's gaze, unflinching. Any disgust or contempt he may have felt lay dormant as lake water beneath a sheen of winter ice. Iman realised he'd probably heard such confessions many times before—probably ones that were a whole lot worse. She pitied him in that moment, to be a stoic witness to such atrocity.

"When he showed the girl to you, what did he say?"

"Does it matter? He spun a line of nonsense, she wouldn't be hurt, blah blah blah. I didn't believe it, and he knew I didn't, and he didn't care. We were alone in the woods. I was as bound as she was."

Moore made a small jot in his notebook and rolled his hand in a move-it-along gesture. "So you had to go on foot from there. Did the girl go with you?"

"He carried her. There was a path through the underbrush, and we followed it. After a while I started to hear things beyond the treeline. Soft rustling sounds. At the time I chalked it up to a heady mix of the wind and my imagination. In hindsight I'm not so sure. Either way, they didn't last long before another sound overtook them. It was a sound I'm sure we're all quite familiar with, given our proximity to the Niagara cataract. The low, steady roar of water spilling from a great height."

"Whitetooth Falls," Iman said.

"So it was named, though there was no town there to speak of. I never saw so much as a road. A few forestry maps list it as a body of water, but no one has ever been registered as living there, as far as I've seen."

"So it was deserted."

This time Motes' smile didn't just lack humor; it strangled humor in its crib. His lips barely parted, yet they seemed to Iman to yawn like some great abyss, sucking away the room's warmth and light. "Oh, they were far from deserted. But the things that live there never answered any census."

"Things?" asked Moore.

"People, or so they seemed when I first saw them. Fair-skinned men and women of impressive height, clad in the skins of moose and deer and musk ox. They appeared silently as the evening wore on, gathering about the three of us one after another. None spoke to us, nor responded to my greetings in any language I know—and I know a few of them. I asked Luka if these were the people he wanted to meet, and he told me to shut up."

Moore made a note. "What did you do then?"

"I shut up. Whoever these people were, I didn't think they'd have much interest in helping me. They certainly didn't seem off-put by the young woman sobbing through her gag.

"We waited what seemed like forever. Eventually, a sort of hush descended on the forest people. That's the best way to describe it, even though they weren't making any noise to begin with. An old woman emerged from the trees. The other people all seemed to just appear out of nowhere, but this lady made no effort to hide her approach. I could hear her footsteps as she came towards us."

"This woman, what did she look like?" asked Moore.

"Ancient. Wizened eyes, leathery skin, scraggly grey hair. She stood maybe five feet tall, but straight-backed. She didn't hunch over or totter the way a lot of elderly people do. When I say ancient, I don't mean infirm. She walked and moved like a twenty-year old woman. Slower, maybe, but out of grace more than age. I got the impression she could run a mile uphill and not be out of breath.

"She sniffed the air and favored Luka with a warm smile. She spoke to him directly, ignoring me and the girl altogether. 'Blood of my blood. Tooth of my tooth. You smell of my sister, and the smell is sweet.'

"She said this in Russian. The dialect was strange, but I could make it out. Luka, on the other hand, didn't understand a word. He just sort of smiled stupidly at her while she was talking. It gave me some petty satisfaction, I must admit, to have some leverage over him, but I couldn't see how to use it. She knew him as her grand-nephew, knew just by the smell of him. If I tried to play them false as interpreter, I was pretty sure I'd get found out.

"'You must be Natasya Volchyin,' I said. 'My name's Enoch Motes. Your grand-nephew brought me along as an interpreter.'

"She looked me up and down like I was something unappetizing served to her at a buffet. 'He doesn't speak the tongue,' she said.

"'I'm afraid not.'

"I could tell Luka was growing impatient. He turned to me, his lips shrunken to a thin line. 'What's she saying?'

"'She knows who you are. She could tell by the smell, I think. She welcomes you to her home.'

"He smiled at that. 'Tell her my grandma spoke well of her. She was sad they fought, and always wanted to make up with her.'

"Natasya frowned at this news when I relayed it. 'My sister is dead?'

"Luka clenched his fists. He seemed to get her meaning by her tone. 'Tell her a bad man burned her alive. An Italian. No, a man from the south. One of the Old Empire. Use those words.'

"It wasn't the sort of news I wanted to break, but I did as told. Her face darkened. It seemed to me I'd never seen something so old as this woman. And I mean some*thing*. She seemed older than the Sphinx, than the ziggurats of Mesoamerica. Staring at her, I felt like some scrawny Cro-Magnon warming myself by a peat fire, jumping at the shadows beyond the mouth of my cave. Does that sound ridiculous? It does to me, but it's exactly how I felt. How I still feel, some nights, when I think of her.

"'What do you wish of me?' she asked Luka.

"'My birthright. The silver tonic. Vengeance.'

"I gave this order to Natasya. She beamed with awful maternal pride. 'He shall have all this and more.' She pointed to the sky, where the last rays of evening sunlight were vanishing. Her finger drifted towards the moon. It was then I noticed how ugly the moon was, blotchy and bloated, like a big fat boil on the face of the sky."

Motes paused. He arranged the papers nearest to him in a neat pile, shoring up the edges with fussy taps of his index finger. He pinched the corners square, smoothed the top of the stack with his palm. When he raised his hands again, Iman saw his fingers tremble.

"It got bad after that. The forest people . . . changed. It looked excruciating. They doubled backwards, every muscle and tendon taut, howling at the sky. Their bones made a cracking sound as they turned into . . . well, you two know what they turned into. You faced one of them. Imagine half a hundred, led by one twice as big as the rest."

"Natasya Volchyin," Moore said.

"They just called her Mother."

"They could talk?"

"A few of them could. It was growly and garbled, but I could make it out. They had a hierarchy much the way actual wolves do, only theirs had something to do with how much of their . . . I was going to say *humanity*, but that's not right. How much of their sentience they retained. Mother retained the most, enough to keep the wildest ones from tearing us apart. She led us to the mouth of Whitetooth Falls and into the muddy banks of a river bend. She sank one foot—paw, claw, whatever—into the silt, leaving a print that soon filled with water. The liquid was silvery and strangely radiant, as if mixed with the chemical slurry inside a child's glowstick."

"And the girl, was she still with you?"

Motes closed his eyes. "She was. Luka carried her to the river and tossed her down. The poor woman was just about out of her mind with terror. She started throwing herself down the bank, wriggling into the water. Luka dragged her back and planted a leg on her to keep her still. I . . . " Motes broke off, buried his face in another handful of tissue. "I'm sorry. I deserve this. I should have helped her and I didn't, damn my cowardice. I deserve what I got."

He steadied himself with a long, slow breath. "Excuse me. Anyway, Luka seemed to know what to do without further prompting. He knelt down in the muck, put his face to Mother's paw print, and drank. The change hit him soon after. It was much like the others, but more violent. I suspect he wasn't prepared for it. When it was done, he turned his eyes on me, and I saw in them a hunger I'd just as soon never see again. In that glance, I could tell he wanted with all his heart to pounce on me, rip my flesh from my bones, bury his muzzle in my belly."

Moore tapped the tip of his pen on his notepad. "What stopped him?"

"Mother did. She growled something at him that he seemed to understand, then turned to me and spoke in her strange, antiquated Russian. I found it hard to look at her as she talked. Her voice coming from that face was too surreal.

"'He is the true strain,' she said. 'The silver water mixes nobly in his blood.

Your time will not be so easy. Cur blood curdles in the silver water. A warped and runty thing you will be, but better than you are now by far. It is a gift I give to few outside the breed, but you have been tongue to my blood, and we have words to share yet before he learns to speak the howl of the steppe outside the hours of the moon.'

"I tried, as politely as I could manage, to refuse. She didn't take it well.

"'None may see the silver water,' she snarled, 'save two breeds: predators and prey. My nephew, robbed of his strength, has still brought prey enough for the pack. But if you will not eat with us, you will find we have great appetites.'"

"So she gave you a choice," Moore said. "Eat or be eaten. Or, I guess, drink or be eaten."

"That's what it came down to."

"So hold on," Myers said. "She didn't bite you, or anything like that?"

"If she'd bitten me, I assure you I wouldn't be here now. Does their bite impart the curse or disease or what-have-you? I have no idea. I only know what happened to me, though it's not without literary precedent. The transformative power of certain streams appears often in folklore, as does drinking from an enchanted animal's footprint."

"Which is what you did," said Moore, more statement than question.

"The taste . . . how do I describe it? Like cancer and moonlight, blood and gold and bile. It wasn't even a taste, really, so much as a pivot of perception. I suspect LSD feels the same way, though I've never tried it.

"I . . . I can't remember much after that. It all gets sort of foggy. I've heard fighters refer to the red mist that clouds their vision during a particularly savage bout. This was more than a mist. This was a red blizzard. Occasional images burst through the driving sleet, and some sounds slipped through the howling wind. But mostly what I recall is that . . . red."

A silence thick as velvet fell over the room. Motes continued shuffling papers. Moore repeatedly clicked the trigger of his ballpoint pen.

"I woke up in a field somewhere, naked and covered in shed fur. Everything ached. My head felt like it had been stuffed full of a thousand hangovers. I stumbled along until I found a road and followed it; whether north or south, I had no idea. I just needed to walk. Eventually I heard a car coming. I couldn't decide whether to try and flag it down or hide in the woods. The driver spotted me before I'd made my decision. It was Luka. He seemed different somehow. Sharper. My brain was stuffed with straw and cotton; his seemed honed to a deadly edge. He motioned wordlessly to the door and tossed me a spare set of clothes he'd packed. I got dressed and got in and we drove home."

"I don't get it," Myers said. "How'd he find you?"

"He said he smelled me." Motes wiped his forehead, and flicked the excess sweat from his fingertips. "I told you he'd changed. Drinking from the puddle took something away from me. I think it did the opposite for him."

"What happened to the girl?" Iman asked. "The one who was tied up."

Motes shuffled his papers. "I have my suspicions. I'm sure yours aren't far removed from them. But I never saw. I was away, running through the forest."

Iman figured he had more than just suspicions. But Moore seemed uninterested in grilling him on it, instead carrying on with his line of questioning. "He drove you back to St. Catharines?"

"Right. We did it in one day this time. He dropped me off without a word."

"Is that the last you've seen of him?"

"I wish it were. He came by my office a few weeks ago. He wants to go back."

"What for?"

"He wouldn't tell me. All he said was he wants his full birthright. He expects me to come with him and translate again."

Moore leaned forward. "He's arranged this with you?"

Motes gave a small laugh. "If by arranged, you mean ordered. He's not the sort of man who negotiates. I'm to go with him at the end of this month, two days before the full moon." Motes' hands formed a prim pile on the desk. His eyes grew shimmery and damp, and his voice came out in a reedy whisper. "I'm not sure I can stand going back there again. Not after last time."

Moore rubbed his chin, tapped his lips with his index finger. "Maybe you won't have to."

"I don't have much choice. He's not human anymore. He's something more than that. Wherever I run, he'll find me."

"Probably," Moore admitted. "But maybe, when he does, you won't be the only thing he finds."

37: THE SUCCESSFUL HITMAN'S TOOLBOX

DURING HIS LONELY inverted exile in Niagara Falls, when he'd been friendless and squeezed mercilessly between Ballaro's rock and the homicide cops' hard place, Derek had figured things couldn't get any worse. And in some ways, he was right. Life in the Volchyin pack lacked the relentless itch of anxiety slithering up his spine, or the hope-swallowing chasm yawning open in his belly. Those things were gone—well, not gone, but certainly diluted—thanks to Volchyin's protection, and that counted for something. So he supposed it wasn't worse, per se.

But it was sure as hell more annoying.

They spent their days squatting in whatever distant shack or squalid flophouse would have them, mooching floor space, booze, and cigarettes off of associates and abusing these gifts with an audacity that Derek found both appalling and sort of impressive. Derek wasn't above using people—God had made chumps for a reason, after all—but at least he showed some decorum. Luka's pack weren't just slovenly or neglectful; they were outright malicious. They pissed on carpets and in potted plants, kicked in television screens if they didn't like what was on, set furniture alight for the simple pleasure of watching it burn. Derek had heard of loose cannons, but here was a deck full of them. It was only a matter of time before one of them crushed him beneath its wheels or blew a hole through his belly for a laugh.

In a sort of circular irony, the pack were currently holed up in the Jupiter Motel, the very same place where the shitstorm engulfing Derek's life had first blown in from parts unknown. The owner, driven by that unique mixture of friendship and stark terror that Luka tended to inspire in people, had lent him the use of two suites at the back corner of his motel free of charge. As repayment for this kind act, Nails and a bug-eyed asthmatic with blotchy skin named Wheeze were busy cutting open the lining of their mattresses and yanking out handfuls of stuffing. They threw the white fluff in the air, giggling like children as it rained down on them. Sarah, still the only woman among them, watched with amused contempt, a cigarette burning between slender fingers. She flicked the accumulating ashes onto the floor, ignoring the ashtray set roughly two feet to her left.

Stepping over empty beer cans and chip bags and other detritus, Derek went out for some air. Packmates loitered in the parking lot, trading cigarettes and blaring music from the sound systems of their cars. A few tipped a wave at Derek, but most shot him dirty looks or simply ignored him. After a tense first few days, he was beginning to sense that none of these pricks had the balls to step to him directly, but that didn't mean they'd all be friends any time soon.

Luka stood by the curb, watching the intermittent flow of traffic down Lundy's Lane. Derek hadn't known the man well before their recent encounter, but even their passing acquaintance was enough to tell him something had changed. And that something went beyond Luka's miraculous regenerative abilities. He seemed sturdier than before, his edges sharper, his gaze keener and more piercing. Strength simmered from his pores like a jungle fever, ravenous and deadly. Derek had no idea how much of his story was bullshit and how much was true—he believed that almost nothing in life existed purely in one camp or the other—though he accepted the core of it without much trouble. When it came to the supernatural, he had no innate leanings toward skepticism or belief; he'd never spared much thought for such matters. But it was easy to see that old Luka had hit on something big, and Derek intended to get a piece of it if he could. Once he'd figured out how to do so, he could ditch the loony brigade and go about things his own way.

"Yo, Matchstick, 'sup?" Luka asked without looking.

Derek scratched the back of his head. "I gotta be honest, man. I'm gettin' restless here. How much longer 'til we get this plan of yours rolling?"

"She's already rollin', bro. The wait's part of it."

"Okay, good to know. But shouldn't we be, like, preparing for something? We got a big trip ahead of us, don't we?"

"Nothin' to it. I've done it once before already. In a couple weeks we grab the professor and we go. Give ourselves two days to make the drive."

"And then what?"

Luka flashed an enigmatic smile. "You'll see, bro. Before this month's out, we're gonna be a pack for real."

Derek hid his frustration beneath a nod and a question. "This professor you talked about, he's critical to your plan?"

"For now, yeah. Unless you know someone else who speaks Russian, he's our guy."

"How's he feel about that?"

Luka seesawed his hand. "He'll do what he's told. Dude's a pussy. I had words with him a few days before you and I hooked up. He knows what the score is."

A twitch rippled through Derek's fingers. "You've talked to him about this already?"

"Like I said, bro."

"And he agreed to it?"

"Dude's opinions don't mean shit. He's nothin' but a walkin', talkin' dictionary."

Derek chewed the inside of his lower lip. Did this numbskull really not see the risk he was taking here? "What if he bolts?"

Luka snorted. "He hasn't got the balls."

"In my experience, not having balls is a pretty good sign someone's gonna run for it."

Luka slapped a hand on Derek's shoulder. "You worry too much, Matchbook. That asshole isn't gonna do shit but sit at his desk writin' his fuckin' papers until we go and collect his ass. I've got some important shit to say to my great-aunt, and with luck we'll be speakin' the same language before long. Then we won't have to worry about Motes anymore."

You're not worried about him now, *you moron.* "All the same, we should have someone camped at his house, his work, wherever else he spends a lot of his time. We've got the manpower, why not make use of it?"

Luka cocked a thumb over his shoulder. "Any of those guys seem like spies to you?"

"They're your pack, aren't they? They should do what you tell 'em."

"They will."

Derek extended his hands, palms out. "So tell 'em to keep a low profile. What kind of wolf can't stalk its prey, right?"

Luka pondered the horizon. He squirted a jet of saliva through his front teeth, wiped his hands on the seat of his jeans. "It's gettin' late, dude's probably home by now. You and me'll take a cruise down there. I'll get Nails and Sarah to scope out the university. Happy?"

"For sure."

Though not half as happy as I'll be after I've seen your face for the last time.

After a brief detour into the motel room to issue Nails and Sarah their marching orders, Luka and Derek piled into a beat-to-hell '96 BMW that Luka had co-opted from one of his more flush pack-members. Being the alpha male had its perks. He gunned the engine with a scattershot rumble of pistons. Smoked coughed out the rust-fringed exhaust pipe, plumes of it like carcinogenic breadcrumbs marking their path.

The drive to Motes' house took ten minutes, tops. On Derek's suggestion, they parked a few houses down and walked the rest of the way. No sense spooking the guy unnecessarily. Luka led them to a ranch-style bungalow near the end of the street. He pointed to the driveway, where a modest beige sedan sat atop the faded asphalt.

"Bingo, dude. Guy's curled up watching Netflix or reading one of his papers or some shit. No worries."

Derek stuck his hands in his pockets. He scanned the house, noting the drawn blinds, the free dailies piled on the doorstep, the junk mail bulging from the mailbox. Tiny signs that told him nothing and everything, aligning in some atavistic magnetism that guided Derek's intuition. The house *felt* empty. Years spent successfully navigating his treacherous trade had taught him to trust his gut, and his gut said this bird had flown. "Who keeps their blinds drawn in the afternoon?"

"Shut-ins, bro. Dude's not exactly a chat-with-the-neighbours type."

"Yeah, but all of them?"

"Haven't seen the back, have we?"

"Good point." Derek strolled across Motes' lawn, hands still in his pockets. The shades in the back yard were also drawn, save for one window where plywood stood affixed to the inner frame. *Weird, but still doesn't tell me much.* He completed the circuit, trying the back and garage doors and finding them locked, and climbed onto the stoop.

"Dude," Luka warned. "I didn't say you could talk to the guy. All we're doing here is proving he's at home."

"So let's prove it," Derek said, and knocked. He waited half a minute before trying the bell and knocking a second time. Stillness thrummed inside the house, silent save for the purr of the air exchanger.

Luka shoved Derek aside and pounded on the door with the bottom of his fist. "Yo, Motes! It's Luka. Open the fuck up."

Nothing. Luka pounded again, harder this time. "Don't fuck with me, bro. Do *not* fuck with me."

Derek looked over his shoulder, half expecting to see a police cruiser rolling up in response to a noise complaint. "Quit it, man. Someone's gonna call the cops. The guy's not home."

Luka shrugged, his outburst from a moment earlier forgotten. "No surprise. Dude's fuckin' married to his job. Probably campin' out in his office."

"Then why's his car here?"

Something grim and spiny crept into Luka's voice. "He probably takes the bus to work, try to save fuel. Those academic types are always doin' shit like that, tryin' to save the environment."

Derek doubted this, but tactful deception was yet another of the shopworn tools in the successful hitman's toolbox. "Great. Sarah's probably found as much already. Why don't we call her and get our asses out of here?"

Luka dialled. Sarah picked up on the second ring. Even with the ambient noise of the wind and the occasional passing car, the speaker was loud enough for Derek to catch both sides of the conversation.

"Hey, boss."

"Yo, Sarah. You scope our boy at Brock?"

"His name's Motes, right?"

"Yeah."

"He's not in his office. We asked the admin about him, and she said he's sick or something. Cancelled all his classes for the next two weeks."

Luka thumbed the disconnect button. He pursed his lips, the fingers of his free hand clenching and unclenching. Derek heard a brittle crunch, followed by the delicate patter of plastic on the wooden floorboards. Luka unclenched his fist.

The remains of the broken cell phone fell like wreckage from a shot-down plane.

38: THE SECOND COMING

IMAN HAD ALWAYS considered her apartment to be cozy. For her and Brian—quiet people with compatible taste in music, movies, and allowance for personal space—its narrow halls and open concept sweep of living room, dining room, and kitchen offered a sense of snugness, a burrow in which she could gladly sleep away a cold and ugly winter. But with Motes camping out on the couch, alongside the frequent drop-ins by Moore and Myers, she quickly realised that *cozy* was, when you came right down to it, nothing but a gussied-up synonym for *small*.

Motes, to his credit, did his best to be unobtrusive. He spent most of his time reading or typing away on his laptop, and made a point to tidy up the bathroom and kitchen whenever he used them. But even the most conscientious houseguest couldn't conjure extra space, and there was nothing Iman and Brian could do but plaster on accommodating grins while tripping over one another.

Another day or two, max, Iman thought. Moore was as eager to move Motes elsewhere as she was, albeit for more pragmatic reasons. Motes, for his part, hadn't wanted to leave his house at all.

"I understand my importance in your plan," he'd said, once they'd laid out the groundwork. "But I don't see why I need to be passed around like some unwelcome relation. Luka told me quite clearly when he intends to collect me for his trip. I can give you the time and place, practically to within the hour."

"Not good enough," said Moore. "If the guy's even halfway bright, he'll pop by sometime when you're not expecting it, make sure you're not cooking up any surprises for him."

"Halfway seems a stretch," Motes drawled.

"A guy who went to this extent for revenge is crafty, if nothing else. So long as he can't grab you at his leisure, we've got a pin on him. If he nabs you while we're not looking, the only time and place we can nail him with any certainty is Whitetooth Falls on the cusp of a full moon. And I'd just as soon not try him there."

Reluctantly, Motes had agreed, and Iman's apartment became a sort of makeshift witness protection program while Moore and Myers arranged for something a little more secure. Myers was working connections to try and score him protective custody, but she considered this a long shot at best.

"They normally only swing it for people testifying against the mob, or someone equally dangerous," she said. "The ironic thing is, that's exactly what you're doing, but the guys in charge are going to want written testimony. We bring them your story as-is, we may well all end up in protective custody. The kind with padded walls."

"There's also my . . . *condition* to consider," said Motes. "Anywhere I stay will have to be equipped with a cellar or bunker of some sort, somewhere I won't be able to break out of. At least until I find a cure," he added, his voice stinging with hope

Moore promised to work on alternative arrangements. In the meantime, he and Myers would take guard duty on opposite shifts, twelve hours on and twelve off, though Myers doubted they could do much good.

"I'm not trying to back out, but what exactly are we supposed to do if he shows up? We've already seen they guy shake off three clips' worth of bullets like they were pebbles."

"As a wolf, yeah. But what about when he's a man?" Moore turned to Motes for his opinion.

"I suspect not to the same extent, although I really can't be sure. I can attest that I'm far from invulnerable, though cuts and bruises do seem to heal quicker than they used to. But I'm a sorry specimen compared to Luka."

"Nevertheless, I think it's best if we stay with you as much as possible. If nothing else, a few shots to the trunk should give the guy a seriously bad day."

"If we're going to pull your plan," said Myers, "I'd like to do a little more than give the guy a bad day."

"I'm working on something a bit more potent. In the meantime, plain old lead is gonna have to do."

The twelve-on-twelve-off schedule proved unworkable, as the pressures of Moore's home life and Myers' work pulled them away more than once. Still, they were there more often than they were gone. Iman appreciated the security their presence offered, however illusory, although stuffing an extra body into an already cramped apartment didn't help their space issues.

At the moment, Myers sat at their kitchen table, absently shuffling and reshuffling a deck of playing cards she'd found in their kitchen drawer. The flutter-snap of her riffling dulled the sound of the television, making it difficult to hear. Iman resisted turning it up. She was on thin ice with her neighbours already, given the constant coming and going, and didn't want to get into any sort of altercation. Brian sat on the futon beside her, his leg jittering—a common outlet for his stress. She put a hand on his thigh, stilling it, and gave a conciliatory smile.

I'm sorry, she mouthed.

Brian tossed his hands palms-up in reply, offering condolence in the private semaphore of their relationship: *meh, what are you gonna do?* He was being a champ about the imposition Motes posed—especially since she'd dragged him into the whole mess in the first place.

Myers set down the cards with a final snap and rapped her knuckles on the bathroom door. "Open up, Motes. You've been in there like ten minutes already."

"Just a second!" Motes called. Iman threaded her fingers through her hair and tugged. She needed some air.

Iman's apartment was contained within a sprawling brick manor house: once the occupancy for a single wealthy family, but partitioned sometime in the late 60s into a hodgepodge succession of student apartments. For this reason, the layout was often eccentric, with much of the plumbing and wiring wedged in wherever it would fit. Likewise, a series of wooden balconies crept up the walls like vines, narrow petals of deck space blooming from support beams bolted into the brick. Iman's balcony was north-facing—exactly the opposite of ideal for an urban garden—and offered a commanding view of a neighbour's driveway and derelict backyard.

A lawn chair leaned against the railing. Iman unfolded it with a few practiced motions and slid it to her usual spot in the left corner. The joists beneath the bannister formed a shelf, where several paperbacks huddled out of the worst of the weather, their pages swollen and warped from nights left inhospitably out in the rain. Iman grabbed one at random—*The Collected Works of W.B. Yeats*—and began reading. After idly flipping back and forth, she settled on "The Second Coming," a familiar favourite to ease her into the headier verse.

She was halfway through "Under Ben Bulben" when a strange creaking pulled her from her reading. She set the book on her lap. The deck shifted slightly beneath her feet, as if jiggled to and fro by some giant invisible hand. It didn't seem in danger of collapse, but the sensation was still unnerving. She stood gingerly and crept to the railing, where she could get a better view of the bracing.

A man clung to the side of the deck. His blond hair hung in disarray from his head, locks flapping in the steady breeze. Sighing, he pulled a gun from beneath his jacket and pointed it at Iman.

"Nothing's ever easy, is it?" he asked.

39: BAD JUJU

BALLARO LOOKED OLDER. He stood in the doorway of his home, one hand clutching the doorframe. The passing months had pulled on him with preternatural force, dragging down jowls and carving lines with the indelicate taps of a clumsy and belligerent sculptor. Streaks of grey-white tarnished his sleek black hair, and stubble stained his cheeks like smudges of charcoal. *Christ, he looks like hell.* By the way Ballaro looked him up and down, David assumed the man was thinking the same thing about him.

"Detective. I guess it's my turn to offer you my condolences."

"Thanks," said David.

"Don't count for shit, do they? Come in if you're coming in. This an official visit? If so, say the word. I've got my lawyer on speed dial."

David shook his head. "As unofficial as it comes. If it was on the books, I'd burn 'em."

"That's sexy talk from an officer of the law. You tryin' to juice me up for something?"

"I guess you could say that."

They sat in the same places they had for their last two meetings. Ballaro offered David the comfier of the two guest chairs, but the thought of taking Walter's spot was unbearable. David settled into the cushion, crossing one leg over the other and swallowing the grimace the motion brought to his lips. His ribs felt like shards of broken pottery clumsily glued back together.

"I know what killed your sons."

Ballaro made a steeple of his fingers, pressed it to his lips. "What, but not who?"

"What. Who. Where. When. Everything but why."

"Always the hardest itch to scratch, ain't it?"

David clamped a cigarette between his teeth and held up a lighter. He pointed to it and looked at Ballaro, a non-verbal request for permission. Ballaro shrugged.

"Yeah, sure. Ruin my upholstery, what the fuck do I care?"

David lit the smoke, inhaled. Smoke hugged his lungs, the nicotine like rubber caps sheathing the jagged edges of his ribcage. He watched Ballaro as the mask of nonchalance ran from his face like wax under a heat lamp. His plump fingers toyed with their many rings, scratched at the lip of his armrest. David gave the man a few moments to sweat before playing his hand. "Tell me what you know about Luka Volchyin."

Ballaro pressed his hands together as if in prayer. His gaze wandered somewhere far away, returning with reluctance several moments later. "Fuck. Volchyin. You're sure?"

"About what? I just asked what you know about him."

"Don't shit a shitter, kid."

"The name means something, then."

Ballaro rubbed his face. "He hung around Main and Ferry, slingin' weed. Had a few girls turned tricks for him. Small shit, but he was real impertinent about it, some fucking nobody actin' like he was Scarface. Some of the fellas had words with him, but the kid wouldn't learn his lesson."

"He wouldn't learn?" David asked. "Or your boys couldn't teach him?"

"Kid was slippery as hell, I'll give him that. Guys chased him up and down town, but no one could ever nail him. Rumor stared goin' around that the kid had protection, and I don't mean one of the families. His grandma was supposed to be some sort of gypsy or somethin', one of those babushka Slav hags, you know. Kind that can brew a tea can grow your hair back or make your dick fall off. Bad juju."

"You believed it?"

Ballaro exhaled through pursed lips. "Fuck, no. But if the mokes on the street start buyin' it, truth or lie don't make that much difference. Anyway, people started askin' around, found out that granny was holed up in one of the local old folks' homes."

"That wouldn't be Stanford Acres, would it?"

"Good guess, detective. You deducted the shit out of that one."

"You like that, how about this one. That fire they had a few months back? I'm guessing grandma Volchyin was one of the victims."

Ballaro scraped a bit of dirt from beneath his fingernails. "Y'know, I think she was. As I recall, the fire started in her room. Old biddy musta been smokin' in bed. Careless."

"You burned an old woman alive to send a message," David said, as if by speaking the act aloud he could better measure the scope of its cruelty.

Ballaro dug a strand of dirt from the nail of his middle finger, flicked it away. "That's a pretty big accusation, detective, and I gotta say I resent it. I'm a legitimate businessman. Why the fuck would I want to burn up some old lady? But I will say this. There are some guys on the streets of this city'll do anything if the price is right. If someone needed a building torched, say, to collect the insurance, they wouldn't have to look far."

They sat ensconced in a brief silence. Ballaro shook his head, tutting to himself. "Volchyin. I should've fucking known."

"You want this guy, right?"

"And I'll get him. Thanks for your visit, detective, but I don't have anything for you."

"I hope that's not true. Otherwise we're both going to be pretty disappointed."

"How d'you figure?"

"I've got something the guy wants. I know how he became . . . whatever the hell he is, and what he plans to do next. I can fix it for him to show up at a time and place of my choosing. When he does, I can nail him."

"Yeah, and lock him up so's he can sit on his ass and watch the tube for fifty years? He murdered my boys, detective. I don't want him behind bars. I want him in the fucking *ground*."

"So do I."

Ballaro fingered the crease of flesh beside his lips, contemplative. "Yeah?"

"If I wanted the guy put in jail, I'd be talking to my sergeant, trying to get a warrant typed up. That's not gonna cut it here. We're not talking about a normal criminal. This is more like dealing with a rabid dog. And you don't lock a rabid dog in the pound. You put it down."

Ballaro cocked an eyebrow. "You're pissed about Pulaski, huh? Buddy killed your partner, got you out for blood?"

David said nothing, his face a stone mask.

The Mafioso chuckled to himself. "Take your moral high ground, see if I fuckin' care. Hatred ain't something to be ashamed of. It's our most human emotion. Animals don't hold grudges. They kill for food, run from fear. Death ain't nothin' to them. It happens when it happens. Not us humans, detective. Death offends us. It spits on me and mine, I spit right back in its face."

Ballaro leaned forward. Age sloughed off him like shed skin, revealing something sharp and toned and hungry beneath.

"Tell me what you need, detective," he said. "And it's yours."

40: DIRTY BIRD

NORMALLY DEREK ENJOYED being right—what sort of masochistic asshole doesn't?—but frankly, he would have preferred it if this particular hunch had panned out to be nothing more than paranoia. Standing in front of Motes' office door, staring into the whorls of dull blue and purple behind frosted glass, he felt only the profound weariness of a man confronting a big and unsightly mess, none of it of his own making.

One small mercy: Luka had finally accepted that the professor had bailed. Things would go a lot smoother if they didn't have to drag the moron's petulant doubts behind them everywhere.

"He ain't on campus. I'd smell him."

Too bad your sniffer wasn't up to the task twenty minutes ago. Derek checked the nameplate next to the door. It read: *E. Motes, Languages Professor.*

"E. Motes?" He shook his head. *Outfoxed by a man with a goddamn pun for a name.*

Below Motes, the sign continued: *Iman al-Qaddari, Research Assistant.* His killer's antennae twitched. Derek kept them well-honed, and he trusted their calibration implicitly. He pointed to the name. "You know anything about this girl?"

"What, the assistant chick? She's a Paki or something.' Not bad lookin', though."

"How old?"

"Mid-twenties, I guess. Way younger than Motes."

"Are they close?"

"How the fuck should I know?"

Derek tapped his chin with his index finger. Loners find friends in unusual places. And even if not, an assistant would be just the sort of person who'd know the guy's travel plans. It was the best lead they had.

"Wait here," he told Luka, who grabbed his wrist and squeezed, stopping just short of causing pain.

"I think you're forgettin' your place here, Matchbook," he whispered.

Derek met Luka's gaze easily. He replied at a normal speaking volume. "You want to find Motes or not?"

The pressure on Derek's wrist tightened. His veins thrummed against the added pressure, bulging like kinked hoses. He swallowed a grunt and held still until Luka's grip relaxed.

"Show me what you got, bro."

He found a payphone on the first floor, checked the phonebook, and was less than surprised to find no one named al-Qaddari. Luka had said young, and people under thirty almost never listed their numbers. Landlines were for dinosaurs like Motes. He laced his fingers together and pulled gently downward on the back of his head. The pressure against his scalp helped him focus.

Back upstairs, he wandered the halls near Motes' office until he found a room marked *Administration*. He ambled inside and waved to the woman behind the desk. Her mohair sweater heaved allergens into the air with every twitch of her hand on the computer mouse. An itch burrowed into the back of Derek's throat. He ran his tongue fruitlessly over the tender skin there and swallowed a cough.

"How you doing?" he asked, all smiles and workaday camaraderie. "I'm wondering if you could help me."

"Sure," the woman said. "What do you need?"

"I'm having some trouble with the pay system. Apparently someone from your department has stopped getting her direct deposits."

The woman clucked sympathetically, a good sign. "Oh dear, that's frustrating."

"Don't I know it. We're migrating systems, and this sort of thing happens sometimes. I've got the lady's name and room number, but I think her employee ID might be copied down wrong. It's giving me a bum result."

"Okay." A little more cautious now.

"I'd check with her myself, but she's not in, and if we don't make the change today the server won't be able to process her cheque until the next pay period. I was wondering if I could maybe grab it from you?"

The woman bit her lower lip. "Yeah, I guess that's okay. What's the employee's name?"

"Iman al-Qaddari."

"Jeez. Iman never told me she wasn't getting paid. That girl needs to stand up for herself."

"She seemed polite in her email. We're sorry we didn't catch it ourselves."

The woman brought up Iman's account details. She began reading the ID out loud.

"It's okay," Derek interrupted. "I got it."

He leaned over the desk and ran his finger conspicuously underneath the employee number, muttering digits to himself low enough to obscure the fact that they bore no resemblance to the numbers on the screen. During this bit of pantomime, he studied the address listed in the lower left corner and jotted it down in a single spaceless line. The woman looked a little put out but didn't say anything. Derek didn't give her time. He tucked the paper away.

"Thanks a bunch!" he said, disappearing around the corner.

Neither Luka nor Derek had a smartphone, so they fumbled their way to the al-Qaddari girl's house using a roadmap they found in the glove box. They pulled up to it as the sun was setting, a ramshackle manor jury-rigged into multiple apartments.

"He's in there," Luka said, his face lengthening in a lupine snarl. "I can smell the cowardly little fucker." He stepped forward. Derek restrained him with a hand on the shoulder. Luka whirled, his lips pulled back to expose overdeveloped incisors.

"Hold up, Luka."

"Not your call, bro. I'm gonna go in there and tell that Ivy League piece of shit what's what."

And leave a carpet of corpses for the morning, I bet. "There's a better way, man. Let me take a stab first, see if I can sneak my way in. Maybe we can pull this off without leaving any bodies behind."

Luka flashed a condescending smile. "You gettin' squeamish, Matchbook?"

"Fuck that. In my line of work, you don't do the deed 'less you stand to gain from it. We drop some bodies for the fuck of it, the PD cranks up the heat on us."

Luka shrugged. "Whatever turns you on, bro. Take your shot."

Derek gave a thumbs up. Inside, he was less pleased. By the look of it, Luka had acquiesced not because he saw the sense of Derek's plan, but simply to avoid an argument. If Derek had proposed shooting up the whole street, the big man would've been just as likely to go for it. That kind of indifference to carnage was more than a little troubling. The crazy asshole couldn't see more than a week or two ahead. The way he acted, it was as if anything beyond that point was irrelevant.

Derek scoped out the building. The place was surprisingly tough to crack. The front door was solid oak, and if Derek finessed it open, there'd still be the apartment door inside to contend with. The apartment he wanted was number three, which logic placed on the topmost floor, making window entry impractical. He could try getting buzzed in, but under what excuse? A locked-out neighbour? Pizza delivery?

He spotted the balconies. They were ugly things, two-by-fours bolted into brick, but they provided decent handholds, and a brief tug proved them sturdy. Stepping back, he walked himself mentally through the climb until he reached the top floor. Slip inside if the door's unlocked, kick it in if it's not. Round up the professor and his little study buddy at gunpoint and buzz Luka in for some quick interrogation. It could work.

Derek spat into his palms and rubbed them together. He grabbed the highest support beam he could reach and hoisted himself aloft. The tips of his shoes found footing in the brickwork. Dislodged pebbles and bits of crumbly mortar tumbled into the garden below. He clambered from strut to strut, legs bicycling through the air in search of purchase. It crossed his mind how conspicuous—not to mention stupid—he looked to anyone who might be watching in the next building, but the thought didn't worry him much. He could easily be a locked-out tenant or innocuous eccentric. A bigger issue would be falling, which at his current height could easily break his leg or worse. Somehow, he didn't think the Volchyin pack had much in the way of health benefits. A bullet to put you out of your misery probably covered it. *Why do I always end up working for guys who like to shoot people in the head?*

The balconies sprouted out around existing apertures in the brick—expanded former windows, by the look of them—and didn't line up neatly atop one another. Derek pulled himself onto the second-floor balcony, poised, and leapt for the third. His fingers closed around a support beam. He wriggled his lower body until his feet found a protruding brick, and used it to shimmy upward. Another few feet and he'd be there.

Movement overhead caught his eye. He looked up to see a young Middle Eastern woman staring down at him.

Derek had spent half his life crushing panic beneath his heel. He did so now, calmly shifting his weight onto one arm to allow himself to draw the Governor.

"Nothing's ever easy, is it?" he sighed, pointing the barrel squarely at the girl.

The girl backed up. That was bad; if she got out of his line of sight, he was fucked. He waggled the gun and tutted. The girl froze.

"Easy there, kid. We're gonna do this thing slow and safe, otherwise someone's gonna get hurt. First, you've gotta give me some room here. Take two steps back, no more, no less. Stay in my line of sight now. No sudden movements, no screams. There's a girl."

Derek hoisted himself up until his arms hugged the railing. He kept one hand cocked out awkwardly, the gun aimed vaguely in the girl's direction. This was the trickiest moment. If she darted for the door, he could do fuck all about it—his aim was hopelessly compromised, and if he tried a shot, he'd risk dropping the gun or snapping his wrist from the recoil. She stood motionless while he threw a leg over the railing and came down securely on the balcony, gun once again trained on her solar plexus.

"I don't suppose you'd invite me inside, eh?"

Silently, the girl opened the door. She made no move to run or lock him out. He pushed his way in and took a quick survey of the room.

An Asian kid about the same age as the girl sat on the couch. His body seized up at the sight of the Governor. Derek could tell he wouldn't be any trouble—he had the doughy, knock-kneed posture of a kid averse to any sort of conflict. The girl was harder to read, but her paralysis struck him as a good sign. If he kept her scared, she'd do as she was told.

Motes was the X factor. He sat on an ottoman, a book open in his lap. The guy wasn't much to look at—reed-thin beneath a tweed jacket, hollow-cheeked and myopic—but desperation could harden the softest men. What's more, he was apparently afflicted with Luka's strange illness, which might convey all sorts of unexpected advantages. The silver slugs lay in the Governor's back chambers. Derek was loath to use them up, but they comforted him all the same.

"Evening, professor."

Motes jabbed Derek with a look of utter contempt. "Am I supposed to know you?"

"Not by name, maybe. But a smart guy like you should be able to figure out why I'm here." Derek found the intercom and pressed the button marked "door." The speaker buzzed. He flicked open the deadbolt, pulled the chain from the door, and crossed back to his original spot between his captives and the balcony.

The girl moved toward the futon. Derek blocked her path with his hand and motioned for her to sit at the kitchen table. He wondered if they had any duct tape. Things would go smoother if he could bind them up. He'd probably still have to kill them at this point, but he could do it quietly, use a kitchen knife. A mask would've been good, too. Motes would know Luka, but there was no need to let him ID Derek as well. He kicked himself for not stopping by a hardware store on the way over.

Luka came upstairs. His anger and agitation were gone, drowned beneath a wave of sinister glee. "Motes, what's up, bro?"

Motes swallowed.

"I went by your house, but I couldn't find you. Your office, too. I didn't think you were the kind of guy to dip your pen in the company ink." He pointed to the Asian kid, who sat as still as possible, hands buried in his lap. "And a three-way, too! You dirty bird!"

"These two have nothing to do with our arrangement. I'll come with you, no questions asked, but leave them be."

"You'll come with me, all right, but what I do to them or not ain't on your say-so. I'm in charge here, not you."

"Wrong."

A woman stepped into view through the narrow hallway, Beretta pointed at Luka. Derek recognized the outfit before his eyes happened on the badge pinned above her heart.

Oh fuck, squeaked a voice in his head. *Oh fuck oh fuck oh fuck.* A cop?! A goddamn *cop?!* It wasn't fair! How could this asshole have police protection? What cop in her right mind would believe his story enough to bother?

The sort that got attacked by a half-wolf-half-human and lived to snub the papers about it, sneered another voice in rebuttal.

Luka grinned at the officer. "Hey, baby, I remember you. How's your boyfriend? I hear he got beat up pretty bad."

"Detective Moore? He's fine. Had a vermin problem, but it's sorted."

"Is it?"

"It is. You're under arrest, both of you. Breaking and entering, assault, and forced confinement for starters. We'll see what your rap sheets have for you from there. I'd advise you to drop the gun, blondie, and put your hands behind your head."

Derek's mind shook like an overheating engine. The Governor was still in his hand, though he'd let his aim drop once the girl was seated. The cop could get a pin on him and fire before he raised it—assuming she was a halfway decent shot—unless Luka distracted her. She was savvy enough to keep both of them in the same line of sight. He could try a rolling shot, but that was risky, and there wasn't much in the way of cover. The other option was—

Luka short-circuited Derek's thinking by pulling out a gun of his own and firing at the cop. The cop shot him twice in the process, two slugs to the chest that knocked him back against the door. He shuddered like a man swallowing something unpleasant before taking aim and firing again. The first shot went high. The second would have connected if the cop hadn't dropped to her knees and slid behind the futon. The Asian kid leapt aside to get out of the crossfire. He tripped over the coffee table and hit his head on the floor with an alarming thud. Motes threw his arms over his head and dove for the corner.

The cop peeked over the futon, taking time to sight a headshot. Derek didn't know if that would be enough to kill Luka or not, but he wasn't keen to find out. He raised the Governor and fired twice, taking the cop in the hip and shoulder. She fell to the side, screaming through gritted teeth, and crawled from view.

I shot a cop, thought Derek, stunned. *I'll be a goddamn folk hero at the Copper Penny. Assuming I make it out of here alive.*

Clutching his bleeding belly with one hand, Luka lurched after Motes, who skittered away on his hands and knees. Luka kicked the professor onto his back and dragged him upright, firing sporadically over the couch to keep the cop pinned down. The Asian kid tried to dart out the front door, but Luka tripped him with a deftly-placed ankle. He tossed the professor onto the kid and planted a foot atop them both, stomping down every time they struggled.

"Let's go, bro," he said, casual as anything. As if he were leaving a party and didn't want to be late getting home.

Derek studied the gap between the futon and the wall. He'd fired twice and hit both times. The cop was probably dead or dying, but Derek wanted to be sure. The only thing worse than shooting a cop was shooting one who lived. Two more shots should be enough. He wanted to save his silver bullets for tonight in case things went south. More than they already had, anyway. *Christ, if they go much farther south than this, I'll be chilling with the penguins.*

"Hold on," he said.

He rounded the kitchen table, putting himself in view of the cop. A trail of blood marked her progress to the far end of the couch, where she'd hoisted herself to a hunched sitting position. Her gun wavered just below the lip of cushions, trying for a clean shot at Luka. She didn't notice Derek until he'd squared her in his sights.

A sharp pain bored into Derek's temple. He stumbled sideways, discharging his gun into the wall with a puff of exploding plaster. His fingers flew to his skull, expecting to come back sticky with blood and brain matter. The skin was tender but unbroken. He looked down and saw a frying pan at his feet, still tottering with the momentum of its landing. The girl hefted a pot from a kitchen drawer, wound up, and hurled it towards him. Derek fired at the girl, forcing her into the bathroom and nearly losing the top of his skull as the cop lit him up. The hornet buzz of passing bullets filled his ears, louder in a sense than the report of the shots. Displaced air buffeted his scalp.

"Bro, give it up," Luka barked. He had Motes under one arm and the Asian kid under the other. Derek ran for the door and helped Luka manhandle the two men down the stairs. Motes put up a struggle, albeit a feeble one, but the kid seemed to have lost what little fight he'd possessed. Carrying him was like lugging a fleshy mannequin down a flight of stairs.

They loaded the professor and the kid into the trunk and slammed the lid. All the while an internal siren bellowed its shrill warning in Derek's ears. *The cop's still alive! She could ID you! The cop's still alive!* Leaving witnesses to their failed massacre was insane, but what was he supposed to do? They had five minutes, tops, until more cops showed up.

An aluminium shed hunched beneath the shade of an oak tree. Derek ran to it and delivered a sharp kick to the latch. The thin metal buckled. He had one shot at this. If he was lucky, his problems might be solved. If not, they'd just have to book it and hope for the best. Tearing the door from its hinges, Derek scrambled inside and scoped the shed's contents.

A smile floated to his lips.

41: BIRD OF PREY

IMAN FELL TO her knees in front of the toilet, unsure exactly how she'd gotten there.

That guy just shot at me. He had a gun and he shot at me.

She recalled hurling the frying pan, her rage obscuring the memory like streaks of grease across the lens of her mind. The throw had landed true, a shot she never could have made without adrenaline twanging her muscles. The man had turned to her and fired, and now she was kneeling on the cold bathroom tile, her stomach a slipknot pulled ruthlessly tight. Her belly hitched, and everything she'd eaten poured out of her mouth in a bilious stream. Stomach acid stung her throat, left her lips feeling stringy and chapped. She wiped her face with her forearm, aware the guy with the gun could be bearing down on her that very instant but too wracked by belly cramps to do much about it. When the worst of them passed and she still wasn't shot, she pulled herself to her feet and staggered into the hall.

The two men were gone. Silence rang in their absence, broken by a low liquid moaning from behind the futon. Officer Myers lay in a stagnant pool of her own blood. The right half of her uniform was soaked from chest to knee, the saturated fabric drying to a dull, velvety maroon. She stirred like a woman in the throes of a bad dream, head flopping from side to side, legs kicking restlessly. Iman shoved the futon aside and crouched down next to her, shaking her shoulder harder than intended in an effort to bring her back to her senses.

"Officer Myers. Officer Myers! Brian and Professor Motes are gone! Did those men take them? Hey?"

"Nngh." Myers tried to shrug free of Iman's grip. Iman shook harder.

"You have to get up. We need to go to the hospital."

"C . . . call . . . backup," Myers breathed. Her voice came out weak and tinny, as if played through blown speakers. A coppery stink wafted from her lips.

Iman fumbled through the wreckage of her apartment for her cell phone. She found it beneath the overturned coffee table and dialled 9-1-1. The operator came on after a single ring.

"Hi, a couple guys just broke into my apartment! They shot one of my friends and I think took the others with them!" She rattled off her address and hung up before the operator could ask more questions.

Myers pulled herself upright, grunting with the effort. Her skin grew waxy and pale, her eyes bloodshot and glossy. Iman eased her back down, tucking a pillow under her head.

"Stay still. The paramedics will be here soon. You shouldn't move until they get here or you might do more damage."

"Smell . . . smoke . . . " Myers said, and coughed. A mist of spittle hit Iman's chin. She wiped it away as discreetly as possible, sniffing the air. It *did* smell like smoke. Standing up, she saw eddies of it flowing along her ceiling from the cracks in her front door. She threw the door open, admitting a torrent of billowing grey soot. It lapped at her face, stinging her eyes and filling her nostrils. She ducked down beneath the curtain of ash and crawled to the third floor bannister.

A fire raged in the building's front landing, consuming the stairs and singeing the walls a charcoal black. Empty canisters of paint thinner littered the floor, and a plastic jerry can of gasoline sat on the stoop. She glimpsed the building's fire extinguisher and laughed. It was a puny thing. Even if she reached it, she doubted it could put all this out.

A bulbous, off-white object smashed through the lobby window. It came to rest in the nest of flames, its rounded edges peeling in the heat. *What the hell?* Squinting through the smoke, Iman spotted the steel valve sprouting from its narrow end, surrounded by the metal frills of a protective collar.

"Ah, fuck," she groaned, and threw her arm over her face moments before the propane tank exploded.

Heat raked her like the talons of some hellish bird of prey. She fell backwards, grabbing a bannister to keep from tumbling into the fire's crackling gullet. Flames twined up the stairs, time lapse tendrils of some nightmare vine. Iman scurried back into her apartment and kicked the door shut. She yanked fistfuls of hair and tried to think. The building was brick, but its fixtures were mostly wood and old as hell. They'd go up like so much kindling. The front door was impassable, the back door non-existent. The apartment was the definition of jury-rigged. It abided by no fire codes, had no contingencies for evacuation. She could theoretically climb down from the balcony—the guy with the gun had made it up that way easily enough—but not with Myers on her back.

Unless . . .

Running into her bedroom, Iman tore her sheets off the bed and ransacked her linen closet, grabbing every spare blanket and beach towel. She wound them into crude strands and knotted them together, corner to corner, until she had a rope thirty or so feet long. At each knot, she grabbed a hank of fabric to either side and pulled as hard as she could. They all held, though she exerted much less tensile strain with her arms than she would with her full body weight—not to mention Myers'.

The air in the living room had grown hazy with smoke. It covered the ceiling in crenulated waves, sheets and strata morphing with the caprices of the wind blowing in from the balcony. She considered trying to manhandle the mattress over the edge to give herself something soft to land on, but there wasn't enough time. Even at the threshold of the balcony, she could hear the dull roar of the flames in the hall, feel their heat snorting through the cracks in the door. The doorknob glowed a dull molten red.

She locked her forearms under Myers' armpits and dragged her upright. The cop's feet slipped and flopped against the floor, clumsy as an infant's. Her heart pounded a frenetic, irregular beat. Step by dragging step, they managed a herky-jerky shuffle to the balcony, the autumn wind a balm on Iman's blistered forehead.

Iman looped the sheet-rope around Myer's chest and triple-knotted it. She pulled the rope tight until Myers grunted from the pressure and helped the officer climb over the railing.

"This is . . . fucking nuts . . . " Myers heaved.

"Better than burning alive. Just hold still, okay? I'll lower you down."

Myers eased herself over the precipice, slowly giving the sheets her full weight. Iman bit her lower lip and held the rope taut, leaning backwards to leverage her meager weight against Myers'. Her feet slid over the wooden deck before catching on a baluster. She dropped to her knees, using the guardrail as a crude pulley, and fed the rope through her hands inch by endless inch. The passing fabric scraped her palms raw. She bit down on the pain until her lower lip bled. Cramps gnarled her shoulders, set her thigh muscles aflame.

Eventually Myers touched ground and the rope went slack. Iman's arms sang with sudden relief. She allowed herself a moment's breath before tying the sheet-rope to a baluster. Her body cried out for rest, but she could afford none. Behind her the apartment door burst inward, spewing splinters of flaming wood. Tentacles of flame probed through the opening, ensnaring her kitchen table and slinking across her carpet. She slipped over the balustrade and abseiled down the wall, shimmying where her feet failed to touch the brick. As she set down beside Myers, her legs gave out, and Iman collapsed beside the officer. She lay there as the approaching sirens swelled in volume, their lights casting red-blue palls on the tree overhead. A thin, throaty laugh escaped her as the paramedics arrived. It seemed about all she had left to lose.

42: A CHEAP SHOT

THE SENSATION CREPT up on David slowly, closing on him like the hungry petals of a Venus fly trap. By the time he noticed it, he was already neck-deep in its leathery folds. It was a feeling unmistakable but nameless, a malformed cousin of déjà vu—a sense of past events replayed with the roles reversed. Melissa lay in the same bed he'd used to recuperate from his broken ribs. Iman sat next to her in the very same chair Melissa herself had occupied a few scant weeks before. And David stood in the doorway, intruding on a conversation neither party wanted overheard.

Melissa spotted him and waved feebly. An IV fed into her wrist, its needle held flush to her skin by a triple wrapping of medical adhesive. Her complexion was blotched and milky, her eyes ringed with purplish bags, but her smile seemed genuine. Iman's wounds were less obvious, but they seemed to cut deeper. David could smell the anguish festering in her belly, a damp and pungent stench undiminished by the antiseptic sting of hospital air. Her face bore a blank, catatonic look. She wrapped a piece of receipt paper around one finger until it formed a tube and let it unspool. Her hands performed the task independently. The rips and wrinkles marring the paper suggested she'd been doing it for some time.

"Hey," Melissa said. "I wasn't sure they'd let you in. Visiting hours and all."

"Police business. We've got all the time we need." He dragged a chair from a nearby table and sat down next to Iman. Her fingers continued their ceaseless winding and unwinding of the receipt paper. "So. What does Delduca know?"

"As much truth as we needed to spill, and not a drop more. A couple guys broke into Iman's apartment, demanding money. They looked strung out, desperate, probably tweaked out of their gourd."

"What about you?"

"I was happening by when I heard gunshots. I attempted to apprehend the suspects but was injured in the line of duty. The thugs panicked and tried to torch the building. We believe they took Brian as a hostage to aid their escape."

"And Motes?"

Melissa plucked at a loose thread in her bedsheets. "We left him out of it."

"What, altogether?"

"There was no plausible way to put him in the apartment. Even my 'happening by' is pretty weak."

"I guess, but every cop in the city is looking for those guys. They should know exactly who they're after. Motes could even get mistaken for a perp."

"Only if they find them, and I don't think that's too likely. We're the only ones who know where they're going, and it's not the sort of place the cops are likely to stumble across."

"So we tell them where to look."

Melissa threw her hands in the air. "How? You think they'd believe us? 'Oh, by the way chief, the kidnappers are a couple of werewolves, let me show you their lair on Google Maps.'"

David twiddled his silver alligator ring. "We'd leave that part out of it, obviously."

"Then what's left? If they bugged out for another city, that's one thing, we could fudge a CI or anonymous tip. But to sweep the fucking Canadian Shield for a couple of hopheads? I don't see them buying it."

"Still, we need to try—"

No," Iman said. Her receipt paper ripped in half. She dropped the pieces into her lap and swept them onto the floor. "Melissa's right. We can't spill everything."

David took Iman's hand in both of his. "Motes and Brian—"

"You think I don't know?" Iman said, pulling her hand away. "You think I'm not worried about them? If I could get the best SWAT team in the world on it, I would. But we can't. No one will believe us. If we convince the cops to check it out at all, the search'll be half-assed. And what if Luka feels the walls closing in? He might decide it's best to cut and run. And if they do that . . . "

"Okay," David said. "Okay. We leave Delduca out of it, for now. At least we aren't entirely unprepared."

David reached into his pocket and spilled half a dozen bits of shiny oblong metal onto the bedspread. Melissa picked one up and inspected it between thumb and forefinger. Its curves were cool and sleek, reflective as the surface of a still lake.

"Silver bullets?" she asked.

"Silver-*plated*," corrected David. "Pure silver's too soft. The ballistics on these aren't amazing as it is, but it shouldn't matter much under a hundred yards or so."

"Where in God's name did you even get these?"

"Ballaro. We came to a little arrangement yesterday."

"And he managed to get his hands on silver bullets on short notice? The man's connected, but I didn't think anyone was *that* connected."

"He had his hands on them already. Turns out Iman wasn't the only one to spot the full moon connection."

Melissa's jaw dropped open. "So that asshole knew?"

"No. I wouldn't even say he really suspected, not on the surface of things. But some superstitious bit of him got through enough to make the order. Just six. He told his jeweller they were for his mantelpiece. Maybe it raised an eyebrow, but any craftsman who works with criminals is gonna get no shortage of weird and tacky orders."

Melissa danced the bullet between her fingers. "Can he get more?"

"He thinks so. But in the meantime, we'll have to make do with what we've got."

"Half a dozen bullets won't do much good against a whole pack."

"True. In my original plan, that wouldn't have been an issue. We'd get Motes to call him, act contrite, say he's sorry he ran but he's willing to get with the program. They pick a time and place to meet, and bam! Instant ambush. But now . . . "

"Uh-huh."

Melissa smoothed a crease in the covers of her hospital bed. Beside her Iman clasped her hands in her lap, legs squeezed primly together.

David swallowed. "I mean, if I'd known—"

Melissa raised a hand. "Stop. No self-pity, please. We both know damn well that you would've helped if you were there. You weren't. It wasn't your shift. That's not on you. I was there, and all I managed to do was just about get myself killed."

"Not true," Iman said.

Melissa silenced her with a look. "Point is, we can't blame ourselves for what happened. This is on Luka and that blond prick with the gun."

"Blond prick?" David asked.

"Luka had a guy with him," Iman explained. "He's the one who climbed up the balcony. Blond, early thirties maybe. Pale blue eyes, but with flecks of gold in them."

The bottom dropped out of David's stomach. He coughed, each burst cinching a band of misery tight around his ribs. *McCulloch. That fucker!*

And who's the asshole that set him loose, hmm?

David grabbed his chest, hoping to pass off the anguished look on his face as lingering pain from his injury.

"Right. If we're not going to Ballaro, let's assess where we're at here. Motes was our hold on the guy, and we've lost him. Even if we could reach out to Luka, he's got no incentive to meet us. He's in the wind, could be hiding out anywhere. But we know one place where he'll eventually go."

"Whitetooth Falls."

"Exactly. He could be heading there now, or not. We can't say. But we do know one time where he's bound to show up. I checked a lunar calendar. The next full moon's in eleven days."

Melissa nodded. "It'll be tight, but I should be able to get out of here by then."

"I wouldn't push it. Besides, even if you are out of the hospital, I think it's probably best if you stay in Niagara."

The bed creaked as Melissa hunched herself upright, her eyes narrowed. "Excuse me?"

"I'm not questioning your ability. Christ knows I'd never do that. But we need to face facts. You've been badly hurt—"

"You're not exactly running marathons yourself, buddy."

"It's not just that. Delduca may have let your story about showing up at Iman's apartment slide, but I doubt he found it easy to swallow. The precinct's gonna be on you, looking for something strange. If you book it for the great white north without a decent explanation, it's only gonna draw more attention to you. It could even wind up tipping off Luka. I'm sorry to be a dick, but I think I need to do this one solo."

"Not solo," Iman said. "I agree about Officer Myers, but I'm going with you."

David shook his head gently. "Again, it's not a good idea."

"Why not? I'm not hurt, aside from a few cuts and bruises. And the cops aren't investigating me."

"You're still connected to the victim. They're going to want to keep tabs on you."

"Well, what they want and what they get are different things."

"You're not a police officer, Iman. I can't just drag you out on some manhunt."

"You're on medical leave, so you're technically not acting as a police officer either."

"She's got you there," Melissa said.

Iman put her hands on her hips. "If you leave without me, I'll call Delduca myself and spill everything. It's you and me or no one at all."

David rubbed his forehead. "This is ludicrous."

"Would you think it was ludicrous if our situations were reversed, and it was your wife they had? Would you wait at home, not knowing where she is or if she's even, you know . . . "

A cheap shot, maybe, but it landed square. David placed a hand on Iman's shoulder. "They bothered to take him with them; that's a good sign. If they wanted him dead they would've just shot him in the apartment or on the lawn. They obviously have other plans."

"Yeah," agreed Melissa. "Maybe they're using him as a hostage, or plan to try putting him up for ransom."

Iman shook her head; her face resumed its pinched, vacant look. "They don't care about that. Don't you remember? Motes told us Luka brought someone with him last time, too. The girl in the trunk. And we know what happened to her."

David looked to Melissa for something to say, and found her staring back at him. Neither spoke.

Iman put her face in her hands and cried.

PART IV: WOLF MOON

43: TRIGGERMEN

GOD, **DEREK WAS** sick of the fucking woods.

Growing up in the urban concretion of Scarborough, with its stunted trees and exhaust-tainted air, Derek had often dreamed of going to summer camps—something for which his tightwad parents would have never dreamed of shelling out money. He pictured the scene in pastel hues of hypothetical nostalgia: paddling canoes along pristine rivers; ranging through acres of old-growth forest, a canopy of leaves overhead; eating sausages musky with campfire smoke; sleeping beneath a canvas tent, chirruping crickets the bucolic surrogate of rattling subways and idling cars. He longed to slice through the GTA's fog of glass and steel and concrete, to heave in lungfuls of unblemished air, to live off scavenged berries and hunted deer. To purge himself of the trappings of urban decadence. To rough it.

He was roughing it now, all right. Mosquitos breakfasted on his face and supped on his back, charting constellations in his scabbed and swollen flesh. Northern winds dive-bombed every clearing, raking icy claws against exposed skin. The trees blocked the worst of it if you ventured deep enough into them, but they held between their gnarled trunks a heavy, stifling dimness, where shadows thick as soggy cotton filled your lungs and settled over your face like a caul. Ridges of bedrock broke through the brittle alkali soil, snagging ankles and cracking shins and making flat stretches large enough to sleep on comfortably all but non-existent.

The urge to bail on the whole scene grew stronger with each passing hour, though making it back to civilization would be no easy feat. Miles of forest and marshland stood between him and the nearest town, and orienteering was about as far from Derek's strong suit as you could get. Stealing a car was likewise not an option. Shortly after they'd left the last town behind, Luka drove his convoy through logging paths and over rock-studded fields until he found a cliff overlooking a deep and frigid lake. Sunlight bounced off its surface like spilled gems, beneath which fathoms yawned down to a bluish darkness.

"All right, boys," he called. "Unload anything you wanna keep. If you can't carry it, leave it be."

Derek popped the trunk. He held a tire iron in one hand in case the "luggage" made a break for it. He needn't have worried. The professor and the Asian kid mewled and squirmed at the sudden brightness, faces buried in the cruxes of their elbows. He dragged them out and tossed them onto the grass, wondering with abstract curiosity whether one of them would try to run. Neither did.

Once the cars were empty, Luka and half a dozen of his bigger pack members drove them to the precipice, punched out the windows, and shoved them over the edge. One by one, they fell in stunned silence for two hundred feet before slamming into the lake. White fists of foamy water jabbed upward with each impact before dissolving into mist and foam. Derek watched the cars sink into the blue-black abyss, the pit of his stomach sinking right along with them. There went their only safe ticket out of the wilderness, plunging axel-deep into mud and silt beneath two hundred-plus feet of frigid northern lake water. And yet Derek seemed to be the only one at all worried—save for the professor and the kid, of course, but they didn't count.

They went the rest of the way on foot, Luka leading and the others gaggling behind, alone or in chatty clusters. They lugged supplies in plastic bags or Value Village backpacks or simply loose and by the armful. Derek wadded up a few blankets in a canvas grocery bag and aped hauling something heavy. He kept his jacket unfastened and the Governor within reach, its final two chambers still pregnant with their silver payload. The professor and the kid stayed near the front of the pack, hands bound behind their backs with lengths of nylon rope.

The walk took most of the day, culminating on a barren limestone outcrop overlooking a foam-flecked river. Derek helped gather firewood and watched as a heavyset man with a serpent's head tattooed on his neck touched his Zippo to the kindling, unlocking wisps of smoke that coughed into a dull but serviceable flame. They stacked punctured cans of chili and beans in maple syrup around the fire and ate when the contents started to bubble, digging with pocket knives or sticks or their fingers. Derek fished out a can and ate alone beneath the shadow of a pine tree. Shed needles formed a spongy cushion atop the rocky soil.

The air grew frigid away from the fire, but Derek preferred the company of the cold to that of his packmates. The former could still kill him if he wasn't careful, but at least it wouldn't take any pleasure in doing so.

A voice in his head urged him to leave, just figure out which way was south and beat feet. Fuck the pack, fuck the cars, fuck Luka and his cabal of junkies and prison-cot padding. Yet something held him in place. Curiosity was too flippant a word. Call it fascination. Luka exerted a tangible pull on his followers, a microgravity snagging each misfit chunk of human detritus in his orbit. Derek saw it clearly in their obsequious bending to his commands. They were less a street gang than a cult, and Luka their messiah. It was nauseating to observe, but was he entirely immune? Had Luka bound him the same way he'd bound the others, slipped the collar of his charisma over Derek's willing neck?

No way. You see through his bullshit. You call him out when he does something dumb.

He repeated those sentiments to himself, rosaries of self-praise that soothed his battered spirit. He was up here in the woods to lay low, far from the dragnet doubtlessly trawling the whole Golden Horseshoe from Toronto to Niagara in search of Motes—not to mention Ballaro's merry little search party. And, perhaps, to take a little of what Luka was offering. If it was even true.

The radar scanner in Derek's head issued a feeble blip, a note of caution little stronger than background static. Branches rustled behind them, stirred no doubt by the wind or some passing animal. He shifted the cut of his jacket, allowing for an easier draw, and waited. The sound came again, louder this time. It circled the clearing, a low susurrus of pine needles crunching underfoot. The others didn't seem to notice—no surprise there. He skimmed possible causes, assessing each for probability and preferred response. Mounties tipped off to their location? Triggermen on Ballaro's payroll, aiming to engage in the mother of all "hunting accidents"? A set-up by Luka? His tongue circled his lips, leaving them no less parched.

They emerged from the woods as one. Derek counted a dozen before losing track. Men and women, they bore a common build and similar features, a leitmotif of kinship in the slant of their eyes and the slope of their noses, underscored by their common dress: pelts and hides from a dozen breeds of northern mammal, sewn together with rugged sinew stitches. Flint knives and tomahawks and tanned bladders full of water hung from their belts. Some held pikes or axes; others bore bows over their shoulders, crisscrossing quivers stuffed with hand-fletched arrows. Russet hair ran wild on their heads and faces, a colour Derek noticed was similar to Luka's.

Luka's packmates regarded the new arrivals warily. A few reached for weapons—mostly improvised cudgels or the knives they'd been using to eat—while the others looked to Luka for prompting. Luka stood, tossed an empty can into the fire, and extended his arms in a mimed embrace.

"I'm back, brothers and sisters! Where's Mother?"

The newcomers shifted, speaking to one another in a guttural tongue. Sighing, Luka found the professor and dragged him to his feet. Motes' legs were bound along with his arms, forcing him to follow Luka in a series of demeaning hops.

"Tell them to go get Majka," Luka said.

Motes spoke in the same language as the forest people, his voice pinched with discomfort. A burly man answered, fingers twining through his grey-streaked beard. By his demeanor and that of the others, Derek pinned him as the head honcho, excluding "Majka." His reply was terse and even-toned, but the message it conveyed was clearly not a great one. Motes bit his cheek and hunched his shoulders before relaying it to Luka.

"He says she's gone into the wilds."

Luka pursed his lips. "For how long?"

Motes asked. "He says it's not for him to dictate Majka's whereabouts."

"Will she be back before the full moon, at least?"

"I suspect so."

Luka planted a foot on Motes' tailbone and shoved him forward. "I'm asking *him*, not *you*."

Motes spat out a mouthful of dirt and pine needles. He posed the question with head bowed, absorbed the reply, and answered in a voice of hollow tin: "Yes."

Satisfied, Luka stepped over Motes, hand extended. The forest man regarded it without expression. His eyes locked with Luka's. A smile parted the underbrush of his brambled beard. He pulled Luka in by the wrist and wrapped him in a muscular embrace—Derek heard the wind escape Luka's lungs in a huff.

Reluctantly, Derek slid his hand away from the Governor. He picked up his can and resumed eating. Weird or not, the forest people were clearly on Luka's side.

Derek wasn't sure whether to feel worried or relieved.

44: CLEVER LIES

RIGID RED NUMERALS branded the darkness. David watched them flex in their staccato ballet, contorting each minute from one shape to the next. He found himself waiting for the climactic shift from 3:59 to 4:00 with nervous anticipation, unsure if the players could manage such a complex maneuver. Nancy's breath ebbed and flowed beside him, a conscious pattern aping sleep. Neither of them wanted to admit to their restlessness. The awkward remnants of their spat still ached after the conversation trailed off, phantom pain in a severed limb.

It was hard to blame her. David's announcement had been uncharacteristically terse, the only way he could get it out without blurting the whole thing. He was going out of town for a few days. Where? Up north. What city? No city, just a stretch of rural highway. Why? Police business. A convenient feint, that. Intangible as a cloak of mist, conforming to the shape of any story. He could've cobbled together a better lie, but chose not to. The deceit felt gentler if he kept it clumsy. Clever lies hurt less but cut deeper.

Nancy rolled onto her side. David turned to face her. They regarded one another across the valley of loose blanket dipping between their bodies.

"There's something you're not telling me," Nancy said.

"I guess that's true."

"Why?"

David stared at the darkened ceiling. Whorls of motion and colour danced over the stucco, ocular white noise. "Because I'm afraid you wouldn't believe me."

Nancy mulled this over, a wrinkle folding the ridge between her eyes. "I don't think you're having an affair, if that's what you're afraid of."

David took her hand in his. "I didn't think you would."

"Is it about what happened to Walter?"

After a moment's pause, David nodded.

"Is it a . . . some kind of a gang thing? Like cop killers or something?"

"No, nothing like that," David said, unsure whether or not to call this a lie.

"Are you in danger?"

David let his gaze drift back to the ceiling. "I guess that depends on what you're asking. Is what I'm doing dangerous? Yeah, probably. But I've got a dangerous job. You know that. But am I *in danger*, are you and Brandon in danger?" He squeezed her hand, his eyes meeting hers again. "No. Absolutely not."

She squeezed back. "I love you."

"I love you too."

Sleep came soon after.

45: SERIOUS AS A HEART ATTACK

THE CAR PULLED up shortly after dawn. Iman heard it from her spot on the futon. She cradled a mug of tea in her lap. It was many hours before the typical start to her day, yet she was grateful her ride had come. Her sleep had been patchy and sour, a roundabout wander through a wasteland of exhaustion and bad dreams, and her once-cozy apartment now felt hostile and alien, thin sheets of domesticity wallpapering over war-zone rubble. Even her morning tea smelled burnt and ugly. The car honked once, a ginger tap on the horn. Iman grabbed her bag, dumped her tea in the sink, and left.

By the looks of him, Moore had slept no better than she had. Baggy flesh waddled the hollows beneath heavy-lidded eyes, and stubble tinted his jaw a ruddy brown. A cigarette dangled between his index and middle fingers, smoke curling out the rolled-down window. He took a drag and flicked the butt into the street as Iman got inside, stuffing her bag into the back seat.

"I wasn't sure you'd be up," he said.

"Yeah, well. Couldn't sleep."

"I guess it's catching."

"I guess."

They drove in silence, pulsing along the arterial stretch of the QEW before hooking north on the 400. City became suburbs became farmers' fields gone fallow, autumn's harvest plowed under and the cover crops yet to grow. The radio grew warbled and patchy with static. Moore punched around some other stations and, dissatisfied with the selection, switched over to the CD player. Iman braced herself for a barrage of macho hard rock. Instead, the sound of a revving car engine preceded a nervous, jazzy bassline she recognized immediately. She listened to the opening vocals for confirmation. Sure enough, they kicked in with a hoarse, breathy rush, barking the first line in a single gust: "Seriousasaheartattack! Makes me feel this way . . . "

"Is this Double Nickels?"

Moore smiled. "Good ear."

"I didn't know cops liked good music."

He shrugged "I think there's a Bad Company CD in the glove box if this is blowing your mind."

The Minutemen's frenetic, desultory opus took her mind off of the trip for a while, but she eventually found herself picking at scabs of anxiety until the blood ran fresh. Was Brian okay? What were they doing to him? She assumed Luka and his cronies were heading to Whitetooth Falls, but what if she and Moore got there and found it abandoned?

Moreover, what if they got there and found it wasn't?

Moore seemed to sense her apprehension. "I can still turn around, you know. I've got time. There's a GO Train station in Barrie that'll get you home. I can spot you the fare."

Iman listened for the voice of rational self-interest to pipe up, to try and goad her into accepting. She heard only silence. "My mind's made up, detective."

"At this point, I think you might as well start calling me David." He reached across her lap and opened the glove compartment. "And if you're set on coming, you're going to need this."

In the glove box, resting atop a cradle of folded maps and insurance slips, was a handgun. Its bore, though pointed away from Iman toward some arbitrary point in the back seat, seemed to peer at her like an accusing eye.

"It's got a full clip. The first three in the chamber'll be silver-plated. The rest are just your regular hollow points. I got the other silvers in mine. With luck, my supplier will get us more, but for now we've each got a three-wolf limit on our permits. You ever shoot a gun before?"

Iman shook her head.

David clucked his tongue. "I guessed as much. It's not rocket science. It's an automatic, no need to rack it. Point and shoot. The trick is to get as close as possible. Pistols aren't meant for shooting more than twenty yards or so, anyway. That gunslinger stuff's for the movies."

Iman picked up the gun, her finger conscientiously keeping clear of the trigger. She rested it on open palms, studying its angles and the graceful fluting of its barrel. It was heavier than she expected, as if its deadly potential compounded its density.

"Is that what we're going to do? Shoot them, I mean?"

"If we have to. I'd prefer we didn't."

"But you think we will."

David didn't reply. Iman ran her thumb along the length of the barrel.

"What if there's a lot of them? I mean, we already know Luka has this other guy with him, plus the woods people Motes told us about."

"My beef is with Luka and the man who shot Melissa. The others can pitch a tent and stay the winter, for all I care."

"I'm not so sure they'll feel the same way about you."

"Probably not."

Iman nodded. "So it's you and me against the world, huh? Like Thelma and Louise."

Moore laughed. "Hopefully we won't need to drive off a cliff. And it's not just you and me. I've got backup."

Iman arched an eyebrow. "Backup? Like other cops?"

"About the exact opposite. But an ally's an ally."

I wonder if your precinct would agree, Iman thought, though the idea of any sort of ally was immeasurably comforting—she would've buddied up with Hitler at this point if he agreed to watch her back. "Where are they?"

"Making their own way north. I can't say for sure where Luka might have eyes once we get into the boonies, and I'd just as soon not make the connection too obvious."

Iman felt like she was inundating the man with questions, but there was one more she needed to ask if she was to have any hope of feeling better about the situation. "These people, do they know what they're up against? I mean, are they, I dunno . . . werewolf hunters?"

"No, but they will be soon."

She felt no better. "Okay, but what if they're not cut out to be werewolf hunters? What if they don't have what it takes?"

David kept his eyes locked on the road ahead of him, his voice calm and square. "Then they'll be prey."

46: THE MAIN COURSE

"**BEAT THAT, CHUMPS**," said Nails, slamming down an ace. The tattered remnants of his earlobes wobbled obscenely.

"Pass," muttered Sarah, sitting cross-legged to his left. An ursine biker with flaming skulls tattooed on each elbow shrugged off his turn with a grumble and a twitch of his red-brown beard. That left only Derek to play or concede. He pondered his cards with phony indecision, baiting Nails with a speckle of hope, and laid down the two of diamonds. He swept the pot without waiting for Nails to top him, and laid down a trio of fours. A smug smile glimmered on his lips as he scanned his opponents.

"Anyone?"

As expected, the trio responded with sullen silence. He followed up his play with a more prosaic pair of eights, ignored their ripostes of nines, jacks, and queens, slammed down a joker and held up his now empty hands, twiddling his fingers tauntingly.

"Another term for El Presidente. The will of the people triumphs again."

Nails pounced on the vacuum left by Derek's victory, playing a pair of otherwise unplayable threes. Derek's sally had sapped the players of their upper pairs, leaving Sarah to toss down two sixes and the biker—Derek thought his name might be Stanley—to growl out another pass. Nails popped down a two and finished with a six.

"Vice Presidente!" he cried, and raised his palm for a high five, which Derek ignored. Sarah played an ace, ten, and six to empty her hand, leaving the biker clutching the remnants of his defeat. He threw the cards down in disgust and stalked off. Derek watched him go, wondering to himself if he shouldn't make a bit more of an effort to be civil. These three were the only members of Luka's pack currently willing to sit down with him. Now it appeared that number had shrunk to two. His survivor's instinct should be crying out for allies, but for whatever reason, he couldn't bring himself to care.

Sarah gathered up the cards and gave them a brisk overhand shuffle. Derek waved her off before she had a chance to deal out the next hand. "I'm with whats-his-face on this one. Time to retire undefeated."

Sarah snorted. "You were asshole three times, vice asshole another two."

"Undefeated in recent memory, then."

"C'mon, Matchbook," said Nails. "We can switch to crazy eights."

"You two enjoy." Derek stood up, wiped dry pine needles from the seat of his pants, and left the cramped hollow they'd designated their games parlor. He took out his phone to check the time, remembered the battery was long dead, and took a ballpark estimate from the position of the sun instead. He pegged it at a little before noon, sighed. The minutes oozed by like ketchup from a glass bottle. Tonight, at least, was the night. Luka would either make good on his promise or prove the whole thing a crock. Doubtless he could cook up some story to keep some of his lackeys in thrall for another month, but Derek wouldn't be among them. He'd spent the last days squirreling away a cache of canned goods and dried fruit beneath the cavernous roots of an oak tree, and had acquired enough to last him, by his estimation, three days—five if he stretched it. A far cry from a woodsman, he'd nevertheless familiarized himself enough with the forest to know north from south, and three days of solid walking should get him within kissing distance of civilization. From there he had money to buy a ride to the nearest Coach Canada junction, or the Governor to steal a ride if the townsfolk were less than accommodating.

Luka paced a crescent-shaped ridge of limestone thrusting from the clearing's topsoil, hands clasped behind his back. His mouth grew thinner and more pinched with each passing hour. The stink of his impatience drove everyone to the fringes of the clearing, leaving the center his and his alone. The pack's view of him mutated as his spirits darkened, swelling from reverence to a kind of superstitious dread. Even the forest people seemed wary of him. Motes—shed of his nylon bindings and instead attached to a tree by a length of chain—was the only person, apart from Derek, who dared to enter Luka's inner radius. The anger or bitterness he'd first exhibited was gone, but so too, it seemed, was his fear.

Derek gave the pack leader a wide berth. He was no sycophant, but he knew better than to poke a bear when its blood was up, and Luka's veins were a few PSI short of blowing a gasket. "Majka" was still nowhere to be found. Derek failed to grasp her role, but he took it by Luka's relentless pacing to be an important one. And if the full moon was her deadline, she was cutting it awfully close.

The land sloped down at the southern edge of the clearing, descending into clutches of cedar and fir and pine, between which packmates and forest people eked out accommodations—always like with like. The two groups barely commingled, lacking a common language or even a general grasp of the nature of the other's existence. The forest people lay on beds of bare earth, or skinned rabbits speared by deftly-fired arrows; the packmates scratched solemnly at bug bites or strung spare shirt awnings ineptly from branches or sprayed lighter fluid into dying fires. Derek dodged both camps and wound along a rocky cleft towards the pebbled shore of a stream. He scooped a handful of water into his mouth, sweet and sharply cold. Trees formed a natural palisade on all sides, breached only by random embrasures through which flew arrows of sunlight. At the far side of the glen sat the Asian kid, his arms and legs bound with handcuffs and twines of nylon rope, respectively, the cuffs further padlocked to a birch tree by ten feet of rusty chain. Derek hunkered down next to him.

"Hey there, slick. How's it hangin'?"

The kid made no reply. His wrists were red and chafed. He never said much, and spent a lot of the time crying, but somehow Derek found his company oddly satisfying. Perhaps the kid's predicament made Derek's situation seem that much more desirable—at least no one had put *him* in shackles.

"It must get pretty boring, eh, just sitting here watching the stream. Well, I gotta tell you, I've been all over this damn forest and there isn't a whole hell of a lot you're missing. The rail shots and blow jobs are conspicuously absent, you could say. I mean, you could always ask around with them forest people, but I'm guessing they wouldn't be all that accommodating."

The kid's head snapped up. His voice creaked out gravelly and hoarse.

"Look, if you let me go, I swear I'll tell everyone I ran away, had like a nervous breakdown or something. I won't say anything about you or any of these people, I promise."

"Of course you won't. Who the fuck would believe you? I mean, you'd probably peg me in a lineup if you ever got the chance—"

"I wouldn't!"

Derek touched a finger to the kid's lips, silencing him. "You would, and you'd love it. Don't shit a shitter, kid. I'd do the same thing, I was you. Point is, you could say me and Luka kidnapped you, some sort of half-baked ransom plan maybe, but the rest of it? Dragging you up north to meet half the fucking cast of Lord of the Rings? Please. If it were just that, maybe I would let you go." In truth, Derek would under no circumstances let someone in the kid's situation leave his sight alive, but why let facts ruin a good bit of rhetoric? "But the boss man, he's got some big plans a-brewing, and as I understand it you feature in 'em pretty prominently."

The kid rubbed the line of abraded skin circling his wrists. He hid his face from Derek, but the liquid warble of his voice betrayed his tears. "That doesn't make any sense. I'm nothing to the guy. He only knows I even exist because I was in the apartment when he showed up."

"What can I say? Wrong place, wrong time, friend. I've been there."

"But Motes was the guy he was after, and he's got him now. What could he want with me?"

Derek polished his fingernails on the lapel of his shirt. "The guy said something about a ritual later tonight, after dark. Some sort of religious ceremony. And a feast. I'm guessing you're an important part of that."

"Like . . . like a guest of honor?"

Derek's smile was merciless, vulpine. "More like the main course." He patted the boy on the head and left him to shit himself in peace. He felt several pounds lighter, as if he'd just hired a porter to take a burdensome piece of luggage off his hands.

The gulley was easier to descend than ascend, lined as it was with a dermis of loose stones and powdery gravel. Hot wires of exertion crisscrossed his thighs as he huffed his way back to higher ground. The pockets of idlers had disappeared from the trees, drawn inward to a chattering cluster ringing the limestone clearing. Derek muscled his way into the center—taking care to shoulder only packmates and not the more formidably-armed and mercurially-countenanced forest folk—where Luka stood in a posture of unchecked rapture, arms drawn rigidly down and out, fingers splayed, chest thrust forward. He dropped to his knees before a phalanx of aged forest people, hands resting solemnly on the handles of their weapons. They parted in a fluid ripple, revealing the slow but stately totter of a woman aged beyond possible reckoning. She stood compact but unbent, her movements slow in a manner that seemed to Derek wizened and graceful, rather than infirm. Her skin, deeply lined, looked less like leather than the pitted granite of a statue dredged from the silt-sheathed ruins of some sunken kingdom. She touched two fingers to Luka's forehead and spoke briefly in a language Derek couldn't understand.

Majka, it seemed, had finally arrived.

47: NO ACCIDENT

THE FOREST SWALLOWED the world. It spread on either side of the road like the jaws of a great green whale, filter-feeding on sojourners foolhardy enough to drive into its impossible expanse. Outcrops of limestone poked tiny carbuncles into its flank, and a network of varicose rivers pumped through the overgrowth. The highway sloped into a valley where the trees rose up and eclipsed the view. After that initial glimpse, the forest's immensity could no longer be seen but only felt, the crushing weight of timber squeezing in on them like deep water against a submarine's hull. Iman put a hand to the cold window, her face close enough to paint splotches of fog on the glass.

"Jesus," she said. "How the hell are we going to even find this place?"

"The GPS'll get us close," David said, tapping the unit suctioned to the windshield. "But according to it, a few of the roads we need to take don't actually exist. So from there we follow the ordinance maps I printed out. You'll see 'em in the glove compartment."

Iman pulled out a piece of glossy accordion-folded paper, unfolding a section and spreading it out flat against her lap. Blue highlighter zigzagged over a network of thin black lines. A few bits of road had been circled, question marks scrawled next to the indicated area.

"I tried to verify the path as much as possible using Google Earth. The images this far north are pretty low-res, though, so not everything could be scouted out that well. The circles are the bits that looked sketchiest to me. Roads that might be washed out or have grown over or just don't exist at all."

Iman bit her lip. "That's a lot of places to get stuck."

"True, but I tried to be cautious. Plus a lot of those are pretty deep into the bush. As long as we get the car farther than the first few, we should have enough time to go on foot from there."

Overgrowth whittled the road down to a single lane, its shorn edges ragged with cattails and Queen Anne's lace. A dusting of snow bleached the foliage white and lent a physical character to the wind, its myriad fingers stirring up road dust and ruffling the trees. The car rounded a bend and nearly collided with the trunk of a toppled cedar.

David slammed on the brakes. A rush of expletive-tinged air wheezed through his lips. Tires squealed over gravelly asphalt. The car lurched to a halt inches from the mangled branches, their ends snapped into caltrops keen to puncture a tire. The seatbelt bit into Iman's chest. She worked a hand into the gap between the belt and her. When it gave a little, she undid the clasp. The nylon strip retracted with a prim *whizz!*

"Well, shit," David said. He drummed his fingers on the steering wheel, primed a cigarette, and took a drag, exhaling as he stepped outside to keep the smoke from backdrafting into the cab. Particles of fine powdery snow piled on the windshield, giving the world outside a faint and ghostly appearance. David pondered the tree, hands on hips, cigarette dangling from the corner of his mouth. He paced its length, hunkered down, stared for some time at a spot beyond the treeline. The cigarette jigged from one side of his mouth to the other, trailing a thin filament of smoke. He ventured into the trees, vanishing from sight for a few endless minutes, leaving Iman alone to concoct various horror movie plots in her head until he re-emerged, wiping pine needles from the shoulder of his jacket. A gust of chilled air probed its fingers into the car as David slipped back inside. He severed them with a brisk tug on the handle and snubbed out his cigarette, half-smoked, in the ashtray.

"That tree's no accident. Someone dragged it across the road. Several someones, judging by the size of it."

Iman peered over the dashboard at the felled cedar. It stretched well past the shoulders of the road in both directions, its trunk too wide for her to wrap her arms around. "Are you sure it didn't just fall over? It looks too big for people to move it by hand."

David shook his head. "There's drag marks. Subtle, but they're there. Also, there's no stump matching where the tree was cut. Whoever moved it dragged it a long way, likely through bush as thick as this, or thicker."

"So what do we do?"

"Well, we can't move the thing. And the angle's all wrong for a winch, even if we managed to rig one up."

David blew air through both nostrils. He pulled his phone out of his jacket. "At least I've got some signal, gods be praised." He dialled a number. Iman heard a voice answer, its words too muffled to make out. David and the speaker had a terse exchange, of which Iman only caught David's half. "The road's blocked. Logging route off the 63. Too damn far. I'm gonna try another route, but I'm not optimistic. We may need to walk in. Meet-up's the same, but we may not have as much buffer as I'd hoped. Right." David pocketed the phone. He hooked one arm over his seat's headrest and backed up for the better part of a kilometre. Eventually the road widened enough to allow a three-point—or in this case, more like a seven-point—turn.

They retraced their steps for half an hour while Iman scouted possible alternate routes on the ordinance map. A left turn led to a gravel road that bounced them up a steep incline and down a furrowed cleft in the rocky soil. The suspension bobbed and trembled like a punch-drunk boxer as the chassis caught potholes on its chin. They bottomed out on several occasions with a sickening scrape of gravel against the car's undercarriage, but the road was wide and cut a true and fairly straight line north towards an old quarry, which gaped like a giant pockmark on the cheek of the Boreal Shield. The road skirted around the quarry and narrowed to a logging route cut into the forest floor. They followed it for half an hour until another felled tree once again blocked their path. David chewed the corner of his mouth. He checked the time on his phone and looked up to the sun. Blowing snow draped the sky in an albino haze.

"What now?" Iman asked.

David shrugged. "Now we walk."

48: THE MOON WINS

THE SUN SKIMMED over the treetops, allowing shadows to seep from the forest's interior and pool in its clefts and clearings. The cold air made phantoms of Derek's breath, each exhalation twisted and tangible and doomed. He rubbed his hands together and jammed them in the pockets of his jeans, positioning his thumb in a streamlined fashion that permitted a quick draw if needed. The sense of impending change was palpable. It rumbled through the earth, the flywheel of some vast machine gradually gathering speed.

Majka led the party through the woods, cutting a pathless trajectory effortlessly through the thickest growth. Brambles parted for her like mist, and trees swung aside like strings of beads decorating a doorway. The forest people followed with similar grace. Luka and his pack struggled to keep up, stumbling over roots and stubbing toes on nodules of moss-draped limestone and swatting aside low-hanging branches, their needles raking across naked cheeks. Trundling behind the eerie silence of the forest folk, the city-dwellers seemed almost deliberately noisy, a chorus of groans and grunted epithets and rustling clothing. Frost-stiffened twigs crunched underfoot, each snap a gunshot in the sylvan stillness. The Asian kid walked with his face scrunched in obvious discomfort. Though his legs had been unshackled, his hands remained bound behind his back, leaving him prey to every gouging branch and bramble that happened upon his unprotected face. Motes, though likewise bound, seemed not to notice the branches at all. He muscled through them not with strength so much as a kind of sublime numbness, his face bearing the expressionless countenance of a man reading a news article of no great interest.

The forest thickened as they progressed, congealing into a semi-solid tangle of hedge and bark and boughs before yielding in an instant to the sharp decline of a gravelly bank over which the forest folk flowed neat as water. Luka's pack took the drop less nimbly, catching frantically at tree limbs or sliding on sore asses or tumbling headfirst over the edge. The descent was steep but brief, five feet where the ground lurched downward before resuming its gentler gait, trees replaced by bulrushes and sprigs of hemlock and dandelion. A shallow but briskly flowing stream cut through the bedrock, its current dappled with foamy bergs of white water. The hoarse and constant roar of falling water crackled its organic static somewhere upriver.

Majka waded knee-deep into the water, her bare feet cradling the pebbled riverbed, and began walking upstream. The forest folk followed, indifferent to the water's glacial chill. Derek preferred to walk along the riverbank where the ground was less even but dry, as did much of Luka's pack. Scarped earth hemmed them towards the water as they progressed, forcing a protracted slog through a churning sludge of silt and sediment. River mud clung to the bottom of Derek's boots, transforming his feet into misshapen hooves. He scraped the treads clean on passing trees at each patch of dry ground, only to accumulate a fresh layer a few metres down the way. Mosquitoes whined in his ear, their silence followed by the itchy sting of a proboscis piercing some unguarded parcel of flesh. He fluttered his hands around his head like a lunatic and slapped the back of his neck at random, hoping to nail a few of the bastards through the law of averages.

The steep earth fell back from the river, smoothing into a mud-caked amphitheatre bordered by a ring of burly evergreens, stern and gladiatorial in their cheek-by-jowl stance. The escarpment remained on one side, over which a torrent of rushing white water plunged endlessly, stirring the shallow water below into a mania of pale foam. The waterfall, bifurcated by a horn of dolostone, fell in two white pillars resembling tusks.

"Whitetooth Falls, I'm guessing," Derek said.

Luka grinned back at him, his own incisors a mirror of the waterfall's alabaster flow. "Good name, ain't it?"

"Call it Swinging Dick River for all I care, so long as it means we don't gotta keep walking."

Luka grabbed Motes by the shoulder and manhandled him into the water, where Majka stood calmly parting the current. Slipping off his boots and socks—wet but not quite soaked through yet, which was how he wanted to keep it—Derek followed, interested in catching this exchange.

The three stood in a rough triangle. Majka and Luka faced one another, while Motes adopted a moderator's stance between them, his back to the falls. Though the water barely passed his knees, the current was swift, forcing him to continually shift his weight and adjust his footing to avoid toppling face-first into the water. His bound arms made this even more of a challenge, and he nearly slipped twice before turning to Luka with a snort of annoyance.

"Are the handcuffs strictly necessary? I'll only break them in an hour or so."

Luka considered a moment, then fished a key from his pocket and unlocked Motes' hands. "You try to run on me before the moon takes you, you're a dead man, translator or not."

Motes rubbed his freed wrists. "Trust me. I've nowhere worth running to."

With Motes unshackled, Luka turned and spoke directly to Majka. Motes followed on the heel of his words, interpreting in his stiff but confident Russian.

"I brought my pack like I promised, Majka. I'm ready to claim my rights as True Silver."

Mother's reply filtered through Motes' tonally flat delivery. "She says you're still young yet, but she admires your spirit. The right's yours if you want it. Your pack must drink the silver water from your hands before the moon rises. They'll drink again from your paw print once you've undergone the change. The moon will take them and bind them to you."

Derek didn't like the sound of that last part. It sounded awfully . . . permanent. His bare feet, inoculated to the water's chill, squeezed river mud between their toes. He watched as Luka flagged over his pack and raised handful after handful of river water to their lips. They lapped and sipped the liquid one by one, their eyes alight with an almost religious fervor. Sarah shot him a small ironic smile before taking her own brief baptism, though the look on her face as she drank was no less earnest than the others. Something beneath her skin seemed to change, a subdermal contortion of muscles and connective tissue. As if a creature still half-formed shifted in its chrysalis, its minute postural adjustments meant to accommodate its coming metamorphosis.

Luka motioned Derek forward with a finger. He scooped a fresh handful of water from the river and held it under Derek's nose, close enough to reveal the bits of dirt imbedded in the whorls and ridges of his callused fingertips. The liquid in his cupped palms was so clear it seemed almost luminescent, a quicksilver tonic pregnant with a queer glow. A sharp, pungent, musky odour wafted from it, a smell of blood and moonlight. His parted lips hung suspended over the water's still surface. The Governor seemed to pulse against his chest with its own cold heartbeat, two silver bullets glinting in the darkness of its chambers. A quick glance around confirmed such a move would be suicide, and Luka's posture made it clear he would brook no backpedalling.

The water was flavourless despite its smell, though alive with its peculiar effervescence, as if carbonated with a gas heavier than air. Derek felt it settle in a heavy mist beneath his tongue, tendrils ebbing and whirlpooling on the currents of his breath. He mimed a swallow and wiped his lips with a theatrical swipe of his wrist, allowing the bulk of the liquid to trickle down his forearm. Its tingling residue remained on his gums, a mouthwash sizzle that lingered no matter how much saliva he rinsed across it. He had no idea whether the amount he'd spat out mitigated the water's effect, or even what that effect might be. All he knew was that this shit was seriously hinky.

A svelte old man in furs jogged into the river, his ornately braided beard penduluming with each step. Muscles twitched and rippled beneath wrinkled flesh. He barked a torrent of hoarse Russian at Majka, who listened impassively, nodding to herself. Luka glanced over at Motes, who knew what was expected of him without prompting.

"There are people in the woods. A couple dozen of them, about half a kilometre south of here."

Luka cracked his knuckles. He directed his words to Majka. "That's on me. You want me and my boys to deal with 'em, Majka?"

Motes related the question. Majka shook her head, spoke a few words in terse Russian.

"She says let them come," Motes said, glancing at the darkening sky. "They'll know us as we are."

Luka's smile bore an impossible quantity of teeth. "Bet your ass they will."

He whistled, gathering his pack. Derek stood to his right as he spoke, cheating half towards him and half towards the crowd.

"You guys got your first taste, but the real fun comes once the moon's full. In the meantime, I want you to take Motes and the kid upriver a bit, on the far bank. Find a spot out of the way and hang tight."

"There gonna be words, chief?" asked a scraggly-armed packmate awash with tattoos.

"Could be. Either way, I want our offering protected. You lot keep a close eye on him. The professor too. He don't so much as go for a piss without my say-so, get it?"

The packmates tromped into the woods, carrying the Asian kid in tow and nudging Motes along ahead of them. Luka watched them go with the air of a parent whose child has done something foolish but endearing.

"They're a good bunch, eh?"

"I guess," said Derek, who in truth couldn't disagree more.

"But they ain't blooded like you, bro. That'll change, but for now they're better off out of the way. You, on the other hand, I want right here. If shit goes south, find a safe spot and cover my ass. With luck, the assholes won't get here 'til full dark."

"I'm guessing they're gonna aim for daylight, if they got any idea what they're up against."

Luka shrugged. "They're fucked either way, but I'd like my own little piece of the action. And I won't get it unless that bad boy is shinin' full and unimpeded."

He thrust his thumb skyward. The moon, full and clearly visible, dangled above a cauldron of orange-red sky. Luka licked his lips, fingers flexing. "It sort of itches. In the back of my eyeballs, mostly. Like it's tuggin' on me and the sun's tuggin' back."

"So what happens when the sun sets?"

Luka's lips disappeared into his mouth, reappeared red and slick with saliva. "The moon wins."

49: JUSTICE

THE FOREST WAS daunting enough in a car; on foot, it was positively predatory. It had loomed over them from the first, invisible eyes staring from a million outposts along its branches, towering trunks cutting the sunlight to ribbons. The windshield had muted their presence somewhat, rendered them inert and passive, trapped them under glass. Seen over the steering wheel, the trees took on the sensory flatness of movies, mere images of immensity projected on a screen.

Without the car, things changed. No barrier stood between the forest and David's other senses. He could hear the crunch of dead pine needles, the scurrying of unseen creatures through the underbrush, the distant fighter-jet whine of mosquitos buzzing past his ears; smell the wintergreen snap of autumn foliage draped like a coroner's sheet over summer's corpse; feel the nip of the wind as it stalked him, whispering its hoarse threats of a coming blizzard. He smoothed out the front of his jacket to block out a draft worming between its buttons and did his best to ignore the solemn gaze of the trees.

A cleft in the treeline allowed him a passing glimpse at the sun. He winced at its low vantage in the sky. A peek at his cell phone's clock confirmed how much of the afternoon had passed, ground to dust beneath time's implacable millstone. He checked the map without breaking stride, confirming to the best of his ability where they were and how much farther they had to go before moonrise—the answers being "who the fuck knows?" and "too fucking far," respectively.

He'd deliberately avoided venturing into the woods too far in advance, knowing the alien terrain put him at an immense disadvantage, and that the odds of his being spotted, tracked, and eliminated grew with every extra minute he spent within its stifling grip. The thought of a roadblock hadn't even occurred to him. A dumb oversight, sure—but what oversight wasn't, in retrospect?

"Are we okay?" Iman asked. She'd clearly noticed his reaction to the time. David ironed the creases of worry from the corners of his mouth.

"It'll be tight," he admitted. "Motes said the change doesn't happen until the sun's fully set, but he could be off by a few minutes. I'd like to hedge our bets as much as possible."

"What if the sun goes down and we still haven't found them?"

David scratched beneath his chin. "Then we hunt in the dark."

Iman swallowed audibly but didn't protest. She held the Beretta with the white-knuckled grip of a civilian without any firearm experience, treating it less like a tool than a vicious and semi-feral animal on a frayed leash.

For his own part, David felt no hesitation whatsoever, though he barely knew where he was going and had no idea what he'd find when he got there. His usual approach to dicey situations, planning for all conceivable contingencies and acquiring all possible foreknowledge, fell flat in the face of this sort of primordial conflict. How do you plan for a fight against werewolves? Where do you get intelligence on something that isn't even supposed to exist? The answer, it seemed to him, was raw instinct, and his was bristling like a dog at its chain.

Just let me get Luka. The others can run back to Russia or wherever they come from, but Luka has to go. Please. He wondered, not for the first time, how much of his decision not to go to Chief Delduca was logic and how much was vendetta. No matter how deep he dug into his own motivations, he couldn't find an acceptable answer.

His cell phone chirped in his pants pocket. He pulled it out and answered. "Yeah?"

"Where the fuck are you, man?" crackled a voice, its corners rough and pixelated with static.

"Can't you see me? I've got signal, the GPS app should pick me up."

"Yeah, I see your little blip. Why can't I see you face to face? We've been waiting an hour here."

David doubted this but didn't question it; he was too tired and it didn't matter. "I told you, we hit a roadblock."

"You think *we* didn't?"

"Maybe you got a lot farther before you did. How should I know?"

"I don't care, buddy, but you best leg it up here double-time. There's guys in the woods."

"Shit."

"Yeah. Shaggy fuckers, dressed like Indians outta them old Western flicks, 'cept they're white."

"They spotted you?"

"Let 'em look, man. I'm just sayin', you best get here pronto. Sun's settin', and as far as I'm concerned this show goes on with or without you, *capisce*?"

"Just hold on. I'm almost there."

David picked up his pace, walking with a brisk but stiff-legged stride. Aches clenched their thorny fists around his knees, squeezing the fluid in his kneecaps into wads of pulpy misery. His ribcage felt like something crudely hodgepodged together using twine and scrap metal. He fished two Percodan from the bottle in his jacket pocket and dry-swallowed them.

After forty-five minutes of walking, they finally found Ballaro leaning against the trunk of a cedar. He looked almost surreally out of place in his double-breasted suit and wingtip loafers. The forest's scant light gave his many rings a firefly gleam. A black duffel bag hung from one shoulder, its bottom bulging with an uneven payload. He raised an eyebrow upon seeing Iman, but neither introduced himself nor asked what she was doing there. An aura of grim focus hung about him, palpable as the musky odour emanating from the pits of his suit.

"You don't go hiking much, do you?" David asked.

"This'll be the only time, one way or the other."

David nodded at the truth of this. "You get more silver?"

"Cleared half the mines in South America. I'd rather do the fuckers with lead if I can help it, though. It's cheaper."

"You got any to spare?"

Ballaro looked at David's pistol and smiled. "Not in that puny calibre. Sorry, pal. Custom orders are tricky, and it was easier to make one batch." He patted his bag affectionately. "Looks like you're stuck with your half dozen."

David gave a noncommittal shrug in reply, though beneath the surface he was annoyed. There was likely some truth to the claim, but he caught a whiff of bullshit along with it. Likely Ballaro wanted to call the shots, and he'd have an easier time of it if he controlled the bulk of the firepower. Well, let him make his little power play. Three bullets should be enough for David's business anyway. If it wasn't, he was probably doomed no matter how much heat he was packing.

"Where the posse?" he asked.

"Fanned out. Just gotta say the word, we can ice these motherfuckers in thirty seconds."

"Let's hope it doesn't come to that."

"The hell you mean, doesn't come to that? I didn't come out to the woods for a fuckin' social visit. These assholes are meat."

"A lot of those guys are petty criminals, nothing more. I'm not going to have them murdered without cause."

"And Luka? You gonna try and snap the cuffs on wolfy too?"

David said nothing. His pistol seemed to pound against his ribcage with its own quickening pulse.

Ballaro laughed, a hard barking sound that seemed to fall out of his mouth. "Thought so. You want blood for blood, same as me. Well, I lost two sons, buddy, and one pelt ain't gonna cover it."

"Our plan works out, you'll get a lot more than one. Shooting a wolf isn't murder. But the guys in Luka's pack are still people."

"Don't be stupid. When my papa fought the krauts in Normandy, you think he walked up onto the beach and asked 'em to turn in their weapons peacefully?"

"This isn't war, Frank. This is justice."

"Peh. Cops. What do any of you know about justice?" Ballaro spat onto the forest floor. "Fine, then. You want to march out there talkin' Miranda rights or whatever, get your brains blown out, be my guest. But we ain't cartin' your dumb corpse home with us."

"I'm glad you approve." David walked off without waiting for Ballaro to reply. He expected the mafioso's pudgy hand to fall on his shoulder, followed by a whispered warning about being flippant with a man of his stature. But the hand never came. Perhaps he felt a begrudging respect for David's bravery.

Or maybe he just looked forward to seeing a cop get shot.

David walked and Iman walked beside him, the two nearly shoulder to shoulder but saying nothing. Sound fell away, the twitter of birds and rustle of squirrels scampering along high branches and the drone of winged insects subsumed by a dense and sludgy roar so constant and inert it could be mistaken for silence: a sound less heard than felt, one that stuffed itself into your ears like cotton and sopped up anything that tried to pass.

Iman stuck a finger in her ear and swivelled it. "You hear that?" she asked.

"Uh-huh." His hand migrated to his belt, where a pistol hung from its police-issue holster.

"What is it?"

"Don't know." He scanned the woods, probing each crook and shadow for the presence of something hostile.

"It almost sounds like running water."

Understanding tolled in his head, crisp and funereal. It echoed off Iman's face a moment later.

"Whitetooth Falls," they said, their voices synchronized and oddly harmonic.

David drew his gun. He walked with it held in a posture of casual readiness, his arms raised but loose, coiled muscles ready to snap into firing position. Iman aped his pose, her grip on the butt awkward and slightly off-kilter. They followed the roar, stepping off the overgrown path and into the thick of the woods for the last fifty metres. David paused at the forest's threshold. He dialed Ballaro.

"I'm going out there."

"God go with you, kid."

David holstered his gun. He pulled out a cigarette and smoked a quarter of it in a single immense drag. The smoke seemed to fill every corner of him, puffing him up to illusory stature. The filter settled in its familiar groove at the side of his mouth.

"So we're doing this?" Iman asked.

David shook his head, the gesture gentle but the will behind it inexorable. "No, Iman. This last bit has to be me alone. I'm acting as an officer of the law."

"So what am I supposed to do? Just watch?"

"Find Motes and Brian. Things could get ugly here, and we're gonna want to keep them as far out of the action as possible."

Iman adjusted her grip on the gun, bringing her index finger in line with the trigger. She ran a thumb along the barrel, picked a fleck of dust off of the sight. "Do you think they're okay?"

"I wish I knew. I sure hope so."

Iman seemed to accept this. She dropped her gun hand to her side, tapping the barrel against her thigh.

David's cigarette burned down to the filter. He dropped the butt and snubbed out the embers with the heel of his shoe. A final curl of tobacco escaped through his nostrils. He looked at Iman and gave what he hoped was a reassuring smile.

"You find those guys, bring 'em back the way we came. Keep Ballaro and his boys between Luka's people and you. If they fall back, you fall back faster. Got it?"

Iman nodded. "Good luck."

They shook hands. Sweat slickened David's palm—whether it was his or hers, he couldn't say.

50: BLOOD FOR BLOOD

WHEN THE MAN stepped into plain sight, Derek could scarcely believe his audacity. He came alone, his gun undrawn, hands stuffed in the pockets of his tan overcoat. Stepping cautiously to avoid the mud slicks and shin-snagging crevices in the bedrock, he regarded the two dozen fur-clad warriors with the detached interest of a visiting anthropologist. After roaming their breadth, his gaze settled in on Majka, Luka, and Derek himself, who grinned savagely and mimed a mocking finger-waggle wave.

"Derek McCulloch. You're under arrest for the kidnapping of Brian Wong and Enoch Motes, assault with a deadly weapon, and attempted murder." His voice carried well through the clearing, rising buoyant over the dull roar of Whitetooth Falls. "Lay down any and all weapons and place your hands behind your head."

Luka ran his tongue along the back of his teeth. It made a wet, ugly sound. "You're a little outside your jurisdiction, eh, detective?"

"I could say the same thing about the two of you. Shouldn't you be running petty cons on Ferry Street or gunning down washed-up wise guys in the bus station bathroom?"

Luka extended his arms. "Bigger and better things, bro."

"A funny way to describe life in prison."

Laughing, Luka brushed a rogue pine needle from his shirt. "We'll see how that goes. So yeah, you've given your little cop spiel. And I'm officially resisting arrest. Derek, what about you?"

Derek pressed his tongue to the roof of his mouth, forcing a jet of spittle through the gap in his front teeth. "Shit, what's one more felony at this point, right?"

Luka shrugged. "I see one cop, two perps, and no paddy wagon. Where do we go from here?"

"I suppose I call in my deputies." The detective raised one hand and snapped his fingers. The sound echoed across the clearing. Rustles in the treeline revealed men in full camo, MP5s braced tight against their padded shoulders. Even putting aside the knock-off fatigues, Derek could tell at a glance these weren't enlisted officers. They moved without the stiff-shouldered bravado of badges, their stride sleek and predatory. He struggled to place them in some sort of context. Mercs? Even if Moore's professional ethics bent far enough to permit them, surely a Niagara Falls cop didn't have that sort of coin lying around.

The answer appeared shortly after the camouflaged men did. Resplendent in a finely-tailored black suit, Frank Ballaro stepped from the foliage. A smile of savage hunger tore across his face. He held an MP7 in his pudgy, ring-encrusted hands, his fingers twiddling compulsively against the handle and barrel.

"Good to see you again, Volchyin. Lucky Luke they called you, right? Looks like your luck's run out."

Pain needled through Derek's jaw. He realised he was clenching his teeth hard enough to crack enamel. Pulling them apart felt like prying up a rusty sewer lid; every muscle in his body threw itself into the action. His finger wriggled into the Governor's trigger guard, traced lovingly up and down the crescent of metal. Even if everything else about this lunatic expedition turned out to be a bust, putting a bullet in that smug asshole's fat face would make the whole thing worthwhile.

Luka, for his part, was unfazed by Ballaro's presence. "I guess we'll see, won't we?"

The smile sutured shut into a wrinkled frown. The man's whole face seemed to collapse, become almost orc-like in its animosity. "You coward piece of shit. You think you can kill my boys and I'm just gonna forget?"

"Blood for blood, padre. My babushka sends her regards."

The cop spoke in the placating tones of a salesman who senses a client getting away from him. "Still not too late to give yourself up, Derek. I've got Ballaro's word you can turn yourself in with no harm to you. But if you opt out, well . . . sunset's still a few minutes away. More than enough time for Ballaro's boys to punch your boss's ticket."

Luka smiled. "That's where you're wrong, bro. These guys? They're old country, man. Pure bloodline. I ran with them in the silver. I know. They don't bow to the moon. The moon bows to them."

With that, he dropped to his knees and hell leapfrogged over him.

51: SILVER SLUGS

A RIPPLE RAN along David's spine. The air turned prickly and cold, as if each molecule gained a sudden static charge. A surfeit of gigawatts poised on some precarious electromagnetic precipice, ready to surge out and incinerate its unwitting target with the slightest jostling. David froze to an extent he didn't know himself capable. Even the flora in his gut seemed to pause, a stasis so absolute his thoughts themselves hung suspended.

The moment didn't so much pass as get torn to shreds by the shrapnel of lunatic howling. Two dozen fur-clad sojourners writhed in hellish metamorphosis. The clearing crackled with an agony of popping joints and lengthening bones and stretching sinew. Ballaro's men clutched their MP5s to their chest and watched, transfixed, as a motley mess of savages transformed into shapes their minds could scarcely digest.

Ballaro was the first to break his paralysis. He stepped into the oncoming tsunami of fur and teeth, submachine gun levelled to chest height. Not a speck of fear or uncertainty blemished his face, his cheeks and forehead still and lineless as a warrior's bronze mask.

"You fucks, you kill my boys, huh? Fuck you!" he bellowed, his finger tight around the trigger.

David dove onto his belly to avoid the crossfire. His elbows sank into river muck. A current-tussled wave splashed his face and he came up sputtering, eyes blinking back the silty water.

The MP7's muzzle strobed madly, filling the clearing with a percussive roar. Ballaro raked bullets back and forth over the monstrous wolf-people, who absorbed their punishments with shudders and grimaces but kept coming. The others soon joined in to the same pitiful effect.

David rose to his knees, took aim at the nearest creature, and fired. The report of his shot carried no louder than the scores of others—was probably in anything quieter, being lower calibre—but seemed fuller, somehow. It kicked in his chest like a kettle drum. The slug took the wolf-thing in the jaw and exploded in a starburst of silver-white radiance. The wolf-thing's head vanished from the snout up, replaced by a fountain of blood and brain matter. It toppled into the water, its long limbs withering and shedding clumps of greyish hair.

Two left, he thought, his eyes sweeping the horde. *Two to kill two dozen. How's that add up?*

"The silver!" he screamed, his voice a ragged whisper beneath the pounding gunfire. "Use the fucking silver!"

The silver slugs were in separate magazines—they hadn't been able to mint nearly enough to waste on bursts of full auto. The plan was to thin the herd with a submachine spray of good ol' fashioned lead, then switch ammo and pick off any changelings with single-shot precision. In his rage, Ballaro seemed to either have forgotten this or decided he didn't care, the simple act of spewing lead at his children's killer sufficient to scratch the visceral itch of vengeance plaguing his soul. His men looked less invested, but in their terror they too had forgotten the plan. They worked their MP5s back and forth as if using them to swat at a swarm of hornets, their eyes huge and white. David watched helplessly as the wolf-things closed in, rage and hunger dribbling from their open jaws.

52: HUNT

"**JESUS CHRIST,**" Derek whispered as the spectacle unfurled before him.

By rights Ballaro had the monsters hopelessly outgunned, but he and his might as well have been packing pea shooters for all the good their subbies were doing. Barrels flopped this way and that like hoses in the hands of incompetent firemen, spraying water over a grease fire of canine fury. A few of the men turned and fled; others dug desperately in the pockets of their camouflage jumpsuits. Those who stayed faced the first wave of charging wolf-things, who sank fangs into bellies with obvious hunger, eviscerating the wise guys as they stared in disbelief at their exposed entrails, some still firing their guns pointlessly into the air.

Derek swallowed. His tongue stuck to the roof of his mouth. His saliva had congealed into a parched and sticky film, salt and moisture rendered into sour glue. He was more comfortable in the presence of death than most men, but the display beyond the river sickened him somewhere deep in his core. Yes, he had killed—for preservation and for profit, in anger and in an assassin's icy calmness—but the killing he'd done had always served some human interest, if not necessarily his own. Did that make it moral? Did that make it just? He expected the answers were no and no, and if a divine judge sat the throne of heaven, he doubted the sentence would fall in his favor. But for all his flaws, he remained an agent of man against other men. In following Luka, Derek realised he'd raised a far darker flag. Whatever was attacking Ballaro beyond the river, it was not his brother. To fight on its side was to betray everyone he'd ever known, including himself. The lowest folds of his cerebellum cried out in Cro-Magnon revulsion, that he might forge an alliance with such beasts.

Traitor, they said. *If you weren't damned before, you sure as hell are now.*

Across the river, Ballaro ejected a half-spent magazine and slammed another into the housing, all the while screaming "You fucks, you kill my fuckin' boys, huh?!" A wolf-thing raked his face while diving onto the man beside him, curled claws peeling back his cheek like wax paper. Ballaro barely flinched. He finished loading and plugged a single shot into the side of the leaping wolf-thing. Its ribcage exploded with silvery light. Though Frank Ballaro just about topped the list of people Derek longed to see ripped to shreds, he still felt in his heart a savage thrust of jubilation as the mobster's bullets found their mark. He buried his celebration in a noncommittal grunt.

Luka had no need to mask such feelings. He growled low in his throat, an inhuman sound that rattled Derek's spine, and narrowed his eyes at the kingpin, his lips curling upward as the other wolves rounded on him. Two leapt for his throat and were pulled back by one of their own, a creature far larger than the rest, with sleek grey fur hackled spine-stiff along its muscular back.

Majka.

She loomed over Ballaro like a great steel sickle, teeth and fangs converging into a single ruinous arc. Ballaro brandished his gun as if it were a conquering knight's sword, thrusting towards her heart. He fired twice before her claws met his throat, parting him into twin curtains of meat and bone. Exit wounds burst from her back, spewing columns of white light.

"Motherfucker!" Luka charged into the river, pausing as Majka rose on her haunches, locked eyes with him, and slowly shook her head. She limped into the woods after the retreating gunmen, leaking dollops of sticky blood.

Luka turned back and marched towards the woods on the bank opposite the action, his face a stone mask. "C'mon," he grunted.

"Where we going?"

"To round up the boys. It's almost time for your baptism."

"What, *now?*"

"Majka needs help, and blood don't leave blood hangin' like that. The pack's gonna have its first real hunt."

Luka stormed off. Derek paused for a moment, casting his gaze back across the river. Luka's words echoed in his ears: *blood don't leave blood hangin'.*

A bilious wad wormed its way up Derek's throat. He swallowed it down, wincing against its stinging residue, and followed Luka into the woods.

53: RUN

IMAN SLINKED THROUGH the trees, hunching below the worst of the intermingled branches. She held the pistol cocked upward at a forty-five degree angle—probably not the best position, but holding it straight outward took a toll on her wrists and shoulders. Every move she made, no matter how measured or minor, seemed to produce some sort of sound: the rustle of pine needles against her jacket, the crinkle of displaced underbrush, the fireplace crackle of twigs snapping beneath the soles of her running shoes. She felt dumb and clumsy and bovine, a brainless piece of livestock that had wandered away from its farm.

She grew disoriented within minutes of venturing into the stifling undergrowth, though it hardly mattered, since she didn't know where to look in the first place. It wasn't as if she had a map to Luka's hideout. Her best hope was to sweep the forest in search of a telltale footprint or piece of ripped clothing snagged on a jutting tree branch, the sort of thing that inevitably guided a movie protagonist to their MacGuffin. The stupidity of this plan became increasingly evident as the minutes ground on and her surroundings grew more and more anonymous and unfamiliar.

A chorus of howls and gunfire sounded to her left. She jumped at the sudden and sustained crescendo, her back pressed up against the trunk of a pine tree. Spurs of rough bark dug into the tender skin between her shoulder blades. She levelled her pistol at the underbrush, sweeping her arms from side to side. The sound of fighting grew more intense, but came no closer. She used it to place herself a hundred metres or so east of the clearing. Lowering her gun, she resumed her northeastern trajectory.

A beige blur shot through the brush and tangled its clammy tendrils through her hair. Iman whipped her head sideways, but the hand pulled with greater force. Her follicles shrieked, their cries muted by the *clong!* of her head striking the trunk of a cedar. Black forms dotted with glittering stars galloped across her field of vision. She was dimly aware of a firm grip on her wrists, hands twisting her arms behind her and up the crest of her spine, pinning them at an angle just shy of painful.

"Drop it, sweetmeats. You drop it now."

For a panicked instant Iman had no idea what the man was saying. The words hit her ears like the blather of a foreign tongue, discrete syllables lacking the connective tissue of grammar or syntax. She assumed "drop it" to be some sort of aggressor's argot, a term ominous and commanding and opaque. It was only as her fingers tightened on the pistol that she realised the phrase was meant literally. She obeyed. The pistol slipped from her fingers, which were fast going numb from the pressure on her kinked arm. Her captor patted her shoulder.

"Good girl," he said, and in a smooth motion shoved her forward and dipped down for the gun. He had the barrel pressed to her temple before she'd fully regained her footing. A nip of frigid metal stung her skin. He resumed his grip on her arm, which he folded up behind her back like a broken wing, and marched her through the undergrowth to a small clearing, where several derelicts hunkered around a small fire. The men eyed her with a mixture of amusement and hunger, the woman—there was only one, Iman noticed, apart from herself—with a kind of bored disdain.

The man shoved Iman into the circle. The fire licked its heat against her shins. Light from the flames danced over the faces of her onlookers, laying down shifting topographies of shadow. She turned, trapped, and got her first good look at her captor. He had the leather-skinned, permanently dirty look Iman associated with homeless people, as if his body had adapted a layer of grime into its dermal makeup. His earlobes hung in gruesome tatters from the sides of his face, stringy bits of atrophying flesh wriggling with each twitch and bob of his head.

"I found this one skulkin' around our camp," the ragged-eared man said. He spoke in a stentorian tone that was clearly forced, the ersatz militia-speak of children playing war. "She must be one o' Ballaro's spies or somethin'."

The men in the circle rubbed their chins and leered at her above scraggly beards and neck tattoos.

"She ain't no Ballaro spy," said a burly man in a leather vest that had, by the look of its tattered armholes, once been a jacket. "She's a Paki. Ballaro don't hire no Pakis."

"She ain't a Paki," said a scrawny chicken-faced one in army fatigues, his fingers absently twiddling a pocket-knife. His Adam's apple, enormous and peninsular, bobbled with each syllable. "Pakis got dots. She's one o' them Muslims."

"Pakis *are* Muslims, dipshit, you're thinkin' Arabs."

"Then why ain't she got a scarf on her head?"

"Some of 'em don't do the scarf."

The woman, sitting slightly back from the others, rolled her eyes at this exchange. Behind her, Iman noticed a stirring among a pile of bags and refuse. A figure sat in the gloom, his hands draped limply over his bony knees. It was a posture of exhaustion and defeat, though the voice that issued from its bearer held an incongruent bearing of confidence and control. Disdain dripped like acid from its barbed edges.

"The woman in question is an Arab *and* a Muslim," said Professor Motes. "Albeit a non-practicing one, from my understanding. As enlightening as your little exchange of geopolitical commentary was, it's also wholly irrelevant. She has nothing to do with Frank Ballaro or Luka Volchyin or any of this sorry business. I'd thank you to let her be."

The man with ragged ears stomped over to Motes, who somehow managed to glower down at Iman's captor despite being seated. A damp glottal gurgling issued from deep in the ragged-eared man's throat. He gathered a payload of mucus, reared back, and spat a sticky yellow wad onto Motes' shoulder. The professor wiped it away, flicking his fingers in an attempt to shake off the residue. "Charming."

"You ain't in charge here, you stuck-up limp-dick motherfucker!" The man waggled the gun in Motes' face.

"I'm merely pointing out the girl's status as a non-combatant."

"Would you shut that faggot up already, Nails?" said the scrawny kid. He thrust his tongue out the side of his mouth and worked the blade of his pocketknife under a yellowing thumbnail. "He's givin' me a headache."

"By all means, *Nails,*" Motes said, speaking the man's name as if it were a dirty term in a foreign language. "Put a bullet in my head. It would spare me your further company, and in that sense could be considered merciful. Luka gave you orders to the contrary, of course, but who is he to stand in your way?"

"Hey, I respect my pack chief, buddy. But ol' Luka didn't' say nothin' about keeping hands off your butt buddy here."

Nails reached forward and lifted the trussed, wriggling figure beside Motes to his knees. A young face, bruised and gagged, looked out with eyes dulled by an overdose of fear. They zeroed in on Iman and the clouds before them evaporated. He let out a garbled sound rendered unintelligible by his gag.

"Brian!" Iman cried, and rushed forward. Nails drove an elbow into her gut and caught her as she tumbled forward. She landed on her knees in front of him. He grabbed hold of a hank of her hair and held it as if it were a leash.

"Well, hey, this is interesting," said Nails. "You and chinky know each other, huh?"

"Shit," said the scrawny kid, a laugh stretching the word into multiple hunched syllables. "That's like, some of that 'misogynation' goin' on. Ain't natural."

"Get with the times, R.B.," said Nails. "Kid your age should be fuckin' whoever he can find'll take his money."

"Hey, fuck you!"

Nails ignored this. He tightened his grip on Iman's hair. "You wouldn't want your little Asian fuck buddy gettin' hurt, would you, girly? Problem is, I'm feelin' pretty, whattayacall, pent up. I need to relax. Normally, I start feelin' like that, I get my jollies stompin' heads. But lucky for you, I ain't all that hard to distract."

He unzipped his fly and pulled out a stumpy, semi-flaccid penis, its head purplish and fringed with red, painful-looking foreskin. A sweetly rancid odour emanated from its tip. The men around the fire hooted and shouted lewd commentary that hit Iman's ears like the hushed roar of waves crashing on a distant beach, hoarse and senseless. She yanked her head back, but Nails' grip on her hair was firm. A sense of whimpering, helpless rage welled up within her. She knew if she opened her mouth she'd vomit, and feared what Nails might do in retaliation. *Maybe he'd be into it,* chirped a voice in her head. She bit her lip to strangle a deranged laugh.

Motes stood next to Nails, nose to nose. He didn't so much as glance at Iman; his eyes remained locked on the furrowed brow and sneering, upturned lip opposite him.

"I believe I've made the girl's status as non-combatant abundantly clear. She has no quarrel with you, one way or the other."

"Don't overplay your hand here, teach. Luka said I ain't s'posed to ice you, but that don't mean you got the final say-so. I got half a dozen witnesses'd say you were makin' a run for it. Ain't that right, boys?"

The men around the fire murmured agreement in dismal chorus.

"Looks like a runner to me."

"You better get him back here, Nails."

Motes showed no sign of intimidation. He kept his gaze level with Nails. After a brief stalemate, Nails let go of Iman's hair and walked into Motes, his chest thrust outward and arms extended in the numbskull posture of beta males seeking alpha status. Motes didn't push back, but nor did he relent. Iman scurried over to Brian, her hands working their way beneath the bindings. Flecks of dried blood sloughed away where the rope had cut into him.

"So what's your plan, teach? You think you can take the lot of us?"

Motes ran his tongue along his top teeth and drew a slow, even breath through his nostrils. He held his shoulders in the squared, rigid mold of a man contemplating a leap from a great height.

"As a matter of fact, I'm pretty sure I can. Maybe not a minute ago, but now?" Motes shook his head. "You should've acted when you had the chance." He turned to Iman, his face soft and strangely tender. "Run, Iman. Run as far and fast as you can."

"Oh, she's not—" Nails began, his words cut off as Motes ensnared him in a bear hug. His nose wrinkled in distaste. "Jesus Christ, what the fuck—"

"Much too late for him to help you, boy," Motes said. His body trembled in the throes of some cataclysmic seismic event, the tectonic plates of his muscles grinding and shifting. Hair erupted along his cheeks, his hands, his forearms. Nails' eyes grew impossibly wide, whites spreading outwards like two eggs cracked on a hot skillet. He struggled fruitlessly to free himself from the shifting column of hair and muscle.

Claws burst through the crescents of flesh beneath Motes' fingernails. No sooner had they emerged than they disappeared again, vanishing into the meat of Nails' chest. Nails screamed as his bones cracked inside Motes' iron embrace. With a howl Motes dug his claws in deeper and pulled them sharply downward. Iman heard the distinct wishbone snap of each rib breaking. Nails' penis waggled as raking claws plucked it from his pelvis. It landed with a cartoonish plop near the scrawny kid's foot. The kid puked in his lap. Still retching, he jumped upright, tripped over his own tangled feet, and fell face-first into the fire. His cohorts exhibited more grace in fleeing—despite some light trampling that kept the scrawny kid pinned against the flames—but Motes possessed a speed far exceeding human. He leapt nimbly over the campfire and onto the chest of the man with neck tattoos. The man fell backwards as Motes' wide jaws closed on his head, swallowing up every scrap of flesh and sinew from forehead to jaw with a greedy smacking of his tongue. The man, his skull grinning nakedly beneath his scalp, let out a shrill cry that couldn't quite be called a scream—his lack of cheeks gave the sound some interesting tonal properties.

Motes leapt and clawed and killed and ate. The few shots the fleeing packmates bothered to fire struck him with all the force and impact of pebbles flung by schoolchildren. Nails, cockless and carved open from stem to sternum, gasped and flopped on the dirt like a dying fish. Iman felt neither hatred nor pity. She barely even felt revulsion. Her brain was a cloth rinsed clean of all emotion, sopping and inert. She fumbled with the rope binding Brian's wrists, her fingers shaking and slippery with sweat. The knots refused to loosen. She dug a nail into the seam. It bent backwards and snapped off at the cuticle. She thrust her thumb in her mouth and sucked until the pain receded. Brian wriggled, speaking garbled noise through his gag.

"I'm trying, hun," Iman said.

Brian wriggled harder, motioning with exaggerated nods.

The thing that had been Motes loomed opposite the fire pit. Blood and froth slickened the hair around his muzzle. His stance was simian and semi-erect, wiry arms grazing the dirt. A tweed jacket hung in tatters from his shoulders, while his pants and shoes had come free altogether, slipping from his sleek and foreshortened lower half.

A glint of metal shone in the grass at Iman's feet. With meticulous slowness, she bent her knees, bringing her hand inch by endless inch closer to the object. Motes' breath came loud and lustful, the sound of a man whose appetites had been coiled to irrepressible tightness and would, at the slightest nudge, spring into violent motion. Her fingers grazed the object. She seized it, slid a rapid shuffle-step backwards, and raised the Beretta to chest height. Motes stared down the barrel.

"There's silver in here," Iman said, unsure whether Motes could even understand her. "If I shoot you, you won't just shrug it off. You'll die. I don't want to do that, though. Shoot you, I mean."

She licked her lips, made minute adjustments to her grip on the gun.

"Please, professor. You went after those guys and not me, even though I was closer. You've got to still be in there somewhere. Just go. Leave us alone. Please."

Motes tilted his head. His tongue lolled out the side of his mouth like a bright pink worm. His back rose and fell in time with his humid breathing. Black smoke plumed from the fire pit, humid with the aromatic stick of the scrawny kid's upper body, which had already rendered into a crust of craggled black char. The sound of crackling flames filled the clearing, punctuated with the greasy pops of human fat sloughing into the coals. Iman tightened her grip on the trigger.

"Please, professor."

Motes bent his knees and leapt over the fire. Iman closed her eyes in the same instant she squeezed the trigger. A single shot rattled the air. White light flashed across her eyelids. Something hard and heavy landed in front of her. She kept her eyes firmly shut, awaiting the sudden pressure of fangs closing around her throat. It didn't come.

Motes lay at her feet. Not a wolf thing or a chimeric abomination, but Motes—a man who drank coffee from fussy espresso cups and insisted on printing everything he edited. Who left sardonic comments in naked margins with a nimble, spidery hand. Who guarded his sense of humor closely, revealing it in small smiles and flickers of wit. A man she had respected, reviled, and ultimately pitied. He looked up at her, naked save the tattered remnants of his jacket, lying in a nest of blood and shed fur, a singed hole about where his heart should be.

"Th . . . tha . . . " he said, and died.

Iman managed to cut Brian loose before she broke down weeping. But it was a close thing.

54: WHITE LIGHT

DAVID WATCHED THE wolves' advance on Ballaro with growing dismay, so absorbed in the folly he didn't notice the mud-matted nightmare to his right until it had nearly gutted him. He lurched backwards, feeling the sharp tug of its claws as they snagged his jacket, rending ribbons of ruined fabric that flapped flag-like in the steady breeze.

The world grew still and crystalline, its clockwork innards trundling in a glass housing. David could see individual molecules of air fold and part as he raised his pistol, chart the Rube Goldberg system of nerves and muscles and tendons ferrying commands from his brain to his fingertips, taste the sour tang of gunpowder undergoing its chemical changes, hear the *tear-crunch-squish-sizzle* of the bullet's impact as distinct notes in a bitter melody. The bullet's silver enamel, catalysed by whatever ungodly enzyme populated the wolf-thing's cells, burned with the blinding intensity of magnesium. A snippet of Velvet Underground unspooled in some long-forgotten tape deck in the back of David's subconscious, setting a hip soundtrack to the lunatic proceedings. *(White light) White light goin' messin' up my miiiind. (White light) and don't you know it's gonna make me go bliiiiind . . .*

The wolf-thing's blood, tainted with Christ only knows what unearthly ichor, coated David's right arm from cuff to collar. Bits of splatter pimpled his right cheek. A mix of howls and screams soaked the forest behind him, though David was too intent on the receding figures of Luka and Derek to turn and check on the fight. He saw-felt the holy flare of silver bullets meeting their targets, a light so brilliant its photons seemed to penetrate his cheeks and set them abuzz, suggesting at least a few of Ballaro's boys had found the presence of mind to load up the right ammo. The air wafting from the shore stank of blood and cordite.

He followed the two men across the stream and into the forest. His last remaining silver bullet called to him from its silent black chamber. *One good shot. That's all I need. Give me Luka and keep the rest for all I care. Even that scumbag McCulloch.*

David broke through the treeline at a run, shoulders hunched and arms tucked in to block the fusillade of branches. The hyper-awareness that had surged through him moments before leaked away. The world grew blurred and dim and runny, a wash of greens and browns. Flitting branches and crunching foliage lay a furry shroud over the subtler sounds of the forest, drowned out only by the mad jungle-drum pounding of his pulse.

After a slight but steady incline, the ground crested briefly before dropping down once again. David's sprinter strides became vaults as the earth struggled to evade his feet. His momentum nearly threw him headfirst into a limestone protrusion. He caught himself inches before his jaw made contact with the ridge, sparing him several broken teeth. His fingers tightened compulsively, firing his last silver bullet into the treetops.

He stared with dismay at the bullet's vanished trajectory. To have missed his shot would have been one thing, but losing this way was just too much. He leaned against the jutting stone. Urgency drained from him like air from a leaking tire. Moving forward seemed impossible; inertia's chains hung too heavily. He remained that way for a while, slumped forward to fit in the tapered space between the mossy ground and the cantilevered outcrop of stone.

Voices slipped through gaps in the undergrowth, faint but audible.

" . . . think it was farther back that way."

"You don't gotta direct me, bro. They're my pack. I can smell 'em like they're right under my nose."

David threw himself against the stone, wiggling into the crevice beneath its overhang. Matted wads of dirt sprinkled over him. He held the Beretta upward in the prescribed two-armed stance. Its barrel lay cold and firm against his cheek, the touch of a reassuring finger. His breath slowed until it flowed silent and without audible pauses, a cadence too low and constant to detect.

"What about the gunshot?"

"Probably echoed from the camp site. Don't worry about it. We just—" Luka broke off. The sound of their footsteps ceased. David heard a sharp, inquisitive intake of breath. It came again, closer. "That you behind there, detective? We playin' hide and go seek?"

David bit his lower lip. Knowledge of his gun's uselessness burst to the surface of his mind, flailing and panicked. *He knows you're not armed! He'll smell it on you!* David thrust the thought down into the muck and drowned it. He remembered Walter as he'd last seen him, bleeding out atop an asphalt parking lot. *Let him smell this,* he thought. *Let him take a whiff of how bad I want him dead.*

"If we are, then I guess you called me out." He stood, forcing every muscle fibre into a pose of contemptuous nonchalance. He told himself he had the upper hand until he actually half-believed it. Luka raised an eyebrow as David aimed the gun at his chest. Derek, half hidden behind Luka, drew a large revolver and pointed it at David.

"Not the best situation you're in, bro. The moon's callin' to me, and you've seen what sort of piss-poor work a bullet does."

"I've seen what lead does, yeah. I've seen what silver does, too."

The right side of Luka's mouth turned up in a coy demi-smile, pulling the pinkish weal of scar tissue on his face to canvas tautness. "Silver bullet, huh? Musta been one hell of a specialty shop sold you that."

"Actually, they were a gift. Courtesy of one Frank Ballaro."

"That so? I noticed you ain't shot me with it yet."

"Tell your buddy there to put the gun down and we've got a deal."

"No chance," hissed Derek.

Luka raised a dismissive hand. "I got this, bro."

"I dunno if I agree with you there, Luka," said David. "We've got a lot of dead on both sides here. And for what? Some petty turf war?"

"For vengeance. You know about vengeance, don't you, detective? He murdered my babushka. Burned her alive. Can you imagine burning alive? What that musta been like?"

"You killed his sons. Tore them limb from limb. I'm guessing that was no picnic either. What good does more death do either of you?"

"Spare me your pacifist bullshit. I'm gonna see that dumb wop and everyone he ever cared about dead, and then I'm gonna take his town. There's blood on all of 'em." His face drifted skyward. Moonlight infused it with a pale, sepulchral glow. His skin bulged and bent and pitted as horrid contortions worked beneath its surface. Shoots of grey-brown hair grew from every pore with time lapse urgency. Bones cracked and shifted like sheets of arctic ice. A shout became a shriek became a howl, a wretched umbilicus of sound that seemed to stretch to the darkness beyond the moon. Derek backed away from the abomination, revolver hanging stupidly at his side. David ignored the wail of every atavistic impulse to turn and flee, the collective cry of a million simian ancestors bending as one to such a primordial menace. He kept his pistol raised, but he knew in his heart it was just a prop. He would live or die by his words and his will.

An idea slithered through David's muddied thoughts. He grabbed it and thrust it into the light. "You're so worried about vengeance, why are you focused on some fat-assed bureaucrat who ordered a hit? Why aren't you going after the man who actually did the killing?"

The question sliced Luka's snarl in two. Its withered halves fell mutely to the ground. David laughed, a deep rolling chuckle that surprised him as much as it did Luka.

"You dumb Cossack piece of shit. You never stopped to think who might've actually put the torch to your grandma's old folks' home? You think it was Frank Ballaro out there with a can of gas and a lighter? Please. Who had the stomach—the gall—to do something that vile? Maybe a guy who made his living doing Ballaro's dirty work? A guy who uses arson to take out targets and evidence right along with them? A guy who people call, I dunno, *Matchbook* McCulloch?"

Volchyin loomed huge and terrible. His growl shook snow from the treetops.

Flames filled his pupils, onyx embers that burned darker than black. They seemed to swallow light, boundless apertures into which you could fall and fall and never reach bottom. His jaws gnashed. His muscles tensed.

Six gunshots crackled through the forest air. Every bullet found its mark. With the preternatural keenness of adrenalin, David witnessed the impact each made on the wolf-thing's hide. The first four landed with all the force of BBs; the last two struck like cannonfire. Silver-white radiance hemorrhaged from entrance and exit wounds. The thing that had been Luka howled with rage and pain, back arching against the spears of light driven through it.

Derek stood with his legs planted shoulder width apart, the Governor cupped in both hands. He gazed down with almost clinical curiosity as the wolf-thing withered. Fur fell from it in clumps, and its skin made a slithering sound as it shrank back down to Luka's less prodigious dimensions. When the body settled to its ruin, he looked up and cocked the barrel of the revolver towards David's chest. David gazed back, unimpressed.

"You think I haven't seen Dirty Harry? You fired six shots. That thing's empty." He held up his own automatic, wiggled it demonstratively. "Mine isn't."

"So you say." Derek scratched his chin with the front sight of his pistol. "I saved your life, you know."

"You saved your own life. He was coming for you."

"Probably, yeah. But he would've gotten you first."

"Probably," David agreed. The wind stirred the branches overhead, sending a brief flurry of snow showering over the stretch of cold earth between them. "You did it, didn't you? Burned Stanford Acres down?"

"Does it matter?"

"Of course it matters. People died."

"People die all the time, man. How many people died up here on your say-so?"

David had nothing to say to that. The whole conversation was pointless. He had Derek on any number of charges, attempted murder not the least of them. The man was a hired killer. It was his duty to bring him in.

David considered the pistol, its metal barrel prickling with cold. He slipped it back in its holster. Derek looked at him with a masterful poker face, betraying no expression.

"Go," David said.

Derek paused, his head tilted slightly, and studied David's face. He nodded once, to himself by the look of it, and tucked the Governor into the waistband of his jeans.

"Thanks." He rubbed his hands together for warmth, blew into his cupped palms. Turning to leave, he nodded again, this time to David. "See ya."

"Better if you don't," David replied. "For both of us."

55: DAYLIGHT

DAYLIGHT PEEKED OVER the treetops and dipped its tentative toe into the landscape's rocky clefts. Iman jerked awake as the first rays grazed her cheek. Her lower back bulged and throbbed like a kinked hose. She stretched, tugging three sharp cracks from her cramped vertebrae and flooding her leg with pins-and-needles numbness from the thigh down. Brian's head slipped from the crook between her shoulder and breast. He woke with a snort and a tremble, hands raised defensively to his face before settling groggily on his chest. The two of them blinked at their surroundings, gradually recalling where they were and why. Iman's hand rested on the pistol as they shrugged their way out of the nest of itchy tartan blankets and spare clothes they'd pilfered from the camp site.

Despite the anguished cries and sporadic gunfire that had continued long into the night, they'd each managed to doze for a while, and had even had frantic, urgent sex on the bare earth, breath mingling between locked mouths as they fumbled at one another's half-clothed bodies. Now it was morning and the fighting had long ceased, and Iman felt anxiety seep back into the crevices of her mind that relief and exhaustion had previously sealed tight.

She sat up and experimented with the gun until she figured out how to remove the magazine. Only one bullet was missing. Tucking the gun into her waistband, she stood and walked toward the trees.

"Where are you going?" Brian asked.

"Back to the camp."

"Why? There's nothing there but a bunch of dead bodies."

"Exactly."

The forest was easier to navigate in the daylight, its undergrowth less oppressive, its curtains of shadow pulled aside. They found the campsite after only fifteen minutes of looking, drawn as much by smell as by sight. Iman hiked up the collar of her shirt and used it as a makeshift filter. A few embers still smouldered in the fire pit's ashen belly. The predawn chill suppressed the worst of the odour, but the first shoots of foetid stink had already begun to sprout up, nourished by the morning dew. Keeping the other corpses on the periphery of her vision, Iman approached Motes and knelt down beside him. His skin had taken on a greyish pallor, and his chin looked smudgy with stubble. He lay face-up on the ground, his eyes closed, his face oddly neutral, almost placid. A small dark hole dotted his chest. In the dim light it could have been a splash of red wine clumsily spilt. Iman smoothed a lock of hair from his forehead, alarmed at the cold marble cast of his skin.

"I killed him," Iman said.

Brian put a firm hand on her shoulder. "Hey, not fair."

"I did, though. I killed him."

"I think you did exactly what he wanted you to do. He was just afraid to ask."

Iman sniffed. She ran a finger beneath her eyelid, the skin there red and puffy. "What do you mean?"

"I saw him attack those other guys. He was so fast you could hardly keep track of him. But when he came at you . . . I dunno. It was like he was moving in slow motion."

Iman stuck the tip of her tongue between her teeth and bit down, stopping just short of pain. "He looks peaceful."

Brian's hand caressed her neck. "He's just Motes again, right? That's got to count for something."

"I guess."

A twig snapped beyond the underbrush. Iman whirled, pointing her gun in the direction of the sound. Her finger tightened around the trigger.

"Don't shoot, please," said David. He stepped into the clearing with arms raised. Heavy bags hung from his eyes and lines of exhaustion crisscrossed his face, but he looked otherwise unhurt. He looked from Iman and Brian to Motes. His smile sagged. "Shit."

"He's at rest now," Brian said, tugging awkwardly at his shirtsleeve. "That's what they say, right? When someone dies?"

"Yeah. It'll have to do."

The three of them stood over the body. A cool wind stirred the branches of the surrounding trees. Gusts of crisp, clean air whisked away the smells of corruption, though a lingering odour remained.

"Do we bury him?" Brian asked.

David clucked his tongue. "We don't have a shovel. Even if we did, you'd never get six feet down up here. We're standing on solid limestone."

"Then . . . we carry him? I'm guessing you guys have a car?"

"It's hours away by foot, and my ribs are shot to hell. I'm not so sure I could do it."

"Well, we can't just *leave* him," Iman said.

"No," David agreed. "Not here. Come on."

With a groan, David locked his elbows beneath Motes' armpits and lifted the professor. Brian and Iman each took a leg, and the three of them carried him out of the clearing.

They found a quiet spot beneath the shade of a spruce tree, far from the bloodshed of the riverbanks. There they washed Motes' face and hands with water from a canteen, raising days' worth of dirt in a brownish foam. David went back to the campsite and returned with supplies. Iman trimmed Motes' nails with the scissors of a Swiss Army knife—halfway through, she realised with a shudder that it may well have belonged to the scrawny kid who'd burned alive in the camp fire—and scraped away most of his chin stubble with the blade. David laid down the cleanest blanket he could find and used it to bind Motes in a shroud. They positioned him in the crook of the tree's raised roots, his tranquil face peeking out between the folds of his chrysalis. After a moment's consideration, David worked the silver alligator ring from his finger and placed it gently in the hollow of Motes' neck. It glinted like a gem in the morning sun.

"What now?" Brian asked.

"First thing, I'm going home, taking a shower, and sleeping for about a month. Beyond that, who knows?"

"It sounds like a good plan to me," said Iman.

The walk back to the car took most of the morning, during which none of them spoke. Iman and Brian walked hand in hand, casting occasional glances at one another. The few remaining finches and sparrows dotted the stillness with their song, sparse melodies played atop the lazy rhythm of their footsteps.

56: UNCLEAN

THE MAN CRAWLED across the forest floor. A susurrus of crunching leaves marked his progress, punctuated by the crisp snap of twigs and the soft moans issuing from his throat. An accretion of dirt and dried blood covered the right half of his face and stained his bear-pelt coat in grim motley. His legs and belly gasped with welts where they dragged over the rocky earth, and blood trickled from beneath his fingernails. He clawed his way across the small clearing, his left leg working like an inchworm while his right hung useless, its dead and frozen flesh already turning an ugly shade of grey. A few metres away stood a dry culvert curtained with holly and bristly underbrush—a good place to rest, out of the wind and hidden from predators.

Derek waited until the man had almost made it before stepping out from behind the tree. The man looked up at him, confusion blurring his broken face. Derek smiled. He hefted the barrel of the MP5 he'd pilfered from one of Ballaro's boys. On his back hung a rucksack bulging with food and ammo, though mostly food. There'd been enough standard rounds to supply a small army, but Derek mostly ignored these, favoring the dearer slugs of silver.

"Hey there, buddy," he said. "Where you goin'? Crawlin' back to the Kremlin?"

Derek expected panic, but as the man grasped the situation, his face settled into sullen truculence. He'd lost several teeth, which gave his pursed lips a caved-in look.

"Ah, you're no fun." He raised the MP5 and fired a single shot. The man's head evaporated. Derek spat through clenched teeth, regretting his action. He should've tried plain old lead first. It would behoove him to learn whether normal bullets sufficed when they weren't transformed. Oh well. Next time.

He paced the woods to either side of the creek until mid-afternoon, when heavy snowfall drove him to seek cover beneath a limestone outcrop. He encountered no one else in that time, only footprints and bodies half-buried by drifting snow. Most of the latter belonged to Luka's ill-fated pack, of whom Derek appeared to be the sole surviving member. He didn't notice Sarah's body among the corpses, but that hardly said much in this forest primeval. It could've been five feet away from him at some point and he'd never know it.

The forest folk had their losses, too, but they were relatively few considering the numbers they'd started with. Most had made their way deeper into the woods, following their grievously wounded Majka. Ballaro's bullets should've been fatal, but from the last Derek saw of the old bitch, she still had some fight left in her.

Rubbing his frigid hands together for warmth, Derek gathered an armful of deadwood and lit a fire. He cupped the warm air rising from the flames, sighing as the heat breathed fresh life into his cold-stiffened fingers. Once the weather calmed down, he'd best move south. The forest was in a state of slow lockdown. A couple more snowfalls, and the roads would be all but impassable. In a few more days he'd be stuck up here, left to freeze or starve as the caprices of circumstance dictated. But that was okay. He needed time to think. To equip himself. To plan. To atone.

He'd stood apart from his species, and in so doing felt a shame he'd never felt before. The few drops of silver water he'd swallowed sizzled on the root of his tongue. He was unclean, but he was still a man, and one man really shouldn't kill another. Not when beasts still roamed the plains beyond the safety of firelight.

Spring would come again soon enough, and the woods were far from empty. He had a lot of work to do.

ACKNOWLEDGMENTS

Of all the novels I've written (only a fraction of which are currently published), Whitetooth Falls had the shortest journey from rough concept to finished manuscript. The pace was breakneck, but that doesn't undercut the immense and invaluable help I've had along the way.

Thanks first of all to Scarlett R. Algee, Chris Payne, and the whole team at JournalStone for their support and guidance throughout the publication process.

To Alec Shane, my agent and unflinching editor, who cuts out all the weak spots and smoothes out the rough edges.

To my friends and family in Niagara Falls. Writing this book was a little bit like visiting home, and you were all on my mind even more than usual.

Lastly, to my wife, Chantal, for being a great partner and putting up with my frantic and desultory note-scribbling, and to my children: Lavender, Hannela, and Leo, who finally gets a namecheck.

CPSIA information can be obtained
at www.ICGtesting.com
Printed in the USA
FFHW021442191119
56069892-62081FF

ABOUT THE AUTHOR

Justin Joschko is an author from Niagara Falls, Ontario. His writing has appeared in newspapers and literary journals across Canada. He currently lives in Ottawa with his wife and three children.